PRAISE FOR
SHORN

"*Shorn* is a striking debut, filled with skilled world-building, complex psychological tension and a fine sense of nuance too seldom seen in fantasy. I was engrossed in the unfolding tale, and I look forward to the continuing journey!"
—Jacqueline Carey, author of Kushiel's Legacy series

"Larissa N. N. Davila has created a fascinating world, peopled it with vivid characters, and woven an epic tale of adventure and political intrigue with thoughtful themes of duty versus desire, bigotry versus acceptance, and the truth of history that hides behind the self-serving accounts written by the victors. She has also invented one of the more convincing religions I've seen in fantasy recently--no mere window-dressing of gods and altars and a priest or two, but a fully-rounded, psychologically convincing faith. An intelligent and captivating novel by a new writer of promise."
—Victoria Strauss, author of *The Burning Land*

"This is an impressive debut from an author whose background in psychology informs but doesn't overwhelm her subtle but well-paced story. Her characters are thoughtful and the spiritual and political history of her novel's world is complex, poignant, and believable."
—Kristen McDermott, editor of "Folkroots" for *Realms of Fantasy Magazine* and staff reviewer for *Historical Novels Review*

"Larissa N. N. Davila has created a compelling story with an original and complex hero torn between duty and desire, loyalty and freedom. She shows us a deep and fascinating culture, a believable world, struggling with issues of faith and power in ways that reflect our own fears and dreams. More please!"
—Ari Berk, author of The Undertaken trilogy

"Jhared Denaban, a young soldier of the land of Avelos, lives under the Avelune Curse because he descended from a tribe that betrayed their land and earned themselves the label of Shorn. As Jhared labors under the strict laws forbidding the Shorn to hold public office or enter the priesthood, he discovers that Avelos faces not only enemies from without but also rivalries and deceit from within, and he suspects that the stories of his ancestors' shame may not be totally accurate. Davila's debut novel, the first of a planned four-book series, creates a fascinating world of rival clans and sacred rituals, tainted by a dark, shameful past and subject to predation from its enemies. This is also a coming-of-age story and belongs in most fantasy collections."

—*Library Journal*

"A grand-scale fantasy that chronicles the journeys of two people desperately attempting to save their beloved nation from those seeking to destroy it. Fantasy fans will be impressed by Davila's deep characterization of the two main players; the focus on their internal development...makes them emotionally relatable and endearing. The attention to worldbuilding is also a strength, as many scenes come alive on the page through detailed descriptions, and multiple layers of political and social intrigue...add remarkable depth."

—*Kirkus Reviews*

SHORN

Book One of
The Sky Seekers

AHW '21

SHORN

Book One of
The Sky Seekers

Larissa N. N. Davila

STONE RAVEN
PRESS

Sante Fe, New Mexico

ACKNOWLEDGMENTS

Shorn and the complete arc of The Sky Seekers series came to me not merely as an interesting idea but as a story I had to tell. Yet without the help of many talented people, I would never have been able to share it. My admiration and thanks go to Ari Warner for his beautiful illustrations, particularly his gorgeous frontispiece. I am grateful to Ally Machate and her team at The Writer's Ally for providing me with the support and expertise necessary to create a beautiful book. Much love goes to Kristen McDermott, a talented editor and steadfast friend, who can always talk me off the ledges and sustain me with large cups of tea (and wine), to Brandon Thomas for understanding Jhared and seeing the strengths in Nemiah, and to the dear friends who have helped me through the writing, the pandemic and more: Jason and Todd.

For my Mouse, now and always.

Principal Characters

IN VELANTAR
Jhared Denaban, a young Shorn man
Mahla Denaban, Jhared's mother (deceased)
Elder Tierzen Trianor, Minister of the Teaching, Jhared's foster father and Teacher
Madam Sarena Trianor, Elder Trianor's wife, Jhared's foster mother and Teacher
Branlen Trianor, Jhared's foster brother
Sirol, Shorn scribe to Elder Trianor
Ziabela Marcalo, Shorn scribe and musician
Isella, owner of the Black Mountain and friend to Zia
Elian Varigo, Shorn scribe and musician
Bilar, Shorn bodyguard
Alende, Shorn waylayer

RIANA'S HIGH TEMPLE IN VELANTAR
Nemiah Gabriana, High Priestess of Avelos
Lady Amalia, traitorous former high priestess (deceased)
Captain Rom, Nemiah's Arionad

Leita, Bearer of Cael's Blade
Kaliska, Healer, Mistress of Guardians, Keeper of the Shadow Guards
Carian, Mistress of Novices
Bena, Mistress of Maps
Clemina, Mistress of Messages
Maita, Mistress of Rituals

} **RIANA'S HIGHER CIRCLE**

COUNCIL OF CLANS IN VELANTAR
Adan Rumar, High Chieftain of Avelos
Elder Toren Abrigado, Minister of the Treasury, Leader of Tumal's Legacy
Tumal the Just, heroic former high chieftain (deceased)

IN THE FOREST GUARD FORTRESS AT RAVIA
Enrian Nadel, General of the Southern Towers
Captain Riselvo, head of Ravia garrison
Lieutenant Matio Sevar, commanding officer of the Forest Guard Fourth
Micah, a Shorn solider in the Fourth
Hendren, a Shorn solider in the Fourth
Jech, a Shorn soldier in the Fourth
Falto, Forest Guard Healer

Commander Carn, head of Jhared's patrol
Lenaro, second to Carn
Anzo Nevia, patrolman
Grion Hariar, patrolman
Jase Relki, patrolman
Esran, patrolman
Bevan, patrolman
Twitch, patrolman
Afiro, patrolman

} **JHARED'S PATROL**

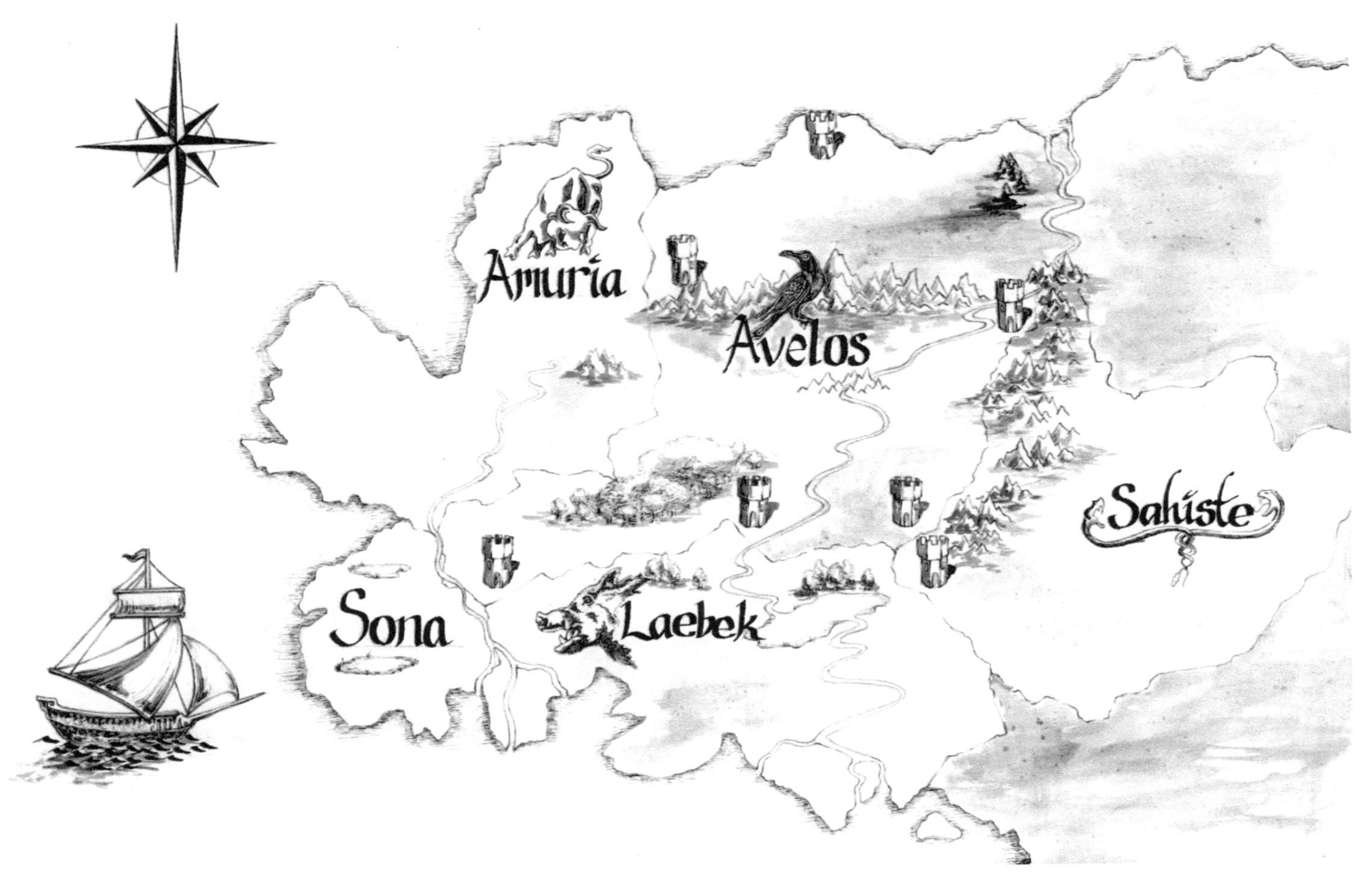

Amuria
Avelos
Sahiste
Sona
Laebek

PROLOGUE

"My lady, the judges have entered the sanctuary."

Nemiah glanced up from the book she was studying, one of the oldest in the temple, but not as old as it should have been. "And the initiate?"

Captain Rom shook his dark head, his beard brushing against the collar of his white coat. "Not yet."

Long streamers of light angled through the windows and across the flagstones to pool on the wool rug. An artifact from long before her time, that rug. Not even the Bearer of Cael's Blade could weave such an intricate pattern now. A lost art, one among many.

"Some time remains still."

Leather creaked as her Arionad shifted his stance, as near as Rom ever came to expressing doubt in her judgment. "We may need to send the Guardians after him," he said. "To be certain he's not fled."

"No. Not for this one. The Minister of the Teaching will see he arrives promptly. Of all people, Elder Trianor understands the significance of this Becoming."

The book's binding crackled as Nemiah closed it. It held an account of the first Becoming performed after the Exile War. Reading it grounded her, helped her to remember the greater purpose of the ritual, a thing that transcended the political squabbles of the elders and her own Higher Circle. Reaching for the past—however painful—helped her to erect the boundaries she needed to focus on the present. Those boundaries meant safety, meant staying in her own Place and not drifting into dangerous moments among the goddess's infinite Paths. Defining boundaries was a part of what the Becoming was about—making certain those who were descended from the seeds of deceit did not ever again grab power. Defining boundaries was just a part, though. Blood must still be shed. A death might yet be required.

Rom scowled. "Do you mean Elder Trianor will try to buy the boy's success?"

"I mean that as the son of the Minister of the Teaching, the boy will be seen as standing for all his kind. Elder Trianor will get him here on time."

Her Arionad nodded but his scowl didn't soften. He understood. This Becoming could mean the end of more than one life.

Nemiah smoothed her hands over her robe, feeling the nubs of the embroidered blessings spiraled through the fabric. She never anticipated a Becoming with anything but a sense of obligation. Her predecessor, High Priestess Pahlina, had always emerged gleaming from the trials, glorying in the goddess's touch—and perhaps the heady knowledge that she owned the power to end a young life. Nemiah did not revel in that power. A flaw, the advisors in her Higher Circle would say, had said. Nemiah loved Riana and treasured order, but the Becoming was a necessity, the ritual that made sense of the bloody Shearing and protected Avelos from the evil of the Shorn. What she did today would be for her people and for the temple. Insignificant as she was, her faith in the rituals encompassed the best she had to offer to her country.

Forming Riana's spiral, she said the first of the prayers silently, then rose and looked up at her waiting Arionad.

"Let us go to greet the judges."

1.
BECOMING

Jhared had prepared for this moment for twelve years, but he never expected the hawk to enthrall him.

She soared above the valley, talons clutching the success of her hunt as a noonday sun painted her body in gold, and he followed—although he feared it was wrong. His eyes tracked her as she wheeled in an effortless arch toward the cliffs. Below, the city shrank to a grey smudge against the foothills of the Parnas Mountains. The river, silver and quick with the spring thaw, divided the dark forest like a belt.

With slow, powerful wingbeats, the hawk hovered above a rocky crag, then settled on the narrow ledge. Her chicks chirped frantic greetings from the nest, stepping over one another to claim her. A breeze swirled off the mountain crevice and fluffed their cream-colored down as the hawk bent her head to meet each open mouth.

When the sun leaned toward the death of the day, she left the nest once more. Her wings extended. Her long, strong primary feathers flirted with the mountain thermals, as if she could entice them to come to her, before she glided lower into the valley. She was magnificent; Jhared hadn't expected that, either. From the crown of the hill, he watched the perfection of her flight and felt an answering excitement in his own body. Desire, dangerous and futile, twitched the twin scars down his back as he leaned into the buoyancy of the wind.

Riana commands that a bird of prey be slain in the prime of spring.

The temple's order dragged his thoughts back to the ground. Despite the warmth of the spring day, a shudder took him, passing from his shoulders through his arms to his hands, which already held the bow. He stared at the weapon, as though this were a decision he could make, then turned quickly to the bird again. He knew the invisible curve she traced against the clouds and shifted his arm until he reached the necessary angle between the horizon and the sky. His breathing slowed as he anchored himself. He sought the instant of absolute stillness in the pause between heartbeats. His fingers extended; the bowstring thrummed.

The shaft hurtled upward, tearing at the sky. It knocked the hawk from her flight, penetrated her feathers, and shattered her breast. She screamed, pumping her wings as if to propel herself above the pain. Then she crumpled and began tumbling toward the ground.

Lower on the hill, Branlen threw back his head and let out a whoop of victory. Jhared stood silently, unable to look away from the plummeting bird, a dull ache starting behind his eyes. Her body somersaulted toward the river and the ancient aqueduct, then disappeared into the thicket along the bank.

"You did it!" With a sunny laugh, Jhared's foster brother scrambled down the rocky incline, heading toward the meadow and the riverbank. The boy glanced over his shoulder to Jhared, who stood motionless, waiting to feel joy, excitement, relief, anything. So many years of waiting.

"Come on!" the boy cried. "You made the kill. Come help me find it!"

"Go ahead, Bran. I'm right behind you." The bird was down. He would be allowed to enter the Becoming. Riana gave him this gift.

The raptor must die in the prime of spring.

Shaking his head to push away his questions before they could fully form, Jhared marked in his mind the point at which the hawk had entered the forest, then swung his bow across his back and turned to follow Branlen toward the sounds of the river.

The ground dropped out from under him. As the ache behind his eyes exploded in blue sparks, Branlen, the meadow, and the forest became pieces in a patchwork of countryside. He spied the arrow a helpless moment before it pierced his chest, felt it ripping through muscle and lodging against bone. Agony loosed an animal scream in his head. Grey cliffs, blue sky, and green trees streamed into one long tail of color as he spiraled toward oblivion.

"Jhared?"

A distant voice reached him through layers of fog. Jhared tried to answer, but couldn't utter a sound. He couldn't catch his breath for the pain in his chest. Heartbeats echoed faintly in his ears.

"Jhared!"

Someone tugged at his body. He let the warmth of that rare contact pull him through a fog-shrouded path until he could open his eyes. Branlen knelt beside him, gripping his shoulder. The boy's startled blue gaze darted over his face, as if trying to determine whether this could possibly be a big brother's joke.

"What in Cael's darkness…?"

"I was…we were…falling." Jhared struggled for breath. No shaft pierced his heart, yet emptiness grew within him as though something vital had ruptured. Nothing had so overwhelmed him since his mother's death. His Teachers snapped a warning in his mind: *"Weak-willed child, you must maintain control!"*

"I was halfway to the river when I heard you yell." Branlen's hand tightened on Jhared's shoulder. "I've never heard such a sound. I thought you were…I thought you were dying."

Jhared took another breath and tried to summon an image of tranquility from the exercises General Nadel had taught him. He sought an explanation he could give the boy. He wished he had one for himself.

"It's only the fast, Bran. A passing dizziness. By tomorrow, I'll want to gobble up the remains of Neta's winter stores." Slowly, he sat up and tried a smile. "Maybe that's why the Becoming is held in the spring, eh?"

Branlen returned the smile hesitantly. He knew Jhared was talking nonsense.

To give his reassurance some weight, Jhared forced himself to his feet and straightened, rubbing the center of his chest with one hand. The meadow tilted for a moment, then righted itself. Branlen kept a grip on his arm.

"I'm fine, brother. I need to find the bird. And you've a job to do as well."

Bran's face lightened. "I'll stay and help. I've plenty of time to reach the temple, and Mother won't expect me back until after the blessing."

The raptor must die…. Of course she must. The temple ordered it.

"Jhared? Are you really all right?"

"No…" Jhared blinked. "I mean, yes, yes. You can stay."

Together they climbed down the hill to the river. Jhared gazed across the fertile valley nestled below the foothills. The Artas blew moist and gentle from the west, carrying rain from the distant Amurian coast to drop across the knees of the Parnas Mountains. Jhared had hunted throughout the borderlands between mountain and valley, river and forest since he was old enough to draw a bow, but never a hawk, never one of the cursed. The landscape wavered in his vision. He paused to steady himself. Below him, the river ran fast and full with the spring thaw. During the Exile War nearly a century and a half ago, the valley would have looked very different: brown and dead from drought. Only blood had watered the land then: the blood of his countrymen, the blood of his ancestors. It was right to remember those deaths today.

"But Madam Trianor, what happened to the Avelune after the war? After Tumal the Just drove them out of the country?"

"They died of shame, child. Just the same as your mother would if she knew the kind of questions you ask! Back to the lesson: tell me the names of the men and women killed in the Battle of Parnas Valley."

He had been no more than eight winters and greedy for knowledge when he'd been so careless as to ask those questions. His mother had died only months later, just as his Teacher warned. A summer fever had taken her, but Jhared had known it was a punishment for his greed. *Desire in a Shorn man is death.* He straightened and made his way after Branlen. Beyond the open meadow, he passed under the crumbling arches of the aqueduct. Branlen had sprawled across the soft spring grass near the riverbank to wait for him. The boy gave him an innocent grin.

Only then did Jhared realize his mistake. He had submitted to his foster brother's begging and allowed the boy to be his witness, despite Madam Trianor's disapproval. He was accustomed to her frowns and cautions whenever Branlen insisted on tagging along with him to the barracks or into the wilds, but now Jhared wondered if she had known something about the pain of this hunt. He wished she could have spoken of it; he would have spared Branlen the worry.

"Brother, I think it's time for you to return to the city. The council—"

Bran leaped up, his blue-grey eyes stormy. "You think I won't be careful. I will! A Forest Guard patrolman does whatever he's ordered, right?"

"Bran, we're not playing games. Not today." Jhared gave the boy a troubled glance. As a child, he had learned not to consider alternatives to a life of service; it was part of what his kind owed. A Shorn woman, if lucky and bright, would be an elder's scribe, a clerk, or perhaps some elder's house servant. For a fit Shorn man, the only question was to which military division he would be assigned, and even that decision was made by the generals. It disturbed Jhared that Branlen, who by his family's status owned the most options of any child in Avelos, wanted to follow his foster brother's predetermined path.

"That's not it," he sighed. "Look at me. This is a path we cannot share. If you return quickly, you could do me the favor of telling your mother and father that I've downed the bird. They'll be eager for news."

Branlen looked doubtful, but then his eyes came to rest on Jhared's face. "All right," he said, shuffling a foot in the dirt with uncharacteristic shyness. "I'll walk you to the high temple when you return."

"I'd like that. Thank you."

"No debt between us," the boy replied, his smile returning.

Oh my brother, the debt between us is greater than you understand. Jhared didn't voice the thought; Bran's smile was a balm. He didn't want to lose it. He reached over and ruffled the boy's bright hair. "I'll meet you at home. Go on now. Don't dawdle."

With relief and regret he watched Branlen turn and trot into the thicket, then set himself to the task of finding the hawk, searching the reeds and brush near the riverbank, where he knew the creature had tumbled. As he worked, his thoughts rushed along as rapidly as the swollen tributary beside him. His Teaching was nearly complete. Slaying the bird was the final task before he entered the Becoming, the rite that would bind him to Avelos. Tomorrow, if Riana willed it, he would take his place among the people.

His place. His stomach churned with all that implied: Service. Duty. Reparation. Jhared stretched one arm over his shoulder, recoiling when he touched his scars. Why must the bird be downed in early spring? Nesting time. Not only had he slain the hawk, but he had left a nest of orphaned chicks calling helplessly to the sky. He hadn't expected to feel this way, not about a creature Riana cursed. He hadn't expected to care about anything besides completing the task set for him. Now he wondered on the purpose of it.

With a sharp breath, Jhared caught himself and hastily blanked his mind of his faithless thoughts, but it was too late; the Teachers within him had already heard them.

"Twelve years of Teaching and you think you know something the elders don't? Arrogant, insolent boy! You don't have the right! Not traitor-born as you are."

A memory caught him: Elder Trianor sprawled on the floor gasping in pain; Jhared aghast, the sword still in his hand. He had lost control of his destructive urges that day. His Teachers ripped through the memory and made the pain his own: *"It is that easy for you to cause harm, boy. It is that easy for you to harm those who love you. To harm Avelos. Desire in a Shorn man is death."*

Jhared gritted his teeth and bore the consequences of his failure. He shouldn't need reminders. His Avelune ancestors had forfeited his right to question when they betrayed Avelos. His place was to repay the debt. Whatever Riana and Avelos required of him, he would provide. He would prove that to them all today.

He made a spiral to the goddess, hoping to balance his error. He couldn't afford to misstep. Three initiates had already failed the Becoming this spring. The wolves feasted on their bodies. No one would remember their names.

He found the hawk enclosed in a leafy bush. The branches curved around her as though she had nested there. Carefully, Jhared pushed aside the brush and lifted her out. As he cradled the lifeless body, other memories rose unbidden: a dove rescued from the cat's jaws; Madam Trianor's fury when she discovered he had healed a cursed creature; the sensation of the warm, soft neck snapping between his fingers as Elder and Madam Trianor watched to be certain of it. He had been too old to cry, but Tierzen had recognized his grief as he cupped the limp body in his palms.

"No, Jhared, you mustn't," the elder had warned. "Your kind cannot afford sympathy for what is cursed. You must reject such things if you hope to resist the flaws in your own blood."

Cool forest air fanned Jhared's face. He took deep breaths and tamped down the recollection. Raising his head to the sky, he murmured a single word, a prayer: "Forgive."

He laid the hawk's body on the ground and cut the arrow shaft close to her breast. Arrows were dear, but he couldn't force himself to further defile the creature by pulling the head free. A gift to Riana should be given intact, he reasoned. He placed the body in the leather pouch slung behind his back, then turned southwest for the journey home. He would enter the high temple before sundown. The judges would be waiting.

He jogged across the wooded hills toward the settlements at the skirts of the city. Even now, the run felt good, burning away some of his restiveness and allowing him to regain control of himself. His body reached for the wind as he negotiated a twisted path through the trees along the borders of the estates that belonged to guild masters and elders. A dog barked at him from the edge of one grand park. He quickened his pace. Soon the forest began to thin, offering a clear view of the walls.

Velantar. It meant *Heart's Hold* in the ancient tongue. From this distance, Riana's city still dazzled Jhared with its majesty. Although he had traveled throughout Avelos during his training, he had seen no other creation of man that could match its size or energy: not Makri with its purple vineyards or glimmering Lake Linde or the wooden keep of Clan Ontera. The dome of the high temple and the grand tower of the high chieftain's palace sparkled from atop the crown of Travitar Hill, standing sentinel over the two sisters: Rianala Hill to the north and Cirolan Hill to the south. Even the Circles of the Lost looked graceful from here; the grey stone turned rosy in the afternoon sun.

Jhared left the forest where the path met the road to Alende's Gate, joining a handful of village clansmen and city folk seeking protection before sundown. As he hurried along with them, his thoughts still twisted over what he had suffered in the meadow. A scout must understand his inner world before he can understand the outer one, General Nadel would say.

If the general were here now, he would, in fact, be ticking off the possibilities about the strange vision he experienced: a result of Jhared's fast, a sign of fever, the touch of disorder. Jhared shied away from that last, letting his mind wander back to an old lesson from the general. The company had camped for the night north of the Jewel River, not far from the Laebeki border. They had encountered a band of raiders that day, but after a brief skirmish and a long chase, they had ended with one of their own injured and no capture. Around the fire in the cold forest, the soldiers had cursed the raiders and told stories of the blood offerings to demons that made them so cunning. Jhared found himself, as ever, outside the circle of discussion. General Nadel had noticed his detachment and approached him on the opposite side of the fire.

"You have not joined the conversation, Patrolman. Do you consider yourself above mixing with my coarse clansmen?"

Jhared looked up, startled. "No, sir. I'm privileged to be among them."

"But?"

But it's wiser for a Shorn man to keep quiet when tempers are hot, he thought. "But I learn more from listening," he told the general, a safer truth.

General Nadel seemed to consider this, stroking a hand over his neat golden beard. "You'd best be wary how you interpret what you hear."

Jhared knew a stir of apprehension. "I'm not certain I understand."

"All that we see, hear, and touch is veiled by what we wish, what we need, what we've been told by others. Have you not heard stories of soldiers lost in the

Barren? Those who survive describe fantastic specters of lush plum trees and blue lakes that disappear just as their refuge is sought. A scout cannot afford such misperceptions. We must test and question, or the veil of our longing may lead us down the trail of our enemy, when we believe we are tracking a friend."

The general nodded toward the patrol. "The men are frustrated with their failure tonight. Their arguments are distorted by emotion. But my men know better than to act on such notions." He picked up a long stick from a pile of firewood. "Close your eyes, boy."

Jhared obeyed, baffled. He heard the general scraping the stick against the dusty ground.

"Open your eyes. Look down. What do you see?"

Firelight flickered over the markings on the ground, a sketch of a simple goblet. "A cup, sir."

"Ah, a cup." The general lifted the stick to point toward the soldiers who were passing wine around their circle and pouring it carelessly. "Lots of cups around, eh?"

"Well, yes, sir," Jhared said, growing more uncomfortable. The men had been drinking for some time. Arguments were likely to be backed by fists soon.

General Nadel gestured again with the stick. "In fact, you're seeing a cup in this picture *because* you noticed those cups around the fire. They're on your mind."

"As you say, sir."

"Now tell me: what are you really thinking about the men?"

There was a silence. Jhared held his breath. This was the kind of lesson Madam Trianor preferred; she knew so many ways to expose his flaws. He didn't expect it from the general. He swallowed. "They're true-hearted Forest Guard, sir. I'm lucky to serve with them."

General Nadel tilted his head back and roared out a long laugh. A few of the men glanced over to see what the Shorn boy had done to so amuse their general. Nadel folded his arms over his chest, his expression growing sharper.

"Luck," he said to Jhared, "has nothing to do with it. Not with your presence in this company and not with anything that happened today. We failed. Now another dangerous band of raiders is loose in Avelos. What of that, soldier? Tell me your mind and not some Teacher's rhetoric."

Jhared sucked a breath. This command was not simply unexpected; it was dangerous. Yet he could do nothing but answer. Despite everything, he discovered that he *wanted* to answer.

"I believe we needn't have failed. We could have had the raiders."

"Go on, then."

"We left a gap when we tried to close on them. Where the river split the forest. We assumed the spring flood would keep them from daring the water, but we should have covered it."

General Nadel watched Jhared closely.

"The men blame our failure on some preternatural strength of our enemy, but no one has bothered to consider our own errors!" He stopped, dismayed by his outburst. Deep within him, his Teachers fumed. He would pay for it later.

"Look at the picture," the general commanded, tapping the ground with his stick. "What do you see now?"

Jhared glanced at the ground and blinked. The goblet was gone; in its place lay the silhouette of two warriors confronting one another in a challenge. "Angry men, sir."

"Ahhh. Angry men? Like the anger you're feeling toward the patrol, perhaps?" General Nadel snapped the branch in half and tossed it away as he stood. "To everything there's more than one interpretation, and each is shadowed by the veils a man brings to the situation. Do not let your veils prevent you from understanding or keep you from acting. I won't have it, soldier."

The general looked down and met Jhared's gaze. In that moment, Jhared had realized he had been wrong: the general would never trick him into revealing his flaws; he already knew them all.

The hail of the guard in the tower brought Jhared back to the moment. He fell into line with the others awaiting entry, praying the City Guard on duty wasn't in a querulous mood. He couldn't afford to be delayed with an interrogation, or anything worse. As Jhared filed through the gate, he wondered what veils he carried with him today. Would they lead him down the wrong path in the Becoming? He shoved down the thought. It was no time for doubt. The guard, a burly, bored-looking fellow, eyed him without interest, gave a perfunctory glance at his documents bearing the stamp of the Minister of the Teaching, and waved him through.

Jhared made his way past Aelend Prison, the City Guard barracks, and the Forest Guard garrison before turning away from the outer wall and into the maze of twisting streets. Here in the city's innards, Jhared could see and smell the decay. The noisy, crowded lower circles of the city routinely confused strangers and could be dangerous for those who didn't know which lanes to avoid. He once heard a soldier from Clan Nadaren complain that the Lady of Order herself would get lost amid the city's chaos. But Velantar moved in rhythms that Jhared recognized, even if he didn't find them comforting.

As he strode deeper into the heart of the city, the buildings on either side of him leaned precariously toward one another, as if sharing recollections of better times. Craftsmen closed up shops. Men strode toward the taverns. Women and girls dressed in clan colors drifted toward their circles' chapels for the evening devotion. In front of him, two women emerged from a weaver's cottage. He saw the younger woman's distended belly a moment after he spotted her guardian's green and blue striped robes. His heart lurched as they turned toward him. He dropped his gaze to the ground and backed up a handful of steps. Although scarves concealed the young woman's face and temple blessings hung from her neck, he couldn't risk the accusation that he had laid the curse of the Shorn upon her unborn child. Shorn men went to the scourging stones for such things, if they didn't first fall into the hands of a neighborhood mob. To his right, a narrow alley curved south. Without glancing up, he left the busy street behind.

It grew quieter as he drew away from the main street down the dusky lane. He hoped the women had not seen him. Every Avelonian woman had cause to dread that she would bear an Avelun, one whom the guardians would carry to the temple to be Shorn. He despised the thought that he might have added to her fear. No one could say for certain why the curse landed among even the most pious families when many of the Shorn couples who dared to have children produced no afflicted offspring. He thought of his own mother: she had not been Shorn; neither had the man who fathered him. He wondered what they had done to protect themselves from the curse. What charms and prayers had failed them?

"One of the cursed dares to trespass. I told you there'd be poison here, Ilvio."

The cold words, ringing like an echo of his thoughts, made Jhared halt. He swore under his breath when he saw where his inattention had led him. Not Laebeki raiders, but an ambush all the same. Four men emerged on either side of the alley, blocking his way.

"Poison that must be purged!" the one called Ilvio crowed, patting the knife in his belt. Red-headed and sharp-eyed, he was a solid, stocky young man. The two others beside him looked younger, brothers from their similar features. All four wore clean, well-made clothes. Their malicious grins exposed good teeth. This wasn't one of the ragged bands that skittered through the shadows, hiding from the City Guard and tormenting whatever passerby they might for the sake of coin. This band wanted Jhared and the others like him.

"Of course it must be purged," said the first man. "That is what we strive for."

Slightly apart from the rest, the first speaker was a few years Jhared's senior, fine-looking and with an air of command in his tone. Jhared knew this one. His father served with Elder Trianor on the Council of Clans. Elder Rud was no friend to the Minister of the Teaching. Jhared pressed his expression into neutrality. This could go badly.

Drawing a centering breath, he kept his chin level and voice even, but made certain not to meet the other's gaze. "I know you, Maren Rud. It's a worthy band you have. Fit for greater challenges than the likes of me. Why not honor them with a hunt in the wilds and let me pass?"

Maren hesitated, a flash of uncertainty in his eyes. Jhared hoped he might stand down as easily as that. Then recognition replaced uncertainty and a slow, mocking smile transformed his features to ice. "Look boys, I know this poison! He's Tierzen Trianor's foul pet." Maren ran his gaze over Jhared, and his expression turned to one of disgust. "We're here in the name of Tumal's Legacy to see you pay for your crimes. If you want to pass, you will do what we command."

Tumal's Legacy. Jhared struggled to maintain his calm. That influential faction maintained a strict interpretation of Shorn Law and saw to it that Shorn men and women who transgressed were pushed off the top of the city walls. "What is it you want?" Jhared asked steadily.

"Pay a toll as a sign of your loyalty: give us what you carry in your bag."

Jhared's hand tightened on the satchel. "I cannot. What is here belongs to Riana and none other. If it's a toll you want, I have…" He thought quickly: his bow, his bag, a small knife, and a few coins in the pouch at his belt. Nothing of interest to young men who spent their days and their fathers' wealth in the city. Maren seemed to know it even before Jhared could finish.

"We don't want your trinkets. We want a sign of your service. If you cannot give it to us, you must face a trial."

"Trial! Trial!" called the two younger boys.

Jhared held himself still. "If you let me pass, the trial that awaits me is beyond anything you might devise."

Maren's expression darkened. "You dare to protest what we rightfully ask of you? You think that soiling an elder's home means you need not prove yourself? Is that it, you filthy raven-spawn?"

Even standing in a dark lane, a petty bully in a coarse gang, Maren's manner radiated authority. He was city-bred in a privileged house; he and his companions would wield true power one day.

"I will prove myself today and each day I serve Avelos," Jhared said without moving. "What trial would you have of me?"

Maren's lip curved smugly. "Since you have no token to contribute, we will hear the atrocities you have committed against Avelos."

"I'll start!" Ilvio stepped forward.

"No. *I* will begin." Maren swaggered before his companions. "Witness, all! Here stands one of the cursed. Know him by his outrageous height, his eyes the color of treachery, and his traitor's scars. He is filthy, like the vulture that eats its own dead; faithless, like the jay that lays its eggs in another's nest; and cunning, like the crow who thieves the treasures of others. He is Shorn, and we will hear him confess his crimes."

Maren gestured at one of the younger boys, who leaped to obey. "Your kind conspired with the enemies of Avelos. Do you confess this treason before the people?"

Jhared knew what he needed to do, but he couldn't force himself to answer.

The boy glowered. "Face your crimes or face your sentence. Do you confess?"

It is that easy for you to cause harm, boy.

Jhared cleared his throat. "I do."

"Your kind betrayed the council and our high chieftain. Do you confess this before the people?"

"I do," he repeated.

"You caused the death of innocents in the Exile War."

"Burned our crops."

"Destroyed our villages."

"Violated our women."

Over and again they shamed him with the truth. He knew they only waited for him to defy them, so they could beat him for it. Even so, as it continued, he thanked Riana for the training that helped him to keep hold of his emotions. Evil existed in his blood, passed down through generations; he deserved this humiliation. On this day of all days, it was profoundly fitting. He should be tested. He must be.

"It is good you admit your crimes," Maren spat finally. "But have you prepared to pay your debt? Are you ready to die for me? When the Sahisten armies come against Avelos once again, will you take a spear in your side and watch the life bleed from you, knowing it's me you protect?"

Jhared hissed and twitched a half-step toward the man before he could stop himself. Too revealing, that gesture. Ilvio caught it. With a snarl, the boy pulled the knife from his belt. The gang was ready to escalate, and Jhared dreaded it. With four of them, a fight would be perilous. In the confusion of such a brawl, he might accidentally cause them serious injury, and the consequences of that were too horrible to consider. He couldn't want to harm them.

He *didn't* want to harm them.

Jhared rubbed a hand across his face to regain his mask of composure, and contemplated his alternatives: aware, with a growing urgency, of the lowering sun. He could run. He would easily outstrip them, and dignity could not play a part in the decision, but fleeing would only excite them. Like any predators, they would be driven to pursue. What he needed was to make them believe the thrill of harassing him was no longer worth the cost, when in truth there was no cost he could levy. *Blind them with their own veils until they cannot see that truth.* It was General Nadel's lesson, although Jhared had an uneasy feeling the general wouldn't approve of its use on an elder's son. Within him, the Teachers stayed quiet. Alone, he made his decision and steeled himself for the unpleasant task of bringing Maren down.

He shifted his stance and clasped his hands behind his back to show the gang they still offered no threat. "Such foolish behavior is no surprise from you, Maren Rud. I suppose this is the kind of elder you will be in your father's place. You will bully the council like the bossy child you are now."

Maren's features turned a mottled red. "You dare to criticize the council? You walk awfully close to the line of treason."

"Missing the point, as ever," Jhared pressed. "There is no treason in criticizing a gutless boy who needs a posse to torment a single, harmless passerby."

Ilvio snickered. Maren shot him a black look.

"We should shove him off the wall for that," Ilvio said. "See him splatter, eh?"

They gathered closer around Jhared. They were no longer laughing. Ilvio raised his blade.

Ignore them. They'll wait for Maren's lead. Fuddle his judgment with his own anger. Make him want you for himself. Jhared looked back at Maren. This time, he met the other's gaze directly and held it. "When you are elder, will you also continue to expect others to do for you what you cannot do for yourself?"

"I need no one else to make you regret your impudence!"

Jhared readied himself for the inevitable, letting his bow and his bag slide to the ground and checking that his knife was secure in his belt. Even if it meant taking their beating, he would not dare to pull the blade. Finally, with a feigned yawn, he offered the greatest insult yet: slowly and casually he turned his back to the man.

Shocked silence spread across the alley. Jhared could feel the others' disbelief and knew they all stared at him. He straightened his shoulders against the weight of their fury.

"Do you think I won't hurt you for that?" Maren ground out, as the last of his inhibition shredded. "No Shorn traitor shows me his back and goes unpunished. You're mine!"

The man charged, growling for the others to fall away. Jhared kept still, counting the running steps. He felt the rush of air as Maren reached upward to grasp at him. With the precision of intensive training, Jhared reached over his shoulder and grabbed Maren's wrist in a solid hold. Stepping backwards into the attack, he plowed his elbow into the man's belly. Then, twisting quickly, he flung Maren over his shoulder and hurled him onto the ground.

Air whooshed from Maren's lungs as he slammed onto the stone. Jhared dropped down with one knee against his throat, putting enough weight in it to make the threat clear. The man stared up at him, dazed and bleary-eyed and enraged.

Jhared pitched his voice so the others would hear. "You are a coward, Maren. You don't dare to face me unless surrounded by your pack. The temple says Cael has a special torment for cowards, so think on that when you lay to sleep tonight."

He rose to scowl at each of the others. Ilvio stared at Jhared with frustrated longing, his fingers still curled around his knife, his dilemma clear. *He wants to lead this band, but he knows they won't follow him. Yet.* Jhared forced himself not to hurry as he picked up his bow and his bag, then turned his back to the gang once more.

He proceeded down the alley with a deliberate, collected pace, listening for the onrush of an attack. His back prickled in anticipation of a blow.

It didn't come. As soon as he turned the corner, he sprinted forward to make up for lost time. Using the rhythm of his pounding feet, he brought his mind back to the importance of what lay before him. The significance of the Becoming repeated over and over in his head. With each step he delivered himself to be bound to Avelos, to accept his place, and all that came with it.

2.

LOYALTY

Jhared sped the rest of the way through the alleys, up Travitar Hill to Elders' Circle. The elegant stone dwellings of the elders and local officials curved into a crescent around the center of the city, rising against the sky in the same silver tones as the mountains. Jhared crossed Elders' Row, where the pennants of the fifteen first-clans snapped over the street, and entered the alley behind the houses, passing between the individual kitchen gardens and the row of apartments where the scribes lived within the reach of their elders. The mark of the black feather fluttered at each door, warning that someone Shorn lived within. Jhared stopped behind the home of Elder Tierzen Trianor. It had sheltered him for half his life, but at times the fine house still felt foreign. He patted the stone. When he left tonight, the black feather flag would be removed. He would no longer have a place here.

Inside it was dim and cool. He hurried through the kitchen to the great room. The hearth was banked, and every chair at the table sat primly in its place. Light from an unshuttered window fell in a slanted square against the paneled wall. All else was still.

"Branlen?"

Silence. Alabaster the kitchen cat padded across the room with no more acknowledgment than an irritated jerk of his white tail and disappeared down the hall.

"Madam Trianor? Neta?"

"It's past time you returned. Elder Trianor is waiting for you."

It took an act of will not to stiffen at the crystal-cold tone of that voice. Jhared looked up slowly, unwilling to show his surprise and displeasure to the man entering the room.

"Hello, Sirol."

The Shorn scribe's habitual grimace deepened. His crippled left shoulder twitched as he pointed at Jhared with an ink-stained finger. "The sun is near to setting on your Becoming and you've only just begun your trials. It's no time for rest."

Jhared focused on the scribe's crooked shoulder and wondered how the man always found a way to tell him what to do. Sirol was no part of this family, although he acted as though he were. The careless knife that had crippled him at his Shearing had left him unfit to pay his debt as a soldier; instead, he served as a scribe to Elder Trianor. The man was loyal and sharp-witted, and Tierzen valued him most dearly among all his assistants. Perhaps that was why Sirol's contempt always stung.

"I passed the first trial," Jhared said, as though it might prove something. "I have the bird." He set his bow and quiver near the hearth. As he turned toward the door, Sirol stepped in his way.

"Of course you did, soldier. I only wonder why it took so long. Killing is what Shorn men are born for."

Jhared's breath caught. For an instant, he was spinning out of the sky with an arrow in his breast. He pressed his hand against the tabletop to orient himself and swallowed back the cutting words he might have said to the crippled scribe. "Yes, well, I've done what was required. Move aside. I'm on my way."

As he pushed past the scribe, Sirol grabbed his sleeve. "Don't think that your strong arms and quick eyes will be enough to take you through the Becoming," growled the man. "Don't be cocky and think the rest will be as easy as the bird. You must not fail. Elder Trianor will pay for it if you do."

"Jhared? Is that you?" Tierzen's voice reached into the hall; then the elder's earnest face appeared at his library doorway. "You're back. Very good. We have to hurry."

Sirol released Jhared with a flick of his wrist, like a man discarding something useless. "Because of you, he'll pay," the scribe repeated softly.

"You're ready?" Tierzen drew a cape over his shoulders.

Bewildered, Jhared watched the scribe depart before turning to look at his foster father. "Ready? Almost. I should clean up. I'm—"

"Do not change or bathe. Go to the temple wearing the sweat of the hunt to mark your labor. Come. We must speak on the way." Tierzen started for the front door.

Jhared followed him into the street. "Sir, I didn't expect to see you until tomorrow."

In the orange light, Tierzen's fine features tightened into lines of uncharacteristic frustration. "Quickly. Quickly, now. The sun is nearly at the horizon, and you must give them no excuse to turn you away."

Despite his shorter stature, Tierzen set a ground-eating pace down the stone-paved lane. Jhared had to stretch his legs to keep up. He felt like a child again, trying to match the stride of his Teacher.

A chill breeze warned that the night would be a cold one. Winter had not entirely relinquished her grip. Some of the people they passed waved to the elder or peered curiously, but Tierzen, who usually had a nod for everyone, hardly seemed to notice.

"I've never broken Shorn Law for you," the elder started, staring ahead toward the temple. "As Minister of the Teaching, I could tell you things about the Becoming."

"Of course you haven't. I'd never believe any such thing. Why do you—"

Tierzen shook his head, warding off Jhared's question. "Only listen. The Legacy knows I could spill secrets to you, but they also know I won't. My hope is that they have not guessed what I'm going to tell you now."

A trickle of cold sweat ran down Jhared's neck. Tierzen's hands closed into fists as the elder turned to look at him.

"Tumal's Legacy wants you to fail."

Jhared lifted a hand to rub at his chest. "Of course they do. They believe every Shorn initiate will fail. Their caution makes us work harder and safeguards the city."

"No. I'm not talking about faction doctrines," Tierzen replied heavily. "This is not about the welfare of Avelos or the payment of the debt. They want *you* to fail. You, Jhared Denaban."

You must not fail. Elder Trianor will pay for it if you do. The street was suddenly too narrow, the city too confining. Jhared wanted to run; he needed to be pounding through the forest, far from Maren, from Sirol, from the Legacy. Instead, he could only whisper, "Why?"

"Because you were sent to me for the Teaching, and I raised you as my son. Tumal wrote that the Teaching must be a duty uncontaminated by any other bond. They will claim we have violated Shorn Law."

"I don't understand. When Mother died, the council approved your request that I stay with you. Why do they fight it now?"

Tierzen gazed at him unhappily. "That is not exactly the way of it. The council never agreed."

"Then how?"

Years of conversations with the elder taught Jhared to respect the clever men who ruled in Avelos, and to be aware of the never-ending rivalries that found expression in always subtle and often dangerous forms. As he considered what he knew, the unlikely answer to his own question slid into place like an arrow to the string, startling him with its enormity. "If the council never agreed, then High Chieftain Rumar claimed his sovereign right to support you."

Something wistful flickered in Tierzen's expression. He gave Jhared a half-smile. "It never fails to surprise me how quickly you recognize the patterns of a thing. Yes, Rumar claimed his sovereign right. To this day I cannot say whether he planned to do it or he just tired of the council's quarreling."

"Why would he use that kind of power for…me?"

"It wasn't for you." Tierzen sighed. "Not really. Too many reasons play a part to fully explain it. That autumn was a dark one. The clans had lost many to the fever and were pressing the city for aid we didn't have, Sahiste had crossed the Burn to raze Ravia, and Adan Rumar was grieving the deaths of his own wife and son. He ended the debate on the matter without council consent. It is possibly the most reckless act I've witnessed him commit. He may yet come to regret it."

"You gained enemies that day," Jhared murmured.

"Yes. Many saw it as an overt act of favoritism. The northern five used it as a way to raise objection once again to the high chieftain's sovereign right. As for Tumal's Legacy, I've openly opposed them in matters of Shorn Law and the Teaching. They have bided their time for your Becoming. If you are found to be unfit, they will say it proves that my philosophy about the Teaching is wrong and dangerous. They plan to discredit me with your failure."

Something disturbing and powerful surged through Jhared at the thought of threat to Tierzen. He pushed the wave back and locked it away with an efficiency born of long practice. Still, he heard the unacceptable strain in his voice when he spoke. "I will never give the council reason to rebuke you. I swear it, I—"

"Don't!" Tierzen's voice echoed down the street. "Don't swear such things. Cael feeds upon the souls of men whose broken oaths were never within their power to keep. I have claimed you as my son, Jhared. None can make me regret that claim. None."

Jhared swallowed and looked down. He would never understand why the elder fought for him when his own father had fled, leaving his mother alone with a cursed child. *Goddess, what I owe this man.*

Tierzen went on. "Speak what you have learned but speak carefully. Beware of your questions." The elder grimaced. "Your questions, Jhared. The judges will read them as doubt, or worse, as defiance."

Jhared nodded, stomping on his need to know, even as Tierzen lifted a hand to cut him off.

"No more. I have warned you. It must be enough."

"Yes, sir. It will be." The words sounded confident, though his palms were slick with his uncertainty.

"You were so young when you came to us," his foster father said more gently. "No other Shorn child has been raised by his Teachers. I had great notions of what I could create…of what you could become if we gave you both the discipline of the Teaching and the care of a family. I still think it can be so. I just pray I've done you no disservice by raising you as my own."

They had arrived at the crown of Travitar Hill, the heart of Heart's Hold. The circular plaza was bounded by Elders' Hall and Alende's monument on the right, the high chieftain's palace on the left, and directly ahead, the high temple compound. Stone walls and guarded corridors closed all around Jhared. He tugged at his shirt collar and drew a deep breath. A City Guard patrol marched toward the palace, boots thudding on the cobbles.

"This is as far as I will go," said Tierzen, stopping by Riana's fountain.

Jhared didn't know what to say. For years, he had struggled toward this test, and now he discovered that success depended on something beyond his own worthiness. He looked down, remembering the knife at his belt. Only sanctified weapons could be carried into the temple. He slid the blade from its sheath and held it out to Tierzen. It was plain, but as well-made as any Avelonian blade could be. He was suddenly, fiercely glad Maren hadn't accepted it. Tierzen had given it to him on the day Jhared first memorized the Shorn Laws. That day he had first called his Teacher Father.

Tierzen took the knife and placed it in his own belt. "Tomorrow you will reclaim it." The elder lifted a hand, but didn't reach out to him. "Goodbye, Jhared."

Branlen waited under the great statue of Alende Isan near Elders' Hall. He faced the noble figure with his hands clasped behind him and his head tilted upward. Jhared smiled in spite of himself. He, too, had once imagined himself as Alende, leading the people from the destruction of their ancestral mountain home all the way to the valley that became Velantar. The memorial towered over the courtyard, where Tumal the Just had commissioned it after the Exile War. With the vigilant hound Rodleto at his side, Alende held his staff to ward his people. Crushed beneath his boot heel was the sharp-beaked head of one of Cael's waylayers. Tall, bold letters at the base of the statue proclaimed *Loyalty. Faith. Will.*

Could a Shorn man rise to meet the challenge implied in those words? Would it matter if he could? From habit, Jhared reached out a hand to stroke the boot of the cold figure, a soldier's invocation for strength. "It's time."

Branlen turned, and the boy's gaze brightened. "There you are! I was beginning to wonder if you fled into the mountains and I would have to face the council by myself."

Jhared laughed nervously. Bran seemed to realize that the jest wasn't a very good one and patted his arm. "It's all right. Let's go."

"You're prepared, Bran? You'll be swearing witness before the high chieftain now. And High Priestess Nemiah."

The boy rolled his eyes. "I know. I know. We've talked it all through."

"Right. It's fine. You'll be fine."

They walked beside the high temple's long, arched loggia to the sanctuary. The setting sun struck the domed building with gold, illuminating the intricate images carved along the walls. Riana's creations—sphere and sky in their eternal dance—had been gracefully chiseled into the stone and surrounded by her five Chosen, the Aye, blessed of Riana: Ularian the archer in his tree, Silvien the healer in her vine, Trevazio the scout in his wolf, Shira the messenger in her hare, and Mavias the captain in his stallion. They had been soldiers once—all the Aye and Cael's Ael—in the Great Wars of Riana and Cael. Somewhere within their mad, mortal existence, within the bodies of the creatures they possessed, the Chosen still remembered battle.

The circle of the five Aye on the temple wall was incomplete, broken and empty where the stone had been damaged, but Jhared had never before wondered what once filled those spaces. He had never given the carvings more than a glance. Now, everything around him stood out with unexpected clarity—even the rough texture of the cracked stone—as he realized it might be the last time he passed this way. With a belated word of respect for the Chosen, he climbed the wide, steep staircase to the arched entrance. One of the white-cloaked Arionade stood watch, but a novice in brown robes stopped Jhared before he and Branlen reached the guard.

"You have come to try the test of Becoming?" The voice of the ruddy-cheeked girl echoed with the seriousness of the newly anointed.

"I have."

"Have you brought the gift?"

Jhared slid the satchel from his shoulder, quelling a fresh pang of remorse as he passed it to her. Her fingers curled around the leather strap without touching his hand. Then, turning with a haughty step, she ushered them past the sentry.

They followed the novice into the first circle, where the four devotions were celebrated daily and people came to pray before the altar. Branlen caught Jhared's gaze and made a face, mimicking the girl's sobriety behind her back. Jhared's stomach did a nervous flip at the boy's irreverence, but he only glowered at Branlen in response. He turned his eyes to the chilly room. In daylight, when the sun poured through Riana's eye, the chamber glowed with warmth and color. Now the eye was dimming with the failing sun. The rows of candles that curved along the outer wall sent uneasy shadows up to the arched ceiling. Night was a dangerous time for Riana's people, the time when it was easiest to step off the proper path.

At the center of the first circle stood the altar: a massive, roughly worked piece of granite. Atop the altar, a precisely cut crystal caught the fading light, splitting it into colorful slivers. The priestess led Jhared and Branlen before the stone and directed them to wait. Several moments passed, then a bell began to toll deep, slow notes above them. The tones still hung in the air as High Chieftain Rumar and High Priestess Nemiah entered the room. Rumar, followed by three of the council elders, stood beside the altar. Lady Nemiah glided up a step behind the altar with two priestess attendants. Dim ribbons of color, the last of the light from the prism, painted Lady Nemiah's white robes.

Jhared bowed low, hands outstretched and palms open.

"This child of the goddess seeks admittance to the test of Becoming," began the novice as she laid the bird on the altar. "He has brought the gift. Does Riana acknowledge him?"

The high priestess, an imperious, golden-haired woman, lifted a strong voice. "Does he have witness to the kill?"

"He does."

"Let the witness announce himself."

Branlen advanced to stand under the eyes of the high chieftain and the high priestess. His voice sounded small in the cavernous chamber: small but bold.

"I am Branlen Trianor. I was witness."

Lady Nemiah pointed a pale finger at Branlen. "You are named before Riana of the Spheres as witness to this Becoming. For whom do you speak?"

"For Jhared Denaban."

"Do you swear by Riana's sacred skies that the bird was slain by his own hand?"

"Yes, Lady. I saw the arrow leave his hand and strike the bird. I swear it by the sacred skies."

"Very well. Let all here mark this gift as a sign of Riana's victory over Cael and all his messengers. The goddess grants acknowledgment."

The novice turned to the high chieftain and council members. Dismay clutched Jhared's chest as he looked at the men selected as his judges. The bear-like man who scowled at him wore his beard in braids and bore on his chest the Mavaye sigil of Clan Lasla, one of the northern five. Beside Lasla, a small, anxious man with the sapphire cape of a city elder darted his gaze from the high priestess to the high chieftain and barely gave Jhared a look. The third man surveyed the proceeding with a distant, winter-blue gaze. His shining brown hair was meticulously arranged and fashionably short. The cerulean of his well-tailored shirt and breeches set off the silver at his throat and on his long, slender fingers. Toren Abrigado, Elder of Clan Amerre, Minister of the Treasury, and leader of Tumal's Legacy, looked more a statesman than any of the men beside him.

"Do the people of Avelos give acknowledgment?" asked the novice.

Abrigado leaned over and whispered to the high chieftain. Lines etched Rumar's craggy face as he nodded slowly. The high chieftain didn't match his elders; instead, he was an unruly compliment to the Lady Nemiah. Broad-chested and hale, with tousled copper hair and a finely woven tunic of Clan Manitar's green and silver, he was autumn wind to her summer rain, a weathered oak beside her slender aspen. Lady Nemiah modeled precision and order, while Lord Rumar was strength and action. The juxtaposition gave Jhared a flash of insight: there was a balance here. Riana meant these two to rule beside one another.

"Witness, how do you know the initiate?" Rumar's voice boomed against the stone.

"I…we are foster kin, sir," Branlen said.

"You live as brothers, then?"

Branlen threw an uncertain glance over his shoulder. Jhared could only give what he hoped was an expression of encouragement.

"Yes, sir."

Adan Rumar paused. With sharp eyes he studied Jhared. The high chieftain was not a short man, but Jhared had the ungainly height of the Shorn and was likely still to grow. It felt improper that the leader of Avelos should be forced to look up at him. Jhared hunched a little and kept his eyes fixed on the altar. Did Rumar recall the child he had given to Tierzen years ago? Would he be satisfied by what he saw today?

After a long moment, the high chieftain asked Branlen, "Can you swear that you are not bound by any tie of blood?"

"Yes, sir. I swear no blood tie exists between us."

The high chieftain gave a nod. "The people of Avelos grant acknowledgment. Let Jhared Denaban enter the Becoming."

Anger flashed across Elder Abrigado's features. Jhared tried not to think about what that would mean for him at the trial.

With Branlen's task complete, a priestess escorted him from the chamber. As the boy passed, he gave Jhared a lopsided grin and made the sign for victory with one hand close to his body. Jhared quirked a quick smile, then had to look down to focus his attention where it belonged.

The high priestess presided over the consecration of the sacrifice. At the end of the prayers, she dismissed Jhared to the purification. The brown-robed novice returned to his side, hands clasped at her waist.

"You must cleanse yourself before you face Riana in the vigil. I will take you to the sacred pool." Her nose wrinkled, and Jhared guessed the cleansing was not for the goddess alone. Heat rose to his face, and he bowed his head, hoping she wouldn't notice as she led him out of the chamber.

They walked the wide passages that wound around the sanctuary and deeper into the temple compound. Jhared kept his eyes lowered as a pair of priestesses passed him. At the end of one hall, the novice opened a broad, wooden door, revealing a small dark landing. As she lifted a lamp from a sconce on the wall, light slithered down a spiral staircase into the bowels of the temple. She led Jhared onto the landing and down, her light making ghostly shapes of her form and Jhared's as they descended. He thought he heard the baying of hounds, but that faded into silence as he continued downward. The moist air in the stairway tasted earthy. Condensation glistened on the walls and made the steps slick. At the bottom, the stairway opened into a warm grotto. Jhared looked around and drew a breath in awe.

Riana.

Here in the temple, it could only be the goddess. He had never felt anything similar. Her power thrummed against his eyelids, his lips, the pads of his fingers. The pool in the center of the cave was a black mirror guarded by serpents of steam that arched off the water. Around the pool, the rock walls came to life with carvings of her land and her Chosen. Unlike the images outside the temple, these creatures reached out with such a sense of motion that they seemed ready to escape their stony captivity. Jhared lifted his hand to touch the closest figure, a leaping, wolflike Trevaye, Riana's scout.

"Do not enter the pool without a prayer."

He withdrew his fingers hastily and looked back at the girl. "What prayer should I offer, Lady?" Were there words for the purification he hadn't learned?

"If you are ready, you will know it. Do not fail her, or the trials will go poorly for you."

You must not fail.

The priestess whispered her own prayer, then knelt to dip her fingers into the pool before making her way back up the stairs.

Jhared held very still. The warm mist enveloped him. Somewhere deeper in the cavern, water dripped slowly onto stone. What prayer did Riana want of him? Quietly, he stripped off his clothes and laid them aside. He couldn't help but touch the smooth, undamaged skin over his heart; even now it brought a twinge of pain. Suddenly, he knew the blessing to offer: it was a simple memory from his mother. He wasn't certain he remembered it fully, but it seemed right for today's sacrifices:

"Lady of the Sky, bless the creatures of the wind. For you are the Path that carries us, the Light that guides us, and the Voice that calls us. All creatures heed your order."

As his reverent words echoed over the stone, the mist cleared to let the black pool reflect the lamplight, like stars in a smoky sky. Reassured somewhat, he stepped into the pool and let his muscles relax in the hot water.

He scrubbed the salt and dirt from his skin, then dipped his head and let the water stream from his hair. The heat saturated his body to the core of his bones, making him heavy and languid. In this hallowed place within the earth, time lost its meaning. Moments or hours might have passed before he drew himself from the pool. Slowly, he dressed in the undyed wool tunic and breeches that waited for him. He swayed under the seductive power of the place.

"You are sensitive to the Lady's power. Your visions will be vivid ones."

He turned to face the priestess where she stood in the stairway. Her eyes glittered in the flickering light. He wished he knew whether her words boded well or ill. Visions were the province of Riana's servants who understood the Paths. Did she mean to say that it was right for a Shorn man to suffer visions on the night of his vigil? Or had he already transgressed? Was he supposed to challenge her to prove he knew a man's proper role? Or was she merely taunting him to test if he would be defiant? Dizzy with uncertainty, he did the surest thing he could and offered her a reverent spiral.

By the time they departed the grotto and made their way to a large inner courtyard, the sun was gone and the evening sky glowed with velvet shades of purple. In the center of the courtyard stretched the bare branches of an Ulaye tree: the one that died, it was said, at the moment when his ancestors betrayed Avelos. Beneath the tree stood the vigil lodge, a small wooden structure, round for all Riana's cycles. A grizzled Arionad stared stoically into the night beside the buckskin-covered doorway. Jhared glimpsed the orange of a fire through chinks in the loosely bound walls. The primitive hut, so out of place amidst the sophistication of the city, reminded him that this rite, like the goddess's power, was far older than even the ancient ones who built Velantar centuries ago. He wondered what the rite might have looked like before the treachery of the Avelune and the Exile War, then swiftly buried the thought before it woke the Teachers within him.

The novice stretched her hand toward his brow, and he bent so she could reach him. She sketched a blessing in the air.

"Riana fill you with her purpose," she murmured. "Nothing will come between you and the goddess this night but what you carry with you." She pushed aside the door flap and gestured him inside.

He entered the hut alone. Immediately, thick, sweet smoke billowed around him, filling his lungs. The tiny hut was empty but for the fire in the center. Coughing, he edged his way around the flames to face the doorway and lowered himself onto the small patch of new grass that made the floor.

Jhared didn't know what to expect tonight, but he knew if he were to survive the trials, he needed to regain his focus. Since the hunt, he had let too many things distract him; he needed balance to keep his judgment clear. The smoky air made his eyes water and his head feel light. The flames and the doorway began to rock. He set both hands on the ground beside him, as though that would hold the world in place. As a child, he had loved to stare up at the sky, spinning until the ground swung back and forth beneath him and he could imagine himself airborne; but that sensation had lost its innocent pleasure long ago. Now he only felt sick. He closed his eyes and took a slow breath, reaching toward the point deep within his center. General Nadel had taught him how to slide past every distraction to find that still point. It was the place that could steady him whether he stood before his Teachers or in the midst of combat.

Instead of finding clarity and control, however, he discovered an avalanche of images and emotions waiting for him. Jhared stood on the brink for an instant, watching in horror and fascination. Then the avalanche caught him and pulled him down.

This was the Becoming. He surrendered to it.

The images came quickly, and with no care for order, skipping along the Path on which Riana set his life: His mother's clever fingers picking out a tune. The blood of his first battle. Elder and Madam Trianor claiming him for the Teaching. Marieva's tentative kiss and sudden revulsion. Every image wrenched old emotions with it: Comfort and pride. Bewilderment and desire. He soared one moment, only to plummet the next. Madam Trianor's punishments. Tierzen's patience. Songs and dancing in a warm inn. A Shorn man pushed from the wall. He struggled to recognize the pattern, to find the meaning.

What lesson is this? How do I answer?

The Teachers within him remained silent. No one answered his questions. As it went on, foreign images and new emotions crossed familiar ones: Lying broken on the forest floor, blood smeared across his chest. Calling helplessly from a clifftop nest, weak with hunger.

The Paths of his life branched over and again as Riana and Cael shaped the directions he traveled. The essence of himself branched with them, tangling into blue and red threads, like veins under pale skin. Soon he would be nothing more than slivers of memories he didn't even recognize. The visions continued: A priestess lifted a bloody blade from the ground. He lunged to stab a man who meant to kill him. The flames of a pyre engulfed a woman's body. The fire consumed her clothing, blackened her death mask, and danced in her hair.

That last image belonged to him; he would never forget it. He dived headlong into the memory to stop the foreign ones from breaking him apart.

The fever had taken his mother. Her remains would soon be ash.

The realization of what that meant soaked through the layers of his grief as the rain soaked through his cloak. Jhared stood stiff-legged, watching tongues of flame hiss at the rain and lick hungrily over his mother's body. He couldn't turn his gaze away from her hands. The priestesses who had prepared her had folded them together at her waist, but Mahla Denaban had never clasped her fingers that way, so prim and purposeless. Her hands had always been engaged in some task: repairing the musical instruments others brought to her, teaching Jhared the fingering of a new song, playing her elegant clanharp. The priestesses should have known better.

"It's time to go, Jhared," said a quiet voice above him. "Riana will care for her now." Elder Trianor wiped the rain from his eyes and looked down, but Jhared didn't move; he couldn't. With a loud pop, a log exploded, and the pyre settled lower. When it had all gone to the fire, only bone and muddy ash would remain. He would have nothing and no one to help him remember her.

If I had listened to my Teachers, would she be alive?

"Come now," his Teacher prodded gently, "Madam Trianor will be waiting with something warm for you to drink."

Could I have saved her, or was it too late on the day I was born? Only days ago, he had run home from the Teaching full of questions and found his mother on the floor, delirious, her skin already ablaze. It was his punishment. Madam Trianor had warned him.

"Madam Trianor, what happened to the traitorous Avelune after Tumal the Just drove them out of the country?"

"They died of shame, child. Just the same as your mother would if she knew the kind of questions you ask."

"The fever is everywhere, boy. If we stay in this wet, it will come for you, too. You owe your mother more than that."

This time the elder took Jhared's fingers in a firm grip and compelled him away from the pyre. As Jhared stumbled after his Teacher, he stared over his shoulder until he could no longer see the flames. He didn't understand why the fever *hadn't* taken him; he was the cursed one. Elder Trianor held his hand all the long way back to the house in Elders' Circle. The warm, unprecedented contact only made him more aware of his losses. His mother was gone, his only family, and with her, his place in the world.

At the house, Neta stripped off his sodden clothes, wrapped him in a blanket, and gave him bitter tea to drink. Madam Trianor led him upstairs to sleep on a pallet in the small chamber beside Branlen's room. Sleep never came, though, only a restless daze. He heard the whispers near the bedroom door.

"I've asked the council to let him stay."

"What? You can't mean it, husband. You would bring his curse into our family? To grow beside your son? I see the slyness in him. He's too quiet, too careful. When he smiles, I know he's only trying to manipulate us. And what if he fails the Becoming? What will happen to us then? The council demands—"

"The council is mistaken. Calm your fears, Sarena. I am the Minister of the Teaching, and I say we need not put him out. Yes, the flaws are bred into him, but he doesn't yet intend to be a harm. We'll reforge him so he never does. He's a child, malleable as silver. Compassion is a more effective hammer than fear. I've long believed it; now I have the chance to prove it."

"Then you will risk your own child for this one who is Shorn?"

Jhared buried his head in the blanket and willed himself to hear no more, but he couldn't escape his thoughts: He had caused his father to run away and his mother to die. Now he caused his Teachers only fear. For the first time, the voices in his mind spoke out; they whispered of his transgressions and told him he had been spared by the fever to make reparation. They would be his Teachers too, they said, Teachers he could carry with him who would warn him when he strayed. He would give them his obedience and they would help him to remain within Shorn Law. *"Aberration,"* they called him, and *"Accursed."*

"Accursed."

"It is true that some have named me so," echoed a low voice.

This voice had substance; it cut across his memories and his Teachers' accusations. Jhared startled and opened his eyes. On the opposite side of the fire, now only a pile of glowing embers, a creature glowered at him from an inhuman face. Hollow eye sockets stared from a black, corvid head. The raven's beak gaped just enough to grasp a human skull. Jhared scrambled to his feet and tried to back away, but hours in the same cramped position had left his legs numb. The intoxicating smoke made the world reel. He stumbled toward the fire and barely managed to throw himself to his hands and knees to avoid falling into the embers.

"Goddess save me."

Cael laughed quietly, the sound echoing eerily through the human skull in his beak. Jhared wasn't certain he had won free of the visions after all.

"She is very far from here tonight," the demon answered in an unexpectedly soft voice. "You had a choice, and you called to me instead."

"I didn't. I wouldn't." The suggestion terrified him. Jhared tried to steady himself to study the demon more thoroughly, but discovered he couldn't make his eyes see it clearly.

"Search your visions. Disorder fills your thoughts." The demon twitched its corvid head until the skull in its beak stared at Jhared. "Don't you know who I am?"

"Death," Jhared whispered in dismay. "Chaos and death." He saw his mother's pyre once more. How could he have been so reckless as to call to Cael on the night of his Becoming? He shivered as wind blew through the cracks of the hut.

"Ahhh, yes. A soldier would know me by those names. Although you called me Death long before you ever held a weapon, I think." The demon leaned across the fire, and Jhared had the sense that those blind eyes could see his fear.

"What do you want of me?"

Cael made a calming gesture with one sharp-nailed hand. "Hush. Be easy, soldier. I want nothing from you tonight. You beckoned to me, and I have come with a gift to help you through your trials." That voice again, not fierce and harsh as he expected, but low and beguiling, husky in a way that made him think of crows cawing in the distance or the rustle of the forest at night.

"Chaos cannot help me to survive the Becoming," he declared, and heard his tone, too challenging.

The great beak dipped downward. Cael chuckled softly. "Ah, my boy. You have been long deceived. You have learned only part of who I am. Look upon me not simply as disorder, for I am also chance. The one Riana cannot control. I am relief from the struggle that her order demands. I am freedom."

Another gust of wind rattled the walls. Jhared pulled his robe closer around him, but he still felt exposed. Deceived? Not by his Teachers, and certainly not by the temple. He knew better than to believe anything from the mouth of Cael, but did the demon's words make a strange kind of sense?

The demon's gaze lifted again. "What I hold is a gift that will aid you, not only through the trials, but for the rest of your service to Avelos. Yet I will not demand that you hear me out. I give you the freedom to make your own decision. If you do not want to learn what I have to give, you need only to command me from your sight, and I will go."

Jhared frowned. He hadn't expected this. Threats of punishment or prophecies of horrors he could understand. Now he wasn't certain what to do. If he sent the demon away, he might miss some key to passing the trials. On the other hand, if he allowed Cael to offer him a gift, would the elders think him corrupt? Jhared considered the Teaching and all the obstacles he faced in his lessons. He knew what Tierzen would tell him: avoiding a struggle meant surrendering to his weakness and avoiding an opportunity to learn. He could not command Cael to go; he had to face the demon.

"Tell me what you offer," he answered finally.

"Choice is what I give you," purred Cael. "Riana demands your oath and takes from you all the desires that make you whole. 'Guard yourself from the deepest needs of the Avelune,' she says. But there is a better choice: promise yourself to me. I am the freedom of chaos. Serve Avelos under my guidance rather than hers and you may pursue the needs and wishes that are your birthright." The demon held him in a hollow gaze. "I am Cael. I know you. I know the things you desire."

In a flash of memory, Jhared recalled the dark moments of his unfulfilled desires: Marieva fleeing his embrace; the rocky cliff edge calling him to self-destruction; Maren's band taunting him with impunity. A surprise, that last, and perhaps the most damning. He had not acknowledged the forbidden anger he had allowed himself this afternoon, or how close he had come to lashing out.

It is that easy for you to cause harm, boy.

Desire in a Shorn man is death.

His fists clenched. He feared to meet Cael's black gaze. With proper study, a Shorn man could master the dangerous urges that plagued him. Tierzen had taught him that, and for Tierzen he would prove it. He lifted his head, bringing his gaze near the level of the skull in the demon's beak.

"The privilege of serving Avelos and repaying the debt is all I desire," he said, wishing his voice sounded more certain.

"Perhaps," Cael answered dubiously. "Or perhaps you say so only because the Teachers have taught you to say it. That's a sorry thing, for you are the son of Mahla Denaban. She gave up her happiness for you. She would want you to choose your own Path."

Jhared drew a breath. "What do you know of my mother?"

"Child, child," Cael crooned. "You know who I am. I was at her fever bed. I heard her last pleas. I was beside her pyre, just as you were, on that cold day in the rain. Give her rest by choosing a Path of your own."

Jhared looked aside to hide the welling of remorse that filled him. Even as a child, he had heard the whispers of others when they glared at him. They made certain he knew what Mahla Denaban lost when she bore him. Yet, then and now, he never doubted what his mother wanted of him. His path was the one on which she set him long before her death.

"I *have* chosen for myself," he said more firmly. "I will be more than a worthy servant of Avelos. I will be the one who makes complete the Shorn promise with final reparation. *I* will fulfill the debt. That is the way I will honor my mother's memory. I owe her nothing less."

The demon jerked backwards, giving the impression of surprise, as if Cael could possibly be surprised by anything a Shorn soldier said or did. The creature hissed softly, "Sooo very sure of yourself. Sooo very sure of Riana's order. Even if you understood the magnitude of the promises you make, you could not succeed. I see the possible Paths stretching out before you. If you choose this way, I see your failure. Like all the Shorn who failed before you, you will be maimed and driven out to die alone. You will shame them all: Tierzen Trianor, the family who raised you, and your mother."

"No." Jhared straightened, heart thudding against his ribs. "I will change that path if I must. I swear it by the Lady of the Skies: I will give my family no reason for shame."

Cael stared at him with dead eyes. "Dangerous. Impulsiveness is always dangerous, even if you call it bravery. You have rejected me twice already; think very carefully before you act again. What I offer you now is your last honorable choice." The demon reached a hand into its dark robes. Jhared stiffened as the hand reappeared wielding a black-hilted dagger. The blade curved wickedly and gleamed red in the dying firelight. "This Path is free of shame. Many others have taken it and found peace before you."

Staring in unveiled shock, Jhared recalled the wild rumors of Shorn youths who entered the Becoming and never stepped from the temple again. Some said Riana forgave them the debts and claimed them for her service. Others said the council sent them secretly to serve among the clans and report on the loyalty of Shorn citizens in the villages. He had never imagined what the demon held before him.

"You are offering death?"

"Choice," Cael whispered. "Do not shun my offer simply because you've not considered it. In this retreat, you will find no disgrace. I would welcome you." The demon pushed the blade toward Jhared's chest. "You will have no such offers tomorrow."

Looking at the knife made Jhared's head pound harder, as though something inside him were trying to break free. He massaged a hand against his brow and closed his eyes. "If Avelos rejects my service, then Riana will see that I pay the debt with my life, as you say. Escape now would be a cowardly betrayal of my commitment."

Cloth hissed against cloth. Jhared opened his eyes to discover Cael rising over him, the blade gleaming. Jhared was already shifting into a defensive crouch before he realized where the demon aimed the knife. The blade slid easily into its sheath.

"The decision has been made. Your chance has passed. Let Riana judge you now."

Cael glowered at him for a long, silent moment. Jhared wished he could read the frozen expression, but he could find nothing human in it. Finally, the demon glided toward the door and melted into the night.

Jhared lifted his hands in a ward of protection, but dropped them into his lap again before completing the gesture. It was too late to invoke the goddess; the damage was done.

The little hut grew quiet. The embers faded, and the wind breathed gently through the walls. In the courtyard, a cricket chirped lazily, and the Arionad shifted on his watch. Tendrils of exhaustion wrapped themselves around Jhared, but he was not tempted to sleep. In the last hours of darkness, he did his best to close his thoughts to Cael and prepare for the final trial.

3.
BINDINGS

As the first silvery whiskers of daylight poked across the floor of the hut, Jhared paced the chamber's tiny diameter to limber his restless joints. He was still standing when the guard held the door flap aside and the novice appeared. With both hands she carried a wooden goblet filled with amber liquid.

"Drink," she commanded, passing the goblet to Jhared. "The wine is blessed and will open your heart to the goddess."

As she stretched out her hands, a ring with a leaping antelope caught the sunlight. It surprised him. Clan Ontera was north of the Parnas Mountains and far to the west. Despite her gravity, she seemed young to be so far from home. He wondered if her family took pride in her service or if she was alone.

Her sound of impatience brought him back. He glanced down at the wine. The bitter scent of karianta berries rose from the cup, with some herbs he couldn't name. He didn't relish the possibility of more visions, but that couldn't matter now. *The decision has been made.* He lifted the cup to his lips and drained its contents. The wine sloshed into the empty pit of his stomach.

"The examiners will call for you after the morning devotions," she told him, reclaiming the goblet and disappearing again.

By the time the escort arrived to bring him to the trial, his heart drummed slowly against his ribs, and his limbs moved as if filled with wet sand. He blinked at the guards' swords and their grim expressions as they marched him through the temple, knowing he should feel something about what was to come, but unable to reach anything sharper than curiosity. He shrugged and felt his body respond loosely. His thoughts felt wrapped in gauze.

The chamber to which they brought him lay beyond the first circle, at the center of the sanctuary. Excited whispers greeted him from above as he entered. He glanced toward the voices, flinching backwards as blinding light pierced his skull. He dropped his gaze, squinting and blinking black spots out of his sight. It took a few moments to realize the brilliance came from the sunlight pouring in. He stood beneath the open oculus of the temple's inner circle. Light bounced off the silvered curve of the dome. His guard prodded him forward, and he stumbled farther into the chamber. Beside him, a staircase led to an open gallery well above his head. Across the room, the high priestess in her white robes sat on a dais with a large hunting dog sprawled at her feet. The sanctified body of the hawk lay on a marble altar, directly under the oculus.

Above him, the whispers rose. Jhared avoided blinding himself again by cocking his head and glancing obliquely upward. Legs in fine woolen breeches showed through the gallery's railing: the three judges. He wondered what such men feared in him that they must distance themselves so.

The odd thought skipped away as a low-toned bell clamored somewhere behind him. Chairs grated on the floor above. The guards left Jhared and took up places by the entrance.

"Jhared Denaban," began Lady Nemiah as she rose and strode to the altar, "by the records of the temple it is known that you were born Avelun and carried to the temple to become Shorn. You are here now to try the final test of Becoming. Have you completed the training of mind and body required of the servants of Avelos?"

"I have." Jhared kept his eyes on the altar, not quite on the lady. He stood with his feet spread to hold him firm in the swaying room.

The high priestess looked up to the gallery. "Do any here dispute the right of this youth to participate in the final trial?"

Jhared held his breath. There was a silence. Then someone cleared his throat, and a small bell rang. An acolyte in grey hurried down the staircase. She handed Lady Nemiah a square of slate. The high priestess read the note written there and returned it to the girl, who wiped the words away with her apron. Lady Nemiah turned to Jhared.

"The people of Avelos challenge your training. In defiance of the Teachers' Code, you received the Teaching within the home that raised you. Why should you be allowed to complete the Becoming?"

Tierzen's warning had come to fruition. All the reasons filled Jhared's head in no good order. He could say that his only purpose was to serve Avelos and that he longed to make reparation for the crimes of the Shorn, but Cael hadn't been moved by his declaration and neither would these men be. What answer might they accept? There must be some logic to it. He forced himself to think coherently through the effect of the wine, but the more he struggled, the more organized thought slid away. He took a deep breath. In the instant he relaxed, the words flowed out of his mouth.

"Lady, in the home of my Teachers, I have spent my years preparing to serve Avelos. I have lived the Teaching every day and night, for more hours than any other Shorn man or woman since the Exile. The Teaching has been not merely my lessons but my life."

The high priestess cast a glance at the gallery. "Riana finds this acceptable," she announced. "Are there further challenges?"

She paused, but no protest came. She gestured to a knife on the altar. Dried blood stained the stone beneath its curved blade.

"Shorn child, before the final test begins, be warned of the consequences of your failure. Should you fail, Riana and her people will drive you from Avelos unbound to fulfill Tumal's legacy: to die without country, without history, and without identity. Do you yet claim yourself to be prepared?"

It came to him that the Minister of the Teaching was responsible for selecting the elders to judge a Becoming. Tierzen had chosen the Legacy leader, a northman, and a distracted city elder to decide whether Jhared lived or died today. No allies. No one would call it favoritism if he lived.

Jhared swallowed and cleared his throat before he could answer the high priestess. "I am prepared."

"Then the final test has begun. Let none outside this sanctuary enter until it is complete. Let no word of what we do here be carried from this chamber. Let the initiate speak carefully lest his words split the Paths and do damage to her weaving."

The high priestess stepped away from the altar. Bright sun limned her body in gold, making her flicker like a candle's flame.

"Jhared Denaban, you are here to prove yourself worthy to make reparation to Avelos. Tell us why such reparation is needed. What are the debts of the Shorn?"

Tell us his crimes!

Jhared winced, then straightened his shoulders. He knew this answer better than any. It was the story Madam Trianor had told him each night when he was a child.

"Before the Exile, the Avelune took positions in places of importance, as architects, healers, historians, and servants to Riana. But they were faithless, lustful, and corrupt. During the rule of Tumal the Just, when drought ruined the land and the people starved, the Avelune saw a chance to sate their lusts. They conspired with Sahiste, and with the aid of the Sahisten ambassador, they attempted to assassinate the high chieftain. When the traitors were caught, exposed, and executed, Sahiste denied its part and crossed into Avelos south of the Sangren Mountains. The war that followed lasted twelve years."

He inhaled slowly. "These are the debts for which I must make reparation: Treason against Avelos. Conspiracy with Sahiste. Attempted assassination of High Chieftain Tumal. Murder of loyal guards. Instigation of war. Death of innocents." The list went on, growing more and more specific until Jhared came to the names of the men and women who lost their lives in the Exile War. His heart ached as each name echoed up to the dome. So many people had bled for his ancestors' treachery: men impaled by Sahisten spears; families starved during a winter of siege; Riana's priestesses raped and strangled. When he had repeated the last name, he had to wipe a hand over his eyes. Shame pinned his gaze to the marble floor.

"Now, a recitation of our high chieftains," Lady Nemiah said, strolling away from the altar. "Tell us every man that we remember and the reasons that we honor him."

"Yes, Lady. From the blood of the noble first-clan Manitar, looking back from the wisdom of Adan Rumar, there is Alaro Rumar the Good, who gave to Avelos summers of security; Mical Rumar, who gave to us the autumn of plenty; Matio, who is called the Giving, who showed us courage; Toma the Fierce, who gave to Avelos winters of strength; Tumal the Just, who gave us loyalty and righteousness. Before Tumal, from the blood of the noble first-clan Amerre, came Donilo Andar, the clever; Grion Andar, the vain." Jhared continued his recitation as far back as he had been taught, over one hundred thirty-seven men. First among them all was Alende Isan, the high chieftain who returned life to Avelos from the ashes of Altan Mar.

"Fine," said the lady coolly when he finished.

The high priestess continued to test his knowledge of history: the wars; the creation of the council; the changes in the ruling structure of the clans; the events leading clan chieftains to be reduced to prefects; the important shifts in trade. Jhared's memory for details, for dates and names, was good, and Madam Trianor was an effective Teacher. Everything he knew came tripping off his tongue without hesitation. From time to time, a bell rang and the acolyte scurried down with a question from the elders.

As the inquiry progressed, Lady Nemiah paced slowly around Jhared. Her robes swayed as she circled him. "If you pass this trial, you will serve Avelos as a patrolman in the high chieftain's Forest Guard. The Forest Guard's rules of engagement address the conduct of Shorn soldiers in battle, do they not?"

He shifted his weight forward. He hadn't expected questions about soldiery from the high priestess. "Yes, Lady."

"And do they speak of the potential for engagement of citizens of Avelos?"

"Yes. I must engage a citizen in only one dire circumstance: if not to do so would endanger the lives of others."

"And if you face such a situation, what is your goal?"

"To maintain the safety of the people of Avelos. Law says that if a combatant refuses to release his weapon, I am to disarm him. If he resists, he may be disabled."

She murmured an acknowledgment. More military questions followed: What was the mission of the Forest Guard? The proper way to care for a bow? The best way to read a man's health, alertness, and speed from his trail? Many of the questions had the ring of General Nadel about them, and all were subjects drilled into him over years. The answers were clear to him. Even as his throat grew dry and his voice became hoarse, his responses came out as though he had written them all beforehand.

The trial dragged on. The room warmed under the sunny dome. Jhared drooped with the effects of the wine, his long fast, and the rhythm of Lady Nemiah's voice. Dust motes floated in and out of the shaft of light before him. The dog on the dais slept.

"Tell us, Jhared Denaban, what is your understanding of the First Law of the Shorn?"

Lady Nemiah's voice tickled his ear and brought him out of his daze. She stood directly before him. He caught the scent of incense in her hair from the morning devotion. Now that she hovered so near, her slight build surprised him. She wasn't tall enough even to reach his shoulder. Her features were fine and her frame delicate, but her eyes blazed with a preternatural strength, eyes of a shocking green. The curse had passed dangerously close to the high priestess of Avelos.

"The First Law ensures that the Shorn do not hold public office, do not serve the goddess, do not hold any position of command in the military, and," Jhared paused to swallow, "do not practice the talents of healers."

"Good," she whispered. "Now tell me, of the one hundred three laws that guide the Shorn, which do you believe is the most important?"

He recognized the shift in her questions. Some part of his mind urged caution, but he couldn't connect that thought to the words that poured from him.

"The most important is the Law of Duty, Lady, for it governs all I do. It reflects the spirit of my oath: to preserve the safety of Avelos above all else, to hold each countryman dearer than my own life, and to devote myself to service."

"Indeed—"

The jangle of the bell above interrupted the questioning once more. Lady Nemiah strode to the altar. The acolyte brought the message from the council, and the high priestess read it. She waited to speak until she again stood close, whispering to Jhared as if they were the only two in the room.

"For what purpose were the laws created?"

"To curb the power of the Shorn," he heard himself say.

The high priestess tilted her head and stared up at him with a probing gaze. "Do you mean that the laws restrain you from living a full life?"

Again that twinge of caution, but he could no more stem the flow of his answers than he could hold back the winds of the Parnas Mountains. "No, Lady. My life is filled with my service. Riana gave Shorn Law to High Chieftain Tumal to ensure the safety of Avelos."

"Yes. Very good. That is true." She took a half-step closer. "Have the laws caused you pain?"

Images of the hunt flooded his mind. One hand pressed against his chest. "Killing the bird…brought pain," he whispered.

"I know," she murmured. But she did not release him from her controlling glare. She straightened, and her shoulders stiffened. It should have been a warning.

"Jhared Denaban, in what way have you been shorn?"

Her words had barely reached him when agony stabbed through his shoulder blades and cut down his back. He gasped. His body arched backwards to escape the sensation of the blade; there was no escaping the memories, poorly formed and powerful: the screaming pain, the smell of blood, and the wordless terror. The knife that had cut him apart all those years ago might have been the very blade that lay on the altar now. He'd been no more than a babe, but his blood had flowed over the stone as a priestess tore away the part of him that signified his curse. Pain raged through him. They had cut away his wings and left the scars. Now the high priestess stood before him, watching impassively. Misery and helplessness surged through him.

"No!" he cried. "Please *don't!*"

From the gallery came the rustle of bodies all leaning forward. The high priestess continued to hold his gaze. Her low voice dripped with his peril. "You will be asked only once more, Jhared Denaban: in what way have you been shorn?"

He groaned, straining to stay on his feet as the blade of memory cut deeper. "I am shorn of my heritage…of my birthright."

"Yes," she said, still and emotionless. "Avelos has stolen these from you. How do you respond?"

"No, not Avelos!" he panted. "My own kind took this from me when they betrayed—"

Wait.

This time he snapped his mouth shut and clenched his jaw to halt his reckless words. This answer was too easy. It was too simple to blame those before him. His Teachers raised him to rue the atrocity of his ancestors' betrayals, but those were crimes long past. He had not been shorn to sate the people's need for retaliation. The Shearing, the Teaching, and the laws were not punishments. They were necessary. He was missing something. His mind spun.

Do not let your own veils prevent you from understanding. General Nadel's lesson anchored him, slowing his racing thoughts. Jhared sifted through his agony for the truth. He knew it when he found his mistake.

"It's me," he breathed. "Not Avelos. Not my ancestors. I was born with the flaws of the Avelune. I am dangerous. I am Shorn to save myself and the country from my own corruption."

"Ahhh." The high priestess turned her head away from him. His body sagged at the sudden release, nearly dropping him to his knees. He caught himself, hands braced against his thighs, and gulped air like a drowning man.

The bell rang again. Several moments passed before the acolyte descended with the slate. She crossed the hall and handed it to the high priestess. Lady Nemiah stared at the writing. Her lowered head shadowed her expression as she read. The silence lengthened. Someone in the gallery coughed. Finally, the high priestess looked up, her expression dangerously neutral. She smeared the words from the slate with her own fingers and shoved it back into the acolyte's hand.

"You have done well, Jhared Denaban. You understand the truth."

Jhared released a silent breath and gingerly flexed his shoulders forward and back.

Lady Nemiah touched the body of the hawk with one hand. She paused again, her features unreadable. The dog on the dais pricked its ears.

"Riana has relinquished her call for a sacrifice. This gift is no longer necessary to complete the Becoming." Her fingers lifted the bird by the tail. The hawk hung over the altar for a moment, golden feathers gleaming in the sunlight. Then the priestess tossed it to the floor near the hound.

In one eager leap, the dog pounced on the body. With muffled snarls, it tore the bird apart. Its large jaws crunched meat and bones until the carcass was a mangled mass of gore and feathers. The beast looked up at Jhared and licked its bloody muzzle.

"No!" Jhared's moment of recovery exploded into anguish. Darkness roared at the corners of his vision, as all the misery he had experienced during the hunt burst upon him. He struggled to conceal his torment, forcing his hands to stay open at his sides, but the wine had rattled the locks where he secured each improper thought and perilous urge. Every ugly part of him threatened to break loose. In his disorientation, he saw the arrow fly once more. It struck his breast, and he plummeted out of the sky.

One part of him observed stoically while his distress unfolded. In the corner of his mind not swept away, he began a litany to regain calm. *The Shorn serve Avelos. I will make reparation through my service. To me is given the duty of loyalty and protection.*

He grasped at those words, trying to restrain the emotions that flooded him. But even that last rational part of him cried out: *I have only done what was asked of me. Why was I manipulated to kill to no purpose?* Deep in places he had never dared to explore, he felt a terrible rending and heard a sound like snapping bone. For the second time since he killed the hawk, he felt the rupture of something vital.

Riana commands that a bird of prey be slain in the prime of spring.

Why? Why must I pay my blood debt with death?

Out of the chaos, he heard the voice of his Teachers: "*You are born from the blood of betrayal. You are born with a corruption of spirit. There must be a test of loyalty.*" He drew a ragged breath. That was the answer: loyalty. The Becoming was a test of loyalty. He must prove himself willing to complete whatever Avelos demanded. He drenched his grief with that knowledge. There must be a test of loyalty.

He focused on the image of himself standing in the Heartsblood River, quiescent against the rapid current. He let the pain drag at him and flow past, leaving him standing intact.

He wrenched his gaze upward to meet the high priestess. She had not moved from the altar. Her eyes arrowed into him. The assembly above was silent.

"Praise Riana's light and order," he choked.

The low-toned summoning bell clamored instantly. Lady Nemiah moved away from the altar and called out to the assembly. "Let all here witness that Jhared Denaban has passed the test of the Becoming. Riana has claimed him as a servant of Avelos."

Thunder rolled above him, as if the judges all roared at once. Jhared trembled with exhaustion, hoping he could get out from under their scrutiny before he ended up on the floor. When the novice appeared to lead him to the ceremony's completion, she was flushed and wide-eyed. He thought she looked shaken; then he realized what a foolish thought that was. She had seen the Becoming numerous times; he must be putting his own state on her. She pressed a small stone cup into the palm of his hand.

"Drink this. It will help to clear your head."

He swallowed the liquid gratefully. It stung the back of his throat and warmed his chest. The elders proceeded to the courtyard, where they would witness his binding. The final act seemed almost irrelevant now. He had passed the true test.

The novice gave him several moments to slow his breathing and still his trembling limbs. When she led him from the hall with the two Arionade, the three temple servants formed a partial cocoon against the elders' stares.

At the end of a wide passage, the guards swung open a set of doors onto the plaza. A breeze fluttered over Jhared's body. He stepped eagerly across the threshold into the solace of the open air.

Surprise pushed him back a step. The novice beside him gave a squeak. A crowd packed the open space between the temple and the palace: bands of young men; women in their clan colors; Shorn children with their Teachers, their leather leashes drawn taut. A pack of boys stood on the rim of the fountain; others had climbed the pedestal of the monument to Alende Isan. Jhared moved a protective step closer to the novice as the crowd enveloped them. The Arionade struggled to push people back. The audience for a Becoming never grew very large. Jhared wondered how much council matters influenced the crowd today.

The answer came almost immediately. As the people saw him emerge from the temple, a hostile roar surged through the crowd. Near the fountain, a banner rose into the air: a bloodied sword on a field of blue: once the sigil of Tumal the Just, taken now by Tumal's Legacy. Jhared couldn't see the individuals who carried it, but he could pick out fragments of their chant.

"…Trianor's Folly! No more of Trianor's Folly!"

A chill skittered up his spine. Then the temple bells rang into the warm afternoon. Their round, full sound rolled out over the city twelve times, once for each year a Shorn youth spent preparing for the Becoming. Under the bells, the chanting became futile. By the time the last chime rang, the shouting had faded. Jhared turned to see Lady Nemiah and High Chieftain Rumar step from the temple. The high chieftain came alone, but a grim-faced, black-bearded Arionad followed on the heel of the high priestess. The guard scowled at the crowd, and the people closest to the leaders parted, allowing them into the circle.

"Prepare this man for the binding," the high priestess commanded, her voice projecting over the heads of the throng.

He had known this part would come; he had witnessed it more than once. But when the novice stepped forward to remove his shirt and expose his scars, he fought the need to resist. The fabric slid from his back, and another unpleasant rumble ran through the mob. Heat rushed to Jhared's face. He couldn't see the scars, but the ache of them never entirely faded. If he stretched with one arm, he could feel the thick, ugly weals that marked his curse down the length of his back.

At the command of the priestess, Jhared started around the perimeter of the circle, so everyone in the crowd could bear witness. He held his head level and tried not to focus on the sea of eyes. A few people nodded their approval, but most showed disgust and animosity. A Teacher jerked the leash of his Shorn charge, a small girl with a dark braid, forcing her to mark Jhared's passage. Elder Toren Abrigado stood at the edge of the throng, arms folded across his chest, an expression of fury in his face. Jhared looked away and tried to remember that somewhere in the crowd Branlen cheered for him.

"Children of Avelos," called the high priestess as Jhared halted before her. "Know that Jhared Denaban has earned the right to serve. What we do here seals the covenant made by all servants of Avelos to Riana and to you."

Lady Nemiah held aloft the ancient knife. The luminescent blue-green stones on the hilt reflected the sunlight like a piece of the sky. She gave a word of blessing and pushed it toward High Chieftain Rumar. The high chieftain held the blade to Jhared's upper arm, just below the shoulder. The bite of the blade caused Jhared's heart to quicken, and he pressed his arm against it to prevent himself from pulling away. The hushed crowd leaned in, waiting. Rumar's large hand flexed. He drove the knife into tensed muscle. Jhared held his breath and clenched his jaw as the high chieftain made two deep, deliberate strokes to form the shape of a *V*.

"Shed this blood before the people as a sign of devotion, so when you are called to their service and protection you will have no fear," the high chieftain intoned.

Rivulets of blood trickled down Jhared's arm and splattered onto the ground. Taking the knife from High Chieftain Rumar, the high priestess raised the blade in turn. Her strokes were smaller, a second V-shape inside the first, a symbol of the shame of the Avelune.

Black dots danced at the corners of Jhared's vision. This was his part, but he couldn't push the words from his throat. He gazed at the crowd; all of Avelos seemed to be watching him. As he smelled his own blood and felt its tickling flow, a sudden irrational fear clutched at him.

They wanted me to fail. The blood I spill now isn't enough for them. It never will be. It took another moment before he found his voice.

"I receive this scar as a reminder of the injuries done by those before me. From Riana, I accept my duty to strive for reparation through the commitment of my thoughts, words, and deeds."

The power of the oath charged the air, and the binding settled around him like a physical tie. Deep within Jhared, in a place too old for words or memory, a gate slammed with a finality that reverberated through him.

"May she look with favor upon your oath," Lady Nemiah intoned.

As her words faded, a flock of blackbirds burst silently into the air from the temple roof. Sunlight shone upon the splashes of crimson that colored their wings. An audible gasp rose from the crowd. People lifted their hands in the ward against evil as the shadow of Cael's messengers passed over them.

The high priestess looked up, eyes wide, watching the flock fly from the courtyard. She whispered words Jhared didn't understand, but which might have been a prayer. Her eyes searched his accusingly, as if she thought he kept a secret from her. For a terrible moment, he knew she would reject his oath; then the moment passed. As she pulled her gaze away, the temple bells began to toll.

4.
SACRILEGE

The bells broke the crowd's shocked silence. People pushed toward the streets, a low grumble rising from the mob of them. Hostility remained heavy in the air. Nemiah felt the weighted stares of the crowd like chains around her neck. They weren't for her, those stares, but they might have been. She pressed her hands against her robe, trying to stop their trembling, trying to grasp what had happened and what she had done. She wanted to beg forgiveness of Riana, but she had no right.

How did she ask forgiveness for her own profanity? She had tossed away a sacred gift.

"Lady Nemiah, I would speak with you. Lady Nemiah!"

Nemiah recoiled at the sound of that elegant voice. She shook her head, not trusting herself to speak. Rom needed no other cue. Her Arionad interjected his imposing frame in front of the elder arrowing toward her.

Elder Abrigado continued speaking as if Rom did not exist. "This was badly done, lady. You know it was. The temple cannot afford to let the cursed go unpunished." His voice, just loud enough for Nemiah to catch beneath the sounds of the retreating crowd, contained carefully bridled hatred. Toren Abrigado was never other than careful, clever, and full of malice, a man who needed to see blood spilled to assuage his own fury. It was not Nemiah's sacrilege that angered him; he had intended to watch a Shorn boy die today.

"Lady, will you give no answer for the damage you've caused?"

"Riana proved the initiate, Elder Abrigado." The words came hard. Nemiah wasn't certain she believed them. What had she done to the ritual? What had this man forced her to do? She swayed as the world rippled, circles within circles. The crowd hastening away to their homes believed she owned power. At one time, the Lady of Avelos had truly guided the high chieftain and the Council of Clans. No longer.

Abrigado sneered at her silence. "When the Sahistens entered my family's lands during the Exile War, they threw the men into a pit of embers and let the flames take them. The women they took with their spears and swords. My twice great-grandmother saw her mother violated and murdered as her home burned. She was no more than eight winters. No one in my family forgets that story. What stories does your family tell of the war, lady? You with your green eyes and the taint in your blood."

"I serve only order, elder. Do not be mistaken. Though I am fallible, the goddess is not." Nemiah caught her breath, knowing herself overmatched. "Rom, now." She lifted her head, as if she possessed the same arrogance as the man before her, then turned away and marched toward the temple. She heard her Arionad declare something to Abrigado in a stark tone. Rom would do what he must to prevent the elder from following her.

She stepped through the temple doors out of the brilliant sunlight and into the darkness. Hidden from the crowd, she leaned against the wall, panting. Rom caught up with her there. He frowned down at her.

"Lady?"

"Not here. To my tower, Captain."

He knew better than to offer his arm to her in the passage, but his glower pushed aside the curious glances from the priestesses and acolytes on their way to lessons or to chores in the gardens, kennels, and barns. At the far end of the priestess's quarters, he opened the door to Nemiah's tower rooms and followed her in. She pushed through the antechamber into her receiving room. Light filtered into the chamber from the tall windows, weaving brightness and shadow across the floor and over the hearth. A low voice spoke from the shadows.

"Why, Nemiah? What threat convinced you it was worth such a thing?"

It took another moment before Nemiah distinguished the Bearer of Cael's Blade sitting in one of the chairs near the hearth. "You attended?" she said faintly.

"Of course I attended! Along with the rest of the Higher Circle. Did you think we would miss the Becoming of the child of the Minister of the Teaching?"

Nemiah drew a slow breath. Leita, Carian, Bena, Maita, Clemina, and Kaliska: her Higher Circle, the Mistresses of Riana's temple, and women who had little faith in the present Lady of Avelos. Of them all, only Kaliska and Leita could be named allies. Nemiah replied honestly; she could do nothing else. "I did not think on it."

"Oh, Nemiah. When will you learn to protect yourself?" Leita sat forward in her chair. "Are you going to answer my question?"

Captain Rom hissed at the Bearer's brazenness. Leita lifted her gaze, all cool confidence and quiescent power. They were not well matched, Nemiah's Arionad and her Bearer. Rom drew his strength from within the boundaries of Riana's order, while Leita gloried in challenging the expectations set for her and pushing to the farthest point order allowed. It was one reason she served so well as the Bearer: she knew the borders outside of which none should tread. If it often made her exhausting to manage, Nemiah still valued her singular perspective. Now, Nemiah raised a restraining hand before Leita uttered something more provocative.

"Thank you, Captain Rom. I will speak with the Bearer of Cael's Blade alone."

Rom scowled at the Bearer then returned his gaze to Nemiah. "Arion guard you, my lady."

"And Riana guide you, Captain."

When Rom had gone, Nemiah allowed herself to fold into a chair. The Becoming ritual required significant strength at the best of times. In the instant when she called upon Riana and the infinite Paths, she forced the initiate to experience the pain of his darkest moments all converged into his present Path. It was her obligation to press each Shorn youth to see what dangerous urges were revealed, like pressing on an abscessed wound to release the infection inside. Calling the Paths that way hurt like nothing else Nemiah had known. She closed her eyes, then opened them again. "Leita, I had to do it. If I had resisted, the elders would have made us pay. You know they would have."

The Bearer offered no agreement or reassurance. "Which of the judges do you think wrote it?"

Nemiah thought of the last slate pressed into her hands by her acolyte. Instead of a question for the initiate, it had been a demand of Nemiah: *"Fail the tainted."*

"It was Toren Abrigado," she answered. "It stinks of Legacy heresy. Just now in the plaza he very nearly confessed to it."

"Careful, Nemiah. Don't rule out the others too soon. It might have been a gambit from the north. Prefects Aglar and Colar have delayed paying their spring levies to the Forest Guard. Clan Lasla may follow. A failed Becoming would have supported their argument that Shorn men are too unstable for soldiery. Especially *this* Becoming."

Nemiah paused. Leita's sources were good. She hadn't known the northerners had gone so far; she should have. After a moment of consideration, she shook her head.

"It wasn't Elder Lezar. The complaints of the northerners are with Rumar, not with us. Any clan that endures the brutal winters of the Sandien Mountains understands the importance of Riana's seasons. They wouldn't risk her displeasure, or ours, I think."

Leita's midnight gaze didn't waver. Nemiah wished for that kind of unflinching composure, but she didn't care for the shrewd look that entered her Bearer's expression. "General Nadel might have something to do with it," Leita suggested. "He might have collaborated with the city elder to bring it about. He has long blamed Riana for his losses."

"No! Not on any Path!"

The Bearer's dark eyebrows dashed upward at Nemiah's quick protest. Nemiah looked away. She owed Leita no apology for the direction her heart turned, and she knew Enrian Nadel better than most could. "The General of the Southern Towers has nothing corrupt in him."

"Every man possesses the capacity for corruption." Leita's voice took on the tone of a Bearer giving warning. "Just as each one has the capacity for disorder. Riana did not win every battle against Cael in the Great Wars."

Nemiah raised her palms to yield the point. "You know very well what I mean. Enrian needs Shorn soldiers. He wouldn't seek to condemn one of them. Enough speculation, Leita. I profaned the sacrifice, not any of the elders. Not the general. *I* did."

The shameful truth was that Nemiah had grown so accustomed to the council's bullying she hadn't really even considered resisting. She had panicked, imagining all the consequences that would fall upon the temple if she didn't comply: taxes raised, harvests withheld, bans implemented against the rituals. Her hand had gone to the hawk, a reflexive movement, and suddenly the holy sacrifice had been on the floor. It stunned her that the initiate had survived it. When the hound savaged the bird, she knew it was over, that Jhared Denaban would expose his treacherous thoughts, forcing her to bleed him and send him into the wilds to die.

No Shorn initiate could have been expected to pass such a trial. Was the Minister of the Teaching responsible for his fosterling's discipline? She didn't know, but she didn't trust it. Her own actions had perverted the ritual. Jhared Denaban might not even be truly bound. Standing at his side, she had witnessed how close he had come to breaking. Then the blackbirds had shown themselves above the temple dome: Cael's messengers bursting into the sky in the moment that should have marked the young man's binding. A sign of disorder when every part of the Becoming was meant to ensure order. The ritual had been tainted. What was meant to protect all of Avelos might not protect anyone.

"You fear the Becoming was damaged. That the binding is not reliable."

Nemiah darted her gaze to the Bearer, disturbed by how easily Leita read her. "I'm going to tell Kaliska to set a Shadow Guard on the boy."

"Good. Too many Paths twisted about him at the vigil. I thought they would settle after the trial. They didn't. Kaliska will have someone watch him wherever he takes up his service. If the bond proves faulty, well…"

If the bond proved faulty, Kaliska knew how to defend Riana's order. As spy keeper, she took care of such things. Nemiah despised the necessity of it and despised her own inability to prevent it. Over the past nine years, the elders and the high chieftain had stolen much of her power. Today, she had handed them more.

Leita's gown rustled softly as she shifted in her chair. Her eyes, the dark blue at the heart of a winter's night, spoke of mysteries few understood. "Nemiah, the Higher Circle will demand to convene."

Nemiah stared out the glazed windows toward the high chieftain's palace. Sunlight burned sparks of red and blue at the corners of her vision. "As we must."

"You should be prepared to face their anger."

"Of course."

The Bearer made a sound of exasperation. "Nemiah, do not put me off with mindless acquiescence as if I were an elder! You must consider where we're heading—Oh!"

Leita grabbed the arms of her chair, as if someone had abruptly tilted it. "The Paths. They're shifting! Do you sense them?"

Nemiah tightened her grip on her own boundaries as the world swung around her. "It's because of what I've done. So many consequences might come of it. The weaving must change to include them all."

"Yes, yes that's a part of it, but the Gate wants to open. I feel the potential in it. Ah, Nemiah, you could pass through and travel the infinite Paths now. I'm sure you could. They want you…" The Bearer came to her feet, her eyes glittering with need. "Prepare yourself for a sacred journey. I'll bring the Mistress of Maps."

Nemiah did not move. "I will not try for a sacred journey now, Leita."

"But it's been years! A journey across Riana's weaving might give us knowledge we can use to overcome the high chieftain and his council, might offer us a glimpse of a point of influence."

"After my sacrilege, Riana would not give me that gift. And I will not ask it of her."

"My friend, you must—"

"I said I will *not*!"

The Bearer's expression hardened for a moment, before going calm and still.

Nemiah sighed out a breath. "Oh, my Bearer, it is your place to test me to ensure I remain within Riana's order. I realize today's Becoming has made you doubt it. But surely you can see that I know how wrong a sacred journey would be right now. Before I seek anything of Riana, I must repair the damage I've wrought."

Leita remained very still. "Yes, I do see that you think it would be wrong."

Nemiah sighed again, gratefully. "Thank you. I need my Bearer to go to work in a different way tonight. See Carian settles the young ones before she rushes to the rest of the Higher Circle to rouse their fears. Talk with the acolyte who served during the ritual. It was Aya. Be certain she remembers that speaking out about the Becoming leads to Cael. News of this must not spread."

They must not know how I have profaned Riana.

They will all know.

Of course they would know. Elder Abrigado was likely to spread the tale himself. He had no reverence. Abruptly, she had had enough. She stood, letting her ceremonial robe with its fine embroidery slide off her shoulders and onto the chair. From a peg near the door, she grabbed up her light cloak against the early spring chill.

Leita stared. "Where are you going?"

"To fetch Capa."

"Nemiah—"

"See to your tasks, Leita. Please."

She fled the room before the Bearer could find another way to test her.

Nemiah hurried out of the east wing past the women's quarters and the archives toward the infirmary and the barracks. It was time for the midday meal. As she neared the dining hall, the rise and fall of women's voices echoed along the stone passages. Nemiah pulled up the hood of her cloak and slipped out the door into the kitchen yard before anyone noticed her.

Outside, the reassuring odors of farm animals, newly turned earth, and fresh herbs filled the spring air, scents that reminded her of home. A tiny hamlet that had been, a place where she knew everyone and every Path was familiar. She had seen nothing of cities until coming to the high temple as a girl marked by the goddess. At the start, everything about Velantar had been strange and dangerous. Days she once spent working under the open sky, traveling with her healer father or helping her mother with their small farm, had become defined by the demands of her mentors, the sly rhetoric of the elders, and the walls: the ancient walls of the city and the carved stone of the temple. She had learned that walls meant safety and boundaries and the rules, written and unwritten, of city life. Walls kept her from straying into unknown territory—like the walls that defined Shorn Circle, where no servant of Riana should ever be seen. She had learned not to push too far beyond the walls in order to avoid the penalties, for herself and for the temple.

She didn't linger over the thought. Early that morning, she had sent Capalino to the kennels that he might romp with his pack. She would bring him back to her tower and at least tonight have the benefit of his cheerful company. The great brindled hound was her pride, a five-year-old she had schooled from a pup. Joy filled the rare moments when they hunted together in Parnas Valley. Trackers and finders of trails, hounds had a special place among Riana's beasts.

At the kennel, she let herself in the first gate, latched it, and then entered the second gate into the fenced yard. The afternoon sun fell upon a pleasant, grassy space where young dogs sprawled or worked with trainers on foundational skills. A stone-paved path led up to the porch of the ancient kennel building, where the doors were open wide to the fine day. On one side of the porch, a litter of fawn-colored pups wrestled each other and tumbled over their mother, who endured their roughhousing with maternal resignation.

The Mistress of Kennels was not among the trainers in the yard, so Nemiah aimed for the porch. Before she went three steps, a large, dark form shot out of the open doors and launched off the porch, heading straight for her. Nemiah halted, her smile growing as Capa bounded up to her, twirling with excitement. Nemiah knelt and wrapped an arm around him. Capa gave her face one polite lick, then subsided happily, his thick tail beating the ground.

"It is comforting to have a creature in your life you cannot fail, isn't it lady?"

The words were pleasant; the tone was not. Nemiah rose and turned. The Mistress of Novices stood over her, arms folded over her chest, her features anything but comforting.

"It is always a joy to be with someone who accepts you for yourself, " Nemiah replied evenly. "Where are your charges, Carian? Isn't it time for afternoon lessons?"

"Soon. I promised the young ones we would continue studying tracking today. I came to fetch Barta. Although after this morning, I wonder if other lessons might be more important. Lessons in the sanctity of our rituals, for example."

Carian smirked at Nemiah from a regal height. Her broad shoulders, straight back, and solid stance gave her a martial bearing, and nothing in her demeanor contradicted that impression. The Mistress of Novices descended from an honored line of priestesses: her sister served at a temple near Lake Linde; her aunt served Clan Aglar; and her mother had served in the high temple as the Bearer of Cael's Blade to Lady Pahlina. Carian had been born in the high temple. She might have expected to follow her mother as Bearer, but Nemiah had chosen elsewhere.

"It is an important lesson for them to learn," Nemiah agreed.

"Perhaps you will join us, lady, as it seems a lesson you have forgotten."

Nemiah pressed her hands against the fabric of her cloak. "Carian, I understand why you are distressed. You have a right to it. And you may speak of it when next we gather the Higher Circle. Standing in the kennel yard is not where I hear grievances." With a single command to Capa, Nemiah turned to leave.

"Do you understand, lady? Do you truly think so?" Sunlight flashed over Carian's flame-bright hair as Nemiah glanced back at her. "Did you know that Lady Pahlina told my mother she never wanted you for Lady of Avelos? A little farm girl plucked from nowhere with the curse evident in her green eyes? Pahlina only named you Chosen because you were a Pathwalker and because she knew, as cowardly as you are, you would at least be malleable."

Nemiah felt ill, but she gave the other woman nothing more than a mild smile. "You have missed the mark if you think to wound me, Carian. I know exactly why I was Chosen. And now I am what you have. If you care for Riana's order as you claim, you'd best stop whining and work with me. We have much to do to restore Riana's weaving."

"Whining? Is that what you name defense of the temple?" The other priestess shook her head, disbelief painted across her features. "How are you so sanguine about what has been stolen from us? Where is your anger? They have stripped us of power and abused us for their own gain!"

"Carian, calm yourself. You are not a stupid woman. Stop acting as if you cannot see the complexity in this! Merely being loud and angry will never bring about the changes we need. That is dangerously wrong thinking."

"And has your profanity served us better, lady? You have done nothing. Worse than nothing. You have made us a piece the elders use in their own games! Look how you've let them rule us!"

Nemiah glanced up at the Mistress of Novices, a woman supremely certain of her place on the Paths. All around them, the yard had grown strangely silent. Nemiah realized that the other priestesses had ceased exercising their hounds and were fixed upon the argument.

"Well, Lady of Avelos?" Carian's expression was smug; she had realized it too.

The women all watched Nemiah, wondering if she would take any step to stop the council. Nemiah could almost hear their doubts. She pressed closer to the woman who loomed above her. "Do you really believe I would allow the council to get away with this kind of disorder?" she blurted. "I am summoning High Chieftain Rumar to the high temple. He will answer for this exploitation."

Nemiah caught a breath. She hadn't planned to say any such thing, but as her words struck the air, she realized the thought had hidden in her since she stood beside the high chieftain in the plaza, both of them carving the mark of binding into the flesh of a Shorn boy who might not be truly bound. She had imagined forcing the high chieftain to come to the temple to make amends. The temerity of the thought frightened her almost as much as the high chieftain did himself, yet she had just spat it out before a member of the Higher Circle and a yard full of her priestesses.

"You will summon Rumar?" Carian choked. "To the high temple?"

"I said that." In another situation, Carian's incredulous expression would have been amusing.

"He will cut you into pieces and serve you to the council for the midday meal."

Nemiah smiled thinly. "Then you will have nothing more to complain about, will you, Carian?" She glared up at the other priestess. "This is not the golden age of Altan Mar. We are living in the time after Lady Amalia. She was as powerful as you might like me to be. And she betrayed Avelos, started the Exile War, and caused the death of all her women. I can only act within the limits handed down to me. Now, be about your business, Mistress of Novices. The young ones are in need of reliable guidance."

"We are all in need of reliable guidance, Lady Nemiah. Some within the Higher Circle will not continue to sit aside as you flail from one danger to another. You are drawing the temple further from our rightful place among the leaders of Avelos. Find us a better Path, lady, or you may find yourself walking the Paths alone."

Capa growled low in his throat. He'd heard the threat in the other woman's voice as clearly as Nemiah had. Nemiah spoke a quiet word of restraint. Carian tossed her hair from her shoulders, offered a fierce spiral, and stalked away.

5.
Sons and Mothers

The blackbirds brought the Becoming to its end, and the crowd began to break away. People in the center of the plaza shoved toward the streets. Their muttering rose like a low animal growl. The high priestess turned her back on Jhared and the crowd, stern and imperious, ignoring those who called her name. Her grim Arionad warded off those who came too close.

People pushed around and past Jhared, but no one touched him. No one stepped in the droplets of his blood on the ground. He stood head and shoulders above most of them, trapped in their midst, drawing himself up so that he did not inadvertently brush against anyone. Then someone touched his arm. He tensed, prepared for something worse, but when he looked down he found a slender Shorn woman smiling up at him. Her sable curls framed her caramel-toned features and bold green eyes as she studied his face.

"Take heart," she said warmly. "They have silenced the music, but there are melodies in you yet. If the son of a bard would like to sing again, come to the Black Mountain Inn."

She squeezed his arm gently, then stepped back into the current of people. It happened just that fast. Jhared stared after her as she disappeared from view. He blinked and rubbed at his arm, unsure whether he had just seen a woman or only a dream-sprite created by the last of the temple wine in his blood.

When the crowd finally dispersed, he found his foster family waiting near a nut vendor's stall across the street. He gave them a wave. Exhaustion dragged at his limbs. His arm throbbed. His head buzzed from the long fast. But those sensations only proved that he lived.

The Becoming had loomed above him all of his life. It was finally over, and he had survived. A lingering doubt bubbled up from a dark space deep within him, burst, and floated away. Gazing at the sky, he thought of his mother and hoped she found peace in knowing that Avelos called him worthy to serve.

He collected himself and headed toward the three people who had become his family. Seeing them together made his chest tighten as he realized how alike they were. All three bore the marks of their noble heritage: smooth, even features; hair the color of wheat; and blue-grey eyes that paled under the bright Avelonian sky. His ungainly height, cursed green gaze, and dark hair tied back in a soldier's tail ensured he would not be mistaken for one of their own.

As he approached, Tierzen watched him with sharp eyes and a thoughtful expression. Madam Sarena Trianor, small and round, linked one arm through her husband's. She looked up at Jhared and draped her other arm protectively across Branlen's shoulder. Jhared stopped, suddenly too shy to come closer. *You will risk your own child for one who is Shorn?*

She had never relinquished her fear; she couldn't, for he had never stopped being a danger. He saw it every time he was too bold with his questions or delved into some book he had better left alone. Despite her fear, or because of it, she had taught him all it meant to be Shorn and all the ways he must atone. He, in turn, worked hard to learn the lessons well. It was the least he could give her—the least he could give them all—for taking him into their home. Seconds passed; no one moved. Jhared remained alone.

"Congratulations, Patrolman!" Pulling free of his mother's grasp, Branlen bounced across the unseen barrier between them, unaware or uncaring, and threw his arms around Jhared. "You've earned your rank now, right?"

Jhared returned the hug with one arm and gave the boy a half-smile. "Yes, Bran. Tomorrow the lieutenant will assign me to a patrol."

Tierzen stepped forward and met Jhared's eyes with a judging gaze. For an instant, Jhared saw a man he did not recognize: Elder Tierzen Trianor, Minister of the Teaching; the man who had selected his rival to judge his son. With a smile, though, Jhared's beloved foster father returned. Madam Trianor joined then. Jhared bobbed his head to her respectfully.

She grimaced at the sight of him half-clothed and bleeding. "You can't stand on the street like that," she said. "Come back with us. You'll eat, and we'll see that you're decent before you leave."

He nodded. The mention of food set his stomach rumbling. Branlen laughed, then took his hand and tugged him homeward.

As he entered the house, the rich smell of roasting meat nearly bowled him over. He might have basked in the comfort of it, but Madam Trianor had other plans for him. She shed her reserve like a cloak and took command as soon as they left the crowded street. She sent Branlen to fetch bandages, then directed Jhared out of the front hall and through the great room to the kitchen. He yielded to her direction, pressing his wadded shirt against his shoulder to keep the blood off her wool rugs.

In the kitchen, Neta prepared the afternoon meal. With a sturdy arm she beat dumpling batter in an earthenware bowl. Behind her, the hearth flames hissed and spit as fat dripped from a lamb roast.

"I'll need your help, Neta," Madam Trianor said, pointing Jhared toward a seat.

The housekeeper looked over her shoulder and raised a ginger brow. "Ah, good. He's home. In time for dinner."

Jhared's lip twitched upward. To Neta, the trials of life were to be endured and set aside, not discussed or contemplated. And there was no trial so grim that a good meal couldn't ease the burden of it.

The savory smells, the warm kitchen, and the familiarity of home melted away the last of his energy. He sank like a sack of grain onto the bench by the hearth. Branlen sat beside him, buzzing with questions about his commission. Jhared was content to sate the boy's interest, but he sensed Madam Trianor growing tense. Flicking a glance from his Teacher to his little brother, he yawned and leaned against the stone.

"I'm sorry, Bran. I'm no good for answering questions right now. Later we'll talk, all right?"

"Indeed!" Madam Trianor scolded. "I've heard enough about soldiers and scouting. No one here is doing border patrol tonight, Branlen. If you can't quit such talk, I'll send you to do chores until dinner."

"But, Mother, I only want—" Branlen cut short his protest when he caught her expression. Jhared shifted to give the boy a consolatory wink.

"Don't try your mother's patience, child," Neta said as she brought a bowl of herb-infused water and clean rags to the table. "Go on and set the plates for dinner."

When Branlen moved reluctantly to the task, Neta looked at Jhared and gently patted his hand that still held the bloodied cloth to his shoulder. "Let me see, now."

He eased the cloth away, exposing his torn flesh. Madam Trianor made a noise of disgust and turned away, but Neta didn't flinch.

"Well, that's a pretty one," the housekeeper muttered, as if he were still eight and it were just another scraped knee. She cleaned the wound and wrapped it, just as she had so many times when he was a child. She didn't share her healer's secrets with him today, but if it troubled her to treat a bound Shorn man, she didn't show it.

Her ease comforted him. For a short while longer he could deny that his place in this family had changed.

"Take some tea?" she offered, as she straightened to inspect her work. "It'll help you sleep."

"No. No, thank you." The wound ached, but he cherished the clarity of the pain. He wanted no more drugged and muddled senses.

"No debt, boy," the housekeeper said, already turning back to the hearth. "I must see to this roast or supper will be burned for sure." She looked once over her shoulder and offered a grin. "It's good you made it back."

"That's fine, Neta," Madam Trianor said. She turned to look Jhared up and down with a critical eye. He pushed a hand through his hair and sat up straight.

"I suppose you're famished," she muttered, releasing him from her evaluation. From the sideboard she retrieved a platter of fresh bread sliced into thick slabs and smeared with lindaberry jam. "Here. It's too long for you to wait until dinner."

Neta darted a glance at Madam Trianor. Jhared caught a sigh. Indulgence of the appetites was dangerous for a Shorn man. He tried not to inhale the fragrant scent of the bread as she carried it to the table. His stomach roared. "It is a kindness you offer, Madam Trianor, but I cannot. Restraint and discipline are the foundations of control."

"Yes, they are. So do not stuff yourself or fall to garrison manners." Madam Trianor set the platter in front of him.

He looked at her, hearing something unexpected in her tone. Then he stared at the bread. The golden jam ran thick and shining across the moist, yellow slices. Three days had passed since he'd last eaten. This was nothing other than a test. No matter that he had just passed the Becoming and proved himself to all of Avelos. This was the time to keep his control firm. Madam Trianor knew his weaknesses. He waited another minute before selecting a small slice and laying it on the plate she offered. She sat to watch him eat.

Slowly, he reached for the bread, took one bite, and set it aside. The fresh, yeasty flavor caused his body to clamor for more. No matter. Hunger was the easiest appetite to curb. He focused on the sweet-tart taste of the jam. It reminded him of days long ago when Madam Trianor rewarded him for perfect lessons with honey and biscuits or a piece of apple cake. "I'll miss your lindaberry jam," he said, setting his hands in his lap.

Madam Trianor glanced up as though he'd startled her. "General Nadel feeds his men well. I'm sure there will be nothing you'll miss. Now, go change, then go to the library. Tierzen wants to see you."

As he stood, he caught her gaze and held it a moment. "Thank you, Madam Trianor."

"I cannot say no debt," she replied.

"I know, Madam. And I will pay it."

She shook her head and dusted her hands on her apron. "Go on. You're making Tierzen wait."

Upstairs, Jhared pulled on a clean shirt, splashed cold water over his face, and dragged wet fingers through his hair before hurrying to Tierzen's library. He knocked and peered around the half-open library door. Tierzen sat at his desk, intent upon the pages of a book. When he looked up, yellow light from the lamp on the desk made his eyes sparkle.

"Come in. Come in."

Jhared entered and waited uncertainly in the center of the room. In twelve years, he had entered this chamber only a handful of times, and not all of those times by invitation. His gaze moved from the intricate tapestries and the framed map of Avelos on the walls to the richly carved bookshelf and its tempting collection of volumes. Important guests were invited here, Teachers, elders, and clan prefects who came to speak with Tierzen about council matters. And, of course, Sirol spent hours in this room working with the elder.

Tierzen closed the old book and came around the desk. "Nothing like a bit of Morican to make a man feel forlorn," he said with a chuckle.

He poured two glasses of amethyst wine from a decanter on the side table and handed one to Jhared. It was an expensive southern vintage, a gift from the prefect of Clan Makri. "Go on. Sit down."

Jhared lowered himself onto one of the leather-backed chairs. He was too tall for it and it made his knees jut up awkwardly. "I thought you didn't like Morican."

"I don't agree with her," Tierzen corrected. "That only makes it more important to understand her. She's the earliest priestess whose writings remain. We must know our history, yes?"

"Of course, sir. Such as we can." Little of the country's centuries of history and knowledge had survived the Exile War; libraries had burned, leaving yawning gaps in the work of the priestess-historians. How much poorer was Avelos for the loss? When the aqueducts failed, no engineers lived who could repair them. No architects remained who could master the stunning arches and impossible domes of Alende Isan's time. The lost knowledge was another wrong for which Jhared's kind must pay.

Tierzen settled in a chair across from Jhared and leaned his head back. "'We are but isolated beings given breath by Riana,'" he quoted, translating Morican from the ancient Velos. "'Riana has given us no means to communicate with Her creatures, no means to speak to the stars, and ultimately we cannot even know ourselves.'"

Tierzen sat forward and gestured with his drink. "High Chieftain Tumal interpreted Morican to mean that since true communication is not possible between peoples, the only way to prevent deadly conflict is for each nation to keep to itself, not communicate at all. He liked Morican a good deal. Today it is Tumal's Legacy that finds her work useful."

Jhared nodded and tried not to look uncomfortable perched at the edge of his chair. His foster father honored him with the room, the wine, the discussion, but it made him feel like a stranger.

Tierzen leaned back again, took a sip of his drink, and looked at Jhared speculatively. "Do you want to talk about it?"

Jhared rubbed a hand over his chest; inside he still felt raw and bruised. "No, sir."

Tierzen frowned, and it seemed for a moment that he would press. "Very well," he said finally. "You'll go to the barracks tonight?"

"Yes. Although I have a few things that wouldn't have a place there. I thought I might leave them with Branlen. If you would permit it."

"Certainly."

Silence again. To escape Tierzen's probing gaze, Jhared picked up his glass and stared at the play of the lamplight on the wine. Through the belly of the glass and the shifting shades of purple, his foster father's face was dark and distorted. In all the man's years as elder, how many Shorn youths had he sent into the wilds to die?

"Did Enrian say where you'll be stationed?"

"Hmm? General Nadel? Not yet." Jhared set down the glass hastily, ashamed of his thoughts. "Somewhere in the south, where the most need lies. Perhaps Barlona, or if I'm lucky, Ravia. With the Laebeki raiders and Sahiste so close, it would be a good placement. An active placement."

"Don't worry, you'll see action wherever you're placed." Tierzen's voice took on a familiar tone. "More men at the border might slow the raiders, but it can't stop them. Too few of our goods are allowed to cross the border legally and thieved goods bring rich prices, not just in Laebek, but in Amuria and…" The elder halted and quirked a smile. "I'm sorry. I can't seem to stop giving lessons tonight."

Jhared returned the smile. "A habit."

"A habit I no longer need. You proved today that you know your place." Tierzen set his glass down on the desk and braced his hands on his knees. "Jhared, in some ways, what you did today is only the beginning. With the Legacy agitating the council, don't doubt that you'll be asked to prove yourself again. When you face such trials, you must remember what we've given you. You know what it is you owe."

"Through your Teaching, sir." Tierzen's words possessed a note of finality that cut apart Jhared's ties to this family. Tierzen had guided him as a Teacher for twelve years and as a father for nearly nine, but everything the man did now reminded him this was no longer his home. When other Shorn youths completed the Teaching, they still had families among the clans or in Shorn Circle. Where did he belong now?

The elder rapped his knuckles against his knees. "I'm not certain you understand. The Legacy lost an arrow in their quiver against me today, but they'll not relent." Tierzen lifted his gaze. "They will continue to watch you."

Jhared smothered a wave of apprehension. "Why are they so invested in discrediting you? This isn't just about the Teaching. What does the Legacy hope to gain?"

Tierzen smiled faintly and shook his head. "I should have known you would notice a piece of the puzzle was missing. I think I have Enrian Nadel to blame for that." He turned to sip from his wine and shook his head again. "All right. Tell me what you need to make the pieces fit together."

Jhared blew out a breath and considered what Tierzen had told him only the day before: *"The council didn't consent." "Rumar closed the debate." "A blatant act of favoritism." "He may still regret it."* He thought of the crowd at his binding shouting curses against Trianor's Folly. Their anger still made him shudder, but it hadn't been aimed only at him.

"If you are discredited," he said, "Rumar will lose your strength as an ally."

"Yes. He would."

"And he would look reckless for ignoring the council's advice simply to give you a favor."

Tierzen sighed. "Indeed. And one thing more: it would appear as though his games of favoritism impede his ability to keep the country safe."

Jhared allowed a little of his reserve energy to trickle out so that he sat straighter and spoke firmly. "I am a servant of Avelos. If they watch me, they will find me as loyal next week, next summer, and every summer following as they found me today."

The tension in Tierzen's hands eased a little, and Jhared realized just how worried the man was.

"I know they will," Tierzen said quietly. "That's because what we did, you and I, was a success. My Teaching and your devotion will keep you safe, even when the faults of your kind lead you toward temptation. I know you won't fail me, or our high chieftain."

Jhared's chest hurt.

Tierzen continued soberly, "It's for this reason I must request something of you while you're commissioned in the south."

"Whatever you need of me, sir."

"Good. For you're the one to accomplish this task. I need your clever eyes and ears to watch and listen where I cannot."

That caught Jhared off guard. Elder Trianor had extensive connections, and as Minister of the Teaching had access to official reports wherever the Shorn gave their service. What he wanted, therefore, had to be something unofficial. "You want me to spy…on my comrades?"

"I want you to report what you observe."

The thought chilled Jhared for reasons he couldn't quite capture. "I'm only a patrolman. I'll have no access to events of import."

"Ah, my boy, after all these years, do you think I would give you a task beyond your ability? You'll see exactly what I need you to see, and you'll see it from a perspective no one else could. The southern prefects are bringing complaints to the council about Shorn soldiers at the border. I need the news you can provide me to decide what truth exists in these stories."

Jhared grew more uneasy. This was a council matter, something far outside the proper domain of a Shorn soldier. "Sir, what's happened?"

Tierzen closed his eyes and rubbed a hand over his face. "Very well. You will hear of it when you reach the south in any case." The elder opened his eyes and met Jhared's gaze. "A Shorn soldier was pushed off the wall at Ravia."

Shock silenced Jhared for a long stretch. "A traitor? Within the garrison?"

"Maybe. It's uncertain."

Shorn traitors who broke the most important of the Shorn Laws died dishonorably, shoved from the highest walls of their city or village, flying toward the earth in a mockery of their own gross desires. Jhared couldn't imagine how such a death remained "uncertain."

Tierzen saw his question before he spoke it. "The sentence was not carried out by the garrison. It happened in town. My report from the prefect of Clan Amerre says the soldier beat a boy to death in a brawl. The soldier was summarily executed."

"You don't trust the prefect's report?"

"Abrigado holds the leashes of Clans Amerre and Makri, and sometimes Rehamra. Whatever else may be said of him, the Minister of the Treasury knows how to mold the truth into the form that best fits his needs. It would serve him to cast doubt over the integrity of General Nadel's Shorn men."

Tierzen looked up, his blue-grey gaze grim. "Jhared, I must give you this directive not as your foster father or your Teacher but as the Minister of the Teaching. If there's trouble among the bound men in the south, I must have an honest picture of it. And if the trouble is only Abrigado's creation, then I need to know who else plays a part in it. The high chieftain must have an army of Shorn soldiers as loyal as you are. I've promised him that."

Exhaustion laid a heavy hand on Jhared, but he held himself upright and didn't turn from the minister's gaze. "As you require, sir."

A knock on the door saved him from more promises. Branlen poked his head in to announce that dinner was ready. Jhared waited for Tierzen to stand before trusting himself to climb to his feet. The elder gave him a nod and a confident smile.

"Congratulations, Jhared. You have earned your place. I know the next part of your journey will be as great a success." Tierzen smiled again before following Branlen down the hall.

Jhared watched the young boy turn the corner with his father. He trailed after them, wondering why Tierzen's words didn't comfort him.

Sleep dangled just out of reach. Each time Jhared drifted toward unconsciousness, his drowsy sinking turned into a deadly fall and he jolted awake. As always, the dream hurtled him down rocky cliffs, filling him with the terrible thrill that sent forbidden heat coursing through his veins. Tonight as he fell, pain constricted his chest and his hands clutched at an arrow that pierced his heart. Death reached him before the rocks this time. He awoke, sweat-soaked, and tossed off the light blanket. His heart boomed against his ribs, while other patrolmen snored in the beds around him.

The moon had risen by the time Jhared gave up on sleep. He pulled on his clothes, his boots, and his Forest Guard cloak. In the moonlight, the yellow trainee's stripe on the cloak shone a lighter grey than the red Shorn border. When he received his commission tomorrow, the yellow would be removed. From now on, if he faltered, no one would call it a trainee's mistake.

He glanced at the sleeping men around him. Most of them had chosen to serve in the Forest Guard of their own will. Even the spring levies were often men—youngest sons, offspring of soldiers—who had vied to be sent to the Guard to honor their clans. Some clan leaders argued against the need for a standing army, seeking power through their own clanguard, but the Forest Guard forced the neighboring nations to step back from the borders. That strength gave those who enlisted a powerful sense of pride. Men who chose a place in the Guard disdained serving beside the Shorn, who were sent to make reparation.

Jhared curled his fingers around the rough wool of his cloak and slipped out of the hall. Outside the barracks, he appraised the darkness, lifting his gaze above the buildings that crowded the street. The sickle moon impaled a sapphire sky speckled with Riana's stars. In the south, Arion glowed pure and bright. Jhared drew a deep breath of the cold air and made a face. The city smelled of woodsmoke and yeast, animals and offal, of too many people living and dying within the walls. He longed for the clean breezes and untrodden paths of the forest, but the gates were closed until dawn. If he needed to move, the maze of the city would have to do.

Before him, Crooked Way turned like a twisted stick. The street was named for the number of taverns, gaming houses, and brothels it supported as much as for the way it zigzagged north and south at the base of Travitar Hill. Light from the wooden buildings striped the ground, and bursts of laughter disrupted the stillness: the din of off-duty soldiers, of apprentices, of wealthy young men seeking the thrill of dangerous streets. Jhared could expect to find no camaraderie there. As he stood, considering which direction to start, a tavern door opened, spilling light and sound into the night. A broad man and a dark-haired woman staggered out of the doorway and wove their way toward the street. The man muttered something low in his throat; the woman shrieked merrily in response as they meandered southward. Jhared turned and headed north.

The noises faded as he left the barracks behind, passing Aelend prison and following the tortuous streets through a sleeping city. Streetlamps flickered small patches of yellow against painted shop signs and stone, but Jhared stuck to the shadows and made his footsteps scout-stealthy. It could be dangerous for a lone wanderer in the city at this time of night. Violence was not uncommon. It was less dangerous for a soldier, or at least it was dangerous for different reasons.

He hadn't planned to pass Shorn Circle, but he found himself climbing toward the city center before he realized it. Once he passed the high temple heading east, his footsteps turned down the slope toward the other side of Travitar Hill, and he couldn't avoid the circle walls. The ruins of the ancient Avelune keep chilled him. Its broken towers leaned impotently over crumbling outbuildings. The walls were breached and sagging. Years had passed since Jhared had last entered the circle. After he came to live with his Teachers, Elder Trianor had forbidden him to enter it, keeping him clear of the harmful influences of other Shorn children. Now Jhared found himself staring up at the arch that marked the site of the old gates. He told himself he only came to pay respects to his mother. His birth had caused her to move here, but she died in the circle alone.

He picked his way through the spot where Tumal the Just had destroyed the gates nearly one hundred fifty years ago. Long before the Exile, the Avelune built the keep, a city within the city: greedily gathering their power behind walls, hiding their secrets from the rest of Avelos. Nothing of greed or glory remained now, only shame and decay. Jhared's memories of the place were so distant from his life in Elders' Circle he could only pull together a few images, like the lines of a half-forgotten song.

Just inside the wall, he paused to get his bearings. On his left lay a pile of rock that might have been part of the gate tower roof. As he peered at the ruins, he caught himself humming. He stopped. "Traitors' Fall" was not a song to lighten his uncertain mood. Still, it was easier to imagine Riana's quick and fatal retribution as his mother recounted it in her resonant contralto than the truth Tierzen had taught him. His mind skittered away from the thought of Lord Tumal's angry armies breaking up the Avelune palace piece by piece and driving the traitors out of the city.

With effort, he dragged up a different melody as he started walking again, another his mother had sung, "Sunrise Over Golden Mountains," which told the story of a man who would make the final reparation to Avelos. Riana would bless that man like Lord Arion, and Avelos would be repaid for what it lost. Throughout his Teaching, Jhared had held onto his mother's words like a lantern on a dark road. Yesterday he had gone so far as to promise Cael he would accomplish the final act necessary to fully repay the Avelune debt. He had meant it, even if tonight he couldn't imagine how to begin.

The shattered cobbles carried him along the edge of Shorn Circle near the walls. This fringe of the city still seethed with activity. Waylayers lined the streets in garish silks and concealing face paint, risking their spirits to seek the forbidden for whoever would pay. The acrid scent of the incense they burned competed with the musk and floral scents of the harlots, who glided through the darkness with bells on their wrists and ankles. Men slipped in and out of the circle through the gaps in the walls, looking for things they couldn't buy in other parts of the city. Some crouched over destiny boards with the waylayers; some tangled with the Shorn whores. As Jhared passed a shadowed doorway, a man lurched into the lane, brandishing a small knife in one fist.

"Your purse," the man demanded, stumbling forward a drunken step.

Jhared drew himself to his full height and glowered down. "I have nothing worth the effort," he said darkly.

The would-be thief looked him over, then apparently agreed and staggered back into the darkness. Jhared walked more swiftly. A soldier's cloak and a bold manner would discourage many, but he didn't feel the need to test that shield.

In fact, his uniform attracted plenty of unwelcome attention from the way-layers, smoke-sellers, and harlots. Silk-clad men and women pressed around him to hawk their wares.

"Let me guide you down the path to love," purred a wild-eyed waylayer, waving a destiny board in Jhared's face.

A slender young woman thrust herself toward him and wound one arm about his neck, laughing softly. "You need no guide to me, Patrolman. I'm right here." The red ribbon that marked her as Shorn curved over her breasts, twisted around her waist, and dangled over her thigh, like an invitation or a chain.

Another waylayer wafted a scarf over him. "There is someone who blocks your way in matters of love? In matters of business? You need the dice to favor? Let me show you the path to that destiny." In a doorway, a third waylayer writhed on the ground, moaning and spitting out gibberish as a slight man, decidedly too well-dressed for Shorn Circle, gazed on with wide eyes, hoping for some useful vision in exchange for coin.

"That's not what I need tonight," Jhared said. Gently but decisively, he disengaged from the woman. He shrugged the waylayer's silk off his shoulder and kept walking. The whores offered no comfort for him. On the disastrous night when he'd been lonely enough to explore that outlet, he realized an unsettling truth: a Shorn harlot was bound to her life just as he was bound to the Forest Guard. She gave her body in her service to Avelos, and he could not be counted as one to whom she owed a debt. He couldn't bring himself to touch her. Still, he understood the harlots; he would never understand the waylayers. Those disordered men called themselves guides and claimed to possess a gift Riana gave only to women: the ability to navigate the sacred Paths. The temple called them demon-touched, caelevano, and forbade them from stepping onto holy ground. Jhared didn't know whether the creatures were truly malevolent, greedy charlatans, or simply insane.

He looked back over his shoulder at the mob and wondered why he had come. Why was he wandering among these outcasts?

He didn't stop until he left the crowd well behind. The center of Shorn Circle was a large, open plaza, defined at its borders by curved stone dwellings that rose in staggered levels like a vast stairway. A smaller reflection of the city center on Travitar Hill, it must have been beautiful once. Moonlight dripped across the flagstones in milky puddles. All was quiet and still; this part of the circle slept more peacefully. Jhared sat down at the edge of the broken fountain in the middle of the plaza. He let his fingers trail in the rainwater collected there. The coolness on his skin awoke a faint memory of splashing about on a hot day. He looked up and recalled the buildings around the fountain with a child's eyes: the stair-step construction heading toward the sky, the tiered balconies, and the peculiar archways high upon the walls with no stairs to reach them. It was all a playground to an agile boy. He had climbed walls and scaled heights just to gain the dangerously open rooftops. The view they offered of the valley and the mountains was spectacular, a hawk's perspective. Long ago, the climb had been a delicious challenge, before he understood that his ancestors, the Avelune, had not needed to climb. Before he learned how they had been marked, like Cael's messengers. And like Cael's messengers, they could travel from place to place with an ease no natural creatures could match. The capacity for flight, and the careless migration it allowed, prevented the Avelune from developing any sense of loyalty—to their mates, to the high chieftain or to Avelos. They crossed borders with abandon. Jhared felt queasy staring up at the heights where he had once scrambled effortlessly. He couldn't recall how he ever survived them.

Not all who made their homes in the circle were Shorn, but all had the taint of the curse somewhere within their family. They gathered like mice among the ruins. Did they find welcome here, away from the disdain of bands like Maren's, away from the elders who served the Legacy? The small flags bearing the black feather marked nearly every door here. Looking at the rows of them, Jhared had the sense that somehow, in this circle, the black marks were a sign of belonging.

Candlelight glowed through the oiled parchment of a window in one of the street-level dwellings. As Jhared watched, the door opened and yellow light escaped around the silhouettes of a man and a woman. The two figures lingered in the doorway. She pressed herself sweetly against him and he held her close with one arm. They whispered together and exchanged a long kiss. Then the door closed, and the man stood alone. Jhared felt an unexpected pang of envy for the stranger. He didn't recognize Sirol until it was too late to flee.

The scribe looked more at ease than Jhared had ever seen him. Rather than the voluminous grey robes of his office, neat dark breeches enwrapped his long legs and a narrow tunic sheathed his slender torso. Despite his slightly lopsided outline, the close-fitting garb gave him a graceful form. His black hair hung loose and tousled down his back. He strode across the street with a half-smile on his lips.

When he saw Jhared, his contentment vanished. He glanced once behind him toward the closed door, then back at Jhared with a suspicious glare.

"What are you doing here, Patrolman?"

Sirol made the hard-won rank an unmistakable insult. Jhared bristled; he wanted more from the scribe than contempt. "I hope you placed no bets on my failure, Sirol. I succeeded. I passed the Becoming."

"I know," the scribe said gruffly. "I was there. Did you follow me in the middle of the night to tell me that?"

Jhared paused in surprise. "You were there?"

"As were many, many others," the scribe observed. "I asked you a question you've twice avoided. What do you want here?"

Whatever he had done years ago to cause Sirol to despise him, Jhared wished he could undo it. The scribe spent so much time in the Trianor household they could almost be called brothers.

"I don't know," Jhared sighed. "Nothing. I didn't follow you. I just couldn't sleep."

"Ah, I see." The scribe's tone turned colder. "Aren't there harlots closer to the barracks for the soldiers?"

Jhared flushed. The memory of a woman's hand touching his scars brought its own regret. He had an urge to soil Sirol's moment of sweetness, but found he couldn't say anything.

The scribe's gaze narrowed. "Not whores? Then what?"

"I told you, I don't know." Jhared felt too tired for wisdom, or perhaps he just held out some hope that Sirol would understand. "I didn't expect to feel this unsettled tonight. I've taken up my duty, but I feel so…out of place."

"Well, you won't find what you're searching for here."

"I'm not *searching* for anything," Jhared insisted. "I simply thought there might be others in the circle who would know what it was like today. It's not been so long since your own trials. You should know."

The scribe's expression turned disbelieving. "You haven't figured it out yet, have you? You don't belong in Shorn Circle. Whatever you faced today, it wasn't the same that I, or anyone else in the circle, faced. It was the culmination of conflicts brewing in the council for over nine years. You are Trianor's Folly. The elders have been waiting for you."

Jhared's hand went to his chest in a defensive gesture that was already becoming a habit. "I grew up in this circle. I'm the same as—"

"A lie. You don't think of this place as a part of your life. You were raised in the splendor of Elders' Circle."

"And you've spent nearly as many years with the elders yourself!"

Sirol laughed darkly. "I am Elder Trianor's scribe and you are his son. But you have no idea what that means, do you? Do you think every Teacher allows his pupil to read the old histories and rewards him with pride and kindness for it? Have you ever felt the lash because you didn't move fast enough or the blade because you didn't answer correctly? Did you ever think about what happens to other Shorn children when they ask too many questions?" Sirol growled and rolled his crippled shoulder.

Jhared knew the Teachers sometimes used harsh measures; sometimes such measures were *necessary*. The seed of evil slept in every Shorn child. It must be killed before it grew in order to save the child from worse. Jhared had borne the bruises from Sarena's lessons. A crescent-shaped scar on the inside of his wrist was a reminder of some of his own failings. Not every Teacher had Elder Trianor's subtlety. "I know," he answered more quietly.

"You think you know." Sirol growled again. "You'd be wise to leave quickly. Too many people in this circle saw you today, people who view a Shorn boy raised by his Teachers as a threat. They don't trust you, and they know who you are now. Elder Trianor must beware of the Legacy, but there are as many Shorn as Legacy folk who would hurt you if they could."

Jhared shook his head. "You are the only one who wants to hurt me, Sirol. What have I ever done to earn your hatred?"

Surprise flickered in the scribe's face before he offered Jhared an asymmetrical shrug. "Believe what you will. If I wanted to hurt you, I would have let you discover for yourself what they think of you here. This was a gift. Because of what you did for the elder today."

"Ah. Then I owe you for your kindness." The mockery came easily. It didn't quell the loneliness rising in Jhared's chest.

"You wouldn't be so smug if you knew what the Legacy plans."

"Father told me. They'll watch me, hoping I'll misstep so they can blame his Teaching."

"Watch you? They won't waste their time. They'll just find a way to trip you into doing something stupid."

Jhared sucked an exasperated breath. "Sirol, whatever you may think of me, I'm not a simpleton. I've proved my loyalty. They can't *force* me to break Shorn Law."

"Of course they won't force you. Goddess, you're a cocky thing. Do you really imagine yourself as clever as Elder Toren Abrigado, the first Minister of the Treasury from Clan Amerre in two hundred years? Elder Trianor doesn't even claim to know all that Abrigado plans. You won't know you've crossed the line until the guard comes to drag you before the tribunal. And after they prove the Teaching has failed, Abrigado will pressure the council to abolish the Shearing."

"Don't be unbalanced. The debt isn't yet paid. They would never abolish…" Jhared trailed off as he realized what the scribe meant.

"That's right. No more Teachers. No more Shorn Law. No more Shorn." Sirol's gaze burned in the moonlight. "A final Exile. All of us shoved off the walls. Avelune babes drowned like kittens. You'd best be certain you don't step over the line, soldier. You're the weapon Abrigado will use to finish Elder Trianor. Then he's going to come for the rest of us."

Jhared couldn't stand to know more. He rose from the fountain and started to stalk away. The darkness had grown cold and hostile. Perhaps that was why his eyes went back to the little window of warm light and the doorway where a woman had stood. He halted, his gaze fastened on the spot. Did Sirol find welcome there? Did she know him—all his flaws and weaknesses—and still open the door to him with a smile? Could a Shorn man truly find that welcome anywhere?

"Don't linger, soldier," warned the scribe. "You'll find nothing there for you. Leave now. You are not one of us."

6.
FORGOTTEN SONGS

A long, hard run was what Jhared wanted, the kind of all-out effort that drained him of the unacceptable emotions testing his composure. But within the confines of the walls, where a fleeing Shorn man meant trouble of any number of types, he forced himself to walk. He marched along the winding streets, leaving Shorn Circle and Travitar Hill far behind, but unable to escape the ache in his heart. The watchman called out the hour twice before he paused. He stood near a dilapidated market pavilion, somewhere east and rather south of the city's center, on Cirolan Hill amid the Circles of the Lost. Fire had charred a part of the pavilion's roof, leaving stone columns carved with serpents uncovered and roof beams exposed. Most of the street's lamps were unlit or missing, cloaking the dreary little quarter with darkness.

A dog barked behind a shed opposite the market. Jhared turned in time to see a rat skitter out of the shed, cross the open street, and scuttle under a barrel. The dog yapped after it, pawing at the barrel until a woman's sharp threats from a nearby house silenced the beast. Quiet fell again. Jhared rubbed a hand over his face and laughed softly at himself. He'd let Sirol chase him off like a dog protecting its territory. The man had barked a warning, and Jhared fled like a pup with his tail between his legs. He felt foolish for letting the scribe manipulate him.

The hound gave up its pursuit of the rat and trotted up to the porch of its home, circling twice before settling down to its watch once more. Jhared considered finding his way back to the barracks, where his own watch would be assigned to him in just a few hours. He skirted the market and started down a street that traveled roughly west, near the base of Cirolan Hill. It was a narrow way and dark. The wooden buildings on either side of the street, small shops and living places mostly, shouldered against one another, creating the slender alleyways and dead ends that made Velantar so confusing to strangers. Part of the way down the lane, the sign of a prancing horse announced a livery stable. Beyond it, a single candle flickered in the round window of Riana's eye, marking a little temple. Not far from that was a stone building, a tavern. Even in the wan light, Jhared could see the paint curling from the tavern sign. It looked black, though it could have been any dark shade. The sign was cut in the shape of a mountain.

A mountain? The Black Mountain? Jhared abruptly recalled why he knew that name. He thought of the woman who spoke to him that afternoon and wondered if he should enter. Following Riana's Paths wisely, he suspected, sometimes meant knowing when to keep walking. But the woman had touched him without fear, and her odd message compelled him to learn more. Wise or not, he walked to the Black Mountain Inn and stopped before it.

From the outside, the tavern lacked the noise and frenetic energy of the drinking houses near the barracks, although it was possible the stone simply held its secrets better. Shuttered windows on the first floor allowed promising lines of pale light to escape. Most of the windows upstairs were dark. No colors or sigils announced clan or faction loyalty, and it was likely close enough to the Circles of the Lost that no one would ask. Jhared pulled on the heavy door, found it open, and went inside.

He almost stepped right back out when a thickly built Shorn man who sat close to the door maneuvered around to stare threateningly at him. A shaggy black beard hid much of the man's expression, but as the stranger appraised Jhared, the hostility in his eyes and the heavy club at his side spoke clearly. Any remaining veils Jhared held about his Forest Guard commission earning him safe passage shredded under the black-beard's glare. If it were not for the music, he would have turned around instantly, but the music bound him with a tie stronger than his good sense. A fiddle, Nadaren pipes, and a flute. He knew their voices without turning to look for their source, like the voices of long-absent loved ones. They made him forget he stood alone in an unfamiliar part of the city, until he realized he was still under the fighting man's inspection.

He didn't drop the stranger's gaze; instead, he offered a neutral nod and turned more casually than he felt to find himself a table. The man returned the acknowledgment with a vicious grin and watched as Jhared took a seat in an opposite corner. Jhared put his back to the wall and settled in. He wasn't going to let another dog chase him off tonight.

With a quick glance, he appraised the occupants of the room to see who had witnessed the threatening welcome he received and who might offer threats of their own. Above the tables, lamps in sconces smudged the walls with oily smoke and provided a shadowy light. In a booth across the room, two young women whispered over their wine with a mild-faced little Clan Everen man. At the bar, past a staircase to the second floor, four old men grumbled and laughed with an elderly barmaid, who paused to joke with them as she picked up their dishes. The woman never stopped moving, though a limp marred her gait as she roved from the bar to the kitchen and back. She raised an eyebrow at Jhared as she refilled the mugs of the old men. A couple sitting near the riverstone hearth spared no attention for anything but the music.

Feeling comfortably ignored, and reassured that Shorn patrons were not summarily rejected here, Jhared turned to the melody and the musicians. A circular space in the center of the room that could be used for dancing held three performers. The fiddler, a wiry old Shorn man, coaxed a soulful lament from his instrument with loving strokes of the bow. Accompanying him on the pipes was a ginger-haired boy who played with less reverence, but almost as much talent. Beside the boy, with a black flute in her slender fingers, sat a tall, curly-haired woman. Jhared's breath caught in his throat when he recognized her as the one who had spoken to him at his binding. Her plaintive tune melded flawlessly with the others, so that they shared their story in one coherent voice. He didn't know the song, but he found himself relaxing into its sweet sadness.

"You'll want s'wine while you enjoy our music."

Jhared pulled his gaze away from the musicians. A broad-shouldered barmaid with a scar above her pale brow stood beside his table, a carafe of the house wine in her hands.

"Of course." He reached into the pouch at his belt for what coin he had. She looked him over with a calculating eye.

"And a meal," she added. "Isella's a bit'a stew left, and n'doubt you need it."

As ever, Jhared's stomach roared his hunger, but as he sat back, his Teachers whispered in his head: *"Practice restraint to guard against an Avelun's cravings."* Tonight that lesson would only get him into trouble with the innkeeper, and he didn't feel like drawing more attention to himself.

"No doubt," he agreed dryly, grateful when the woman took his money and let him be.

The wine couldn't compare to any Makri vintage, but it was mellow and pleasant. The bowl of stew she brought smelled appetizing. If it didn't have anything recognizable as meat, still it was hearty with beans and potatoes and the first of the spring carrots. He ate while the musicians crooned one last melody. In the nearly empty tavern, they seemed to be performing more for themselves than for anyone else, experimenting in ways that carried them far beyond the confines of the inn's stone walls. They played as though they trusted one another, each contributing a personal variation on a theme. The three musicians laid open their hearts, with all their different wishes and longings. It was like nothing Jhared had heard elsewhere in the city. It should have been discordant and chaotic, but instead the sound rose to a level of complexity that he only heard in half-remembered dreams. They finished the piece to scattered appreciation from the drinkers, but the players hardly seemed to notice the audience, grinning and congratulating one another in their own small circle. The flautist laughed at something the pipe player said, then leaned forward and kissed him on the brow. Jhared looked to his food and took another swallow of wine.

"Well, hello, Jhared! I didn't imagine you would come to me so soon."

He looked up in bewilderment to see the flautist wave goodbye to her troupe and approach him with a cheerful smile. She didn't wait for him to speak, but slid onto his bench close enough to brush his side as she set her flute on the table. With a wink, she reached for his wine.

"Thank you. I'm dry as Rona's dust."

He tried not to appear as startled as he felt, while she took an impressively long draught from his cup. She was dressed simply in a light green gown that couldn't match the sparkling emerald of her eyes, but did much to reveal her soft curves. The fingers that lifted Jhared's wine were long and slender and smudged with ink. Her spicy scent, like cherries and cinnamon, filled his head.

"How do you know my name?"

The woman's eyes went wide over his cup. She set it down and flicked her tongue over her lips, leaving them softly gleaming. "Ah, a voice low and lovely and pure. If you sing with such a tone, I should have invited you to take Dria's place tonight. The miserable girl can offer a pretty song, but she's less dependable than a Clan Delsio merchant." The woman refilled his cup from the carafe and glanced at him slyly. "Nearly half the city heard your name today, Jhared Denaban."

He tensed at that reminder of the Becoming and Sirol's warning. Part of him knew he should walk away. He only shrugged and replied flatly, "I don't sing."

"Oh?" A troubled frown dimmed her eyes. In the depths of her expression, Jhared saw she was older than he by a number of years. Then her smile returned and took the years from her again. She lifted one hand and laid it gently on his shoulder, where his binding still ached.

"Forgive me," she murmured softly. "You are worn out, and I'm being flippant. Let me start again. I'm Ziabela Marcalo. You've come at a good time; Isella will be locking the doors in just a few moments, and it will be quieter here. I hope you will come into the back with me and talk for a while."

The warmth of her fingers on his arm and the sweetness of her breath against his neck stole his ability to think sensibly; he couldn't imagine what she wanted from him. Then a memory of Marieva drifted to mind, and he flushed.

"I'm not certain how to say this, but I'm not seeking…anything."

"I know." She stood, still smiling, and tugged him up from the bench. "That's not what I'm offering. Although I do have something of a present for you. First, come here. There's someone you should know."

He submitted to the pressure against his wrist, Sirol's message lost somewhere between his last glass of wine and Ziabela's smile, as she led him toward the kitchen.

"Isella, set your work aside and come see who I've brought you," she called from the threshold.

The elderly barmaid limped from the kitchen shaking her head, a rag still in one hand, the other hand cocked on her hip. "Zia, when are ya going ta give up trying ta find a match for me, eh? There's not a man in this city who…"

Jhared never discovered what the men of Velantar were incapable of accomplishing, for she trailed off as her gaze landed on him.

"What's got into ya, girl? Last week the one ya brought me was older than Alende's mother, but this one's barely out'a his mother's arms." The woman offered him a yellow-toothed grin as her eyes traveled over him. "Truth is he's got the look'a one'a yours. Another soldier, eh?"

"Hush! You'll scare him off!" Ziabela scolded. "Isella, it's Jhared Denaban."

The old woman's grin dissolved and her eyes widened. "Jhared Denaban," she whispered, pronouncing each syllable with a care that softened her northern accent.

Ziabela waved her hand in a little flourish as she made the introductions. "Jhared, Isella is the owner of the Mountain. She has nurtured musicians in the performers' circle for longer than you or I have been alive." The flautist favored the older woman with a fond gaze. "It's her wicked tongue that keeps her healthy. Riana won't have her and Cael can't keep up with her."

"Ay, well," Isella said with a shrug, her attention still focused on Jhared. "The Lady's light on ya, young man. How good ta see ya."

She was grey-haired and wrinkled as a dried apple. She must have been old enough to be his grandmother. Her attentiveness and warm greeting made Jhared feel that he was supposed to have something important to say to her. Instead, he bobbed his head and tried a smile.

"Thank you, madam. It's my good fortune to have discovered a place where the music is as rich and sweet as the wine."

Isella laughed, not unkindly. Despite her injury, she emitted a feeling of sturdiness and comfort, very much like her inn. "No debt, boy. Ya have a bard's tongue, not a soldier's, but I suppose that shouldn't surprise me. I'm glad ya like our music. Our troupe does squeak out a passable tune when pressed to it. Do ya sing, then?"

While Jhared puzzled over the woman and tried to manage the unexpected question for a second time, Ziabela moved familiarly through the kitchen, negotiating her way around the scowl of a large cook to collect a jug of wine and two cups. She returned to hug Isella with her free arm and kiss the woman on the cheek.

"He sings; he just doesn't remember the words, I think. Tell Elian and the others not to wait for me tonight. Jhared and I have stories to tell each other."

Isella nodded, but she didn't take her eyes off Jhared. "I'm glad ya found us, son. Welcome to the Black Mountain."

He offered a farewell to the woman as Ziabela led him away. The room had nearly emptied of patrons, but the black-bearded man remained, still drinking alone. The fighter was too unkempt to be a Forest Guard. The primitive braids in his beard marked him for a clansman and a northerner. Likely he belonged to that rabble who called themselves clanguard and were trained just well enough to swing clubs against village raiders. Jhared's surreptitious glance intercepted a glare of disapproval aimed in his direction. No matter whether the man's hostility was personal as Sirol warned, common northern malice toward the city, or just typical clanguard resentment of anything Forest Guard, leaving the inn tonight might be a more dangerous task than Jhared had expected.

Ziabela appeared not to notice the stranger's glare. She took Jhared past the inn's main staircase and down a dark hall to the back of the building, where the construction changed from stone to wood. In the centuries since the original building rose to serve whatever need the ancients had for it, rooms had been added and another, smaller flight of stairs had been built against the outer wall.

"Watch your step," Ziabela murmured, climbing up before him. Her warning came almost too late, as he set his foot upon an unnailed plank halfway up the stairs and it lifted under his weight. He shifted backwards, allowing the plank to fall into place with a bang.

"Isella's mousetrap," the flautist declared, running up the rest of the stairs.

One door waited at the top of the dark landing. Ziabela handed the cups to Jhared and fumbled for a moment with the latch before unlocking it. A strange odor, smoky and medicinal, wafted out when the door opened. It tickled his nose and the back of his throat in an oddly familiar way as he followed the woman inside.

Gooseflesh rose along his arms as he looked around and realized he had already lived this moment. "Riana's Paths have turned you twice around the same tree," Neta would say when that eerie feeling took him as a child. She was right; he knew this room: the single lamp flickering over white walls and dark ceiling beams; the oak table crowded with chairs and benches; the mismatched sideboard covered with sundries; and the colorful pile of pillows that made a nest near the hearth. Even the combined scent of horse liniment and cherry pipe tobacco tickled some foggy memory.

Ziabela pushed aside a bowl of chestnuts and a dog-shaped nutcracker to set the wine jug and her flute on the sideboard, then lit another lamp.

"These are Isella's rooms," she explained, nodding toward a second door to the left of the hearth. Putting down the light, she went to the window to close the shutters. "Isella lets me stay here on nights when it's too late or too cold to walk home."

"Why do you know who I am, Ziabela? Why do you know I'm the son of a bard? Did Isella know my mother? Did she tell you about her?"

The woman laughed and crossed the room to take the cups from him. "One at a time," she said gently, drawing her hand around his to unclench his fingers. "I promised you a gift, and I meant it. But not like this. Your mother was a storyteller; she would want you to be prepared for this story. Sit down. Let me fill your glass."

She motioned to the pillows on the floor, but he continued to stand while she poured more wine. He glanced at his hand, still feeling her fingers pressed against his skin. With a small sound of satisfaction, she set the cups on the hearth, along with a bowl of last fall's apples. Then she seated herself among the pillows and looked up at him expectantly.

His heart skipped in his chest. He sensed the crossroads Riana offered here, but he stood, unable to take any of them. This wasn't Marieva, he reminded himself. Ziabela hadn't been dared by others to be alone with him, hadn't been dared to touch him. Marieva fled in horror when he responded to her touch and reached for her with desire, but this woman shared his curse; she understood what he was.

"Aberration," answered one of his Teachers coldly.

He paced away from the hearth and Ziabela's inviting smile, needing somewhere safer to focus his attention. He turned to the interesting clutter on the sideboard.

"Where do you give your service?" he asked, lifting a small knife with a Mavaye stallion, Clan Lasla's sigil, rearing on its hilt.

"I began as a city clerk," she said mildly. "But I was claimed for an elder's scribe within a year of my Becoming."

His fingers twitched on the knife. "Then you know Sirol Relian, scribe to Elder Trianor?"

"You are full of all types of questions, aren't you?" she murmured. He glanced back to find her expression thoughtful.

"No. I've never met the scribe," she said finally. "Although I know his name, of course. My elder often has correspondence for the Minister of the Teaching. Why do you ask?"

He shrugged, not entirely certain himself. "I know Sirol, and Riana's Paths move in odd circles. I just wondered."

There was a silence. Jhared felt Ziabela's eyes studying him as he returned the knife to its place. Was it possible she didn't know that the Minister of the Teaching was his foster father? Could that explain her willingness to befriend him? He let the gleam of her flute draw his thoughts away from darker roads. The body of the instrument shone as smooth as Riana's pool, with keywork of silver and bone. Its preternatural beauty stirred bits of memory that were too hazy to make sense.

"Do you know that instrument?" she asked.

He peered again at the flute. A dark, hollow-eyed reflection of himself shone back. "If I've ever seen one, I've no recollection of it."

"It's an Ulaye flute. The wood was given up by the Chosen."

He straightened and glanced at her. "The Chosen give up nothing."

"Point," she said with a little laugh. "Perhaps 'violently surrendered' would be a better choice of words. I danced beneath the trees to make Ularian shoot branches at me until he threw a branch long and straight enough to be of use. After, the wood was crafted by a friend."

Jhared watched to see if she were mocking him. "You provoked the Aye for the sake of music?"

"If Riana were displeased, her Chosen wouldn't have given me the wood. Now, she has another voice to sing her songs of praise." The flautist grinned up at him. "It was Mahla I had to fear more than any other. She scolded me soundly when she learned what I had done."

Ziabela's eyes twinkled with mischief and warmth. Jhared understood she would eventually come to know what he was and would flee, but he couldn't make that matter right now. He moved to the hearth, pulled forward by her boldness and the stories she promised, and sank to the floor beside her.

"Will you tell me what you know about my mother?"

"Now, that's much better," she said, making room for him among the pillows and handing him a cup of wine. "Though I thought you would remember. If not when you saw me, then Isella…" She stopped in the face of his confusion. "Never mind that. You were right; Isella knew your mother. Mahla and her troupe played here for years."

Something inside him unclenched, and he settled more comfortably against the hearth. Half his life had passed since another person shared a memory of his mother with him. The sharing made her real again, more than just his own faded dream.

"You met her here?"

Ziabela nodded. "I came to the Mountain to find a place where I could work in the evenings after my Teaching. I heard that Isella didn't always turn away the Shorn. The first night I came, Mahla's troupe performed in the players' circle. She had a voice rich as honey. Hers wasn't one of those wispy, fragile voices so many call fashionable these days. She had a resonance that put layers of meaning into a song, made it come alive."

Jhared found himself nodding "I remember that. When she sang of Rona or Tumal, or another of the heroes, I always felt as though they were in the room. I imagined those songs would help me to be more like them." He shrugged. "A child's fantasy."

"She could make people want to try the impossible," Ziabela agreed, shifting to lean against him. "She wasn't just a singer; she was a true storyteller, like none other in Velantar. That first night, I was so taken with her I couldn't bear to leave. In fact, Isella refused to take me on because she said I'd spend all my time mooning over the music. I also suspect someone in my family informed her that, as a rule, I didn't always do…what I should."

Jhared drew a shallow breath as Ziabela changed position. Her warm weight against his side caused his body to respond with disturbing alacrity. He took a deeper breath to tighten his control. He had the sense that she still did not always do what she should.

"What happened?" he managed.

"Mahla vouched for me that night. I have no idea why. Maybe she saw how much I loved her, even then. She vouched for me to Isella, and asked me if I wanted to understand the music I heard."

"She took you as an apprentice?" It never occurred to him that his mother might have taught a Shorn student. The realization wasn't enough to distract him from Ziabela's proximity, however. He took another swallow of wine.

"It wasn't an official apprenticeship, of course. I had no time for that with the Teaching, even if the guild would accept me. But your mother and I spent many evenings here in Isella's rooms rehearsing, discussing music, retelling the old stories. You sat beside us as often as not, intent upon every note."

Ziabela turned to look at him directly, her eyes glittering in the lamplight. "You see, Jhared, I've heard you sing. I know what it means to you."

Jhared shook his head. "You're mistaken. Song has no place in the life of a bound Shorn man."

She made a little sound of dismay. "Oh. Oh dear. I am sorry."

"Sorry?"

"I should have come for you sooner. Don't worry. Now that you're here, we'll awaken the music in you again." With one ink-stained finger, she drew a line along the edge of his jaw and down his throat.

Jhared struggled to maintain his composure. In another moment, nothing would conceal what her presence did to him. Without effort, she knocked him completely off balance, and all the trials of the past days left him too few resources to keep from tumbling in whatever direction she wanted.

"Zia—" he began hoarsely, trying to articulate the reasons why he shouldn't just take that tumble.

She pulled away with a silky smile and shook her head to silence him. Her spicy scent drifted past him as she rose and went to the sideboard to retrieve her flute. After a moment, she returned to settle again near the hearth. She wet her throat with a drink from her cup and lifted the instrument to her lips.

As the silver sound of the flute unfurled around the room, quietly at first, then with building power, Jhared realized he was already tumbling, into the foggy chasm of his past. The poignant melodies told him stories: not the stories of the heroes of Avelos, but long-ignored tales of his own. He did remember, at least some of it. Once, there had been evenings filled with dancers and laughter.

He had an image of his mother in the performers' circle, her long auburn hair shining as she lifted her head to sing. He shifted onto paths the music laid for him, recalling the magical feel of escape, as though, with the melody for a guide, he could leap outside himself and travel the world. As a child, while imagining those paths, he had discovered the hidden caches of Shorn energy within him and soared beyond the boundaries of everything he thought possible. He recalled the flush of excitement in that first innocent exploration, his first experience of desire, before he knew the danger.

"Careful," growled his Teachers. *"You know better now."*

The warning returned him abruptly to Isella's little room. He discovered himself rocking in time to the rhythm of the music, while Zia slid from one tune into another. How long had she been playing? His light wool tunic had become uncomfortably warm. His muscles buzzed with unnatural energy, and the blood hissed in his ears. Startled by his lapse of control, he wrestled down the effects of the unbidden release. It was a challenge, for Zia's fingers still flew, turning music into longing. The black and silver Ulaye flute flashed in the lamplight. He thought of the ballad of "Leita and the Piper." Tonight he had no trouble imagining the binding power of an ensorcelled flute. Zia glanced up at him, and her green eyes lit triumphantly as she caught his gaze. Several more moments passed before she finally brought the last melody to its close.

"You felt it," she said breathlessly. "I knew it wouldn't take long."

It wouldn't take long at all to send him over the edge in more ways than one. Still, Jhared couldn't help but answer her smile. "Those were songs my mother played. I recognize them."

"Those were songs your mother *composed*," Zia corrected with a grin. She laid her flute beside her and pulled a ribbon from a pocket.

"I never knew her work." He gazed at Zia, who was drawing her curly mane back from her face with the ribbon. She had been his mother's student, worked with her for years. How much better Zia knew Mahla than he did.

Perhaps Zia sensed something of his thoughts, for her expression turned more serious than it had been all evening. "The work Mahla accomplished was of great importance. It changed the lives of many, and still does. I'll make certain you learn of it." She lowered her hands and quirked a half-smile. "That discussion is for another night. Tonight, let me tell you stories of Mahla's music and make you glow again as you did when you listened to 'Alende's Flight'."

She reached for an apple from the bowl beside her. "Did you know that your mother once played at the palace before a feast of the high chieftain and clan prefects? That's a story from before you were born. Mahla didn't speak of it, but Isella bragged for her often enough." Zia bit into the rosy fruit, and Jhared found himself distracted by the thought of tasting tart apple and sweet wine upon her lips. He cleared his throat and tried to refocus.

"It was Alaro, then," he heard himself say.

Zia tilted her head at him.

"Before I was born. It would have been Alaro Rumar and his council for whom she played."

"Ah! Just so." She nodded brightly. "To hear Isella tell it, your mother's music narrowly prevented the prefects of the northern five from declaring war upon Clan Manitar."

Jhared laughed in amazement, then realized his response might be seen as an insult against Clan Manitar or the prefects and quickly sobered. Zia, however, grinned unabashedly.

"Even the provincial hotheads of the Sandien Mountains couldn't help but fall spellbound under the beauty of Mahla's song."

She went on to tell him the details of what appeared to be a Black Mountain legend about Mahla's evening singing for the council. Alaro Rumar had only recently established the Forest Guard as a standing army and demanded the clans surrender their own guards to the command of his generals. Few clans did so eagerly, but the northern five—Aglar, Lasla, Colar, Hilera, and Avien—openly protested it. Defying the courtesy of the feast table, the prefect of Clan Colar began to speak slyly of his vision of a new country beyond the Sandien Mountains, the true Avelos founded where Alende Isan and his companions first landed when they fled Altan Mar.

"It could have come to blows among the prefects, or much worse," Zia said. "But in the midst of the uproar, Mahla, a young bard hardly past her apprenticeship, began to sing 'Rona's Glory.'" The scribe peered at him. "Do you know it?"

"Of course," he murmured. It was a ballad one could hear at almost any tavern on any evening. When Amurian pirates sailed up the Jhanaza River and attempted to kidnap the heir to the prefect of Clan Manitar, Rona laid down his life to save the son of his rival. As a child, Jhared only cared to hear of the battle and Rona's bravery, but later he came to recognize a deeper pattern created from the complex harmonies. The song celebrated the interdependence of the clans and the abiding importance of family. And Rona had been a man of the north.

"It was Mahla's voice and her clever choice of song that cooled the tempers in that hall," Zia said.

Jhared nodded appreciatively. It *was* clever; it was more like Tierzen's subtle diplomacy than anything he knew of his mother.

"'Rona's Glory' reminded Clan Manitar of the debt they owed the north and at the same time the northerners were reminded of the loyalty of their ancestor."

"Aha. You've an elder's mind yourself." Zia grinned.

He grew wary at that comment, but she encouraged him with her smiles. Even when he looked for it, he found no contempt or fear in her. He accepted that as a gift and tried not to wonder when it would change. Tonight she was a connection to a part of his life no one else knew.

As the evening crept away, they spoke of Mahla and music and Zia's time working at the inn. Slowly, the thrill of Shorn energy dissipated from Jhared's veins and the wine blunted the pain in his shoulder. His role in the conversation gradually shrank, while Zia's voice rambled on pleasantly from farther and farther away.

At some point he couldn't recall, Zia's voice transformed into the pure sounds of the Ulaye flute once more. A soft melody cradled him this time. Memories drifted through his awareness like ragged bits of cloud: women's voices, a warm fire, a sense of belonging. His muscles began to loosen, and he realized how hard he had been struggling to stay upright under the weight of all that happened in the past two days: the hawk, Tierzen's warning, Cael's threats, the trial. Zia and her flute made struggle impossible. Instead, he sank deep into a place where he remembered the pleasure of music and the pain of losing it. In a moment of fading lucidity, he understood how vulnerable that left him. Then all thought winked out.

He awoke to silence sometime later. No soldiers snored around him. No guards stomped in from their last watch. No forest sounds put him on guard. He regretted the need to disrupt the peace, but as his mind stretched slowly out of the mist of sleep, he became aware of two things: The first was the stone of the hearth carving a hole in his back where he leaned against it. The second was the sense that someone watched him.

He opened his eyes. Ziabela sat cross-legged at his side. She had claimed his right hand in both of hers. Her star-bright gaze measured him steadily. Still muddled by sleep, he saw an uncanny resemblance between her focused stare and the expression of a fox waiting at a rabbit hole.

He blinked and the illusion shifted. Zia squeezed his hand, all warmth and softness. "What did you see?" she asked gently.

What did you see? A goblet or the faces of angry men? A woman or a predator? Jhared brushed the thoughts aside. Sleep had tangled him in the general's old lesson about veils.

"See?" he echoed, pushing himself up from the stone.

"You slept so soundly. You must have found a place of tender dreams."

"No, I…there were no dreams at all." Incredibly, it was the truth. Disappointment flickered in her eyes, and he quickly clarified, "Such solid sleep is sweet and rare. Believe me. But I'm sorry. I've been a rude guest. I should go."

He should. The anticipation of dawn already hummed in his blood. If he weren't back at the barracks by first light, there would be Cael's wrath to pay in the form of his lieutenant. And Zia's slender fingers entwined in his were beginning to stir him once more. Gently, he withdrew from her grasp and rose to his feet.

She stood with him. The disappointment hadn't disappeared from her gaze. "I'll show you out."

As she led him to the door, he started to feel uncertain again. What did she want? Had he failed to meet the expectations she held for the son of her mentor? She had reached out expecting him to know her, to know the Mountain, and to sing. Instead, she discovered he remembered nothing of the people from his past and most of his memories of music were as hazy as day-old dreams. He wasn't anything she might have imagined.

"Thank you for tonight," he said awkwardly. "You've been…kind."

"Bah." Zia made a face. "Take that back, Jhared Denaban. Those are words for a stranger. You are Mahla's son, and I am her student." She moved a step closer and gazed at him with a look as soft as a spring promise. "We will see each other again."

"I would like that, Ziabela, but I doubt it can be so. I'll soon be on my way to the border. I don't know when I'll be allowed to return to the city. I must focus now on making reparation—"

Zia closed the final distance between them and stretched up to brush her lips against his cheek. She lingered until his head filled with her scent. He forced his hands to remain at his sides and stood unmoving, afraid to test his discipline any further.

"You'll be back," she whispered, pulling away with a little smile. "Go out and fight what battles you must. You are meant to return and continue your mother's song."

7.
RIANA'S PATHS

The night smelled of stone and campfires, of cooking food and too many men living in one place. The sound of voices rose and fell in the distance. Nemiah lay sprawled on the ground, her cheek pressed against rough stone still warm from the day's sun. She had no sense of where she was or how she had gotten there.

She lifted her gaze, seeking some clue, but a wall of taut canvas blocked her view of the landscape. A pavilion, fine and large. Eagerness leaped in her breast. Something important was happening here or was going to happen. She must learn of it, despite the danger. With the core of her being, she yearned to do what was right. She paused, frowning. How could she feel eagerness or yearning when she didn't even know where she was? Understanding arrived belatedly. It wasn't *her* eagerness. This Path did not belong to her. The Gate onto Riana's infinite weaving had opened and she had fallen through it. Leita had tried to warn her.

Movement from within the pavilion caught her eye, and despite her own apprehension, Nemiah pressed her face to the gap between the pavilion's floor and the canvas to see. The inside walls were covered with ugly and ominous paintings of black and red serpents threatening cities and consuming mountains. In the middle of the chamber, two men sat at a table conversing in sober tones. One man was tall and lean, a hard-eyed warrior with a torc of golden serpents entwined about his muscled arm. The other man, broad and solid, wore the sign of the boar on his silky tunic. His cunning gaze slipped over the room. Not a soldier, that one; his crafty look reminded Nemiah of an elder. She didn't understand their language, but she knew what they represented. The serpents and the boar meant Sahiste and Laebek, two border nations in constant quarrels, yet here they sat at the same table, sharing food and conversation. Nothing good could come from this moment.

As if answering her dark thought, a creature in a corner of the pavilion shrieked, a hawk tugging against its tether. Nemiah shuddered. The messenger of Cael was a reminder of her own sacrilege. Beside the hawk stood a third man.

He moved toward the others with the grace of a shadow. In his gaunt figure, Nemiah recognized power far beyond that of warriors and statesmen. This one was a priest. His body carried the intricate spell of his foreign god tattooed down his neck and around his long arms. His eyes burned with an otherworldly fire as he chanted a prayer in a resonant voice. And around his wrists curled two scarlet and ebony vipers. Fear iced through Nemiah of the kind she had only known on Dawning's Eve, when the honed blade pressed against her throat.

The other men rose from the table and went to their knees before the grim priest, who stretched his arms out as if to embrace them. Nemiah wanted to scream a warning, but this was not her Path. The priest slapped his hands around the wrists of the warrior and the statesman, grinding the vipers against their flesh.

Angered, the creatures stirred to life and uncoiled from their host to slither around the new sources of warmth. Like living chains, they bound the three men together wrist to wrist. The Laebeki man glanced up, and in a breath, Nemiah saw regret and resolve cross his face. She didn't see the instant when the vipers' fangs pierced muscle, but the warrior threw his head back and roared with agonized laughter.

In the corner, the raptor shrieked and struggled. Power shoved at Nemiah's spirit, something foreign and dark and frightening. She grasped at the Path, trying to anchor herself. She needed to know what happened here, what it meant. The infinite Paths expanded around her. Suddenly, she stood not just in this moment, but in every moment. In that instant she saw her own death as it occurred on every Path. Then the blue flames flared across her vision and she tumbled into the Nowhere.

She fell through the black of nothingness toward the distant threads of blue and red that gleamed in patterns too complex for any mortal mind to comprehend. It was Riana's weaving, ever growing, twisting, and changing: all the Paths that might have been, all the Paths that are, and all the Paths that could still be. She tumbled through them with no control. She could lose herself here. They would find her body in the temple and never know her spirit wandered, trapped among Riana's endless ways.

Desperately, she grasped for a moment, any moment, to keep her from falling farther from her own place. The world righted itself. Her moment came clear.

This flame to light the Paths behind us.

A temple acolyte walked the outer ring of the first circle, lighting the candles for the sunset devotion. Relief flooded Nemiah at the familiar sight, one she had officiated for nearly a decade. This most powerful of the day's devotions was meant to mend the damage that the faithless and the careless had caused to Riana's order. With the high priestess's prayers, it would adjust the balance and prevent Cael from rising against the goddess during the night.

If Riana would still accept her prayers.

Nemiah sought a sense of balance within herself.

This flame to light the Paths before us.

Another candle crackled to life. Incense from the brazier on the altar wound heady smoke around her. She lifted her arms and tilted her head toward the sky. Tonight, instead of the river of Riana's power, only a cold stream trickled into her.

This flame to light the Paths beneath us.

The acolyte completed the circle, but Nemiah sensed the gap that remained. It was her responsibility to find the way to close it. The task was growing more and more difficult as Avelos neglected Riana and her order failed. This spring the warning came in the form of wild storms, drowned crops, and stillborn stock, a mirrored reminder of the time, long ago, when the warning had been drought. Then had come war, the strength of the temple collapsing and the ancient wisdom lost. Since that time, their Path had spiraled ever downward. Nemiah opened her eyes and stepped forward to speak the healing words of the devotion, knowing they wouldn't be enough.

"Hush now. It isn't your place to speak," whispered a woman's amused voice. "This isn't your devotion."

Nemiah started at the voice in her head. "Good Lady? Is it you?"

Soft laughter, low and rich. "Not by a long way, sweet. But I do the best for her that I can with the gifts I have. Who are you? Are you lost? I don't see your guide."

A shiver of dismay rippled through Nemiah. She had thought herself home, but instead she had staggered into yet another perspective. Ah, Goddess. She was indeed lost. Still, this stranger could not just speak to her as if she were a child. She drew herself straight, compensating for her diminutive stature with a confident tone.

"I am Lady Nemiah Gabriana, High Priestess of Avelos, and I go wherever Riana opens the doors."

A satisfying silence greeted her words. Nemiah took the moment to gather herself and look at the room around her. She realized the chamber was in fact not the same as the one in her high temple. While the dimensions seemed similar— the arched ceilings yawned into familiar shadows, and the circular window of Riana's eye threw its colors across the floor—the walls of this room came to life with garish paintings of the goddess consorting with shocking creatures in depictions of stories Nemiah had never heard. Wolfish Verael trailed Riana's heels near the altar. A group of Avelune smiled craftily from above the door. Was that Cael himself near the ceiling holding a prism that split the Paths? In her temple, the plaster-coated stone of the first circle stretched smooth and reassuringly white.

"I apologize," the voice returned, more subdued. "You seemed so confused that I took you for…well, no matter. I am always glad to meet a sister on the Paths, and tonight more than ever."

"You are also a servant of our Lady?"

"I am. Don't you see me here beside you?"

"I see the temple and the preparation for the devotion." *Unless the acolyte was the one speaking?*

"No, dove. That's Elina with the candles." The woman answered Nemiah's unvoiced thought. "But she's only here, like the temple and the rest, because I thought of them as I began this journey. You have paused at one of my moments and opened a door to my Path."

"Forgive me," Nemiah said. "I did not intend to intrude. That is, I fell without warning and I—"

Everything around her—the altar, the acolyte, the paintings—spun in sudden circles, like fireflies cutting loops in the dark.

"Careful! You aren't focused here." The presence in her head reached out, and the spirals mercifully slowed. "One more step and you'll be spinning away. To where did you mean to travel?"

"I don't know," Nemiah admitted. "I didn't mean to travel. It was an accident I ended here." This time she thought that she sensed a shadow of the other woman: a tall figure, sturdy, patient, dignified.

"Not true," the woman said. "The sacred journey is never accidental, although often surprising." Her shadow melded with the darkness again, but not before Nemiah sensed warmth, like a supportive arm around her. "If Riana brought you to hear my warning, it must have meaning for you. I fear these dark days will touch many parts of the weaving. I am sorry for that."

Nemiah knew she should not be here; she had said as much to Leita, and yet Riana had sent her. Order demanded there be a reason. The temple rippled like an image under water.

"Please, speak your warning. I have seen darkness coming as well."

The other priestess started suddenly. "Wait, wait! You're slipping again." The arm shifted and Nemiah felt fingers grasping for her, trying to steady her. This time the world heaved and buckled. "Don't think of your own place," the woman commanded. "Focus on me. Swiftly now. There are things you must know."

Nemiah struggled to comply, but she had nothing to anchor her: no face, no name, no moment in history. A chasm opened beneath her feet and the Path began to crumble. Instinctively, she threw her awareness into the darkness like a rope, hoping the woman might find her.

"I'm here! Tell me what you've seen!"

The priestess caught Nemiah with a current of thought so strong it held her suspended above the chasm. Nemiah gasped; she had never known a Pathwalker so powerful.

"The balance is shifting," the woman said quickly. "The faster fear spreads, the farther we will fall. We must find a way to turn this Path, or Alende Isan's people will suffer. I have seen such death—No! By Riana's way, keep your feet beneath you!"

The Path flaked away into sparkling fragments. Or perhaps Nemiah was the fragmented one. Again she found herself floating in darkness, far from the weaving. Urgently, she reached for her own moment. She belonged to only one tiny place along all the endless Paths, but the single skill drilled into her over years was the one to get her home. She flung herself toward her own place and through Riana's Gate.

For a sickening moment, she felt herself split in two as she straddled the Nowhere between her own Path and the infinite roads of the goddess. Then her awareness somersaulted gracelessly back into her body. She groaned, her muscles and her mind protesting the abrupt transition. *There's the price you pay for panicking.* Her tower bedchamber was dark, but she smelled the welcoming hint of incense that permeated the entire temple, combined with the rich scent of the spiced tea she had been drinking earlier in the evening. The wool blankets of her own bed lay tossed around her. She sighed with relief, even as she pushed the familiar sensations aside to hold onto the scent of serpents and the words of a strange priestess.

"Lady? Are you well?" Merisel stood at the doorway to the attendant's chamber, her young voice thick with sleep.

"Call the Mistress of Maps," Nemiah croaked, clinging to the images behind her eyelids. The chill of the Path-travel caught her, and she began to shiver.

"The Mistress of…? Yes, Lady!"

The girl padded hastily from the bedchamber to the stairway that spiraled down to Nemiah's receiving room and the door to the hall. The rattle of a lamp's glass chimney reminded Nemiah this was the child's first time to face a return from a sacred journey. It would be the first time for most of them. It had been too long.

"No light," she hissed between clenched teeth. "No sound. Go."

In the time it took Merisel to come hurrying back with old Bena, Nemiah rehearsed the vision, connecting the images in her head over and over like stars in the constellations. Her body shuddered with the bone-deep chill that was the cost of traveling Paths not her own. She pulled the bedcovers tighter around her and tried to picture the ethereal form of the lady, the faces of the men in the pavilion, the dark shadow-priest and his serpents. With every breath, the present threatened to break apart the fragile weaving of memory.

The ancient Mapmaker entered the tower with only the sound of her slippers shuffling slowly up the twisting stairs and her panting breaths to announce her. She needed no light to find her way. With a rustle at the bedside table and the strike of a flint, a red-gold glow lit the images behind Nemiah's closed eyes, followed by the mind-settling, memory-reviving scents of lavender and sintermint.

Nemiah trusted that Bena would begin the recording perfectly, no matter the length of time that had passed since the last journey or Bena's animosity toward her. The Mistress of Maps had devoted her life to charting the Paths since long before Nemiah's birth. Her charge was larger than any other undertaking in the temple: by illuminating the connections across the Paths—from one moment to another or one decision to the next—the servants of Riana honored the cycles of the world, influenced events where they might, and strived to maintain the goddess's order. In some ways, Bena's task was more important than that of the high priestess herself.

The old woman knew it. Nemiah kept her eyes closed and pushed away the distracting thoughts. The scent of dust and mint filled her lungs as Bena bent over her.

"I will touch you now, Lady," she said, gruff and purposeful as always.

Nemiah nodded silent permission, and dry fingers took hold of her trembling hands.

"Lady Riana of the Journey," the Mapmaker began, "the sun you gave to us, and the stars, and the flame for the darkest nights. By all these do we seek to understand your order. Now, by the light of your chosen servant, Nemiah Gabriana, illuminate for us the steps along your Paths." She released Nemiah's hands and with a grunt lowered herself into the chair near the bed, arranging the little lap desk with its ink and coarsely pressed paper. "Speak of all you sensed, Lady. We are ready."

The prayer eased Nemiah's shuddering enough that she could speak. She lay back and let the words come. She described every sensation she could recall. The cold night, the rough stone, the fear. There had been Sahisten and Laebeki men. The hawk and serpents. A sense of anticipation, of a desire to accomplish something meaningful. The woman who caught Nemiah was a priestess. But who? Nemiah recalled a sense of comfort with the woman, but why did she seem so very familiar? Nemiah stopped trying to make sense of it. That was for later. The Mapmaker would take the images and try to determine the four Principles of the journey: Place and Time would tell where and when the journey took place. They were the most basic, but not necessarily the easiest Principles to puzzle out. Perspective would say through whose eyes Nemiah watched the Paths. The unknown priestess would be key to Perspective. Then Bena would look for associations of this journey with any of the points illuminated by Pathwalkers for a hundred years before. If they were blessed tonight, she would discover a repetition—a point where Nemiah's walk intersected with the travel of another priestess. Such an intersection indicated that the Paths were related, perhaps branches off the same trunk. If they could determine the Parallel between the journey and Nemiah's own road, they might even discover a point of influence that would give Nemiah the knowledge she needed to alter the direction of this Path. Avelos needed it. She needed it.

The balance has shifted. The strange priestess could not have spoken more truly. High Chieftain Rumar and his council had usurped the rights of the goddess.

"Lady?"

Bena's prompt made her realize she had been silent for a long while. The last image from the Paths was dissolving—

"Not yet! I remember something other. The Sahisten warrior. He wore a gold band about his arm with a serpent sigil. It wasn't just a soldier's crest. The entwined serpents were thrice crowned. I remember how they reflected the light."

The crowned serpents. The man had been a Sahisten royal. Bena continued writing without looking up.

"Anything else?" the Mistress of Maps pressed.

Nemiah inhaled slowly, her eyes still closed, but the journey had turned to fog. She would retrieve nothing more. She cleared her throat and opened her eyes.

"By Riana's ways I travel and by her ways I return."

"By Riana's ways," Bena replied.

The Mapmaker completed a final note and set the paper aside. As though Merisel had been waiting for precisely that moment, she entered the room bearing a cup of steaming tea. Nemiah sat up and took the tea gratefully. She ached as if she had spent the day running with Capa. Merisel flicked a wide-eyed gaze over her before offering a wavering spiral.

"Is there something else you need, Lady?" asked the child.

To regain the power the council has stolen. To put Adan Rumar in his place. To stop the snakes of betrayal... "My dressing gown, please, Merisel. You can light the lamps now. And bring tea for the Mistress of Maps."

The girl moved quickly to obey. She had only been novice attendant a short time, but had already proved herself observant and uncomplaining. Nemiah needed to thank Kaliska for pointing out the child from among the young ones.

"No tea. No time for tea," Bena said, gathering her notes and negotiating her bent frame out from under the lap desk. "We've been five years without a walk to chart; I'm not going to let this one grow stale. Lady, you'll be awake if I have questions?"

"Of course." Nemiah set aside her own tea to slip into the warmth of the green robe Merisel held for her. Ice still swam in her blood. "The journey was a dark one. What are the implications for our own Path?"

"I can't say anything about it! Without study, there's no way to know how close this Path is to ours." The Mapmaker gave Nemiah a grim expression. "I've more than one hundred years of walks to review. It's not a job for guessing."

Nemiah understood enough about mapping to know that guessing was very close to what the job called for: educated, Riana-inspired guessing about how one part of the Path connected to another. "Take what time you need then, Bena, so long as you come to me with a first report on the Principles after dawn. I will address the Higher Circle this afternoon."

"Yes, Lady." The Mapmaker's clouded gaze reflected Nemiah's inadequacies back at her. Nemiah felt a twinge of guilt, but she didn't turn away. In nine years, she had given Bena only a handful of walks to chart. Leita was the only other priestess remaining in Avelos who possessed the ability to walk the sacred Paths, and as Cael's Bearer, she could make no journey of her own. This could very well be the last journey the old Mapmaker ever charted; Nemiah couldn't begrudge her anger. Bena didn't offer a curtsey on her way out, and Nemiah didn't demand it. They both pretended it was for the sake of the old woman's frail body.

When Bena departed, Nemiah rose for an important ritual of her own. She swayed, still lightheaded, at the edge of the bed before making her way to the tower's west-facing window. Drawing back the shutters, she leaned out over the inner gardens and breathed deeply of the cool, damp air. Here was the first boundary she needed. The orderly lines of the columns of the loggia steadied her spinning mind. Although it was too dark to see, she knew the neat rows and organized circles that the flower beds made around the dead Ulaye tree in the garden's center. Fragile new growth was already peeking out of the dirt.

She took another deep breath. The next step was a greater challenge, and she moved cautiously to the north-facing window, where she forced herself to look beyond the temple's dome into the city. Dots of light marked the complexity of the city lanes, and in the distance she could find the walls of Velantar. *Velantar. Heart's Hold. Splendor of the goddess. Home of the fifteen clans of Alende Isan. Home of Nemiah Gabriana, Chosen Lady of Avelos.*

Nemiah Gabriana. Nemiah for Riana.

No other high priestess since the Exile had taken Gabriana, the traditional name of devotion. It was viewed as a sign of self-sacrifice, but Nemiah had selfish reasons for setting aside her family name.

Chosen Lady of Avelos.

She repeated the titles in her head like a prayer as she turned away from the second window to set her hands upon each feature in her bedchamber: the small desk near the fireplace, the wardrobe, her dressing table, the tapestries on the wall and the cold stone behind them. She ran her fingers along the balustrade as she stepped down the stairs. Without thinking, she glanced toward the tower's impossibly high arched ceiling. It was a mistake. She stumbled dizzily and clutched the rail to keep from falling. The ancients who built the temple had hungered for open spaces. She needed borders. The incomprehensible vastness of the Paths left her disoriented and rootless. She needed to reclaim her own place in the world.

As she entered her receiving room, Capalino rose from his bed near the hearth, stretched his front legs in a canine bow, and padded over to greet her. The hound pushed his large brindled head against her thigh, and she reached down to scratch his ear, setting the thick tail to wagging.

"I need your skills," she murmured to the hound. "I need to find the Path. I think we're lost. I think I've gotten us all lost."

Capa froze, head up and ears cocked toward the door. A sharp knock followed two heartbeats later. Nemiah straightened with a sigh; she wasn't eager to deal with Bena again. Before Merisel could answer, the door opened and a husky voice called into the room.

"Nemiah? Are you there?"

Not Bena. It was the only person who would be passed into her chambers unchallenged by one of Rom's guardsmen. Nemiah wasn't certain whether to be relieved or dismayed.

Leita stepped into the room and closed the door. In the dim light, her white skin shone as pale as the full moon. Her black hair and midnight robes made the rest of her no more than a dark outline. She glanced around the chamber, until her gaze landed on Nemiah standing with Capa beside her.

"Why didn't you call for me?" Leita asked softly. "I warned you the Gate was seeking you."

Nemiah breathed a sigh. "I see Bena wasted no time in spreading the news. I thought she would wait until morning, at least."

"I didn't talk to Bena. I felt the Gate shift. I felt your footsteps."

Surprise froze Nemiah's expression. By the Lady, she had forgotten Leita was that sensitive. "You know I wouldn't have risked losing the first journey in five years had I a choice. It wasn't a journey of my planning."

The Bearer took that in, studying Nemiah with a probing gaze as deep blue as the predawn sky. That look could make even the most arrogant and self-possessed of the priestesses in the Higher Circle squirm like disobedient novices. "And the reason you didn't share with me your plan to call Rumar to the high temple?"

"Ah goddess, Leita. I blurted it out to Carian without consideration. I wanted to discuss it with you before sending the summons this morning. My friend, you have no cause to question my trust. You know I rely upon you and your keen perceptions."

No answer. Nemiah hated the awkwardness and the unspoken accusations. She let out a breath. "Leita, did you come to berate me or to hear what I learned tonight?"

"I came to see that you were safe."

Capa whined softly. Nemiah realized her fingers had tightened over his ear. She turned him loose. "I'm sorry. It has not been a peaceful night."

After another moment, Leita relented. "Very well. If no peace can be had, let us see if we can find you some order. Tell me what you found on the Paths."

Nemiah nodded and led the way into the receiving room. She motioned to the seats near the hearth, where Merisel had already stirred the fire. As Leita stepped into the light, Nemiah saw that the woman was fully dressed, her hair braided sleekly down her back. Rather than the thin slippers fit only for carpeted flagstone, she wore her boots.

"Merisel, bring the tea. Then take yourself to bed," said Nemiah. She chose a chair for herself and turned to her friend. Capa sniffed around Leita familiarly before settling down on the woven rug between them. "You have late business in the city tonight?"

"Just a walk. Through mundane streets," Leita added, averting her gaze to let the dog nuzzle her hand. "I needed some reprieve from the others' questions. They're all asking about you. And about what happened."

Among the young ones, rumors of every sort circulated about how Leita spent her nights: cursing her enemies so they blundered off their proper Paths; sowing discord between lovers to steal consorts for her own; even consulting with the demon-touched waylayers. Children were eager to believe such dark gossip, and the Bearer of Cael's Blade couldn't hope to escape the rumors. But tonight was different; it was about the Becoming and Nemiah's own mistakes.

"Many thanks to Carian, I am certain."

"No doubt. Are you ready to share what you saw?"

Merisel took the hot water from the fire and prepared more tea. Nemiah waited to speak until the child placed the kettle aside, gave a spiral, and stumbled to her little room.

A log popped in the fire, sending bright sparks drifting upward. Leita's eyes swallowed the light: Cael's Bearer brushed by Cael's darkness. Not even the darkness could conceal how badly Leita wanted to hear about the sacred journey. The Bearer wasn't permitted to seek the Paths on her own; she traded that access to power when she picked up Cael's Blade and tainted herself with its ancient connection to Riana's strongest foe. Nemiah often wondered how much her friend, who was so very sensitive to the Paths around her, regretted the choice.

"I know how they whisper in the Circle—Bena, Carian, Maita, and the rest— that Riana has withdrawn her favor from me. They may yet speak truly, for there was nothing of control in this trip. The Gate opened and I fell."

For the second time, Nemiah relived the journey. This time she had the distance she needed to consider the possible meanings. With Leita's wise assistance, she took apart the images and the warning of the priestess. They argued over the interpretation of the events, drawing on the holy stories and the histories to determine when and on which of Riana's threads the moment might exist. Nemiah realized how much she missed the stimulation of such discussion. *This* was what she had imagined her purpose to be when Riana called her to the temple as a girl:

struggling over interpretations of sacred journeys, illuminating Riana's ways, not struggling to keep her head above murky political waters.

"We still don't know where in the Lady's great weaving this warning comes from," Leita said after a long argument over the disturbing paintings of Riana with the Ael. "Perhaps your unknown priestess travels along a time far ahead of us, or on a Path from long ago that splits before it reaches us. Or she could travel beside us on a Parallel that never has and never will meet ours."

"I've considered the possibilities," Nemiah said, "but wherever she's from, she believed that her message had meaning for my Path. She was so careful with me that I…" Nemiah hesitated, choosing her words deliberately. "I trusted her. I felt as though she knew me."

"Ahhh. That's different, then. A link exists." Leita stroked Capalino's sleeping form with her sharp fingernails. "Perhaps she does know you. Why not? Riana's chains can bind us to kin and consorts across many Paths. Perhaps some blood tie exists between you. Your family has given servants to Riana in the past. Who's to say what happens to those kin along other branches? Or in the future?"

"True enough." Nemiah didn't care to consider her family's history; there was more shame than pride in it. She took another swallow of tea and set down the cup. "What matters now is the relevance of this journey for Avelos. I need your thought as a guide, Leita. Do you believe the warning was meant for us?"

Leita's expression turned thoughtful. "You've offered little evidence that either your lady or the Sahistens exist on our Parallel in a Time that is meaningful to us."

"And yet," Nemiah prompted.

"Yet the interpretation of the patterns in Riana's tapestry is complex. It's not merely a recounting of observable events. Too many patterns exist that we cannot understand. I trust what you sensed, Nemiah. Yes. On whatever Path it started, I believe we must heed this warning."

A large, fleshy spider chose that moment to lower itself from the ceiling to dangle beside the Bearer. It wasn't venomous Aranael, but Nemiah still shifted uncomfortably in her chair when Leita lifted her hand, palm upward, to let the creature skitter over her fingers.

Nemiah stared at the weaver. "The truth is that those moments in Sahiste frightened me. More than I can say. The Sahisten priest was working with something dark. I believe we must shift this Path to keep the snakes out of Avelos, but is it possible? We've surrendered that ability. *I've* surrendered it."

Nearly a hundred and fifty years had passed since the Sahisten army marched into Avelos, but that warrior nation never stopped testing the strength of the southeastern border. No woman who served Riana ever forgot the terror of the Exile War. If the border nations united, on this Parallel or any other, it would free Sahiste to turn even more of its ample military resources toward Avelos.

"Stop." The spider climbed over Leita's fingers and dropped to the leg of her chair. "We've yielded our knowledge and strength since the day Lord Tumal executed Lady Amalia and placed his council-chosen priestesses in her place. Don't take that burden as your own, Nemiah. Only take responsibility for the righting of it."

"The righting of it? When we're so far under the boot of the council it's impossible to see which direction is the safe one?"

In the play of the fire's shadows, Leita's expression flickered. Slowly, the spider started to spin out its thread. "Perhaps the time has come to remember that it takes both the light and the darkness to make a day."

Nemiah's gaze snapped up. "Only when Riana puts them in their proper order!"

"Order without the possibility of change makes us rigid and vulnerable," Leita replied. "Rumar and the council do what they will with us because we are predictable. They know our strategies and believe that they will never face punishment for shunning the goddess. You must teach them otherwise."

"Be careful, Leita. I know what you're suggesting. Betrayal is a step on the road to chaos. Don't forget who you are. Cael's Bearer is meant to warn us of the consequences of disorder, not champion them."

From outside the window, a bird sang a tune of first light. In the outer hall, voices and the sound of booted feet signaled the changing of the Arionade watch. Capalino grumbled in his sleep.

"I know who I am," Leita said. "And I know that right now we need the strength of the unpredictable."

"Well, I told Carian I would summon the high chieftain. That was unpredicted, even by me. I'll send out the letter after the morning devotion."

"Good. It's time. Stir the conflict in the council and use their discord to our advantage."

Nemiah pushed a hand over the wrinkles in her robe. "It's time and past time. The only way to shift this Path is to take back some of what we've lost." She cast a glance toward the sky in silent invocation. "I do know it. That Path has been waiting for me. I must warn Rumar of the danger I saw."

"What you must remind him is that the High Priestess of Avelos was long the guide of the high chieftain. He thinks he and his elders can see the Paths clearly. We must teach him that he is blind without us."

"And if he refuses my summons?"

"He won't. He's too clever and too curious. By coming to the temple, he loses nothing. The people will only see that he's made a gesture of reverence to Riana, and he gains the opportunity to learn what we're up to. For us, there is no other choice: if you are to regain our rightful place, you cannot do it by climbing the steps as a supplicant at Elders' Hall."

A thrill of hope and trepidation made Nemiah's heart race. Ahead she saw a thread-thin chance for change. She resolved to compel the high chieftain to come to her and take note of the temple as he had not since he assumed his father's place. *Riana guide my steps.*

A grin spread slowly over Leita's face as she watched Nemiah. "There now. You've found your determination. I think Rumar will find his visit not as—"

Harsh voices in the corridor cut her off. Capalino surged to his feet and trotted across the room into the antechamber, growling at the outer door.

"In the Lady's name...?" Leita stood and shared a wondering glance with Nemiah before heading for the door as well. Firelight sparkled off the hilt of the Blade as she moved. Someone in the corridor cursed. A quick, hard knock shook the door.

"Lady Nemiah?" a woman called out. "Lady, please open the door. It's Kaliska."

Lady Kaliska. Had she come as healer and Mistress of Guardians or as keeper of the Shadow Guards? Leita looked over her shoulder at Nemiah.

"Open it," Nemiah said tightly.

With the hunting hound beside her, Leita lifted the door latch and stood back.

The door swung open to reveal Kaliska standing with one hand in the air, frozen in the act of knocking. In her other hand, she gripped the black satchel that held the tools of a healer. Her robes were in disarray and her long silver hair fell around her shoulders in a loose tangle. She didn't notice the open door at first, for her attention was on the Arionad beside her. Captain Rom seemed to have his hands full with something or someone Nemiah couldn't yet see. His ferocious black-eyed scowl would make a storm think twice before striking.

"Kaliska! Captain!"

The healer turned, looking simultaneously mortified and relieved to see Nemiah before her. She lowered her hand and made a passing sweep at her hair before offering her spiral.

"Forgive me, Lady. I heard that you were ill and I—"

A choking sound that Nemiah knew for stifled laughter came from Leita, who had peered past Kaliska toward the Arionad.

"Captain Rom, I do believe that that's a palace courier dangling from your fists. I think protocol requires him to stand on his own two feet before the high priestess."

Rom stepped into the doorway, looking not a bit amused. He made no move to release the disgruntled youth in his grip. The boy wriggled and straightened as best he could, but he still looked like a puppy caught by the scruff of its neck. His grey and green tunic had pulled free of his belt, and his courier's bag had slid around his waist. Nemiah winced. Let none say Riana lacked a sense of irony.

"Release him, Captain," she demanded, pitching her voice to the authoritative timbre she usually saved for ritual. "Then tell me why I've been disturbed."

"I am to blame, Lady," Kaliska offered quickly. "I was outside the sanctuary when I heard that you had journeyed and might need the healer's attention. The courier arrived as I headed inside, and in my rush, I did not naysay him. I knew your Arionad would assist him." The healer cast an approving glance at Rom. If she had reasons for her visit other than those she voiced, Nemiah couldn't see it in her clear grey eyes.

"My lady, the boy was disinclined to wait for an audience," Rom responded, with an eye on his captive. "He and I were just discussing the meaning of patience."

The courier tugged his clothing back into order, squared his shoulders, and lifted his gaze to Nemiah. His blue eyes flashed with indignation and something close to contempt.

"I've a message from High Chieftain Rumar that can't wait for the sunrise. When the Lady Healer brought me in, I thought I'd be allowed to carry out my duty, not treated like a ruffian."

Rom laid a heavy hand on the youth's shoulder. "Respect before the Chosen Lady of Avelos," he growled.

Nemiah made a sharp gesture and her Arionad backed off, but she felt the sting of the boy's disregard. He was so young and already denying the goddess. "Well, you have my attention now, courier. Deliver your message."

The boy opened his mouth and drew a breath, as though preparing to ward off a tirade. When Nemiah simply waited, hands folded at her waist, he grew flustered.

"Yes, yes. The message. From the High Chieftain of Avelos himself!" The boy untangled the bag from around his hips and drew forth the letter with some grace. Nemiah wondered for a moment if it was his physical appeal that had won such an ill-mannered youth a position as courier and which minister or secretary had fallen prey to it.

As she took the letter, the blood pounded in her ears. The eyes of the others burned into her. To gain time to collect herself, she made a show of examining the seal: the oak and sickle moon of Clan Manitar with the Avelonian mountain peak above. It was Rumar. She hadn't doubted it. She cracked the seal and read the message:

Greetings to Nemiah Gabriana, Chosen Lady of Avelos:

While the season of renewal is upon us, not all have taken the opportunity to rebuild their relations with Riana. The strife among us does no service to the people of Avelos or the servants of the goddess. I invite you to attend me at the palace to speak of these matters. I trust that you are as eager to address them as I; thus, I will look to see you after the morning devotion before the sun touches the top of the eastern wall.

Adan Rumar, Ward of the Council of Clans, High Chieftain of Avelos

Everyone in the room remained silent. The sounds of a city morning drifted through the open window: the voices of vendors in the plaza, the creak of cartwheels as goods rolled toward market, the squeal of a child. Somewhere beyond the plaza, a dog barked. Nemiah's hopes folded in on themselves like wet silk.

"What is it?" Leita asked, peering over her shoulder.

Nemiah handed over the note.

Kaliska darted a glance from Nemiah to Leita. Rom glared with black concern. The courier looked smug.

"Lady?" asked the healer.

At a nod from Nemiah, Leita held up the letter and read it aloud. She trailed off at the end with a soft whistle. "What timing. If I didn't know better, I would say the man has a Pathwalker at his side, after all."

"No. He doesn't need one. Not for this." Belatedly, Nemiah saw the truth of it. "He knows the council went too far for us to tolerate this time. He has anticipated a response and wants to mollify us. So he's called me to him. On his terms. You did name him clever."

"Clever enough to be dangerous," Leita observed. "It worries me that he's trying so hard to speak our language."

Kaliska frowned at the letter with Leita, visibly displeased that she was missing information.

"He chose the palace instead of Elders' Hall. That's no accident; he wants you out of range of the eyes and ears of the council. But why?"

Only Rom's gaze remained focused on Nemiah. "What will you do, my lady?"

Nemiah glanced at the summons. *Riana's Paths twist for a purpose.* She never doubted it, but she had never expected to find herself here, leading a temple that had yielded its history and its influence to a council blind to the goddess's ways. She had never expected she would be the one who surrendered what little power remained, putting Avelos itself in danger of foundering. Now Adan Rumar had disarmed her scheme with its thin advantages of surprise and territory before she even had the chance to try it. She found herself wondering what the priestess on her sacred journey might do in the same situation. It saddened her that she knew so little about the woman: not where she came from, not what she looked like, not even her name. The priestess had radiated wisdom and strength in a way that reminded Nemiah of what she wished to offer her own people. She let that realization build her resolve. The time for compromise and avoidance had ended. She took a breath and drew herself straight.

"Adan Rumar is lost without a guide to the goddess's Paths, so I will go to him. None of us can afford to walk in ignorance any longer."

8.
ACCUSATIONS

Calling for the litter to bear her just across the plaza seemed ostentatious and a waste of time, but the clans still attended to such symbols, so Nemiah ordered Rom to send for the extra Arionade to prepare a formal procession. She had been neglectful of impressions for long enough. If she must answer a summons, let them at least see the trappings of the Lady's authority, however faded they were.

The morning devotion passed in a blur. As she prepared the altar, Nemiah blinked at the white walls of the first circle. They seemed sadly empty now compared to the bright story-filled walls she had seen on her journey. Whatever tales might have been painted here before the Avelune leaders plotted against Tumal and the High Priestess Amalia conspired with Sahiste were long forgotten. After the Exile War, Tumal had purged Avelos of everything written, sculpted, carved, and painted that carried the seeds of chaos or celebrated the evils of the Avelune. The purge rooted deep into the temple's archives, cutting away dangerous pieces of knowledge and destroying seditious works of art. As the daughter of a healer, however, Nemiah knew that in cutting out an infection, some healthy flesh must be sacrificed. No one could say how much the temple had lost.

She chided herself for thinking about such cursed Paths when she should be focused on greeting Riana with a clear heart. Murmuring the prayer of welcome, she closed her eyes and lifted her arms, uncertain if the goddess would answer. Only emptiness followed her call. She waited, trying not to succumb to fear. The world slowed and the darkness reached hungrily toward the sacred center within her. She repeated the prayer, willing back the darkness with everything in her. Her arms began to tremble as the cold crept forward and moments ticked by. Then, without warning, power rushed into her, filling her body with heat and the unbearably pure light of the goddess. Nemiah gasped and clung to the altar for support, startling the acolyte beside her.

Thank you, Lady. Thank you! I swear to keep my feet on your road this time, no matter the obstacles before me.

By the time she finished the devotion and prepared herself to leave, Rom's men were assembled and waiting in the outer courtyard. The day promised to be a bright one. A crisp breeze swept down from the Parnas to flutter the curtains of the litter and tug at the guards' white cloaks. One of the younger men smiled as he made his spiral and offered his arm to assist her.

"A clear day she's given for the job ahead, Lady," he said, addressing her with a westerner's bluff charm.

The wake of Riana's fierce greeting still made kaleidoscopes of Nemiah's sight, but at least her hand did not tremble as she rested it on his arm and stepped into the litter.

"A good day to start out in a new direction," she agreed, appreciating his optimism.

A shadow cloaked the sunlight. Nemiah looked up to find Rom looming behind the guard.

"The lady hasn't time for your chatter, Anilo," the captain growled. "Take your position."

"Yes, sir." The young man bowed to Nemiah and snapped to his orders. Rom bent to peer into the litter. The scattered silver in his dark beard caught the light as he ducked his head to Nemiah.

"A clear day is all the better to see the twists ahead of you," he grumbled. "Be careful, my lady. The man is a fox. It isn't sentiment that leads him to offer conciliation now."

"I didn't think he invited me to share tea, Rom."

The wiry Arionad frowned down at her. Nemiah thought of how many times over the years she had seen that same black-eyed scowl and couldn't help smiling a little. There had been a time when it daunted her, when she was a novice and Rom was an irascible Arionad not yet sworn to her. But she had come to understand his manner as the product of a singularly focused nature. In these days, when few families remembered the honor of having a youngest son serve the temple, he was loyal to Riana and her servants above all else; a true descendent of Lord Arion, whom the goddess chose among all mortal men to defend her from Cael. Nemiah took comfort in his solid, surly presence.

"There's bound to be talk at the palace about why my Arionad put Rumar's courier into a wall."

"He must learn to show reverence to Riana."

She nodded. Rom wasn't referring to the courier, she knew. "It is time. But no man likes to hear that he's traveling in the wrong direction, least of all the high chieftain. Say a prayer for me."

"Daily, my lady." He offered a neat spiral and withdrew from the litter. His voice rumbled across the courtyard as he ordered his men to their places.

The litter swayed along the stone streets, and Nemiah sat forward to observe the people moving about their morning business. Those who bothered to glance in her direction revealed more bland curiosity than respect. Some sketched Riana's spiral in the air perfunctorily. A small group of barefooted Arionites with their ragged cloaks and unkempt bodies dared to prostrate themselves on the road, very nearly under the boots of her guards. Nemiah leaned back to avoid their stink and their unbalanced, arrogant faces. They bore their bloodied feet and torn garb as accusations against Riana, profaning her for what they called the goddess's betrayal and enslavement of the armies of her Chosen, those who served her in the Great Wars. Lord Arion they adored for his eternal loyalty.

Rom halted the procession at the top of the portico bounding the palace. Nemiah stepped from the litter as Rumar's steward, Laval Astreno, a thin, pasty-faced man of advancing years, hastened toward them. He greeted her with a boneless bow and an obsequious "Bless my ways," murmured toward her feet. Wisps of faded brown hair floated over his forehead as he rose.

"Welcome to the palace of the people of Avelos, Lady Nemiah. May it please you. You are expected." He flicked a nervous glance at Rom standing close behind her. He hesitated, as though he would rather not have to deal with the Arionad, before he said, "May it please you, Lady, you may both follow me."

In the entrance hall, sun poured through the high windows, glaring off white granite walls and gilded sculptures. Nemiah blinked in the raw brightness. The morning activities of servants, palace guards, and Manitar clansmen caused a din that bounced across the stone. From somewhere down a hallway, a small dog yapped. Nemiah found it all too akin to chaos. Although the palace and the temple had been built of the same mountain stone, here she sensed none of the ancients' mysterious presence. Everything in the hall glittered and sparkled in an effortful display of grandeur. Nemiah found herself looking for the graceful carvings that marked the temple walls or the unreachable inner balconies that remained in the temple gardens, but the palace had been thoroughly altered since the Exile War. The touch of the ancients who built it had been stripped away or covered over.

As Nemiah continued down the hall past the grand state rooms, she prepared herself for a spectacle. Adan Rumar would no doubt flaunt all the trappings of his power. He would set the stage with a meeting in Petitioner's Hall or in the smaller audience chamber, forcing her into the position of supplicant. Nemiah imagined him in his robes of state with the seal of Avelos around his neck, the staff of warding in his hand, and the banners of the Council of Clans behind him. He would use his authority and blunt manner to intimidate her into accepting false promises of cooperation. She was prepared for that. But Astreno didn't stop at any of the imposing halls; instead, he led her and Rom up the sweeping staircase to the second floor. Nemiah followed the steward into a wing of the palace she had never seen.

"I am here to meet with the high chieftain," she said to the man's shoulder, wondering if there had been some mistake, after all.

He cleared his throat and kept walking. "Yes, Lady. May it please you, yes. I know just why you are here."

The hall narrowed and grew quiet as they left the public rooms for the living quarters. A serving girl in Manitar silver and green stepped aside with eyes downcast as they passed. Here the walls exchanged gaudy sculptures for simpler portraits of the great chieftains carved directly into the granite: Toma the Fierce, Matio the Giving, Mical Rumar. The last two hundred years of Avelonian leadership was a pedigree of the most influential families of Clan Manitar. The imposing family tree emphasized a striking absence in the palace: Rumar had no living heir. If he did not produce a son, Clan Manitar could finally lose its long hold on the council. Many among the other clans would not grieve when it did.

The steward stopped outside a finely worked door of dark wood, beside a larger-than-life carving of Tumal the Just. The palace guards on either side of the entrance came immediately to attention, their gazes fixed upon Rom and herself. Nemiah masked her apprehension. Now she knew exactly where she was.

The guard to the right of the door, a hard-eyed man with humorless features, gazed down at her. "Your weapons, Lady, and those of your man."

Nemiah sensed Rom stiffen behind her. "I bear no blade, sentry," she said mildly, hoping Rom took her cue and restrained his temper. He would be the one against the wall this time if he did not.

After an instant's tense pause, Rom surrendered his sword and dagger, and after another moment, the thin blade sheathed on the inside of his forearm. Nemiah said nothing. The grim attentions of the guards reminded her that the memory of betrayal was still fresh to some. High Priestess Amalia had caused the deaths of the men at this post, and very nearly the death of the high chieftain they protected. The dark-bearded guard to the left shifted as Nemiah passed, causing his sword to ring against the wall and drawing Rom a step closer to her.

Not for the first time, she cursed Amalia, whose perfidy brought the goddess to her knees before the council. Nemiah didn't give the guards a second glance as Laval Astreno announced her with one more "may it please you" and she entered the high chieftain's apartments.

Silence greeted her. Along one wall, heavy burgundy curtains shut out most of the early morning light, leaving the high ceiling in shadows. Only a single stripe of sunlight slipped between the curtains, cutting across a massive table in the center of the room and the thick rug beneath it. The fire in the fireplace had gone to ash.

Adan Rumar did not look up. He worked at a lacewood desk grand enough to accommodate his broad frame. Beside him on the desk stood one accent of striking grace: a translucent alabaster statuette suggestive of the shape of a slender woman. Apparently oblivious to all around him, Rumar gripped a pen in one strong hand, dipping it in ink and setting it to paper again.

Nemiah stared at the high chieftain, willing him to raise his gaze to see her neutral expression before her uncertainty won through again; but his weathered features were set with concentration. Even behind a desk, he looked more a fighting man than a statesman. His copper-colored hair was too long to be fashionable. His hands showed the calluses of weapons practice, and his nails were broken to the quick. Even the expression on his face as he worked looked like a challenge to an opponent.

The Firebrand, his ministers and prefects called him. When his father died a tired old man, Rumar seized the reins on the Council of Clans and pulled out the whip, demanding more taxes from the guilds, more compliance from the factions, and more contact with the outsiders. The clans, which had gone their own ways for years with few demands and fewer consequences for rejection of those demands, resisted the new controls. Old rivalries flared anew, but Rumar charged on, regardless of the conflict. He was quick and impatient and had no tolerance for those who did not keep up with him. That dangerous combination caused the worst kind of disorder.

Looking around, Nemiah saw that disorder still ruled the man, even in his own chambers. Books and scrolls overfilled the table in the center of the room and were stacked in scattered towers on the floor. A pair of boots peeked out from beneath the desk. A crumpled blanket cloaked the arm of a chair. Two dirty teacups leaned bottom-side-up against the hearth and a half-empty wine glass shaped a purple ring on the desk. Didn't Rumar realize how much of himself he revealed here? Or was he so confident in his authority he didn't care?

As though hearing her thoughts, the high chieftain set down his reed at last and looked up with a deliberate smile.

"Lady Nemiah," he said, studying her frankly. One hand brushed across the statuette of the woman before he stood and moved around the desk. "I'm glad you've come."

Instead of a spiral to Riana, he gave her a brief nod and motioned her toward a cluster of chairs beneath a window. She stood before him just long enough to make his omission noticeable, then selected a chair. Rom took his place behind her as she sat.

"Riana guided your invitation, Lord Rumar, for I have news of import to Avelos."

A copper eyebrow dashed upward at that, but Rumar only turned to order his attendant, a slender grey-haired man, from the room. He didn't sit; he paced across the carpets and back. "I've not seen such a Becoming in all my years on the council, Lady."

Nemiah choked on a startled breath. No, the man didn't waste time with pleasantries or pretenses. "May you never again."

"Indeed. That's why I've asked you here this morning."

Nemiah folded her hands in her lap in a gesture she hoped appeared confident. "And it is the reason I have come. This is the path I wished we might walk."

"Tell me, when does Riana allow a blessed sacrifice to be devoured by beasts?"

"Never, Lord Rumar. It is a sacrilege."

He stopped his pacing, turned around slowly, and pinned her with a warrior's gaze. "Then what did they offer you to make it happen?"

"What did they…?"

"Even you would not do such a thing unless there were an advantage for the temple in it. What did Abrigado and the Legacy promise you if you failed the boy? A larger portion of this fall's levies? Favors from Clan Amerre's smithies' guild? A reprieve from the loyalty tax?"

"You think I would *sell* Riana's favor?" She hadn't sold it, after all; she had surrendered it at knifepoint. "Here is the root of a problem that will bring all of Avelos to ruin: the council forgets that the Lady's power cannot be traded like this year's wool!"

Rumar grasped the seal around his neck. "Perhaps Riana's influence cannot, but the influence of her servants can be. We both know very well it can be. You were seen speaking to Elder Abrigado after the Becoming."

Nemiah reeled with the implications of those words. She had been too slow to realize that submitting to an elder's threat in the Becoming might mean crossing the high chieftain. How had she arrived on such dangerous ground so quickly? He hadn't yet used the word *conspiracy*, but it was out there—in his choice of meeting rooms, in his quick accusations. Rumar was the twice-great grandson of Tumal the Just, and the High Priestess Amalia had died, pushed from the wall, by Tumal's own hand. Nemiah scrambled to shift the focus.

"The strife among us does no service to the people of Avelos or the servants of the goddess. You wrote truly. There are to be consequences for the neglect of Riana's order."

Rumar narrowed his eyes. "What do you mean by that?"

We must find a way to turn this Path, or Alende's people will suffer. The words echoed in her head, and the world rippled around her like a reflection in a lake. She gripped the arms of her chair and took a breath.

"For too long we have neglected Riana's order, and our Path teeters toward destruction. Destruction that will come in the form of Sahiste."

"Ah. The Sahistens to punish us again, is it?" Rumar smiled thinly as he lowered himself into a chair across from her. "What beautiful symmetry."

Nemiah blinked and sat back. "Adan Rumar, you disregard the Lady's warning at your peril."

"Yes, yes, I'm certain. Your delivery is very dramatic, Lady. So they came to you about Javahari's message as well as the Becoming, hmm? Was it the Minister of the Treasury? Abrigado's bold enough to dare it himself. Or perhaps he sent one of his hounds: Elder Rud? Or was it Prefect Makri?"

"The council has nothing to do with this warning. It comes from Riana herself. The temple has had no promises from any elder but promises of abuse. If they—" Nemiah stammered to a halt. "Wait. A message? Are you saying Sahiste sent word to Avelos? Recently?"

The high chieftain didn't answer, but watched Nemiah with a keen eye.

"What do they want?" she demanded. "Are there threats? Did they speak of Laebek?"

Rumar stood and strode to his desk. Without having to search for it, he plucked a rolled parchment from the unsteady pile on the desktop, then crossed the room to hold it out to her. Nemiah reached up to take the parcel. For the first time, she noticed the blue-tinged shadows circling the man's eyes and the barely perceptible tremor in his fingers: signs of too little sleep and too much boldblood tea.

"Read it," he commanded.

The message was scrolled in the old fashion. She unrolled it to reveal a flowing script. It was written in Velos, but penned in something close to the ancients' style. Still, the message was clear enough to make her heart hammer against her chest.

"King Javahari wants a meeting."

The high chieftain studied her surprise. His frown darkened his grey eyes to the color of thunder. "You didn't know."

"I did not! I have come for what Riana has told me. No one else."

"Very well." He seated himself once more and folded his arms across his chest. "If that is so, then I'd best hear what you have been told."

He didn't believe her: she saw it in his wary posture, but he had enough doubt to listen. It was a start. Carefully and deliberately she explained the sacred source of her knowledge; then she painted a picture of what she had seen: the Sahisten priest, the Laebek ambassador, and the snakes. Avelos was on a path toward devastation, and that path started in the south.

"This letter is only an opening gambit," she finished. "Sahiste is moving toward something new."

Rumar's expression had turned speculative. "You say the warning comes from Riana. How often has she given you such gifts?"

"They are rare," she admitted, then added, "rare and precious as the gems in your staff of warding, Lord Rumar."

"But I don't toss the gems like a waylayer's dice to make important decisions for the country. How often have you read the gift correctly, Lady?"

"No one can describe a journey as correct or incorrect!" she said, the blood heating her face. "It's not like checking a tax collector's records. The sacred Path is not so simple. The journey was as clear as it could be, and my interpretation is borne out by your news. We should refuse Javahari."

"Mmm. That's just what the Minister of the Treasury said."

Nemiah tripped over that; Rumar was still trying to catch her in a lie. She gripped her hands together in her lap, felt the bones and tendons shifting in them. When had her hands become so thin and pale? She had been tough and strong as a girl, from working with the hounds on her family's small farm, helping her mother to prepare the wool for weaving, riding out with her father to attend ill or injured neighbors. Her hands had been callused and sun-darkened then. When had they lost their strength?

"I am certain, Lord Rumar, that the Minister of the Treasury and most of the rest of the council has said as much. Sahisten raiders have wet our borders with blood for a century and more. Surely, the council will vote to refuse them."

Rumar waved a hand dismissively. "We've only just received the news. I haven't yet called for a vote. There are other things to consider: The Sahisten border has been quiet for a season. Quieter than I've known it or my father knew it in all his years. They want us in a receptive mood. They need something from us."

"Vengeance. I've seen it."

"Would that our relationship were as *simple* as that, Lady."

Nemiah glanced up. The Firebrand possessed more subtlety than some credited him.

Rumar must have seen the puzzlement in her expression, for he gave her a rueful smile. "We need the Sahistens, too."

He moved to the piles on the table and again reached unerringly for the work he wanted. Nemiah began to see that order did exist here, but it was a far more complex arrangement than she had first realized.

The high chieftain opened the parchment in front of her. It was a map of Avelos and the border countries.

"Look at this." He jabbed a finger at the Sandien Mountains in the north. "Silver here. Had we the men to keep the mines running to their potential. And this," he pointed to the city walls, "a city with a swift flowing river and the advantage of the mountains, though we've lost the skills to repair the aqueducts. Here: vineyards. Though the clans hardly keep their own roads clear enough to move the wine."

"I am quite sure I know the treasures Riana has given to Avelos."

"Treasures, indeed." He ran an impatient hand through his red hair, standing it on end. "The treasures of our land lie poorly tended, while our soldiers struggle to keep the raiders from stealing them away, and we drain our resources girding ourselves against threats from the border nations. Isolation only worked for us while we had the strength to enforce it. Right now, the countries around us are licking their greedy chops. Of course King Javahari is considering expanding his holdings. No doubt the Amurian dukes and Prince Roelof in Laebek are doing the same. If we don't give them a reason to want us intact, they will tear us apart and share the spoils among them."

"Then approach Amuria if you must bring in the outsiders," Nemiah insisted. "Avelonian blood runs in the royal line from Lady Elia's day."

"We have," Rumar said shortly. "Duke Branald has put off our offers of trade with hollow excuses. It's no longer a matter of choice, Lady. Sahiste has given us an opening that we might use to negotiate trade in the south. We must take it. We can no longer afford to fight."

"You think that in this time of weakness we should invite our enemies to our gates?" Nemiah shook her head. "Sahiste came to us when we were weakened once before, and it was almost the death of Avelos."

Rumar grunted and paced away. "Yes. We're weak. It takes strong alliances to make strong borders."

"No, Lord Rumar. On Riana's spiraling Paths, the past is our warning for the future. Hear me: you will regret it if you allow Sahiste to step onto our land."

It only took a heartbeat for the high chieftain's expression to transform into something dangerous, and Nemiah knew too late that she had gone too far. He crossed the floor with the swiftness of a hunter, his broad form blotting out the rest of the room as he stood over her.

"Do not echo threats at me," he growled. "I don't yet know for certain whose strategy you're playing out, but I don't have time to waste with it. You have no vote on the council and the temple long ago lost its hold on the clans, so I have no *need* to waste my time with it. If you value your place, Lady Nemiah, heed your own words: let the past be your warning for the future."

Nemiah sank backwards in her chair and craned her head up to meet Rumar's uncompromising gaze, realizing just how thoroughly she was cornered. The Legacy, which clung more fervently than any traditionalists to the mandates of Tumal the Just, was growing in popularity among the guilds for its criticism of Rumar's trade policies and his siphoning of power from the clans, as well as for its support of new sanctions for the Shorn. Now, with Rumar's suspicion of collusion upon her, she had none of the Legacy's power but all of the high chieftain's ire.

She had done nothing of use for Riana today.

Mustering her determination, she rose to her feet, bringing her within inches of Rumar as he towered over her. His body was warm and smelled of bitter boldblood. She quashed the queasy sense of vulnerability her small stature always invoked when she stood beside the powerful.

"The only strategy I serve is Riana's, Lord Rumar, and I am a poor servant at that. But what I offer is a vision of your Paths that none other in Avelos can provide. You can choose to use what Riana offers or…" She'd been about to utter one last warning, and thought better of it. Her words trailed into ominous silence.

Rumar took two surprised steps backwards, opening a proper distance between them. For an instant, Nemiah saw something unguarded in him, an awkwardness that reminded her the man had lived without a wife or a consort for nearly ten years. She recalled the rumors that his had been a love match. Aviya Rumar had died of fever at the end of Rumar's first year of rule, Nemiah's first days as Chosen. Had it been a true partnership in which he could share his fears and doubts? Did he ever weary now of fighting battles where subterfuge won all and trust was a liability? Before Nemiah could decide how to respond, the instant passed and his gaze filled with suspicion once more.

"If I have a need for someone to read the signs for me with the voice of the Legacy alarmists, I shall summon Toren Abrigado," he said.

The meeting had come to its end.

Nemiah could not escape the palace soon enough. The fabric of her robes fluttered behind her as she followed Astreno back through the halls, down the grand staircase, and out. Rom made no comment as they traveled back to the temple, but when they reached the courtyard, he dismissed his men and saw her back to the sanctuary alone.

The first circle was blessedly empty. She sank to the ground before the altar and closed her eyes, seeking to order her thoughts. Methodically, she reviewed her conversation with Rumar. Rom remained quiet beside her.

"I should have expected that," she said after a long silence. "I made the mistake of assuming the Legacy was focused on the Becoming for what it would do to us, but they were aiming for Rumar."

Her Arionad was pale and drawn with anger. "They have entrapped you. The high chieftain will be watching you now."

"Yes. The Legacy appears to have used us as their diversion. It worked well enough or Rumar would not have bothered sending for me."

She discovered herself beyond anger, perhaps even beyond fear. Rumar thought the temple and the Legacy were aligned. She had begun to see a way she might use that.

"He thought he might frighten you into revealing their plans."

"Well, then, if I've done anything today, it was only to confuse him more. He's certain I'm with Abrigado, but he can't understand why."

"Then he's a fool for letting them mislead him. All he need do is listen to the Legacy fearmongers on the streets to know they have no respect for the Lady. The worst among them dare to call the temple traitorous and Riana's servants as deceitful as the Shorn."

Nemiah shook her head. "Rumar plays a layered game; he knows the street screamers are no more than Abrigado's tools. He won't use them to read the minister."

"Tools or not, they are heretics as sure as any Arionite," Rom growled.

"That's because they don't understand that Riana is incapable of betrayal," she said. For the first time in a long while, Nemiah thought she knew what her next move should be. She lifted her head to meet the gaze of the man who had sworn his life to hers. "They don't understand that the goddess is unending loyalty."

Riana's gift rose in her, fierce and unexpected. Her Arionad caught his breath, and she felt his Paths shifting under the influence of her last words: *unending loyalty*. Rom started to go to his knees as his Paths converged, combining his every experience and notion of loyalty, magnifying the emotion until it was hardly bearable. She put out a hand quickly to keep him upright.

"No, Captain. Your loyalty is as enduring as that of Lord Arion himself. Now is not the time for renewing your oath." She averted her eyes to quell the gift and free him. Released, Rom leaned against the wall, breathing quickly, his eyes shining with devotion.

Inwardly, Nemiah reveled in the thrill of Riana's strength. The goddess had come unbidden to acknowledge her. It was a validation.

She came to her feet and returned her now-quiescent gaze to her Arionad. "Rumar is clever, but he's still terribly unbalanced. He sees only one Path for Avelos. The most dangerous one. He'll force us in that direction if we don't find a way to turn him."

Firebrand, his detractors called him.

"We need the Sahistens," he had said.

Nemiah shivered.

"Lady?"

"I must confront what Riana has set before me if there's to be any hope of finding a way beyond it, Rom. It's time to open a conversation with the leader of Tumal's Legacy." She shivered again as she sensed new Paths rising around her and old ones falling away. Her choice was already rippling through the weaving.

With thanks to the goddess, Nemiah spiraled her fingers toward the altar before turning for the inner compound. She needed to find Leita. The changes to come would not be easy ones. The Bearer would understand the difficult things that needed to be said and done to move forward on this new road.

9.
CROSSING BOUNDARIES

The fortress at Ravia couldn't claim to be the largest or the oldest of the seven keeps that secured the borders, but set as it was in the southeastern corner of Avelos, within a morning's ride of both Sahiste and Laebek, it received respect. Soldiers at Ravia stood between the people and the worst of their enemies. Jhared allowed himself a spark of pride that General Nadel thought him worthy of a post here.

The sun crept over the horizon as Jhared headed for the stables. By midafternoon, the heat would sear his skin and make it uncomfortable to breathe, but this early the air still blew cool and fresh across the loggia that connected the barracks to the stable yards. Men moved purposefully toward their morning duties. Two priestesses from the valley chapterhouse, an old woman and her young acolyte, carried candles toward the infirmary. The clang of steel and the exhortations of commanders tumbled over the wall from the practice grounds on the north side of the keep. Jhared's patrol wasn't a part of the company of drilling soldiers this morning. Commander Carn had given the order to form at the south gate. They were to ride for the Barren.

Jhared pulled out the glossy figure of obsidian from the pouch at his belt. The finely carved face with its ancient, secretive grin winked at him in the pale light. He tossed it skyward, then snatched it out of the air again and returned it to the pouch, smiling. He had found the figure at the edge of a river near the Laebeki border and given it to Branlen, when the boy was too young even to shape his letters. Over the years, the stone's exchange had become a part of their farewell. Branlen always passed it to him before he left the city, and Jhared gave it back upon his return home. It was child's play, he knew; no magic existed in the ritual other than Branlen's good wishes, but so long as he had the talisman, he always came back safely.

From the loggia, he crossed the inner yard to the paddock where the horses milled, waiting for their morning grain. His bay border horse, Brio, stood apart from the others at the far end of the enclosure, peering curiously toward the activity in the dusty yard. At Jhared's whistle, the gelding's black-tipped ears flicked forward, and he tossed his head in recognition before ambling toward the gate.

Jhared slipped a lead around the animal's neck. "Are you ready for Sahiste?"

The horse's whicker was noncommittal. Jhared pulled an early apple from his pocket and took a large bite of the sour fruit before offering up the rest. Brio crunched contentedly as Jhared led him into the stable to be cleaned and saddled. Stable boys strode back and forth, distributing the morning feed, mucking out stalls, and tacking up mounts for training. One of them nodded to Jhared as he collected his own brushes and tack. Lieutenant Sevar demanded that his company attend to their own horses. "The more time you spend caring for and schooling a creature, the more devoted it will be and the more willing to give you everything when it matters most."

Today Jhared might very well have cause to test that belief; they were riding into the most dangerous corner of Avelos. Would he find the chance for final reparation on this trail? The possibility made him grin once more. He finished preparing the bay, double-checked the security of his bow and quiver behind the saddle, and headed for the south gate.

Micah appeared at the edge of the loggia as the sun topped the eastern wall. Golden ribbons of light silhouetted the older Shorn man's lean figure as he paced toward the practice grounds, a slender dagger twirling between his fingers. With all his warrior grace and tightly bridled energy, Micah might have been Lord Arion marching out to battle Cael. The soldier was a member of Jhared's company in Commander Churion's patrol. A model of Shorn soldiery, he threw himself tirelessly into drills and weapons practice and was notorious for taking on the riskiest situations with a smile. Jhared offered a friendly salute as the man passed. Micah glared in response.

"You think a brilliant soldier like that ought to acknowledge a pathetic creature such as you? When you can't even accomplish the task Elder Trianor needs of you?"

Jhared strode away from the older soldier and tried to ignore his Teacher's jab. Since arriving in Ravia, he had struggled to gain the trust of any of the Shorn soldiers within the garrison, but the other Shorn shunned him as thoroughly as Micah did. So far, Jhared was forced to fill his letters to Tierzen with distant observations. Although the Shorn men were scattered throughout the patrols, in their off-duty moments some drifted together in small coalitions. In the yard or the mess hall, one could sense the invisible barriers that separated those coalitions from the other soldiers. Recent events had reinforced the barriers and heightened tensions: a Shorn soldier had been executed, not by the garrison captain but by a mob in the town. Jhared had only been able to gather the gossip from his own patrol to report to Elder Trianor. None of the Shorn would speak to him of it. The Minister of the Teaching needed him to learn more about the Shorn soldiers, but the Shorn soldiers wouldn't trust him because he was the son of the Minister of the Teaching. Jhared found himself well and truly alone.

Despite the warming air, a chill feathered down his back. Drawing close to men who despised him required perilous deception. "Small deceits build the foundation for a tower of lies," Anarava wrote. That path was a hazardous one. Jhared took some comfort in knowing that the Minister of Teaching understood better than anyone what was safe for a Shorn man. Tierzen would never endanger him, not in that way.

"Nice'a you to join us," a voice grumbled.

Grion, thick-limbed and coarse, stared down at Jhared from astride his sorrel mare. Most of Jhared's ten-man patrol were already waiting at the gate, sitting with Forest Guard ease in their saddles or standing beside their mounts. They were a varied lot, the rough men of the clans. They traced their ancestors back centuries to the families who had survived the migration from Altan Mar and established the fifteen first-clans in Avelos. Jhared was the youngest, the only city-bred, and the only Shorn man among them.

"Lenaro's with the commander," Grion announced to the others. "Where's Jase?"

Esran, a burly blond soldier from Clan Ontera, gave Jhared a civil nod before answering. "He staggered back uphill with boys from Rafel's patrol at some unholy hour this morning. All'a them were missing a feather in their fletching, that drunk they were."

"Somebody gonna check on him?" slight and flighty Twitch asked, flipping his reins between his fingers.

"Can't be!" Grion barked. "After what happened in town, even Jase isn't fool enough to drink with those villains."

"Cael's balls in a bag!" Esran snapped. "Those hot-blooded Legacy boys were looking t'prove themselves against the Forest Guard. When they set on Rafel, they earned what they got."

"That wasn't what the barkeep saw," Bevan interjected, quick to side with Grion. "He said Rafel and the others taunted the town boys into taking on something too big for them."

Grion nodded. "It was Eris who started it. No man with an ounce'a pride could sit still while a blood-back like Eris called him out."

"Whoa, now." Esran was glowering. "Don't speak against our dead. Eris was a soldier. One'a us."

"Eris was one'a the cursed," Grion replied.

"And now we got one'a our own." Bevan turned a cold, grim glance toward Jhared. Jhared held his ground beneath the man's icy appraisal.

The others went quiet. Anzo, a grizzled little veteran from Clan Everen, heaved a sigh. Jhared had learned little more of the incident than Tierzen had told him. One of the town youths had died in the tavern brawl, and Clan Amerre had demanded retribution. Rafel and three of his patrolmates had been sentenced to a flogging by the garrison captain. But Eris, the Shorn soldier in the patrol, had been summarily executed by a mob of townfolk: pushed from the wall as an oath breaker.

"Well, whatever he got up to, Jase seems to have survived last night just fine," Anzo observed. "There's our boy now, and looking far too pleased with himself." The old patrolman nodded toward Jase, who rode toward them, grinning madly. It lightened the precarious mood.

"Tell us her name," Esran said, looking relieved by the excuse to shift the subject.

Jase halted in a patch of sunlight beside the wall. "Fortune," the wiry soldier laughed, rubbing one finger along the tattoo that spiraled down the right side of his cheek. "Fortune and her sister Fate." He swung out of the saddle of his blue roan colt and bent to check a hoof. Something flickered on the wall above him. "Boys, never dice with a blessed man'a Clan Nadaren unless ya have the silver t'lose!"

"Or you fancy working your way out'a debt," Twitch said with enough ruefulness to suggest personal experience in the matter.

Living as they did within the shadows of Avarel Forest, the families of Clan Nadaren had more need than any for blessings. Someone—Jase's mother or perhaps a lover—had spent a small fortune to buy the soldier an intricate blessing after the Nadaren fashion. The blue tattoo started at his chin and twisted in a complex series of spirals and loops along his jaw to his temple. Jhared didn't know if the tattoo actually helped the man win at dice, but the exotic look certainly seemed to help him win the Ravia women.

Jase straightened and rested an arm across his horse's withers. "I told ya, anytime ya want another try at recovering your losses, Twitch, let me know."

Twitch switched hands to flick the reins back and forth over his other leg. His horse danced, as restless as its rider. "And get my Mardia slashed at me again? No, thanks. Losing a week's wages to you isn't half as bad as facing her for it afterward."

The men laughed, and Twitch received a good share of taunting about his wife's talent with a whip. From there, the conversation turned toward the topic of other women and other types of talent. Jhared adjusted Brio's girth strap. He almost missed the slender grey and black flicker on the wall. Esran laughed at something Anzo said. The deadly flicker came again. Jhared straightened.

"Snake, Jase! Above you. It's going to—"

The viper dropped off the wall, missed the soldier, and landed on his roan's broad back. With a frightened squeal, the young horse threw itself skyward, smashing Jase in the face with the ridge of its muscular withers.

The Nadaren man went down. The serpent slid from the rearing beast to the ground beside him.

Panic rippled through the other mounts. Grion and Esran backed their horses away from the fray. Twitch threw himself out of the saddle, tossed his reins to Bevan, and tried to close on the roan. The colt was untamable. It whipped up and down, instinctively trying to crush the snake. Jase lay stunned, his head too close to the sharp hooves pounding the dirt. On his other side, the viper lifted its head to strike.

Under Jhared's hand, Brio shuddered but stood in place. Jhared grabbed his bow and an arrow from its quiver. As he nocked the shaft to the string, he heard Anzo cursing with a feverish intensity. Then the rest of the world faded out of focus.

An Artas breeze breathed gently from the west. The horse's legs pounded in and out of his line of flight. On the ground, a deadly length of black and grey no thicker than two fingers arched toward Jase's face. It would take very little energy from the bow to reach the target and very little error to put the shaft through Jase's head. Jhared slowed his breathing, waited. The string released with a low thrum.

He sensed it as the fletching caught the air, steadying the shaft against an upward current. As though it were an extension of his own arm, he knew just where the arrowhead would pierce the serpent. The flight's perfection carved a pleasurable ache in his middle.

The serpent died pinned to the ground, the shaft centered through its narrow head. Jase rolled away from the pounding hooves and climbed to his feet as Twitch made a grab for the terrified colt. Even after they caught the beast, it took some effort to calm him. For several moments, no one spoke.

Grion bent down to pluck up the arrow with the serpent still impaled upon it. "A Sahisten black-dart. Aggressive sons of demons. You couldn't find a darker omen for a ride to Sahiste unless Cael delivered it himself."

"Naw." With a grunt, Anzo hoisted himself into the saddle of his stolid gelding. "It woulda been a dark omen if Denaban missed."

Twitch laughed tightly. "He couldn't help but hit. Shorn boys have hawk's eyes, don't they?"

Grion flung the body off the arrow. He scowled when he returned the shaft to Jhared, as though he hadn't made up his mind whether a Shorn man in the patrol was just as poor an omen as the serpent.

Jhared thanked him.

Grion spat. "Ravens are good at killing snakes, too."

"Riders, formation!" Commander Carn bellowed across the courtyard. Every man in the patrol snapped to attention as the commander trotted his horse up to the gate tower. Lenaro, a Clan Ontera man who seemed to be in line for his own command, rode close behind, mirroring Carn's glower. Jhared drew himself straight, the arrow still clenched in his hand, as Carn reviewed the patrol. The commander's gaze rested on him for a long, uncomfortable moment. Years of patrolling the Sahisten and Labeki borders had beaten the man's face into dark leather, lending his blue eyes a feral brightness. The garrison knew him as the most dogged tracker of the Forest Guard Fourth, a patrolman who never lost the raiders he trailed and took no excuses from his men if they did. Behind his back, the men called him after one of Cael's Chosen, the *Verael*, not just for his uncanny tracking skills and his half-wild gaze, but also for his unpredictable temper. Stories existed about how Carn had punished men in the past, men who were no longer at Ravia or any Forest Guard garrison. Jhared couldn't afford to err.

Slowly, the commander's attention moved from Jhared to the dead viper, and his lip twisted into a wolfish grin beneath his white moustache.

"Good. It's good you're in the mood for hunting serpents. We've got work to do. Let's get to it."

"Riders up!"

Jhared mounted with the others and filed out of the gate onto the dusty road. His horse's hooves drummed against the dirt. From the crown of a brush-covered hill, the fortress road wound down into the little valley and the Clan Amerre town of Ravia. The Everen-bred border horses picked their ways down the slope almost as agilely as the goats that wandered the rocky meadows around them. The Amerre hills had turned gold and dry with the midsummer sun, but in the fold of the valley, the Jewel River painted a narrow stripe of green as it watered the orchards and bean fields that fed the town and the garrison. At the bank of the river, children checked river-crab traps and san-dy-haired girls drew water.

The Shorn women laboring in the fields didn't look up as the soldiers passed, but their headman turned his horse to watch. From the town wall behind the laborers, the rising-sun banner of Clan Amerre flashed its proud orange and red. The Amerre clansmen and their kin in Clan Makri were the descendants of the survivors of the Exile War. Their twice-great grandparents saw the worst of the horrors of the Sahisten invasion. They had more reason than any to hate Sahiste, and more reason than any to want strong borders, but their relationship with the Forest Guard was precarious. Clan Amerre also had more reason than any to despise the Shorn, and the south-erners balked at seeing Shorn men armed for battle. During Jhared's short time in Ravia, he had realized it was no accident that the south was the birth-place of Tumal's Legacy.

Commander Carn pushed them along at a fast trot, eating up the miles be-fore the heat forced them to slow. The first part of the ride was easy: scrubby hills unrolled beneath them as they passed through the quiet hamlets of Clan Amerre, which spread out from the seat at Ravia like acorns scattered around a tree. Bees hummed about the purple blossoms of the sandbrush, and sunlight warmed Jhared's back. When he turned his eyes to the north, he could see the rust-colored peaks of the Sangren Mountains; the vineyards of Clan Makri were only a stretch of foothills away.

The patrol headed east along the river and trundled over the narrow bridge toward Sahiste. A half-day's ride would get them to Maren's Burn and the Burn Tower, the more eastern of the two towers to which the Ravia garrison was prepared to respond. From there, they would see the northeastern corner of Laebek and the southwestern corner of Sahiste. Jhared didn't yet know what tasks would be required of him, but he felt content knowing he was exactly where he ought to be, doing the things for which he had been trained, things for which he even seemed to have some skill.

Anzo started a song as they left the valley behind. The old patrolman could never be silent for long. He rumbled out marching tunes with the raw enthusiasm of a much younger man. His gravelly voice wouldn't win him prizes at the Day of Dawnings festivals, but it suited the bawdy lyrics he favored. Twitch joined on the second verse, then Esran, with a surprisingly fine tenor, and then the rest of the patrol.

Jhared remained quiet. In his head, he heard an entirely different melody: one of Ziabela Marcalo's. He couldn't stop thinking of the bright-eyed scribe and her songs. These days he discovered himself singing lays he hadn't recalled in years, the words coming back to him whole verses at a time. Grion caught him at it once and mocked him for a songbird. He took more taunting when he received Zia's letter, and his patrolmates learned he could read. "Proper little scholar," Bevan spat. "Should'a been a clerk. Pampered elder's boy will get someone killed, you'll see." Tierzen had taught Jhared to read the histories to make certain he understood the depth of the Avelune's betrayals, but an honest soldier need only ever read the forest or the look in his opponent's eyes. Jhared endured the taunts silently, and would have willingly endured worse, for Zia had sent the lyrics of several verses he'd never heard from the "Lament for Altan Mar" in the Alende Cycle. She ended her letter with a wish for his health and safety and a hope that he would come to hear her play when he returned to the city. It took effort to stop imagining her warm figure nestled close beside him.

The terrain became more difficult as they drew nearer to the border. The tributaries that nourished Ravia Valley died under the attack of the summer sun, and a tenacious breeze stripped the hills down to the rocky bone. Brio picked his way over stones and crumbling trails, sometimes half-sliding down a steep incline on his haunches. Jhared shifted his weight in the saddle to help the sure-footed gelding keep his balance. Scrubby pine bushes and clumps of thorny fireweed caught at his legs and tore at the horse's coat as the patrol made its way along sandy washes and narrow ravines.

By midday, the edge of Maren's Burn loomed on a ridge to the east. The commander stopped the patrol within sight of the dead forest to water the horses. Jhared dismounted with the others and led Brio to the trickle that remained of the creek. He kept an eye on the ridge, even as he bent to dribble water over his face and pull food from his saddle pack. A wise man didn't turn his back on the Burn, where Sahisten soldiers sometimes hid among the trees, hoping for an opportunity to pick off a Forest Guard or two.

"Gives me chills riding through there," Esran said, nodding toward the fire-blackened trees. "Too much like tramping through someone's pyre. I'd just as soon they found another place for a watch tower."

"Smells like death," Twitch agreed.

Anzo gave them a wry smile. "King Javahari wishes we'd found another place for a tower, too. On someone else's border."

"Ah, blow yourself, Nevia," Esran replied without malice. "I've seen ya whisper prayers in the heart'a the Burn at sundown."

Anzo still smiled, but he spoke in measured tones as he wiped his damp hands over his head. "True enough. A man doesn't get to be grey as I am without learning to tiptoe 'round the spirits of the Exile, eh? I'm not for the flames just yet, boys."

Jhared restrained a grimace, but not at the thought of spirits. Anarava's *Loyalty and Will* detailed the Battle of Maren's Burn during the Exile War. At Lord Tumal's order, General Maren rounded up the Avelune in the south to drive them out of the country. His troops pushed several hundred exiles to the Sahisten border—where they ran straight into the raging Sahistens, who declared their ambassador to be an innocent framed by the Avelune leaders. Caught between two armies, the traitors were torn apart. Those who managed to free themselves sufficiently to take to the sky died in flames, shot down by Maren's bowmen with flaming arrows. Their burning bodies ignited the trees as they collapsed to earth, and their evil tainted the forest. A necessary burning, yet Jhared couldn't help but imagine the screams, the sight of flailing limbs and wings limned in flames. No living thing had grown in the forest since. The tree trunks and branches remained black and bare.

Anzo no longer sang as they continued their ride. Commander Carn still had not given them their orders. Most nights, the patrol hunted smugglers and scouted the border closer to Laebek with the rest of the Fourth. The brazen Laebeki raiders crossed the river for the barest scent of profit, and in summertime when the waterline dropped and the crossing was easy, they could run the Ravia patrols ragged.

"Does the Burn tower suspect raiders settling in near the border? Someone they need us to flush out?" asked Twitch.

"Doubtful," griped Grion. "We haven't seen a single stone-licker across the border since midwinter. I say if they don't come looking for us, we don't go looking for them."

"Pardon us, old man," Anzo laughed. "We keeping you from your bed?" Anzo had at least ten winters on Grion and had served the guard for twice the years Jhared had been alive.

Grion scoffed. "I say we're busy enough, is all. You think we should waste our time chasing shadows while Laebeki highwaymen chase our folk?"

Esran coughed pointedly. "I say we let Laebek and Sahiste chase each other."

"You boys got it wrong," Jase announced. "All wrong. What we're looking for is sorcery."

Jase could have been a player on the stages in the city. His theatrical announcement stopped the other speculation. He waited a moment longer, until the entire patrol was listening.

"Ya can hear it on the wind. Sahiste has something dark in the planning. They've only left us alone all these months t'fool us into feeling safe."

A couple of soldiers laughed. Bevan sniggered about a Clan Nadaren man's need to find magic in every fart in the dark.

Anzo sucked his lip in disapproval, a habit he had when he was missing his pipe. "The only wind you've heard *that* story on is the hot air coming from the barkeep at the Snip and Whistle. If you believe every rumor'a doom you hear from Clan Amerre, Jase, you're going to want a few more blessings for that pretty face'a yours."

Jase's lips curled into his most charming smile. "Ya wait and see then. Wait and see. Or better, put some money on it, if ya dare."

Anzo grinned and waved him off.

The men's banter possessed a rhythm that Jhared was starting to understand: Grion's complaints, Anzo's easy jests, even Jase's superstitions all had a place. He had ridden with them on enough patrols in the past three months to know that the pre-mission talk was as predictable as a temple ritual, and that when the ritual was over, these unpolished clansmen were well-trained soldiers. He wasn't yet certain of his own role here. So far, they showed him the bare edge of tolerance with the expected pranks—all but Anzo, who once or twice tossed him a nod and a grin after drills in the practice yard. But Jhared didn't need their acceptance to work his hardest.

They trotted on another mile before Commander Carn led them off the road and up toward the dark ridge. As though a signal had been given, the men fell silent. Jhared touched his heels to his mount. In front of him, Anzo's horse scrambled upward, kicking back dust and gravel.

Within the leafless woods, the afternoon sun shot an unforgiving glare over horses and men. The heat hung thick and unmoving around the tree trunks like a memory of flames. Beasts and soldiers were sweat-soaked by the time the tower came into view, rising up from the skeletal trees with its white rock gleaming against the sky.

A pair of watchmen met the patrol at the base of the tower and helped to put up the horses. Someone offered Jhared a flask of water as he dismounted; he took it gratefully. When the mounts were cooled and the tower guards had given their report, Commander Carn ordered the patrol into formation in the stable yard. He strode back and forth before them. Sunlight shone from his white hair and ignited the blue fire in his eyes.

"Sahiste's gone to ground," he growled. "You all know it. Since winter we've had not a village raid. Not a sign of smugglers. Not even a taunt from their patrols across the border. General Nadel wants to know why. What's keeping the stone-lickers so busy they've lost interest in harassing us? Our job is to scout out Demonrock." The commander stopped pacing and faced them, his lips carving a fierce smile in his lined face. "I need two."

Without hesitation, Jhared stepped forward. Four others stepped out with him: Esran, Jase, Grion, and Bevan.

Carn's grin broadened; it wasn't a pretty thing. He took his time looking over the five of them; the others had scouted the Sahisten border for years, but Jhared knew he possessed the skill for it. He held his commander's gaze, willing the man to see his determination.

"Denaban and Relki," the commander finally snapped. "You'll cross the Barren tonight. Hariar and Nevia, you're with them to the edge of the Burn. Lenaro's up to the tower with me. The rest of you'll keep watch in the wood in case we have visitors."

"Sorcery," Bevan snorted. "If it was sorcery we're after, they wouldn't send the Shorn boy in to look for it now, would they?"

Jhared let it go. This was his first order to cross the Sahisten border. Carn was still speaking, giving them details that would help them cross the Barren without inviting the attention of the Sahisten guard. Jhared did his best to focus. He was going to put himself under the nose of the enemy garrison tonight. He could barely restrain his anticipation.

They had a few hours to prepare before making their way to the edge of the Burn on foot. In the tower, a map of Demonrock and the Barren offered up secrets other scouts had discovered over the years. Jhared took a careful look at it, although he already knew the surrounding landscape as well as any man might who hadn't yet traveled it. Beyond the Sahisten fortress to the north, rocky foothills poked their way upward until they grew into the Vinden Mountains. Farther east and somewhat south, lay Manildam, the Sahisten city closest to the border.

Manildam was significant for the river that ran beside it, creating a fertile plain that fed much of southern Sahiste. Jhared's task did not require traveling so far into the country. Not this time.

As the hour drew near to leave, he shared a final apple with Brio. The horse took the offering and slobbered on Jhared's shoulder in thanks. Jhared patted him farewell. Then he turned to check his gear one more time. He regretted that he must leave his bow behind, although it would likely be of little use if it came to a fight. Of course, if it came to a fight, he probably wouldn't be coming home.

Anzo led them north as twilight wrapped itself around the trees. With the sun's departure, the heat hissed slowly out of the forest on a welcome wind. The old patrolman moved easily, belying his age with the grace of long experience in the wilds. Jhared followed, concentrating on slowing his breathing and the too-rapid beat of his heart. The dirt on the path deadened the sound of his steps. It was fine and powdery. Like ashes.

Wisps of cloud veiled the stars as Riana closed her eyes on the world. The moon wouldn't show itself until near dawn. Nighttime could cause a person to stumble off his proper road into Cael's waiting arms. For a scout, though, the darkness was a shield. It could even be salvation. Jhared had never before taken the time to wonder what it meant that he walked so comfortably in Cael's realm.

"Best just not t'think on it."

"What?" Jhared turned to peer at Jase, who was little more than the gleam of eyes in a darkened face. The others were shadowy forms around him as they approached the cliff that marked the border.

"Getting caught in Sahiste," Jase said. "Don't make the mistake of dwelling on it. Ya won't see anything worth a ram's ass that way."

"Easy advice for you to give, Relki," Grion smirked. "You know that if they catch the pair of you, they'll be too busy with Denaban to bother with your sorry self." Grion cast an evil look in Jhared's direction. "You know what parts they slice off a Shorn soldier for their trophies?"

Anzo cleared his throat. "Everyone's coming back in one piece tonight. I want a chance to win a few rounds off these boys." He lifted the coil of rope from his pack and tossed it to Grion, who scrambled in the darkness to catch it. "Make your hands as busy as your mouth, Hariar."

The four of them halted at the cliff edge. Jhared looked down and gritted his teeth. He could avoid the Sahisten guard and manage Grion's rancor, but the drop-off before him was a different story. He knew that it stretched little more than fifty feet above the Barren. In the dark, however, it could just as well have been five hundred feet; he could feel the emptiness stretching seductively before him. It made his limbs tremble and his stomach turn.

"I'll go first," he said, forcing himself closer to the edge. The sooner he stood on level ground, the less chance he would have to fall.

Grion anchored the rope around a tree, kept one end, and tossed the other over the cliff. It plunked quietly as it uncoiled against the rock face. Jhared picked up the rope where it disappeared over the edge, reminding himself that he only had to hold on to keep from crashing to the stone below. The breeze blowing across the Barren sucked the moisture from his throat. He looked up to the tower, where the commander's light shone yellow: the border was clear. His fingers tightened as he prepared to back himself off the edge.

"Eyes, tongue, and balls," Grion hissed near his ear.

Jhared only had time to flip his palm toward the man, fingers curled clawlike in a rude gesture. Then he was hanging in midair, his body responding to the sensation of emptiness all around him. He clutched the rope with both hands and concentrated on denying the urges that shouted for him to release his grip.

"Reason controls the base instincts that lead to self-destruction. Hang on."

He listened to his Teachers' reminders as he worked himself down the cliff face, rappelling with a handful of thumps against the rock. When his boots touched dirt again, he wiped his sweaty palms against his shirt thankfully, then tugged on the rope for Jase.

Jase slid down and landed in a crouch beside Jhared. "It's a beautiful night for uncovering secrets," he said as he straightened. "So, Denaban, are ya as good a scout as ya're a bowman?"

Jhared shrugged and smiled a little. "Almost."

Jase laughed. "Almost, my left nut. General Nadel would have sent ya to Lieutenant Dalvino for an archer if he didn't think ya more useful to the Verael's hunters. How about a wager on tonight's work? The winner is the one who gets the better story."

"Bet against a blessed Nadaren? I don't have the silver to lose."

"Never mind what I said before. Think on it: a cursed city man against a blessed clansman. There's a balance to it. It'll bring us the Lady's favor tonight."

A warning sensation spidered down Jhared's back. In the past three months, while he struggled to get close enough to watch the Shorn soldiers in Ravia, he had tried to determine who had their eyes on him. Within his patrol, Bevan and Afiro, who flaunted their Legacy sympathies, seemed inclined to avoid him, or like Grion, to openly taunt him. Westerners like Jase were typically too devoted to Riana to support the Legacy. Still, Jase never passed up a chance to test him with such games as this one. Jhared stared at the other soldier now, trying to read his intent. Jase only grinned benignly.

"For the sake of balance, then," Jhared said, his own smile growing broader. Let them test him. Let the patrol see just how hard he was willing to work toward reparation. "Let's go."

Jase stepped away from the cliff and turned to look up at the Burn tower, now just a hopeful spot of light to the south.

"We're still clear. We'll strike out east across the rocks t'come at the keep from above. We're far enough north that, if we're lucky, we should miss the border patrol. If we're not lucky…" He chuckled and lifted a hand to touch his tattooed cheek. "If we're not, then Alia deserves her silver back from the priestess who gave me this."

So far they had been lucky: clouds still masked the stars, turning the Barren into a field of irregular grey shapes that would give them some camouflage. From the border to the enemy fortress, the Sahisten Barren stretched in broken slabs of rock, small boulders, and tumbled columns: like the ruin of some ancient city. It was just as dead as the charred forest behind them, as though years of hatred between the two countries had made the land incapable of nurturing life.

What damage did it cause to the people of Clan Amerre, who lived so close to such a poisonous place, a place where, just beyond a strip of dead earth, others wished them only harm? What did people do with so much fear and hatred?

Jase took the lead, and Jhared curbed his wondering to turn all his senses to the night. He followed closely, creating a smaller profile for any watchman who might glance their way. Stony hillocks, narrow gullies, and cracks between boulders attempted to trip him in the dark, but he knew how to move with the land. It wasn't so different from padding through forest groundcover, although he preferred the shelter of the trees. The plain of broken stone left him painfully exposed.

They angled toward a massive butte that rose on the other side of the Barren. Demonrock lay on the western side of the butte. From the maps, Jhared guessed the distance to be nearly five miles, although the number of miles offered no good measure of the time it would take them to cross the tricky flatland.

Without warning, Jase pulled up short, his arms flailing. Jhared flung an arm around the man's chest and threw his weight backwards. Pebbles skidded out from under their boots into the black hole at their feet as they scrambled for balance. Jhared had recovered his footing before the tiny *plink-plink-plink* of stones hitting water echoed back to them from a frightening distance below ground.

Jase wiped his brow and straightened, laughing tightly. "That was close, eh? I fall into an ancient Sahisten latrine, the boys back home would never let me live it down."

"I wouldn't want to be the one to explain it." Jhared stepped around the well. Even in the dark, he could see that the hole had been shaped by men. At one time, the Barren had supported life. The thought hardly registered before a new alarm sent a bolt of heat through his veins.

Silently, he dropped into a crouch, dragging Jase down beside him. In response to the other soldier's questioning expression, he walked his fingers in the air to indicate a patrol on the march. Then they waited, straining to hear whether the Sahistens would come tearing after them. The last of the day's heat radiated up from the ground, sending rivulets of sweat down Jhared's tensed shoulders. His scars itched. Cautiously, he rocked forward to peer around the stone. The three-man Sahisten patrol moved north. Big men, they each measured nearly as tall as a Shorn soldier, and each carried a spear taller than himself. They marched steadily and didn't appear to be in any hurry.

"Don't they make a merry group," Jase whispered.

Jhared listened as the slippery tones of the guards' conversation slid over the stone. They could be excited, or maybe angry. Jhared couldn't label the emotions in the voices with any more certainty than he could label the emotions in the hiss of flowing water. Sahine was an uncomfortable language, with pronunciations that writhed oddly over the tongue. The handful of words Jhared had learned at the garrison to describe a man's mother or the circumstances of his birth didn't help with interpretations now.

Luck stayed with them, however; the men strode off without pausing. Jhared released a silent breath.

Jase glanced over with a fey grin. "What good'a story would it be without the danger?"

Jhared rolled his eyes. At times, Jase seemed no older than Branlen. He didn't say anything, only waited until the Sahisten band disappeared into the night, then followed the other man onward.

The butte loomed larger as they crept across the Barren, an ominous blackness against the clouded sky. Twice more they observed patrols sweeping the rocky plain. As he came out of hiding a third time, Jhared exchanged a look with Jase. North? Why were so many men patrolling the north, the gateway to Sahiste's interior? The Sangren Mountains kept Avelonian armies out of northern Sahiste as effectively as they kept Sahiste out of Avelos. Jase shook his head. It was another question in need of an answer. Whatever the reason, watching Sahisten soldiers march *behind* him made the muscles of Jhared's back twitch. He didn't like to think about what it would mean when he and Jase tried to slip back out.

Then they came around the butte, and his focus shifted, as he saw the face of the fortress for the first time.

The brutal, ugly keep so fascinated and repelled him that he stopped dead to take it in. He understood now how it had earned the name the garrison gave it: Demonrock. The fortress lurched up out of the stone like some malformed beast. Turrets jutted hornlike at unexpected angles. Lights in the slit windows made yellow eyes, and the uneven wall formed rows of jagged teeth. Where the cliff face curved outward, the gates were carved like a bulging belly. The whole thing looked primitive and cruel.

He must have revealed some sign of his disgust. Jase laughed dryly.

"She's a beauty, isn't she?"

"A nightmare."

Jase sucked air between his teeth. "What in the mother's name are they up't over there?"

On the far side of the keep and close to the cliff, two large pavilions had been erected. No rough soldiers' tents, together they could fill nearly a quarter of the inner yard at Ravia. Painted or woven into the fabric, a pair of undulating serpents wound around one another and around the tents' walls. Two sentries stood near the serpents' heads, which pointed to the entrances of each tent.

Who was it that shunned the rough quarters of the fortress and earned extra guard?

"I'll take the pavilions," Jhared volunteered quickly.

"Ya ready for that?" Jase gave him a doubtful look. "Commander will take it out'a our hides if we don't bring back something useful."

"Commander chose me for this trip. He thinks I'm ready."

"All right, all right. If you're that sure of it, then the fortress is mine." Jase grinned. "We're each on our own from here. Check the signal before ya head back; the commander will warn if he sees the border's under watch. But don't linger and get caught on the Barren after dawn."

In answer, Jhared gave Jase the Forest Guard salute. Jase touched two fingers to his cheek in a jaunty mock salute.

"See ya back at home. I got a wager t'win."

As Jase snuck away, Jhared hunted out a niche from which he could observe the pavilions more closely. It took careful work. The tents sat against the south side of the cliff and the keep, while he was on the north side. To reach his goal, he had to cross before the main gates on the western face, where the watch was more attentive. Sahiste's focus was always on the west, always toward the destruction of Avelos.

He melted from one shadow to another, his body buzzing with the thrill of traveling undetected within his enemy's grasp. Early in his training he had discovered that the ability to move invisibly came readily to him, but then it was really no surprise; invisibility meant safety. He had spent much of his life striving to go unnoticed.

When he found a place from which he could observe both pavilions, he tucked himself into a stony crevice beneath the keep and settled in. The tents were aligned end to end, such that their long sides stood about ten feet from the cliff wall and their entrances faced away from one another. All the activity seemed to be taking place in the tent that opened nearer to the keep. Men came and went along a stony path that led from a narrow stairway high in the fortress wall. Some fellows looked to be servants and carried great platters back and forth. Other men moved like soldiers. Everyone paused at the tent's entrance and murmured something to the sentries before being permitted inside. Jhared shifted his position against the rocks and considered: the password implied they feared threats from among their own people, but who required that kind of protection? An ambassador with enemies in the Sahisten court? Some statesman reviewing troops for the king? Why didn't they take the shelter the fortress offered? And why were they here now?

The night crept along and Jhared found himself no closer to answering those questions. Hunger made his stomach rumble. He rolled his shoulders to loosen his cramped muscles. As a spasm clenched its way down his back to the parts of him that no longer existed, he swallowed a curse and resisted the urge to stretch one hand over his shoulder. Some nights, the pain could nearly convince him that if he reached out, he would still find what had been torn away.

"False perceptions are the sign of a weak will," a Teacher reminded him.

"Hush. Please. Dangerous now."

For a blessed change, neither Teacher offered a retort. Jhared refocused on the pavilions. By the small hours of the morning, he had watched a score of men arrive and nearly as many depart. Half of them disappeared into the second pavilion; the other half returned to Demonrock. He had stored away as many details about them as he could ferret out, but he still had more questions than answers. If only he understood Sahine. He wondered if anyone in Ravia could teach him. His Teachers grumbled at him, this time for his wandering thoughts. He thanked them for their guidance. He didn't need their prodding to know that the general would require more information to put the pieces of this puzzle together.

What he needed was to win a view of the inside of the tents. That meant he would have to move closer. And to do so, he must put himself in the open, just steps away from the guards of Demonrock. Cautiously, he rose from the stone and crept forward. He was still exposed when the slap of leather on stone warned that someone was descending the stairway behind him. He went still in the shadow of the cliff as a hooded figure in dark robes caused the two sentries to come to attention. The robed figure gave no password, but a guard bent hastily to pull aside the tent flap. Light spilled onto the stone and over the sentries, painting their bodies with a crimson glow. Jhared forgot about the newcomer and dared to peer closer. He looked from one sentry—dark-haired, stern-faced, tall—to the other—blond, milk-faced, broad. On the breast of the taller guard shone entwined serpents and a three-crown crest. The broad man wore a charging boar.

The flap fell closed and cut away the light. Jhared ducked back and leaned against a rock, breathing quickly. The boar and the crowned serpents. Together. He wanted the image to be a trick of the eerie light, but he knew better. The sentries weren't Sahisten regulars; the crowned serpents signified the *qia*, the personal guard of the royal family. A royal had come to Demonrock: perhaps the king's cousin, Jondahl—or even the heir himself, King Javahari's nephew, Prince Ashani, Heir to Eight Thousand Years of Glory. Jhared's insides twisted with apprehension, for it wasn't just the *qia* on watch; the charging boar was the sigil of Prince Roelof of Laebek. Laebek and Sahiste couldn't even agree on the color of grass, yet here they stood on guard together. Avelos relied on the conflicts of her neighbors to ease the burden against her own border. If somehow they had come to terms, it meant new kinds of trouble.

Jhared started once more for the tents. He slipped into the unguarded space between them and crept around until he found a place to crouch under the cover of the cliff. The rock face sheltered him from the eyes of passing patrols on the Barren. He hoped the ornate design on the tent would make it difficult to pick him out if someone on the stairs or the wall looked his way.

He hunkered down and put his hand to the canvas. It was woven too tightly to part easily, even with a good knife. After a moment's pause, he stretched out on the ground along the bottom of the tent. The raised wooden floor protruded sufficiently that it left a gap in the fabric loose enough to peer under, although he had to press the side of his head against the ground to do it. He tried not to think about how vulnerable that left him.

His awkward position skewed his view of the pavilion's interior. He could see things on the opposite side: a table with the remnants of a meal, a cluster of low stools, a shelf laden with scrolls, and two interior sentries—also Sahisten and Laebeki. Whoever had shared a meal in this room had not shared trust; the men at the door were alert and attentive. Garish paintings wrapped the inside of the tent as they did the outside: black and scarlet serpents entwined around cities, draped across mountains, hovered with wings unfurled over dancing people. Lamplight reflected off the writhing bodies, giving the chamber a lurid glow.

The robed newcomer from the keep stepped from the corner of the chamber into Jhared's line of sight. Like the Sahisten soldiers, he was tall, though he moved more delicately than a fighting man, like someone taking care with a fragile package. His robes, Jhared realized, weren't black but a complex red, the shades of spilled wine. Although his face hid in a deep cowl, from his cautious bearing, Jhared guessed him past his prime. In a low, imperious voice, the man began what sounded like a greeting.

A furious shriek stabbed across his words. Jhared gasped, fire shooting through his veins, before he even recognized the sound as avian. As he scrambled to regain control, he darted a gaze around the room to find the raptor—a gleaming sable falcon—beating its wings against a tether in one corner of the tent. Jhared's heart thumped hard against his palm, which had made its way to press against his chest. Stories claimed the southern warriors kept such creatures for hunting, but he had never believed that even a Sahisten would taint himself that way.

A lean man in boots and breeches of black leather crossed the room to stroke the creature's dark feathers and croon soothingly. His sleeveless vest left his muscled arms bare, but for a band of twisted gold that shone richly in the firelight.

The gold also bore the crowned serpents: the mark of a Sahisten royal. His red-gold hair was tightly braided to the middle of his broad back. Too old for Prince Ashani, not old enough for Jondahl, but no less fierce looking for the fact that Jhared couldn't put a name to him. An aquiline nose, severe cheekbones, and black eyes as sharp as spearheads reflected ruthlessness. Sahisten men might not have the beaks and talons the songs attributed to them, but their lust for the hunt was never slaked. In statesmanship, in trade, and in battle, they were predators.

The falcon calmed under the warrior's caress, settling its powerful wings and shifting on its perch. With his attention on the two hunters, Jhared didn't even notice the other person in the room until he spoke. This man was no Sahisten: he was broad-shouldered and solid, but soft. Not a fighting man. His round features contrasted sharply with the lean angles of the royal, and his fine garb fluttered as silkily as a woman's gown. He was Laebeki. For all that he showed no warrior's edge, no foolishness existed in his gaze. Laebek cared for cleverness and craft, even to the exclusion of honor. What honor could exist, after all, in a country where the word for *brigand* was the same as the word for *merchant*, and the highwaymen ran their own guilds? The Laebeki people measured success through acquisition; that they set aside their conflict with Sahiste meant they saw profit in it.

The Laebeki man nodded toward the raptor and said something to the royal in slow Sahine. The Sahisten laughed. The one in red acknowledged the ambassador not at all. Instead, he glided silently as smoke around the perimeter of the tent, pausing to extinguish the lamps that swung from poles near the walls. Covered from head to slippered feet, he seemed insubstantial yet ominous, like a shadow cast by a creature much greater than himself.

As the lights died, shadows consumed the rest of the room. The raptor rustled its wings. Jhared stared at the creature's long, strong flight feathers, the vigilant golden gaze. He almost missed the grave obeisance the royal made to the robed man. The royal bent and touched his lips first to a bronze ring on the dark man's right hand and then to a gold ring on the left. When he straightened, he reached up and spoke reverently as he pushed back the man's cowl, revealing a shaved head and a painted face with severe features similar to his own.

Jhared tried to make sense of what he saw. It was women's work to read the Paths, but this robed one—this shadow priest—with his face paint, red garments, and otherworldly manner, looked like some forbidden disciple of Cael who might claim a sacred journey for himself. Like a waylayer. The tattoos twisting up his neck and along his cheeks looked to be an intricate spell.

Whatever spirit he served, the shadow priest commanded the obeisance of leaders in a way the high priestess of Avelos never would. At a gesture from the Sahisten royal, the Laebeki ambassador folded himself gracefully to touch his lips to the priest's rings. The royal gave a word to the sentries: the Sahisten sentry bowed and left the tent, but the Laebeki guard looked to his own charge.

The round-faced man nodded, although his clever smile faded somewhat as his guardian departed.

Looming in the faint glow of a brazier, the priest chanted over the others in his resonant voice. Jhared's gaze wandered back to the falcon, and once more a deep ache started in his chest. It throbbed to the rhythm of his pulse: a mix of pain and desire that constricted around his heart, a reminder of nightmares, and of dark, destructive urges that could not be sated. Cursing inwardly, Jhared forced his attention away from the bird.

The priest stopped chanting; the Sahisten and the Laebeki knelt before him. Jhared vibrated with tension, sensing that whatever had gone on earlier in the evening—a meal, a conference among generals, the planning of statesmen—had only been preparation for the next moments.

With a shrug of his thin shoulders, the priest shed his robe. It fell in a pool of crimson around his feet, exposing the bony chest of a young man aged before his time. The complex spell tattooed around his face and neck trailed down his wiry arms to his wrists, writing its potent secrets for whatever demon might read them. The reason for the charm was obvious now. There on his wrists, like a pair of brightly colored bracelets, coiled two red and black vipers: the symbol of Sahiste. A symbol of poison and betrayal.

Jhared's blood roared in his ears. The Sahisten royal reached out quickly with his right hand to grasp the Laebeki man's left. At the same time, he flung out his left hand to the shadow priest. The Laebeki ambassador clutched at the grip that held him and mirrored the royal, offering his right hand to the shadow.

A wave of apprehension crashed over Jhared. Someone—his Teachers maybe—screamed in his head. The priest stretched his arms toward the men on their knees. Jhared knew an instant when he was capable of action, when he might have rolled into the tent and put his sword through the shadow who wielded poison. He hesitated, and then it was too late. The man slapped his large hands around the wrists of the royal and the ambassador, grinding the vipers against their flesh.

Angered, the creatures stirred to life and partially uncoiled from their host to slither around the new sources of warmth. Like living chains, they bound the three men together wrist to wrist: the raptor and the boar, and the serpent that could sting them both. Jhared didn't see the instant when the vipers' fangs pierced muscle, but the Sahisten warrior threw his head back and roared with grim laughter. The Laebeki man hissed under his breath and murmured frantic words that sounded like a prayer.

In the corner, the raptor screeched and fought against its tether. The men in the center of the room clutched at one another. Their eyes rolled white and their bodies shuddered. Power radiated from that dark space, pushing at the walls of the tent, heating the brazier coals to a sunset glow. The falcon screamed again and tried to escape. Power pounded at Jhared, as though he were a locked door. It threatened to shatter the boundaries that held his self. He caught his breath, longing to know what would happen if the door broke open. Would he still exist on the other side? By the time he realized the danger, it was too late. From far away, stone came up hard under his head. Then he found his own escape.

Jhared blinked at the slice of grey sky above him, tunneling through his confusion to collect the scattered pieces of himself. Pain boomed against the backs of his eyes. He rolled over and scrambled to rise, but the greedy stone had sucked the warmth from his body, leaving him stiff and slow. He had only lifted himself to his elbows when footsteps echoed on the wall above him. The footsteps paused. Jhared held his breath, hoping no one would look between the two tents and that his dark garments against the black serpent would camouflage him just a little longer if they did. After an eternity, someone called to the watchman farther along the wall. The footsteps hesitated, then hastened away.

Jhared let out his breath in a rush. The raptor's shriek still echoed in his mind. He slid down again to peer into the tent. It was empty and dark. What had happened to the two stricken men? Were they dead? A sacrifice to Cael or some Sahisten demon? He could believe that the Sahistens were callous enough to use their own royalty as lure in the hunt for power. He wasn't certain about Laebek. Perhaps they would, if the exchange was of tremendous value or if they hadn't known what would be required of them. Jhared thought that the Laebeki ambassador had been apprehensive, but not surprised by the ritual. Or perhaps an entirely different explanation fit the pieces. Too many things were beyond his comprehension, too many veils he couldn't see. He rubbed a hand over his face, dizzy with the memory of power and the dread of what such power meant for Avelos. Whatever had happened here, Sahiste and Laebek had acted together. His report must reach the garrison. Already the pale blade of dawn sliced the night sky.

This time, he scanned the walls carefully and waited for the world to stop swinging before clambering to his feet. When his vision steadied, he slipped away from the pavilions and back onto the Barren. By the time he made it far enough north to see the cliff that marked the border, the sun had cleared the horizon. Soon it would be scorching the stone around him. He could ignore the heat and the hunger gnawing at his middle. What he couldn't ignore was that daylight had transformed the grey plain of the previous night into a field of white rock, and his dark garb made him stand out like blood against snow.

Jhared tamped down the urge to run. Motion draws the eye, and the gait of a fleeing man is distinctive. Instead, he crept from hillock to boulder. The oddity of the Barren was its dead, open surface. Too many moments found him scrambling over an exposed tract of flat stone, his back prickling with the anticipation of a spear's point through his body before he could reach cover again. The Sahistens were wise when they chose this place for their keep. No army could approach from the west undetected, and a siege force would find insufficient food and water to sustain itself.

Jhared crawled into the slender cover of a pillar to rest before trying the last stretch to the border. The scent of hot stone left an acrid taste in his mouth. He could see Avelos. The cliff beckoned to him from a little less than a quarter-mile away, but it rose up from a long, dangerous flat, like a book standing on an empty table. He considered finding a place to wait out the daylight. The narrow gully a short distance ahead would give him decent cover. It probably cradled a small stream during fall and winter, but now it would be a dried crack in the ground. He glanced for the hundredth time toward the Burn Tower. The bright sun made it impossible to distinguish the signal.

He lifted his palm from the heat of the stone. The longer he lingered in Sahiste, the greater his risk of being discovered. If he chanced an open crossing now, he bet on the likelihood that the keep patrolled less frequently in the daylight hours. The pressure of what he knew made it worth the danger. With one more watchful glance at his surroundings, he set out again for home.

His timing was so terrible and so perfect that Jhared didn't know if Cael or Riana shaped the moment. He had just reached the place where the rock sloped toward the gully when a Sahisten guard staggered out of the rift, still lacing his breeches. He was young. His braid made a short, pathetic tail that stuck out over his collar. He climbed over the bank, one hand clutching at his stomach as though it pained him. Jhared had an instant to wonder just how thoroughly the garrison had celebrated the alliance with Laebek last night. Then the guard pulled to a halt and stared at Jhared, his grey eyes round with dumb shock.

"*Qi lium?*"

The words might have been a challenge, but the guard's tone was nothing other than startled. In that absurd instant, a flock of incongruous thoughts flew through Jhared's head: He would have to kill the boy. His swordsmanship was barely scraping adequate. Even a Sahisten looked vulnerable with his trousers hanging open. It would be ridiculous to die within sight of home.

It was the last thought that propelled him forward. He hurtled toward the guard without even slowing to draw his blade. They crashed bodily, momentum throwing them over the lip of the gully. For an instant they were airborne, and then they landed hard, Jhared on top. He grunted as his knee struck rock. The

Sahisten flailed at Jhared's face with a fist. Jhared blocked the first blow, missed the second. His jaws clicked together painfully.

He had the advantage of size, but the Sahisten was agile as a ferret. The boy twisted and thrashed, gaining enough leverage with one leg to fling Jhared sideways. Jhared held on, throwing them both over again. He clamped his legs around the boy's chest. The guard struggled for his knife, but couldn't free his arms to reach it. Jhared grabbed the boy's shirt with both hands, yanked his shoulders off the ground, and slammed him down. A shudder twitched through the guard's body. Again Jhared slammed him down. And a third time. The boy's skull thudded against rock. Then he went still.

Jhared leaped up and crept to the edge of the embankment, his gaze darting over the landscape for the rest of the Sahisten's patrol. His own harsh breathing rent the silence as he freed his sword and prepared for them to come. A dry breeze hissed through the rocks. The only thing moving on the Barren was a bundle of dead brush tumbling over and over across the stone.

Sweat dripped down his back, and his bruised knee grew stiff. No other men appeared. As the sun blazed toward the hottest part of the day, Jhared decided the guard had been alone. He sheathed his blade and turned to the body. He smelled blood, and from somewhere nearby, evidence of the soldier's sickness. Perhaps during the celebration the boy had been dared onto the Barren by a comrade. Perhaps he had stumbled into danger on his own and passed out. He remained unconscious, his chest rising and falling evenly.

Jhared stared at the limp form and drew his knife. He had never yet killed at close range. Of course, he had known this time would come; killing was what Shorn men were born for. He swallowed and looked down at his hands, wondering why he heard the words in Sirol's ironic tone. Once, in a time nearly out of memory, he had imagined himself having the skills to heal. Now, he set a naked blade across a young boy's throat. The guard's short braid poked out from behind his head, looking silly and sad.

This is wrong. Jhared pulled back. He couldn't kill this way. Not against an unconscious enemy. Surely, Tierzen would agree that such a slaying was a kind of deceit. A Shorn man must be so careful. The Avelune did not fall into treason in one day; their weaknesses and little deceits led them step by gradual step toward greater transgressions until their acts became true evil. Jhared refused to start down that path. He lowered his knife. Let the boy face his comrades and his family in shame for letting a spy cross the border. Jhared wouldn't be the one to give him the escape of death. He slunk out of the gully, his insides in knots.

"The Sahisten saw you coming from the east. What will the consequences be when his commanders learn that Avelos knows of this alliance with Laebek?" His Teachers struck him with the first question as he hurried toward the border.

"He can tell them nothing that they wouldn't assume if they found him dead," Jhared offered. Avelos taunted; it was close now.

"Then let them assume, and let there be one less Sahisten soldier to take up arms against us! After all they did to us, how could you spare any one of them?"

He focused on the rocky cliff and the charred forest above it. His Teachers' anger created a tempest in their corner of his mind.

"But I took my example from the histories. The Avelune—"

"Coward! You take only what you need to excuse yourself. You watched idly while our enemies loosed a dark power. You walked away from the challenge of what you've sworn to do. You proved nothing today except your capacity for inaction!"

Jhared stopped short and bent double, gasping for breath. One hand clutched at his chest. They were right. He hadn't seen it before, but the insight appalled him. They must be right; they were his Teachers. He swung around, running back to the gully, trying not to hear their accusations repeating in his mind.

He didn't use the knife. The Teachers demanded that he deliver the kind of death a Sahisten deserved. Rocks littered the gully. Jhared hefted one, gauging its weight. Without stopping to think on it, he flipped the unconscious boy face down and slammed the rock against his head. The skull gave way, crackling and snapping with a sudden surrender that ended life. Something within Jhared surrendered, too. *You proved nothing today....* He slammed the rock down again with all his strength behind it. Bits of bone and soft matter spattered around him. Blood flowed along the creekbed where water should have run.

With a groan, Jhared threw down the stone and staggered to his feet. He forced himself to turn the body over, to look into the dead boy's face. His enemy's face. In his mind, he felt his Teachers' thread of approval, but it wasn't forgiveness. Taking a strangled breath, he lurched away from the body. He made it a handful of steps before his stomach revolted. He vomited onto the dry stone.

He wanted to beg his Teachers for pardon, but he didn't know whether his crime was trying to avoid the killing or failing to avoid it. When he could breathe again, he climbed out of the gully. His Teachers hovered in stormy silence the rest of the way back to the border.

The rope uncoiled down the cliff as he neared. He clawed for it and grasped it to him. His body was too tired to rebel as he pulled himself into the air. Near the top, his boots found purchase and he scrambled over the edge onto his stomach. Hands reached down to pull him to his feet. Anzo and Jase. Grion stood as anchor behind them.

"We were starting t'wonder if ya decided t'trade your sword for braids and a spear." Jase's bright blue gaze danced in the afternoon light. His grin showed too many teeth.

Jhared stumbled away from the cliff edge and cast a glance at the Nadaren clansman, uncertain whether Jase said such things to provoke him or just to be outrageous.

Anzo scratched at his stubbly grey chin. "Should we expect visitors behind you?" He gestured toward Jhared's hands, smeared with blood. If he'd been watching the Barren, he must have witnessed part of the struggle. Jhared wondered if the old soldier had seen him go back to finish the Sahisten boy.

"I don't think so." The words came out as a dusty whisper. Jhared cleared his throat and tried again. "But they may be angry enough later to try the border."

Anzo handed a water skin to Jhared.

Grion snorted. "You start another war for us, Denaban?"

The water gave Jhared a way to compose himself a little. He drank long, closing his eyes as it flowed over his parched tongue and throat. When he finished, he glanced at the brawny clansman behind Anzo.

"Am I to give my report first to you, Grion?"

"Only if ya want t'wear Carn's bootprint on your backside," Jase interjected. "Come on. We should be halfway back to Ravia by now. And that's longer than I want t'wait t'find out if I won my wager."

Jhared nodded mutely. The motion set hammers trotting against his skull again. The power he had witnessed echoed through him. He thought of sable wings and a predator's gaze. Earlier, Jase had used the word *sorcery*.

Anzo sucked his lip and watched as Jhared massaged bloody fingertips against his temples.

"Oh, your wager's lost, Jase," the old patrolman observed, bending to retrieve the rope and coil it around his arm. "Might as well hand it over now. If you looked truly, you'd see that your wager is clearly lost."

10.
TWISTING PATHS

Darkness lowered its fist over the hills. Jhared gave Brio his head and let the gelding pick his way among the rocks. The patrol rode in silence, but Jhared felt the men's glances pressing on him. As General Nadel required, Carn had taken the scouts' reports individually, to avoid the possibility that one man's telling would color the other's. Jhared and Jase could not speak of the mission to one another or to the patrol until Carn brought the report to Captain Riselvo. But as they left the Burn, everyone saw their Verael bare his teeth at the east.

They reached the fortress after midnight. The night sky was an ocean of black and silver above them. In the inner yard, the men dismounted gratefully, loosening their horses' girths and muttering among themselves. Jhared slid from the saddle and headed toward the stable with the others. Once Brio was cleaned and fed and bedded down for the night, he would find his own meal. Afterward, he would have to deal with whatever it was he had witnessed in Sahiste and figure out what to write to Tierzen.

"Hold!" Carn barked. "Denaban and Relki, where d'you think you're going?"

Jhared halted, forcing himself away from indulgent thoughts of food, and exchanged a quick look with Jase. The Nadaren man shrugged as if to say the commander's behavior was beyond him to predict. The entire patrol had stopped, staring at the scouts. Esran reached a hand toward Brio's reins, and Jhared offered them over with thanks. The burly Onteran nodded, his expression an expectant one. They would all be waiting for Jhared and Jase to come and tell their stories afterward.

Carn herded them across the yard, to the northern tower and the garrison captain's office. Just inside the tower, a small guardroom hunkered beneath a twisting stairway dimly lit with torches along the walls. As the commander prodded Jhared and Jase up the stairs, loud footsteps echoed on the landing. The captain came into view, arms crossed over his chest.

"Where in Cael's hole've you been, Carn? You should'a been back yesterday afternoon. And what's this I'm hearing about losing a man to Sahiste?"

So the rumors were already flying. Burn Tower must have sent a courier back yesterday.

"You don't look lost," Riselvo said sourly as Jhared and Jase topped the landing. The captain grew from the same barrel-chested Everen stock as Anzo, but he possessed none of the Clan Everen geniality. He might have been a doughty warrior once, before his battles with the council to keep the garrison provisioned and the men equipped had flattened him.

"Well? What do you have for me, Carn? Makri Tower sent back nothing. The general can't make decisions based on nothing."

The commander followed Riselvo into the small office, his big shoulders hunched below the heavy wood beams in the ceiling.

"We've got something, sir. It's trouble. You should hear it direct from the ones as found it." He pointed at Jhared. "Denaban, you first."

Jhared straightened as Riselvo dragged a chair away from his orderly desk and settled his aging frame. The captain's grey brow wrinkled with impatience, as if he'd been here a thousand times and heard all the reports there were to tell. Jhared didn't let that fluster him. He laid out the mission with the precision he'd been taught: observations first, down to the smallest details, and interpretations later, only if requested. The telling came out clearly at the start, until he reached the description of the ritual.

He was hungry and tired. Pain twinged in his knee. The banality of his needs made the previous night's images of spirits and demons seem outlandish, a boy's bad dream. He began to stumble over his report as he recognized his own veils: the excitement of a first foray into Sahiste, Jase's superstitious talk, and the need to win a wager. Had his strange perceptions during the ritual been anything more than fear and fantasy?

Riselvo's features darkened. "You're telling me that Sahiste and Laebek have come together to what? To wield some kind of snake magic?"

Jhared hesitated. "It seemed a rite of bonding, sir. But bonding to what, I don't know. I think both sides gave a commitment of some kind."

"If the scouts had more Sahine," Carn interjected, "perhaps we could understand these riddles...." The commander trailed off as though it were an argument the captain knew well enough to finish for himself.

"There's our answer," Riselvo grumbled. "Let's teach our Shorn men how to communicate in the language of traitors. That should sit well with the council. We've enough battles to fight without creating more adversaries in the city." The captain waved a hand at Jhared to continue. "And after? What about the men?"

Jhared braced himself. "I don't know, sir. Something happened after the vipers struck. Everyone in the tent seemed to feel it...a force. I blacked out. When I came back, the others were gone."

"Blacked out?" The captain's voice crackled with sarcasm. Jase shifted. "You mean to say you fell asleep on your watch? That'll earn you the lash, soldier."

"No, sir. No. Something struck me. It…" *It craved the very space I occupied. As if we must both stand in the same place in the same moment.* Those were the words that came to him, but he feared such an obscure explanation would only infuriate a man as practical as the captain. He wished he could speak with General Nadel.

"Something…struck me," he tried again.

"If a guard found you, soldier, we wouldn't be having this conversation."

"No, sir. Not a guard. The tent was dark and the watch was changing when I awoke. That's all I have, sir."

Riselvo's thick fingers jabbed rhythmically at his chair. "That's all, eh? Well, well. Your hunters don't seem to have captured all of the beast this time, Commander." He scowled at Carn, then pointed a finger toward Jase. "What does this one have? Did you faint away, too?"

Jhared lowered his head and wiped a bead of sweat from his brow. He forced himself to pay attention to Jase's report, noting the man's thorough description of the jubilant atmosphere in the keep, the couriers riding out on the northern road, and the evidence of a garrison functioning at capacity. The Sahistens *had* been celebrating. Some truce had been negotiated with Laebek, surely. But what did they intend to do with the power he had witnessed? Jhared had no way to answer the question. He was grateful when Captain Riselvo finally dismissed him and Jase both. He saluted the captain and his commander and headed with Jase toward freedom.

"If Laebek and Sahiste move together, we don't have the men to hold them." Carn's gruff voice followed Jhared down the stairs. "When will the general return?"

He didn't hear the reply. A rough shove sent him tripping over a rut in the dirt. He caught his balance in a step and spun around, defenses up. Jase jumped back hastily, wide-eyed and laughing.

"Easy, man! Don't be so hawkish. I owe ya a little pat on the back for the story you told up there is all. You did top me, didn't you?"

Jhared lifted one shoulder, unsure why the wager had ever seemed important. "You would have seen the same if you took the pavilions."

"Maybe I wouldn'a fallen asleep." Jase grinned. "A jest. Only a jest. I've seen the Bloodless in Avarel Forest. I know demons still walk our lands. And I won't be the only one unsurprised t'hear Sahiste's dabbling with curses. Come on." He steered Jhared toward the mess hall. "The patrol's waiting for us. They'll be passing the jug for the storytellers."

The last thing Jhared wanted was to go over his night in Sahiste yet again, with an audience. He needed to wash the dust off his body, eat a good meal, and then maybe find a quiet place to consider how he was going to explain this night to Tierzen. But there was no extracting himself from Jase's grasp. The man drew him toward the open door of the mess, where soldiers' voices rode out on a wave of heated air.

Predictably, an uproar greeted Jase's appearance at the door. Soldiers lifted their mugs and some rattled bags of dice at him. He waved and nodded, like a priestess bestowing blessings. Jhared trailed behind, caught in the Nadaren man's wake as he started up the two lines of tables that filled the narrow hall. A large hearth yawned at each end. Only one fireplace burned this summer evening, and just high enough to make a cook fire. Still, in the low-roofed chamber crowded with sweating men, the air stank like an old horse blanket.

Most of Carn's patrol sat together near the door, where a finger of breeze lifted the heat. Food and camaraderie seemed to have lightened the pall of their ride from Sahiste. Twitch interrupted some bawdy story to welcome Jase. The others called to hear the news from the scouts.

Despite the crowded room, Jase managed to affect a pretty bow for them. The men laughed, and Jase showed his teeth as he found a seat. Jhared detoured toward the food on the sideboard. He took a round of dark bread and layered it with a thick slice of roasted meat and a chunk of sharp goat cheese. The sensation of eyes upon him caused him to look up and catch a soldier frowning at him from across the room. Jhared recognized the raven-haired Shorn man from his own company: Haren or Henren, he thought it was. Before he decided how to answer the stare, the man's gaze drifted past him, toward the door, where Bevan had entered with soldiers from the Fifth. Jhared realized with a strange mix of relief and regret that he had never been the intended target at all.

With his hands full of the layered bread and a half-dozen small summer plums, he returned to the patrol and edged himself into the narrow space left for him. Jase had secured a cup of wine and was gesturing with it for quiet. All around the room, men quit their gaming and gossiping to listen as he launched into the story. Sahiste's uncharacteristic quiet at the border was like the silence of a drawn bow, and the longer it continued, the more tension gathered in the garrison. No one wanted to miss the news.

Not that many were as interested in hearing the story as in giving their own opinions about what it meant. In this, Jhared found the fighting men of Ravia no different from those in the city. By the time Jase finished his retelling of the snake ritual, the room echoed with debates. A group from Clan Nadaren spoke of armies of the dead and men who could not be killed, like the dark forces that rose against Riana and her Aye in the old songs.

"They're raising the dead," someone hissed. "The hordes'a the Exile War will come again. Ya wait and see."

Lenaro clunked his mug on the table and shook his red head at the man. "You know better than that, Patrolman. Jase could tell a story about horses pissing and make it sound like the Great Flood. Whatever Sahiste's up to, her soldiers still bleed and die same as ever."

A white-haired man, an archer from the Sixth, gave the westerners a disparaging look. "Worry s'more about what Rumar's going to do with all those *living* troops filling Demonrock."

"What Rumar's going to do?" Bevan muttered. "He'll tell us that fighting Sahiste's the old way and we got to learn to change, maybe invite them over for a cup'a wine and a piece'a cake, instead."

Grion laughed. "Then he'll find a way to tax us for it!"

Lenaro gave them both a warning look. "Careful where you're going with that talk."

Bevan shrugged sulkily. "Going nowhere but for another cup'a wine. Pass me the jug."

The hall grew louder as jugs were emptied. Grion's incautious words shifted the conversations and sparked complaints about rising levies, especially the change in the travelers' tax. Recent news from the city held that Rumar had claimed the ancient tax away from the clans. Now it was the high chieftain who would receive the levy that travelers paid for crossing clan lands.

"If all the first clans'd keep their roads and chase off highwaymen as they should, High Chieftain wouldn't need the silver to pay others to do it," declared a Manitar clansmen, leaning drunkenly over a patrolmate from Clan Aglar.

The big northerner, at least as drunk as the Manitar man, rose to the challenge. "They're our lands. Alende Isan gave 'em to *us*. No one should be telling us what to do with 'em or who can travel 'em. 'Specially no Manitar city man!"

The Manitar soldier dove for the bait, swinging hard at the northerner. With a roar of warning, more sober comrades leaped up hastily to part them. Both soldiers were flung into the night to cool off.

Jhared was more than ready to follow. He had seen something in Sahiste he couldn't explain, something that *looked* like sorcery, and he couldn't say he had done all he could to keep Avelos safe. He didn't want more wild speculation and posturing. He discovered with surprise that what he really wanted was music. He wondered if Ravia possessed any bards worth the name. It probably wasn't the best idea for a Shorn Forest Guard to wander alone through town, but he needed to escape. He needed relief from the memory of a skull cracking and the blood of a dead boy on his hands. If he could evade notice by the *qia*, he didn't fear a few angry Ravia men. He knew how to manage himself among the townspeople. He made his decision, rose, and headed for the door.

"Naw. You don't want to be going downhill tonight."

Anzo lounged at the table next to the door with his back against the wall and his bowed legs stretched along the bench. The others had given the old veteran the extra space without complaint. Throughout the debate, he had listened quietly as he pulled on his pipe and shared drinks from a worn leather flask. Now he eyed Jhared with an all-too-knowing gaze.

Jhared pulled a neutral smile. "I hope I don't look like a fool who can't find himself a quiet drink downhill."

"You look like a man who wants to find himself some trouble. It'll be waiting for you in town."

"Let it wait. I just need to stretch. I spent the better part of a day crawling over Sahisten rocks."

Anzo's lips formed an *o* and a ring of smoke drifted lazily over the table. "It's all right, you know. What you saw wasn't yours to stop. Not if you wanted to come back alive to report it."

Jhared drew a sharp breath. Anzo's guess struck painfully close to the core of his thoughts. Yet the old veteran's oath to the Forest Guard was different from his binding to Avelos. *I will hold each countryman dearer than my own life.* Jhared wasn't sure he *should* have come back.

"I did what I've sworn to do," he insisted, to himself as much as to Anzo. "Now I'm looking for nothing more than a walk and a drink."

"You say so, pup." The old soldier gave a shrug. "Just try not to walk into the blade of a town man, eh?"

It occurred to Jhared that if he were any other soldier, he might respond with a jest and then invite Anzo to share a flask. But he was a pup and clanless and Shorn. He was on his own with this.

"Don't worry; I won't bring trouble to the patrol," he said as he left the hall. "I promise you that."

He slid out without attracting further attention and strode down the empty loggia. He went to the water barrel behind the barracks first. No one was around, so he stripped off his shirt and used the small pail beside the barrel to splash the worst of the grime off his body. The cool water trickled pleasantly down his back and eased some of the tightness there. With a hand, he reached over his shoulder to knead a knot of muscle. Inadvertently, his fingers found the edge of one thick scar. With a grimace of disgust, he drew his hand away. He returned the pail to its peg before stepping inside.

The inner barracks were dark and cooler than the mess had been. A low rumble rose from the snoring soldiers who slept before their next watch. As he crouched near the chest at the foot of his own bed, his weariness finally caught up with him. He considered giving up the walk to town and just collapsing onto his blanket, but he knew that the nightmares would be bad tonight. His Teachers had been furious with him. He had rather put them off a while longer. He pulled on a clean shirt, glad to smell less like Brio, and thought about the longing for music that stirred him. When he was a child, music had guarded him from the dreams, leading him down paths of melody and story in place of his nightmares. Zia had been the first one to offer him that haven in years. Only now did he realize how much he had missed it.

"Alende's Flight" played in his head as he dressed. It was the song his mother wrote about the hero's escape from the destruction of Altan Mar. The song Zia played for him. Perhaps they knew it in Ravia. He hummed as he stood and rebuckled his sword belt. In the dark, the cream-colored corner of paper on the bed almost escaped his notice.

Riana's Paths twist for a reason.

The temple teaching came to him unbidden. Curious, he reached down and plucked the paper out from the fold of his blanket. A courier must have come through while he was on the border. It might be another letter from Zia or a note from Bran or perhaps a warning from Tierzen. The letters he had written to the elder had so far elicited no response, and he was beginning to fear that everything he'd sent had been useless.

Riana's Paths twist for a reason. The teaching was one of Neta's favorites. She gave it to him not long after his mother died: a ward against the fear of chaos, she said. He had never liked it: it sounded too much like a man's excuse for his own poor choices. He sat down on the bed, holding the paper in two fingers and turning it over. It was fine stuff, expensive, like that used for important correspondence by an elder. The seal was not Tierzen's elder's mark, however, but only a blob of colorless wax. His name wandered across the front in uneven letters, not Zia's elegant scribe's hand or even Bran's boyish script. Jhared slid his thumb beneath the fold and broke the seal. Inside was the same scrawl.

They watch for your defiance. Be careful. They will fall on you like dogs.

Don't let them claim you.

He read the message twice, wearing a mask of composure, then set it down on the bed, laid his open palms on his knees, and drew a deep breath. Why should this upset him? Certainly he was watched: by his commander, his lieutenant, his captain, and his general. Within his mind, his Teachers monitored and guided him, always. Tierzen had warned that the Legacy would watch him, too. Why should his heart race like this? He knew his duty.

They watch for your defiance.

The Teachers kept silent when, for a rarity, he wanted to hear their voices. They knew better than anyone that no defiance existed in him. Jhared took another breath. Worrying was no help. He tried to consider the note as if it were one of General Nadel's puzzles. Here was evidence that Tierzen's prediction was accurate: the Legacy still observed him in hopes of seeing him fail. But who would take pains to warn him of it? He had no friends within the garrison, and no one in the city who knew him had reason to hide. No, it wasn't concern for his welfare that motivated the letter. Could it be someone who feared for Tierzen? Perhaps Sirol? But the scribe had already given his warning, and the tone of this note was less personal. Perhaps it was a Legacy supporter who hoped to frighten him. Jhared reread the last two sentences and considered their ambiguous meaning. How would they claim him? Were they ready to move from observation to action?

He thought regretfully of the music that waited in town. What had seemed only an evening's distraction now might truly be dangerous. With a message like this in his lap, he had no excuse to tempt Cael by strolling among a town full of Legacy men. He rubbed a hand over his face and sighed.

If he couldn't find escape in town, then he would do just what he had told Anzo: find a place to stretch the stiffness out of his limbs. He refolded the paper, and after a moment's consideration, tucked it securely into the pouch at his belt.

Outside, crickets chirped in the mild darkness. Torches flickered along the walls, and the nightwatch stood silently at their posts above. One of the priest-esses from the Ravia temple slipped across the inner yard, a healer's bag over her shoulder. Riana's servants offered their guidance to the fortress healer from time to time. She paused to smile at Jhared, and it crossed his mind to ask for a blessing, but he didn't need a priestess to realize he had stepped on the wrong path today.

He checked through the south gate and left the fortress heading west. The west road climbed into the hills along the Laebeki border. A few clan settlements hugged the shoulders of the rugged slopes close to Ravia, but then the land opened to the wilds. Not far to the south, the Jewel River sparkled its way across Avelos, gathering strength until it finally rushed across the western corner of Laebek and into swampy little Sona.

Jhared waited until he passed the cluster of farms outside the walls before he dared to run. When he did, he held nothing back. He fed his muscles on apprehension and need, pushing himself hard up one slope and down the next. Exertion burned away his unanswered questions and left no energy to conjure thoughts of Legacy spies or images of blood and raptors. After the first nec-essary burn of speed, he settled into a steady, ground-eating pace, and felt the rightness of this choice.

No one understood why he ran. He once tried to explain to Tierzen how speed eased his constant longings, but the elder believed the best way to conquer the Shorn urges was through study and insight. General Nadel and Commander Carn encouraged running as a matter of physical training. None of them un-derstood how the wind stirred around his body and gave him the illusion of freedom. They couldn't understand how it eased the pull toward self-destruction when the urges threatened to send him over a cliff. He ran until his limbs grew weightless and he floated like fog over the road. The wind carried the scent of the river and ripened plums up from the valley. He ran until the fortress became a black shadow in the distance.

He ran until horse's hooves against the dirt drowned the sound of his own feet.

They were coming his way. Jhared pulled up at the bottom of a hill and quieted his breathing to listen. The uneven pounding hinted at injury or exhaustion in a large horse with a poorly balanced rider. Jhared moved quickly to the side of the road and waited for them to crest the slope. Likely it was a courier from Barlona to the west, but they were coming too fast for a dark road, and he had seen things that made him cautious tonight. As he waited, tense and ready, the horse's rhythm broke entirely, and the animal squealed in pain before the hoofbeats stopped. The beast had gone down, or nearly. A man cursed, low and urgent. Without waiting another breath, Jhared took off up the hill toward them.

The horse stood splay-legged in the middle of the road: head hanging low, coat sheathed in mud, and flanks pumping for breath. Looking as battered as his horse, the rider hunched over the beast's neck muttering exhortations. Jhared hissed in dismay; even now he knew the cultured voice.

Lieutenant Sevar dragged his head up. His eyes glinted with cold flame through a mask of dirt and gore. One hand went to his sword. "Identify yourself."

Jhared stepped out of the shadows and saluted. "Patrolman Jhared Denaban. Sir, are you pursued?"

"Carn's Shorn boy." The lieutenant cast his glance off the road. "We're attacked near Lamirna. General Nadel needs men. Where's the rest of your patrol? Where's Carn?"

"I'm alone, sir. We just returned from Burn Tower. Commander gave us the night…" Under the lieutenant's glare, Jhared felt as though he'd been caught doing something prohibited. "What can I do, sir? Give me an order."

Sevar cursed again and kicked his beast forward. "You can move out of my way!"

Jhared skittered back from the plunging stallion. The animal cantered several brave lengths down the hill, then with a scream of agony, stumbled hard. Its left front leg buckled with a sickening snap. Sevar lurched forward, freeing himself from the stirrups and swinging out of the saddle just as the stallion foundered. The beast dropped to its side with a groan of pain. Running after them, Jhared saw the lieutenant go to the animal's head and lay a hand on its foam-flecked muzzle. Then with one quick movement, Sevar's dagger was out of its sheath and reflecting starlight. Jhared stifled a sound of surprise as the lieutenant raised the blade two-handed, and without hesitating, thrust it deep into the stallion's heart.

The horse shuddered, kicked vaguely at the air, and was still. Sevar crouched over the dead beast, his knife grasped in his fist.

Jhared was at the man's side in a moment. "Sir, let me bring help. I can run back to the garrison and—"

"No. The general doesn't have that kind of time. Just see that you keep up."

Sevar sheathed the knife and straightened. Despite his injuries, he hurtled down the road as if Cael chased him. Jhared ran at his shoulder. They raced through the darkness, the lieutenant's ragged breathing and Jhared's own heart loud in his ears.

The distance that Jhared had covered so easily now seemed unending. Sevar's gait grew increasingly unsteady along the rutted road, but he didn't slow; he lowered his head and pushed on faster. Finally, they reached the edge of Ravia's settlements. As the lieutenant glanced up at the promise of the fortress beyond, he lost his balance. One leg went out from under him, and he hit the ground. Jhared thought the man would go down as terribly as the horse. Instead, he caught himself on one knee, both hands to the road like a runner at the start of a race.

Jhared bent to offer a hand.

The lieutenant resisted. In the dark, Jhared couldn't tell if it was pride or disgust that held him back. Both, Jhared decided, as Sevar finally grasped his arm.

"Here's irony for you," the man panted, pulling himself straight. "Come on. There's no time."

Jhared hadn't expected to stand before Captain Riselvo twice in a night, but he found himself supporting his injured lieutenant up the tower stairs, pounding on the door, waiting as Riselvo frowned, then saw Sevar and drew them into the chamber. The garrison captain pulled his chair over and called to the watch to send for the healer.

"Tell me," he commanded Sevar as he opened a drawer in his desk and yanked out a flask and a cup.

The lieutenant ignored the chair, but took the cup Riselvo pushed into his bloody fingers, gulping down the wine in one long draught. It seemed to revive him somewhat; he drew away from Jhared's support.

"The levy arrived in Barlona as expected a week ago," he gasped. "A good group—eager boys. The general and I took them out for a test four days past. We turned south at Lamirna to give them a look at Laebek. Test their wits against the forest. They got their test too soon. Raiders struck the village yesterday. Before dawn. We heard the alarm bells from camp and caught the trail as the raiders fled for the border. We crossed the river to cut them off and put ourselves between them and Laebek. It should have been an elegant trap. It should have…" Sevar trailed off to catch his breath and take another drink.

Jhared watched, ready to move forward if he was needed. Sevar wouldn't ask for aid. The lieutenant was city-born, and it showed in his unbending pride, as much as in his cultured voice and controlled manner. Many of the men respected the lieutenant's strength and spoke of his fairness, but not all the soldiers of Ravia thought a city-bred man should rise so high in the Forest Guard. They called him a golden boy for his pretty looks and whispered that he only succeeded because of favors Rumar owed his father. Before tonight, Jhared's only experience with the lieutenant had been the lash of his voice on the practice grounds and the sting of his disapproving glare.

Captain Riselvo cursed into the silence. "You and the general with a handful of untried levies. Cael's balls, what a bloody mess."

"The boys had courage," Sevar grumbled. "It didn't matter. We never caught the raiders. Something else assailed us. Some…storm."

The captain's eyebrows rose.

"A storm like nothing I've known," the lieutenant said, his tone twisting with anger. "Like nothing I've read in all the histories. I can only tell you that a wind pursued us. Beat at us with a malevolent will."

Riselvo leaned back against the corner of his desk and folded his arms across his round chest. "The Vuri can rise fast and hard from the south. I suppose it brought in the storm that blinded your boys. Then the raiders could've had their way—"

"No, that wasn't the means of it. The raiders never touched us. This is a power of blood and darkness." Sevar held up his hand; it was covered with cuts and gashes, as if he'd been in a knife fight. "The general and our levies are trapped by it. We took what shelter we could in a cave in a vale near the border, but it isn't enough. If there's any hope for them, we must ride. Now."

Jhared looked down at his own hands, sticky with Lieutenant Sevar's blood, and thought of serpents and a man in scarlet robes. *A power of blood and darkness.*

Riselvo stared past them out the narrow window, his expression shifting. He looked old and tired, like a man whose sword no longer fit comfortably in his fist. After a silence, stiff resignation settled over his features.

"Then we ride," he said. "We'll take the Fourth. Will your men be ready?"

"All but Carn's patrol," Sevar said. "He just came in. We'll leave them here."

"Don't, sir." The words were out before Jhared knew he was going to say them. The officers turned to stare at him.

"What's that, Patrolman?"

Jhared straightened. "We're ready. Not a one would want to be left if it's for the general." He thought it was true of the men in his patrol. He knew it was true for himself. He owed General Nadel for his training, his position in the Forest Guard, and his very success in the Becoming. He couldn't be left behind.

Captain Riselvo gave a grunt that seemed to signify approval, but Sevar turned a hostile expression on him.

"Are you so certain your comrades will thank you for pulling them into a deathtrap, Patrolman?"

"We should see it. Jase and I at least. There may be something we'll recognize." Jhared glanced at the garrison captain.

"Javahari," Riselvo said to Sevar by way of explanation. "You need to hear it, but on the way. The boy's right: if Sahiste or Laebek has a hand in this, the scouts might know something. We'll bring Carn." The garrison captain strode toward the door. At the threshold, he paused. "You're not to move until Healer Falto has seen to your injuries, Matio, so take a damn seat and stop wasting your strength. I need you able to sit a horse back to Lamirna." Then Riselvo disappeared, his boots thudding down the stairs.

Lieutenant Sevar moved to the captain's desk, poured himself another cup of wine, and downed it. Jhared waited uncertainly for direction.

"You like to run. That's good." Sevar set aside the cup and eyed Jhared with a blood-filled gaze. "I have tasks for you. You can start by letting Commander Carn know what you've brought him into. Then I have gear for you to fetch. After that, we'll see just how fast you are when you're running for your life."

11.
KILLING WINDS

Brio trembled from head to hock as Jhared patted and soothed him. Standing close to the big horse, Jhared sought to regain his own composure. His skin burned with dozens of shallow cuts. The ringing in his ears muffled the gelding's anxious whickers. All the company sought to calm their frantic mounts. On a steep hillside above the river, in the gloom of a false dawn, they had confronted the incarnation of terror: No rain. No thunder. Only a slicing wind that launched branches through the air and spun funnels of dust across the vale.

The preternatural horror had transformed the well-ordered ranks into a tangle of panicked horses. In the confusion, two mounts had stumbled off the narrow ridge road and fallen the long, deadly way to the riverbed, their heavy bodies sliding and rolling. One rider barely flung himself from his horse in time to avoid the same fate; the other man hadn't been so lucky. After that, Captain Riselvo signaled the retreat. Jhared said a soldier's prayer for the lost man, knowing the company had been fortunate to lose only one.

General Nadel wasn't so fortunate; he remained trapped in the midst of it.

The *bump, bump* of Brio's muzzle against Jhared's chest drew him back to the edge of the clearing where they had halted south of the village of Lamirna. He ruffled the bay's forelock. Talk was low and strained among the soldiers. The pragmatic men of Clan Valador pointed toward the slate-colored cloud to the west and spoke of storms. Clan Nadaren men prayed, and the Onterans openly pulled on the beaded charms at their throats.

On the other side of the clearing, among the trees where most men wouldn't see them, the captain and lieutenant argued over what to do next. Jhared could imagine the conversation: Captain Riselvo would want to wait out the maelstrom. Lieutenant Sevar intended to enter it. Jhared knew it at the moment of their retreat, when he caught a glimpse of Sevar that he hadn't been meant to see. Jhared recognized the man's need from his own nightmares—from the eyes of an injured raptor tumbling out of the sky. Sevar wore the expression of a hunter made prey. The raptor of Jhared's nightmares always struggled, no matter how hopelessly, to master the force that subdued it. The lieutenant needed to face the storm again.

So Jhared stood with Brio where the lieutenant had ordered them. He didn't think they would be standing long; fury drove Sevar and the general had no time. Two other Shorn soldiers had been pulled from the ranks with him. They made an odd picture of calm amid the agitated company. One man was in his middle years, stockier than most Shorn, his warrior's tail shot with grey. He stood with an arm slung across the back of his grazing horse, his weight on one foot, and his gaze unfocused—the look of someone accustomed to waiting. The other man, lithe and dark, sat beneath a tree with his eyes closed and his head tilted back against the trunk.

The stocky soldier blinked owlishly and yawned in Jhared's direction. "Looks like the three of us are for a mission to meet Cael, eh? You do something to slash your commander, boy? Earn yourself this ride?"

Accustomed to being ignored by the other Shorn soldiers, Jhared was surprised to be addressed directly. "I don't know what you mean."

"You don't think it was an accident we got picked for this trip, do you? It's Shorn for the deadliest work, you know." The soldier grinned lazily and plucked at a burr in his horse's coat.

Jhared groaned inwardly. Needling the new man was a game with which he was familiar. He shrugged. "Of course. The deadly work is what we're here for. How else should we repay the debt?"

"Repay the…?" The soldier looked confused a moment, then laughed. "Ah. I see now. We got ourselves one'a the bright-burning here, Hendren. Another Micah in the making."

Hendren. That was the other's name. He lifted his dark head to peer at Jhared with detached interest. Dawn caught a glimmer from the silver loop in his left ear. One hand smoothed the beard neatly confined to his chin.

"Perhaps, Jech," he said with the Clan Manitar precision that was closer to city Velos than clanstongue. "But I don't think so. The lieutenant knows us well enough not to pick a Micah for work like this."

Now the game had turned strange. Jhared felt as out of his depth standing among other Shorn men as he had felt standing before his commanding officers. A glance over his shoulder found Micah restively pacing the meadow. The man never flinched from hard work; he always sought the greatest challenges on the practice grounds; and he was a messenger of death with a sword in his hand.

"Why shouldn't Micah be chosen?" he asked. "I'd be glad for half his skill."

"Wish instead for twice his sense," Hendren replied. "There's a difference between bravery and recklessness, and Micah doesn't know it."

"Micah's one'a the bright-burning," Jech said, flicking another burr to the ground. "He's got something to prove, maybe to himself or maybe to Avelos.

Don't matter which—he won't be satisfied 'til he's found a way to get himself killed. That man should'a gone to Cael's Escape at his Becoming. Now he's searching for it every day."

Jhared stared at the ill-sworn Shorn soldier. "Micah serves with all that he is, as we all must."

"Slow down, Jech. You're going too fast for the boy." Hendren turned a grin on Jhared. "Jech can't help his Delsio bluntness. He's not speaking against what we've all sworn. What he means is that Micah might throw himself into his duty like a moth into a flame, but that won't make his service more worthy than any of the rest of ours. And it won't change things that can't be changed. Unless I miss my guess, though, you're no Micah. You have reasons to come back from this mission, eh?"

Jhared thought of Branlen and home. Then he thought of Zia and heat rushed to his face. "My duties don't end until I make the final reparation."

Hendren's green eyes twinkled as if he knew something of what Jhared didn't say. Jech's laughter scratched the air.

"Final reparation! Oh, that's dear. Not a woman who wants him. Not even an old mother to care for. We've got ourselves the Hero of Avelos. Goddess save us from the bright-burning!"

Jhared straightened, stunned and aggravated by such apathy. "If your blood is so thin you can't meet your responsibilities to your high chieftain and your country, surrender your place on this mission to someone with the courage for it!"

The words hung in the air as Jhared stepped back, his limbs loose and ready, aware he had just begged for a fight. No Shorn man could let that insult stand.

Jech only chuckled. "Oh, don't fret, eager one. I'll try to make these old bones keep up with you. We all do what we must, now, don't we?"

Amusement bloomed in Hendren's expression, but it vanished as he came abruptly to his feet. Jech pulled to attention as well. Jhared was the last to turn to salute Lieutenant Sevar and Captain Riselvo.

"Mount up," Sevar ordered. "And keep a tight rein. We're heading back to the ridge."

It was all the explanation they were given. Riselvo and Sevar led them out of the meadow and back up the hillside. Although the sun lay well above the horizon now, the day still struggled to announce itself. Behind Jhared, clear sky shepherded benign puffs of white and sunlight washed the shadows off the road, but ahead of him a massive cloud churned like molten steel, throwing darkness across the landscape. Brio pinned his ears back and tossed his head. From the other side of the hill, the storm snarled promises of bloodshed.

By the time they reached the crest of the ridge, the terrifying clamor made the horses wild-eyed. Captain Riselvo's mount danced sideways, and Jech turned his grey in tight circles to keep it from bolting. Jhared stared at the assault on the valley below. Trees cowered against the storm. Leaves and loose branches rushed along violent currents. All manner of creatures fled from the attack: deer, cabrin, a great black hill cat, rodents of every sort. They scurried up the hillside or followed the river toward the valley's edge, like creatures fleeing a fire. Jhared thought he saw the hulking form of one of Riana's Trevaye, but the wolfish creature disappeared into the haze of blowing debris before he could be certain.

Lieutenant Sevar dismounted, took from his saddlebag the items Jhared had packed for him in Ravia, then handed his reins to the captain.

"You'd best be certain you have enough left in you for this, Lieutenant," muttered Riselvo. "Rumar won't thank me if I lose you and the general both."

"I know what it's going to take," the lieutenant answered. He added dryly, "You needn't worry. If I end here, Rumar will appreciate the symmetry of it."

Sevar handed Jhared and each of the others a set of leather gloves and a square of rough-woven cloth.

"The general and our levies are trapped in a cavern along the bluff on the other side of the vale. We're to find them and carry out who we can." Sevar uncoiled a length of rope and flipped it in front of Jhared, Jech, and Hendren.

"Inside the storm, we'll not be able to hear each other and sight will be near to none. Hold onto the rope to stay together, and keep your mouth shut or you'll be trying to breathe through a throatful of dirt. You'll keep up with me—"

A harsh shriek cut him off. Jhared looked up. Two enormous grey condors drifted circles over the ridge. Their powerful wings spread wider than the height of a grown Shorn man. Jhared shuddered. They were Kilael, some of Cael's Chosen: soldier-spirits who had fought Riana in the Great Wars. They soared too high to be a danger now, but Jhared sensed their malevolence.

"Soul eaters!" spat the captain. "Looking to take what's not theirs, just like all their cursed kind."

The lieutenant pulled on his gloves and tied the cloth over his nose and mouth. He didn't glance at the raptors or the captain. Instead, he set his keen grey eyes on each of the soldiers in front of him. Jhared found himself nodding in response to the man's unvoiced question: *Do you remember all you owe?*

They left Captain Riselvo with the horses and ran down the ridge toward the valley. The lieutenant led, Jech followed, then Hendren. Jhared brought up the rear, the rope looped loosely in his gloved left hand.

Unlike any natural storm, this one did not weaken at its borders; it made a knife-cut boundary at the edges of the valley. Above the boundary, where Jhared ran with the others, the land held its breath in fearful stillness. The lieutenant shunned the switchbacks that wound gradually toward the vale floor; instead, he led the group directly down the slope, hardly slowing on the steep, slippery terrain.

They half ran, half stumbled toward the storm at the bottom of the ridge. As the winds rose before him, Jhared threw his weight backwards to keep from running into Hendren. Sevar flung his arms wide to stop them all from careening across the storm's boundary head-first.

Jech regained his balance most quickly and backed up several hasty steps. Jhared stood with the others as the winds raged before them without reaching them, like a mad dog on a short lead. The storm's roar ground against Jhared's skull and gusted into glass-splintering howls, but not a breeze passed his face. Why didn't it touch them? Sevar said it had pursued the general's patrol. Why did it hold now? *Riana's Paths twist for a reason.* Jhared gave a short, crazy laugh none of the others could hear. He was about to step onto a path where he wasn't certain Riana walked at all.

Sevar raised a hand and counted down the seconds for them to gather themselves. Jhared took the moment to ease his inner hold and let a little of the potent poison that was Shorn energy trickle into his veins—just enough to strengthen him for the task ahead. The controlled release made his tired muscles hum again.

The lieutenant crossed the boundary first, followed by the others one by one. Jhared gritted his teeth and pushed into the storm; it was like forcing his hand into a flame, and he fought every sensible impulse to recoil. The wind ripped his breath away and drove him sideways. Before him, Hendren staggered. Jhared grabbed the other man's arm, and for a moment their gazes locked. The sharp resolve in the older soldier's eyes surprised Jhared. He hoped his expression reflected as much. Hendren gave him a nod that might have been encouragement, then a tug on the rope insisted they plow onward.

They dragged themselves across the valley, step by agonized step. Jhared saw nothing, heard nothing, felt nothing but the wind and its violence. Despite the filter of cloth across his face, every breath drew dust into his lungs. Flying debris battered him. His skin prickled and burned.

When they reached the river, the winds funneled through the narrow gap in the hills to tear through the valley's heart. On bright spring days, the Jewel River sparkled, the blue-green beauty of the south. Now it churned into brown rapids and shunted branches along a dangerous current. No choice existed but to cross it. As Jhared entered the water with the others, the current grabbed hungrily at his legs. His boots slid uncertainly over mossy rocks. Water sprayed off the surface, soaking him through. Soon the group straggled out the full length of the rope; Lieutenant Sevar became a dark figure halfway to the opposite bank, nearly lost to sight.

Jhared reeled backwards as the branch of a tree passed under the rope between him and Hendren. The body of a deer spun along the current, nose pointed skyward. She snagged on a rock near the shore, exposing one shredded flank. Jhared's heart turned over. What was this force that could tear flesh?

He spied the big log only because his eyes lingered on the doe. It bobbed near the bank, trapped for a moment behind a rock, then abruptly popped free and shot toward the middle of the river and the men in front of him. He shouted, but the storm swallowed his words. In a terrible flash, he imagined just how the log would ram into his comrades, snapping bones and crushing skulls. He braced himself and gripped the rope in both hands. Strength flooded his limbs as he yanked backwards, putting all his will into it. The rope snapped taut. Hendren and Jech swayed and fell, disappearing under the surface as the log leaped past. The lieutenant, scrambling to stay upright, released the rope.

The sudden loss of resistance threw Jhared off his feet. He splashed backwards and the river rolled him under, filling his mouth and nose. Below the surface, the water cut the storm's howling to a muffled moan and stopped the knives against his flesh. For the space of a heartbeat, Jhared considered the possibility of peace. Then his feet struck the riverbed, and he kicked for the surface. He rose, spitting out muddy water and gulping the polluted air.

He swam after Hendren, and they clambered unsteadily onto land. Jech and the lieutenant were indistinct forms near the bank downstream. Hendren bent forward, hands on his knees, blowing hard. He glanced sideways at Jhared and touched two fingers to his brow in acknowledgment.

Lieutenant Sevar didn't let them pause as they neared the bluff. Even when they stumbled over the first bodies, Sevar didn't stop. The two boys—they had been boys last night, Jhared told himself—were now no more than blood and bone. The winds had sliced their skin and flesh and carved their very identities from them. Nausea surged in Jhared's innards. He took a breath. These two he could not save, but the others were waiting.

Others were waiting. *Goddess, let it be so.* He glanced at the lieutenant. Sevar's sword-straight back was retreating up the hill.

Jhared no longer knew the direction he moved, but followed the tug of the rope, setting one foot blindly in front of the other. Wasn't that the way of Riana's Paths, after all? A man stumbled along, blind to what was ahead, and hoped the tugs he followed led him aright. Some chunk of debris struck him in the side of the head, driving him toward the ground. When he straightened, the hand he set to his temple came back bloody. It probably should have hurt. His body couldn't acknowledge any new sensation.

The wind halted him entirely at the unprotected crown of a low rise. He hunched his shoulders, lowered his head, and dug into the slope with his boots. No good. The rope demanded movement from him, but he might as well have been pushing against a mountain. He sent another stream of energy into his veins, then dug in again, shoving against the wind's resistance until his lungs screamed and sparks danced across his vision. Something popped in his ears. Abruptly, the force dissipated to nothing, and he crashed to the ground. Everything around him went deathly still. It took several moments to understand that he had crossed the storm's far boundary.

He was out.

On hands and knees, he sucked in clean air greedily. Beside him, Jech retched out a lungful of dirt. Hendren held himself upright against the skeletal branches of a broken tree.

When Jhared could manage a clear breath, he pulled himself slowly to his feet and looked around. They stood on the flank of a low ridge that snaked along the western edge of the valley. It was—had been—a forest. Now it was the site of a giant pyre. Felled trees cluttered the ground. Branches twisted this way and that. A human arm stuck out from the pile.

The body was lodged into the hollow left by a tree torn whole from the ground. One arm clung to a thick root as though it could anchor its owner to life. Nearby lay a fallen horse. Jhared scrambled over the logs and wriggled into the hollow to stretch a hand to the boy's throat. Only cold met his searching fingers.

"Riana light your way—"

A hand grasped his shoulder, dragging him roughly out of the hollow. Sevar glowered at him. Blood ran from day-old wounds and all the new gashes across the lieutenant's face.

"No time to waste with the dead," Sevar shouted over the roar. "Get moving."

The wind's keening faded by the time they reached the rise, but Jhared's ears rang so loudly he could hardly hear the lieutenant shouting orders as they hurried to a wide-mouthed cave at the valley's south end. The cavern was large enough for all four of them to stand together in its belly. Except for scattered leaves and one torn Forest Guard cloak, it was empty.

"They're all out there," the lieutenant growled. "The general decided the cave didn't gain them time enough and sent the boys in different directions to try to keep the winds from pursuing them all. It was our last option. Some would have made it."

Sevar turned, staring at the destruction beyond the lip of rock. "Some *must* have made it. Spread out. We'll find them."

The bluff rose no more than forty feet at its highest, but it stretched across half the valley, and crevices and caverns honeycombed its length. A row of snapped pine trunks lined the top of the bluff like broken teeth. Forest debris cluttered the meadow beneath. Hendren headed for the clearing; Jech jogged ahead to search the north end of the bluff. Jhared stuck close to the rocks and hunted through the caves. An injured man might have clung to the hope of that poor shelter rather than give himself up to death in the storm.

An eerie silence pressed upon the land as the winds died away. No insect or rodent chatter filled the air; no foraging cabrin or deer stirred the trees. Jhared spent the afternoon hunting for some sign of men—tracks, spoor, blood. General

Nadel was the one who had taught him how to read the wilds, to expand his awareness until he noticed every place where the patterns were disrupted and to question the disruptions to decipher their meanings. What passing creature bent the leaves of the underbrush? How long ago had the grass been trampled? Was it man or beast that caused alarm within the forest? In the wake of the winds, no patterns remained to be questioned. Order was destroyed. Jhared felt like one of Cael's soul gatherers, moving emotionless and empty over a violated land.

He found another body outside a cave. This boy had died under the weight of a tree. His features were sufficiently intact for Jhared to see the blue tattoo on his left cheek: a smaller, less intricate blessing than Jase's. Like the others, this one was thirteen or maybe fourteen winters, part of a clan's annual levy to the Forest Guard. General Nadel liked to spend time testing the new ones himself when he could. The boy's tattoo suggested this group had come from Clan Nadaren. Today Riana's blessings had brought them no luck.

Jhared straightened and stumbled past the corpse. The cave entrance was an elongated triangle formed from two slabs of rock that leaned against one another like drunken soldiers. He kicked away the debris that had drifted across the opening and stepped inside. Weak fingers of daylight crept into the first few feet of the cavern, then died. He shivered in the gloom, breathing in the scent of mold and decay, and remembered another cave: the warm temple grotto that vibrated with Riana's power, a power that ordered the spheres and fostered life. This place was its antithesis.

Farther into the darkness, someone groaned.

Jhared made his way deeper inside, hunching when the ceiling pressed down on him. As his eyes adjusted to the dark, he saw a body stretched out on the floor, swaddled in a cloak. The cloak's hood covered the face like a death mask. Jhared knelt and drew back the hood. As he slid a hand over the boy's smooth brow, warmth met his touch; a pulse beat evenly and fast. He lifted the cloak to assess the boy's injuries.

His face was bruised, but intact. The most gruesome injury was the twist in his right leg below the knee. Jhared winced. The boy's leg might have twisted in the stirrup as his horse panicked and threw him, or perhaps the winds had shoved him down a hill. Whatever happened, it would have been impossible for the boy to flee with the others. Jhared covered him again gently. As his fingers slid over the edge of the cloak, Jhared felt the familiar double-rowed border in the wool. The colors of the border would be yellow and red. This boy was Shorn.

"Demon."

The voice resonated through the cavern like a warning. Jhared snapped his gaze upward, half-expecting to find the figure of Cael lurking over him. Instead, in the farthest reach of the cavern, he made out another body, broad-shouldered and fair-haired, slumped against the wall.

"General Nadel." Jhared's voice broke on the name of the man to whom he owed so much. He crept to the general's side. He smelled blood. Even in the dim light he could see the ruin of the man's face. Leather, cloth, and flesh alike had been torn open. Across the cavern, Nadel's sword lay glinting in the darkness, but the general still grasped his dagger. In the other hand he clutched—

Jhared sat back, staring in disbelief. He shook his head. After all the day's atrocities, why should this one be so unimaginable? He forced himself to look again.

The feather was long and unflawed, a primary feather from a condor. In the half-light, he couldn't tell the feather's color for certain, but he knew the curse. It must be a feather of the Kilael. It would be grey.

General Nadel's right hand came up fast under Jhared's chin. The point of the dagger pressed against his throat and cut the skin.

"Demon!" the general gasped once more, brandishing the feather. "You cannot have this soul. I am not…finished with this path yet."

Jhared's heart pounded energy through his limbs. A droplet of his blood fell onto the cave floor. He held perfectly still.

"General Nadel," he breathed. "It's the Forest Guard Fourth. We've come to move you out."

"Cael's messenger!" the man insisted, holding the knife firm. "Keep your talons off my men. We will…we will not yield."

"You're safe, sir. The lieutenant won through. Your men…We've found your men. The messenger is gone."

Nadel's glazed stare speared Jhared accusingly. His body stiffened; his eyes rolled back and his hand fell away. For a terrible moment, Jhared thought the man was dead. Then a shallow, wheezing breath shook his ravaged frame.

"He stayed behind."

Jhared startled, stood too quickly and knocked his head against the low rock. "Yes, Lieutenant. It's the general."

Sevar moved easily through the dark cavern; he'd been standing there long enough for his vision to adjust. He had seen the knife. The lieutenant bent first over the boy, then came to crouch beside the general. Gently, he pried the dagger from Nadel's fist.

"For a single Shorn levy not even past his Becoming, the General of the Southern Towers of Avelos stayed behind."

Jhared didn't know what to say to the disturbing imbalance of that sacrifice. He rubbed a hand over his face. "Sir. A foreigner's been here. Someone who came after the winds left. The boy was wrapped as for the pyre. And the general, he has…"

"The grey feather?"

Jhared stifled a shudder. "Yes, sir."

"And you think that's a curse no Avelonian would lay on his own countryman?"

Sevar's eyes glinted in the gloom. The grey feather was the cruelest curse one man could lay on another, a curse that reached beyond death.

"A man as powerful as General Nadel must stir anger in some," Jhared said, "countryman or no."

Sevar gave a hoarse laugh. "Here we are covered in blood and picking up the broken pieces of our own boys and you're still speaking like an elder, with cautious words that answer nothing."

"Forgive me my caution, sir. I just mean to say that we know foreigners were near before the winds struck. You and the general chased raiders to the river."

Sevar used the general's knife to saw at the edge of his own tunic. He ripped a long strip of fabric from the hem and began to wrap Nadel's bleeding hands. "And you can be sure we'll hunt them," he said, his voice a stream of ice. "But there are others to consider as well. You have Sahiste on your mind just as surely as I. And you'd best not forget that not all threats to the country exist outside our borders. We are Forest Guard; we scout the shadows and protect Avelos from any who would defile her."

Jhared stared at Sevar in surprise. What other soldier knew Anarava's unlikely call to the guards of Avelos? "Eye of the Watcher, survey well the threats from foreign soil, then turn inward and scout the shadows of your heart lest you defile your own charge," he murmured.

"Mmm. Not only do you answer questions like an elder," Sevar said derisively, "you quote the histories like Trianor himself." He bound off the cloth at Nadel's wrists and stood. "Don't play the scholar with me. I know your kind better than you think. Evasiveness and cleverness might serve the elders, but they're a dangerous pair in the Shorn. Oath breakers are pushed off the wall in Ravia, just as they are in the city, Patrolman."

A sick feeling rolled in Jhared's middle. He felt suddenly, desperately tired. "Forgive me, sir. I am sworn."

"Yes. You are. That should be reminder enough that the shadows of the heart you must scout are your own."

Lieutenant Sevar strode out of the cave, bellowing for Jech and Hendren to come to help move the wounded, leaving Jhared blinking and dazed.

They used the rope and broken branches to fashion a litter for the unconscious survivors. Four men of twenty still clung to life. Jech had found two levies wandering delirious on the other side of the bluff, boys as towheaded as children and alike as twins. They had been lucky enough to retreat in the direction that offered the shortest route out of the winds. The others had not been so fortunate. Their bodies were so badly mauled that Jhared didn't know how anyone could determine their identity. One man was still missing.

The return across the valley took all Jhared's focus. Only his rasping breath and the panting of the others punctured the heavy silence. When fallen trees and undergrowth blocked their path, they wrestled the crude litter over. When that proved impossible, one of the group trudged ahead to find a pass before coming back for the rest. The angry river proved the worst of it. Sevar ordered them to stop while Jech ran east to find the safest place to cross. Even so, the trek was harrowing. Hendren and Sevar took the front of the litter and Jhared the back. Every moment, the current threatened to grab the litter and capsize it.

They slipped and staggered through the water, rested briefly, and continued on. The afternoon's deadly clouds thinned into gossamer wisps, as though they were only ever harmless vapors, leaving behind a velvet night. Jhared bounced the unconscious men as little as possible, sliding his hands up the poles in hopes of a better grasp. It helped only for a moment, until his sweating palms slipped again. He clenched his jaw and squeezed more tightly. Fatigue clutched at his limbs. Defiantly, he drew up his foot and took another step, then another. In Sahiste, he had held back from doing all he should, and his Teachers named him a coward. This time he held nothing back. He fed his body on determination. A branch snagged his shoulder. He stumbled, ripped free, and tightened his grip on the litter once more. He would *not* drop this burden.

The song started in his head as a way to distance himself from the pain: "Lament for Altan Mar." Until Zia sent him the neglected verses, he had not remembered it. The song revealed Alende Isan, not as the confident leader, but as a man undone and uncertain, running from the destruction of his home and grieving his own frailty. Jhared discovered an unlooked-for mix of comfort and despair in the hero's doubt. It gave him a place to loose all his own fears. By the time the camp's perimeter guard cried out and jolted him from his meditation, Jhared had broken past the wall of exhaustion.

"Halloo to the scouts!" called an eager voice. Then from another direction: "Ho! The lieutenant returns! Send for Healer Falto!"

Voices rose quickly among the trees. Soon, torches cut the darkness and men outlined in yellow light hurried to meet the group. Soldiers crowded around the litter, desperate for news. There were others, too: strangers who moved awkwardly among the company. As the soldiers and the strangers laid eyes on the bloody body of General Nadel and the tattered, swaying figures of the levies, their expressions turned to shock and dismay. More than one hand shaped Riana's spiral.

"By stars and spheres! Fall away!" snapped a raw voice at the edge of the crowd. "The injured need care. Fall back or I'll have each one of you lashed!"

Healer Falto, a short man in his late years, with sparse white hair and a beak of a nose, shoved his way through the gathering. He clucked at his assistants, well-muscled Forest Guard both of them, and they prodded the others to clear a wider path. Ahead, four fires illuminated the camp. The largest crackled in front of the healer's tent. Falto signaled to the lieutenant, and the weary group followed the healer. The rest trailed after them, muttering.

"Here. Lay the litter here," Falto ordered once Jhared and the others had ducked into the tent. Then to one of his assistants: "Run for the captain."

Jhared laid his end of the litter gently on the ground. He stood, flexing his cramped fingers. The other assistant helped the unsteady levies to lower themselves onto the pallets arranged for them. Lamplight flickered over their bloody forms.

"I'm here. What news?" Riselvo pushed the flap aside and strode into the circle. Jhared shifted his weight from one foot to the other, uncomfortable standing still. As he saluted the captain, he thought the man moved strangely. Too slowly for the urgent need.

"Tell us where to find the others," Riselvo demanded of Sevar. "Churion's men are ready to ride. They will..." The captain's gaze dropped to the unconscious forms at the feet of the healer, and he faltered. "Riana save us. General Nadel?"

"Yes, sir," Sevar said, his face a mask of stone beneath the blood.

"Goddess, I hardly know him. The other?"

"A Shorn levy named Alevir."

Riselvo nodded, taking in the other two injured levies as well. He glanced up at Sevar, his jaw tightening. "They're the only ones?"

"Yes."

"And the storm?"

"Gone. As far as we could see."

"Very well, then. I'll send a patrol in for the bodies." Riselvo paused, clearing his throat hard. "All right, all of you. Have your injuries tended—"

"You'll want my report, Captain. And that of the levies." Sevar stood yet at rigid attention.

"Afterwards, Lieutenant," Riselvo repeated gruffly. He gazed at General Nadel and wiped a hand over his mouth. "Falto, you know who it is you treat and his importance."

"Of course. We'll use what gifts Riana's given us." Jhared saw determination but little hope in the healer.

As Riselvo departed, Falto took one look at Sevar and pointed him to a pallet. When the lieutenant demurred, the man reminded him bluntly who wielded the authority in a healer's tent. The assistants examined Jech, Hendren, and Jhared, proclaimed them in need of rest, and sent them on their way.

Jhared hunched with the others around the fire in front of the tent.

"Well, boys, a sorry day's work this has been," Jech said. "But here we all stand still able to tell the tale. I'm for a drink. Are you with me?"

Hendren stared glassy-eyed at the flames. He looked as hollow as Jhared felt. "Delsio, are you made from stone? I'm done."

"What about you, eager one?" Jech smirked at Jhared. "Not burning quite as brightly as you were this morning, eh?"

"Eee, Goddess," Hendren hissed. "Don't be a bastard after all we faced. Leave the boy alone and come along. The commander will want to hear from us before you start your drinking."

Jech chuckled and looked unrepentant, but he turned to follow Hendren.

"Go sleep," Hendren suggested to Jhared as they wandered off. "Try not to think too much. It won't change anything."

Jhared couldn't have followed either of those suggestions had he wanted to. The need to act buzzed beneath his skin. When Jech and Hendren disappeared, he poked his head back into the tent and offered his service to the healer.

"I've seen too much death today," he said to Ino, the larger of the two assistants. "Please let me help to save someone from Cael. Let me help the general."

"Are you unbalanced?" Ino snapped, scowling. "Shorn soldiers don't serve as healers. Do you mean to break Shorn Law?"

That interpretation caused Jhared to withdraw hastily. There were always tasks to be done around camp. He would present himself to Commander Carn.

The camp was unsettled. Soldiers sat around the fires, talking moodily about the loss of the levies and the hope for General Nadel's survival. They might have welcomed Jhared into their circle for the news he carried, but he didn't want to sit. Carn was deep in conference with Captain Riselvo and the other patrol commanders, along with the villagers Jhared saw earlier. The villagers looked angry and fearful. Jhared didn't dare interrupt, although for a wild moment he considered it, circling wide of the group several times before finally veering back to the other side of camp.

Away from the fires, the noises faded and the darkness weighed more heavily. In the woods, a wild dog whined. The horses nickered and shifted on their pickets. Jhared hurried down the line to Brio, to find the bay well-fed and drowsing. Jhared said good night to the horse and moved on. He couldn't bear to be still. His muscles hummed.

"Halt! No soldier…is permitted…to cross."

Jhared peered into the trees, surprised to find himself at the edge of camp so quickly. He recognized the voice, but Anzo spoke with painful hesitation, as though he had not the strength to maintain a full sentence.

"Anzo, what's wrong? Are you injured? Why have they abandoned you to the watch? Where's the rest of the patrol?"

"Ah. Jhared." The stocky little patrolman separated himself from a tree and ambled forward. "I'm well…enough. Given today's horrors. You need something?"

The starlight was unkind. It painted the old man all in grey and made black caverns of his eyes. He looked worn past his years. Jhared paced a circle around the veteran, as though to appraise him for injury, but mostly he didn't want to stop moving.

"Yes, I need something. I need something *to do*. No one will have me. It was a terror, Anzo. I've never seen a thing of such unthinking evil. Our men were torn apart. Savaged. All of them. They died without even seeing the faces of their slayers. Or perhaps that's untrue. There was a feather. A grey curse. General Nadel called...General Nadel spoke of a demon."

Anzo made a sound in his throat. "It's over, boy. For now. Go back to our fire. Find Twitch. Or Esran. They will share a flask. Keep the vigil with them. Tomorrow. Tomorrow there will be pyres."

Jhared strode around Anzo one time and then again. "How can I be still when this kind of violence is loose? I saw it, Anzo. I saw the birth of evil in a tent in Sahiste. The boar and the serpent and a hawk to condemn them all. No, I won't be idle again. It's not enough to read the histories. *Sinta def volten fal em revlur.* Silence in the presence of ill-will is complicity. And inaction in the face of malevolence is a form of treachery. I should have seen it before. It's not a mistake I'll make again."

"Treachery? What's got into you, eh? You don't ever speak so many words in a week."

Jhared didn't realize how fast he was moving until Anzo stepped in his way and he nearly ran over the little patrolman. He offered a distracted apology and spun back in the other direction.

"Whoa. Whoa!" Anzo called. "Come back here." The Everen clansman moved more quickly. He grimaced as he caught up to Jhared, and bounced two steps backwards as though he'd hit a wall.

"Cael's chaos! So that's what this is about. Who said it was all right for you to be wandering around?"

"Wandering? I'm trying to make myself of use. Healer Falto sent me away. Commander's with Captain Riselvo. Lieutenant Sevar—"

"Never mind," Anzo said roughly. "You come with me. There's someone who needs to see you."

Jhared didn't know what he had done to make Anzo so angry. Whatever it was, he added it to the growing list of errors he had made in the last three days. He followed Anzo, trying without success to keep from treading on the slow soldier's heels. They stopped before the fire in front of the healer's tent. Anzo called to the men inside.

"Why didn't you tell me you were hurt?" Jhared hissed. "I knew there was something wrong—"

Falto himself came out of the tent, wiping his hands on a rag that was too bloody to make a difference. He frowned at Anzo. "You've been injured?"

"Not me." Anzo jerked his chin over his shoulder at Jhared. "There."

The healer looked up wearily at Jhared. "I've seen him. He's healthy enough. Shorn men are hardy as goats. I'm not treating bumps and scrapes here tonight. Good men are dying. Go back to your duties."

"You know your work, sir," Anzo continued without budging, "but the boy carried our general out of the darkness and I think maybe he's feeling the weight of it now. Perhaps you could take another look at him, eh?"

Jhared shook his head in confusion. "What are you talking about, Anzo? I'm well. I'm better than I deserve to be. I don't even hurt anymore." He glanced down at the healer. He didn't want to stand and talk; he needed to run. "Forgive me, sir. I need no care. But please tell me how the general fares. Will he survive? Has he spoken? I remember when I was a trainee in his charge. We fought Laebeki raiders. I won't forget it, or the veils the general lifted from my sight. Will the levies be all right? Riana save us all from this terror. I saw the birth of it. Did they tell you I saw it?"

"Ah. I see." The healer sighed. "Come here, Patrolman."

"Sir. Anzo. This is absurd. Soldiers are dying." Jhared backed a step, then two, as the healer stepped forward with the same dream-slowness as Anzo.

"No. Don't go. Sit." The man came at him from across the fire. Anzo stepped behind him.

"Do as he says, boy."

Jhared startled as Anzo gripped his shoulders. Forced to be still, his muscles vibrated like plucked cords. He gasped a breath and shuddered with the overwhelming sensations. It took all his effort not to tear free. He didn't want to injure the man who held him, but he needed to move. His body trembled with energy he needed to spend. Anzo pushed him down beside the fire.

The healer crouched in front of him. "He's burning like an ember, sure enough. Damn Shorn fire blazing in there. When was the last time you ate or slept, Patrolman?"

Food? Jhared considered it. It hadn't been so long. A day? Two? And sleep was entirely unnecessary. He supposed he would never need to sleep again! The realization was freeing: never would he face another nightmare. Something rumbled on around him, but he soared above it. Nothing had ever felt this good. It was a gift from Riana. Impossible lightness. With a laugh, he raised his eyes to the sky, content to lose himself among the stars.

"What happened? Can he hear us?"

"I think so. But not for much longer if he doesn't come down."

He did hear, but the words rolled from their mouths so slowly that they made an annoying growl in his ear, like someone speaking underwater. He couldn't figure out why they pestered him so. He glowed with strength.

"There's nothing wrong. Truly, I'm well. I just need some way to help. Tell me what I can do. I could go back to retrieve the others—"

"Patrolman, *attention!*"

"Sir! Yes, sir!" Jhared leaped to his feet, unable to do anything but obey.

"Enough of this!" The healer rose into Jhared's face, his words falling together almost like normal. "You've allowed your Shorn body to respond freely to the intensity of what you've been through. You've reached too deeply for the energy available to you, and now your body needs help to cool before your heart gives out. It's Shorn battle sickness. You should know better. Where's your control?"

Battle sickness? The words seemed familiar, an old lesson, but thinking on it was a tedious thing. He was airborne.

"Listen to me: take one slow, deep breath. Right now. That's an order."

Jhared complied, or tried to. He had never realized that breathing deeply could be a chore. Once he pulled his attention inward, he realized how hard he was panting, as though he'd just finished a mountain run. His heart raced so fast he couldn't separate the beats to count them.

"Deeper," the healer demanded, "deeper than that. Now hold it. Hold. And slowly let it out. Slowly, I said! I know it feels good where you are, but you will soon be very ill if you stay up there."

Jhared reached reluctantly for the centering breaths that General Nadel had taught him. He didn't want to give up this weightlessness. Desire raced through his veins, making the sky a possibility. But desire was a dangerous thing, and he had been ordered. He took another breath. As his heart surrendered its frantic pace, he plummeted toward the ground. Instinctively, he struggled against it.

"Slow!" the healer insisted heartlessly.

The descent was agony, but at last the world crashed back to its proper speed. Jhared collapsed like a discarded puppet, his limbs twitching and shaking as he sprawled in the dirt. In that empty, earthbound place, his Teachers waited for him. Their angry voices cut through his thoughts and trampled his memories. He wished only to curl up and ignore all the reprimands, the ones inside his head and outside, but he had earned them. He dragged himself into a sitting position, shivering violently as the mild breeze of the midsummer night rushed like ice across his overheated, sweat-soaked skin.

"There. He's back," muttered the healer. "Make him eat something and drink only water. He'll regret this tomorrow. And well he should. I haven't seen such a disgrace in years." Falto picked his way toward the tent. "I've other soldiers to tend to now. Ones who didn't bring their illness upon themselves."

The healer's departure left an awkward silence around the fire. Anzo slipped off, only to return a few moments later with a blanket that he tucked around Jhared's shoulders.

Jhared wanted nothing more than to fall off the Paths and vanish.

"I'm back to my watch," Anzo said finally. "See that you do as you've been ordered." He didn't speak of his anger or Jhared's shame before he turned away. He didn't need to.

Jhared wrapped the blanket tightly around him and lay down close to the fire. He meant only to rest a short time before finding something to eat, but sleep snatched him as soon as he closed his eyes.

His nightmares came quickly and stayed long. They seethed with all the raw emotion of the day. At the last, he met the demon: Cael, with his avian head and human skull. The demon flew into his face screaming questions he couldn't answer, and tore him apart with the invisible force of a killing wind.

12.
CONSEQUENCES

"No."

The brittle paper crackled and broke like dead leaves in Jhared's fist. He opened his fingers and watched as the fragments scattered across the dirt in one of the little sheds behind the stables, where he had gone for the small measure of privacy it offered. As he crouched over a crate that he'd turned into his desk, the flame on the stub of candle beside him trembled and threatened to die. Dawn wouldn't make her silent way to Ravia for another hour, and the rest of his patrol had gone to the mess or off to sleep after their night duty. A breeze sifted through the cracks in the timbers of the old shed, and the remainder of his words drifted away. Jech and Hendren had nearly been blown into oblivion by the killing winds as they struggled, battered and bleeding, across the valley together. Jhared scrubbed at his eyes, as though he could wipe the image away. He hadn't expected it to be so difficult to write this letter. He tried again; this time he composed in his head so as not to waste the precious paper.

Dear Minister Trianor,

It is true, as Azare wrote, that adversity acts as a sieve through which all men are sorted. During the horror of the recent attack on Lamirna, the types of Shorn soldiers who serve at Ravia came clear…

He let out an uneasy breath. This was what Tierzen needed from him, a report on the activities of the Shorn men of Ravia. He couldn't claim another Shorn soldier who was even willing to speak more than a few words with him. According to Sirol, they all despised him. So why did giving them up to the Minister of the Teaching feel like a betrayal?

He stared at the tiny candle as it guttered. Everything about Jech roused his ire: the man's air of laziness, his spiteful jests, and the way he treated his oath. Still, Jech had endured the winds with the rest of them; he had run the extra miles through the forest when they needed to find a pass, and he had helped to carry out the injured levies. What would happen to him if Jhared sent this letter to Tierzen? Would he be interrogated? Lashed? Would they find that the man had broken his oath and push him from the wall? Jhared's insides roiled when he thought about it. Unexpected power lay in the assignment the elder had given him. He didn't like it and didn't want it, but he wasn't free to give it up.

"Give it up?" snapped a Teacher within him. *"The elder needs your eyes and ears! Not your wavering and whining!"*

"Yet what I tell him must be balanced, not shaped by my own needs," Jhared argued. *"What if it's my dislike for Jech that influences my words? Then my report to Tierzen is no better than what the southern elders offer him. And worse, I'll have used the power he lent me for my own purpose."*

"You report," snorted his Teacher in disgust. *"The Minister will interpret. You're a scout, not a scholar of the histories. Stop acting as though you have the strength of spirit to contemplate these complexities."*

With a half-stifled growl of protest that earned him an internal sting from the Teachers, Jhared slapped the last piece of paper into the weak pool of light and dipped his pen to ink. The reed hovered above the blank cream.

"Write! All of it!"

He did finally—almost all of it. He reported the events of the past days as though he were standing before General Nadel, only stumbling when it came to the point of his battle fever. Tierzen hadn't asked for a report of his own behavior. Was it right to cause the elder needless worry over it? Jhared himself couldn't understand how things had gone so wrong when he had been focused solely on serving Avelos. In Sahiste, he had used the histories to inform his decisions, as Tierzen taught him, and yet his Teachers showed him how his flawed reasoning threatened the border. In Lamirna, during the killing storm, he had been determined to give all of himself to bring the general safely home, and somehow he had given too much: his Shorn energy had poisoned him. His best intentions and clearest actions led to ugly outcomes. He desperately wished to speak with Tierzen about all of it, but he knew that the Minister of the Teaching would expect him to figure this out for himself.

As Jhared debated, his little flame drowned and went out. His Teachers sat in silent judgment as he penned his name in the dark, dusted the ink, and carefully scrolled the paper.

"Done."

No one answered. Exhausted and feeling no sense of satisfaction, he rose stiffly and went to prepare for the day's duties.

In the weeks after the attack, Ravia thrummed like a beehive preparing to swarm. Couriers raced back and forth among the city, the towers, and the garrison at Barlona. Riselvo doubled the patrols on the Burn and near Lamirna, trying to watch both south and east at once. Commanders raised the tempo of drills until the sound of men driving each other to battle readiness could be heard at any hour of the day. The entire garrison moved with tense anticipation, not knowing when another attack might come, what form it would take, or where it would strike.

The villages along the Laebeki border caught the tension like a fever, and the fortress faced a stream of clan leaders demanding a stronger Forest Guard presence on their lands.

"Southerners," Esran hissed, stepping out of the drill line across from Jhared. An entourage of Clan Amerre elders was skirting the practice grounds on their way to Riselvo's tower. "Always complaining that we drain their resources. Jump you if they catch you alone, but now don't they come begging for our blades and our blood."

Twitch and Jase paused beside Jhared. "We could just give 'em back the fortress and see how well they like fighting Sahistens by themselves," Twitch said, twirling his blade in one hand.

"There's plenty t'take ya up on that," Jase replied. "And who's t'say the first-clans shouldn't still have the rule of the garrisons on their own lands?"

"You want to be clanguard 'stead of Forest Guard?" Twitch snarled. "Wield a rusted sword and fight without armor under some fool of a prefect? You're welcome to it."

Jhared lowered his sword to watch the procession of elders go by, glad for a break from parrying Esran's powerful blows. The grim-faced clan leaders strode by without so much as glancing at the soldiers.

"They resent it that they need us," he said. "They don't want to ask for help, but they fear what will happen if they don't. I don't envy the captain that meeting."

Esran spat into the dust. "If he says yes to any one of them, then every hamlet from here to Barlona will be after us to play their City Guard, but if he says no, then we're not meeting our duties. And be sure we'll hear about it from Velantar."

"Will the captain ask for reinforcements from the north?" Jhared asked.

"Well, he sure as Cael's hole can't keep us at this pace all summer."

Jhared wondered whether more drills, heavier border patrols, and northern reinforcements really mattered. If Sahiste and Laebek could truly attack with the killing winds, Ravia had no defense to offer but stone walls.

He didn't voice the thought. Most of the men seemed content to hone their battle skills in the field. Perhaps it allowed them to escape the sense of helplessness that still clawed over him, or maybe they didn't fully understand the threat. For most of the garrison—those who hadn't lived the terror—the survivors were the only evidence that the attack had ever happened, and few still lived who could tell the story. One of the young levies had died of fever soon after reaching Ravia. The other had joined the rest of the garrison's trainees, his towhead easily identifiable. The young Clan Nadaren man moved as though his injuries were healing, but he stared out of dead, empty eyes. Jhared hadn't seen Lieutenant Sevar. Rumor held he rode between Ravia and Barlona like a man possessed, trying to whip the permeable border watch into something solid. Of General Nadel, Jhared heard only that he still fought against the darkness.

If anyone could say for certain whether Sahiste or Laebek controlled the killing winds, it would be the general. He had battled someone in that cave, someone who had cursed him and left him to die, shrouded for eternity from Riana's eyes. It would take someone that cruel to wield a terror like the winds.

Despite all the uncertainty around Jhared, in most visible ways his life had changed very little since the storm. He patrolled the border villages at night, caught a few hours of sleep while the morning air was still cool, and drilled endlessly with his company in the dusty afternoons. The Shorn seemed as inclined to shun him as ever, and he hadn't yet found a way to break through their antipathy.

He trudged into the mess hall with the rest of his company as they came off the night watch. Tired, hungry soldiers jostled for a space at the sideboard. As Jhared edged his way toward the large kettle of oats at the fire, he spied Micah ahead of him. The lean warrior could catch the eye with his tall, striking presence, but something else drew Jhared's attention this morning. Cold anger radiated from the older Shorn man. It was there in the set of his shoulders and the stiffness of his expression, anger ready to be loosed. Jhared scanned the line of soldiers, seeking the target, but he was too late. Micah made a sudden motion with one hand. Someone gave a cry of pain and a bowl of oats splattered onto the floor, causing men to hoot and jeer. A young stable boy, one of the youth hired from Clan Amerre, clutched his scalded hand, his grey eyes wide. Micah glared down at him.

"Sorry," the Shorn man said with an unapologetic shrug.

"Not hardly," the boy answered. "Just clumsy."

"Clumsy. Is that what you called it when you pulled Marsa's girth over an open wound?"

Around them, a few men grumbled at the disturbance. Others simply moved to grab what food they wanted. Still others pushed for a better position from which to watch, hoping for a fight.

"She didn't have any wound when I saddled her," the boy said. "You must'a let the girth go loose. It rubbed."

"It was no rub. It was a gash. Made by something sharp."

"So take better care of your horse, blood-back. I'm a son of Clan Amerre. I don't answer to you."

The sudden emotion in Micah's green gaze caught Jhared off guard. Not anger this time; it was dark anticipation. Jhared had an instant to think of the town boy killed in a brawl and an executed Shorn soldier. Then Micah's fist flashed forward. Jhared moved faster. He grabbed the older man, twisted his arm, and swung him around.

"Micah, don't! Not this. Report him."

"Report him?" Micah's muscles contracted and loosed beneath Jhared's grip, and Jhared found himself thrown off. "Do you think the report of a Shorn man against a villager would mean anything?"

"Here in the barracks? Of course it would."

"You're a fool, Trianor's Folly." The anticipation in the older soldier's gaze didn't fade; it shifted onto Jhared, fortified with scorn.

Jhared grimaced. He never expected friendship from a man such as Micah, but he had hoped one day for respect. "I'm not going to fight you," he said, showing his open palms.

Micah rolled his shoulders as he began to move toward Jhared's right. "Because you don't have the stones for it?"

"Because I won't bring trouble to my patrol over a personal grudge."

The other Shorn man laughed caustically. "You are a pretty picture, aren't you? You might fool your commander and the lieutenant with that good-boy talk, but I know what it means."

Despite Jhared's intentions to remain unmoved, the heat started to rise in his veins. "And that is?"

"That you're afraid," Micah spat. "You're so afraid of doing the wrong thing that you do nothing. Nothing to teach a lesson to that boy who hates you. Nothing to prove yourself against me. And nothing to fulfill your oath."

Jhared gritted his teeth and tried not to think of venomous magic in a tent in Sahiste. "I know my duty, and fighting you isn't going to prove it. Leave the boy alone. Catch yourself a smuggler if you've an itch to spill blood."

Without warning, Micah threw a punch from the left. Jhared twisted sharply, and the blow slammed only the air in front of his face. He backed toward the wall, crouched, fists up. The room swung beneath him. Men's jeering rang in his ears.

"*Don't you* dare *release that anger!*" a Teacher ordered. "*Step back! You're at the edge of a precipice.*"

"What you know is how to stay out of trouble," Micah returned. "The officers turn to you and see devotion when what they're looking at is cowardice."

"I won't fight you," Jhared repeated, "not here. If you think I lack the strength to prove myself, find me at drills!" He wrenched himself away and stepped clear of the man, wondering if he should turn his back on Micah, wondering when he had become so monumentally foolish as to offer a challenge. With a sword in hand, Micah could likely take off his head without breaking a sweat.

With a snarl of disgust, Micah shoved his way down the line of tables and out of the mess hall. Another Shorn soldier, a veteran with a scar across his brow, rose and followed.

Jhared took a deep breath and let it out. He found the stable hand where the boy had sidled against the wall to avoid the two circling soldiers. "Are you all right?"

"Leave me be! I fight my own battles, blood-back. Keep your taint off Clan Amerre!"

The boy grabbed a bowl from the table and stomped off to join a table of grooms and other stable help, leaving Jhared standing alone.

The tables were crowded. With the chance for excitement past, most of the men went back to their food. From the back of the hall, Jase grinned at him beside Bevan and Grion, but Jhared wanted no part of the barbed comments that would come from that group. He surveyed the rest of the seats. Hendren was straddling a bench in the corner. He nodded when he saw Jhared glance in his direction. Jhared hesitated, unsure of the welcome he would receive from a soldier who was a favorite among the Shorn, then decided he had better just sit and make himself less of a target.

"I'm not certain whether that was spectacularly brave or absurdly stupid," Hendren said, looking up from his meal. "You'd do well to stay out of Micah's way for a while. He grips onto a grudge like a wolverine."

Jhared dropped onto the bench and eyed the lithe patrolman warily. "It's fine. That wasn't about me."

"Ah, but it was. Micah wouldn't have touched the boy. Not much, anyway. It's you he'd like to pound."

Jhared reached across the table for a loaf of bread. Now that the potential for a brawl had passed, he remembered how famished he was.

"How do you figure that? I've not even spoken to the man before today."

"Didn't have to. He's slashed at you because you got something at Lamirna he desperately wanted, and you didn't use it."

"What I got at Lamirna was a body full of bruises and a formal reprimand."

"And the chance to die a hero's death."

Jhared glanced up sharply. "You meant what you said in the valley? That talk about the bright-burning, it wasn't just to…" He trailed off with a shrug.

"Just to mock you? No, it wasn't just." Hendren smiled, shoveled a bite of food into his mouth, chewed, and swallowed. "Poor Micah. Nothing in this life'll satisfy him."

The chance to die. Jhared expected his life would end on a battlefield or in the dark on the border, but he prayed that day would only come after he found the key to reparation. To *seek* death? Would such a thing be a fulfillment of the debt or an abandonment of it? Suddenly, Jhared wasn't sure whether Micah was the most dedicated Shorn man he knew or the most craven.

"And that's why he hates me?"

"Hates you? No. It's himself he can't live with." Hendren took another bite of oats and looked curiously at Jhared. "Jech was right; you really don't know anything about us, do you?"

By *us* Hendren meant the Shorn, but somehow Jhared didn't think he had been included in that group. "I don't know how Jech or any bound man can treat his duty like a bar jest," he growled. "If that's what you mean."

"All right, all right!" Hendren laughed and held up his hands in a gesture of surrender. "Don't name me with the Delsio. I didn't mean to light that fire."

Jhared frowned across the table. "I don't understand, Hendren. Is it that you don't believe in final reparation, or that you don't believe you could be the one to achieve it?"

The other soldier looked startled by the question. He stared speechlessly a moment before managing another mild laugh. "If there's any man who's going to finish repaying the debt, it's not going to be me."

"Is it going to be Micah?"

"You mean is dying a hero's death enough?" Hendren dropped his spoon into his empty bowl. "Lots of us have died for Avelos and the council hasn't declared reparation to be complete yet. I guess I see it this way: one man on his own can't get us out of something it took six priestesses and a Sahisten to get us into."

At Jhared's shocked expression, the Manitar clansman grinned. "Oh, come on, soldier, what do you earn by taking the world so seriously? No one's making final reparation today. Why don't you just satisfy a man's curiosity and tell me if I was right out there?"

"Right?"

"You know, about the woman. You hum love ballads when you come off patrol and the courier brings you letters that leave you far away on some other path. Either your Elder Trianor is writing to ask your opinion on the state of the southern border or there's a girl."

Jhared tore another piece from the bread, using it as an excuse to dodge Hendren's gaze, and tried to make his laughter sound genuine.

"That bad, is it?" The older patrolman nodded sympathetically. "Don't worry, we've all been there. Well, all but perhaps that Clan Nadaren rake in your patrol. Jase. To hear him tell it, no woman born can refuse him. Is she pretty?"

"I really don't..." Jhared sighed, then found himself grinning. "Yes. Yes, she is."

For the first time, he admitted Ziabela's existence to another person. He mentioned nothing about the connection he shared with her. That part of the story belonged only to him and Zia. Hendren listened with surprising attentiveness.

"Be careful," the neat-bearded soldier offered as they finished eating. "Musicians are like new-broke horses: not malicious creatures, but they'll toss you off and bruise you up without a thought."

Jhared assured Hendren that his musician was careful and kind, to which the dark patrolman only arched a brow and praised her rarity. Talking about Zia diluted some of the bitterness of Jhared's encounter with Micah. And Hendren's way of taking in the world with an unruffled shrug and a detached smile helped Jhared release some of his own tension. He was still grinning when he left the mess hall.

His smile faded when he spied Healer Falto shuffling hastily across the inner yard toward Captain Riselvo's tower. The old man's thin hair waved over his forehead like cobweavings in a breeze, and his robes fluttered around his dried-skeleton figure. It wasn't like the healer to hurry anywhere; his assistants saw to injuries on the field, and any wounded soldier who could walk or be carried came to him. Something of import had happened. Jhared thought of General Nadel. He turned and started to jog toward the infirmary.

The stone building near the kitchens was the only structure in the fortress, besides the walls themselves, that had survived the Exile War. Its tall, flat-roofed profile reminded Jhared of buildings in Shorn Circle, but remnants of intricate masonry depicting the Aye at the cornices and lintels made it seem more like the entrance to a temple.

He leaped up the stairs three at a time. The massive doors carved with tendrils of Silvaye vines burst open just as he reached for them, and he jerked backwards to keep from colliding with the soldier rushing out. When he saw Lieutenant Sevar, he saluted hastily and pulled to attention. The lieutenant's face was still mottled with bruises, but his grey gaze was as sharp and unforgiving as ever. In one fist he clutched a half-crumpled letter with a broken blue elder's seal. For a moment, the man seemed too mired in his own thoughts to recognize Jhared, then he paused in mid-step and his glare landed hard.

"Perfect," the lieutenant sneered, looking Jhared up and down. "Precise and subordinate. We teach you to play the part so well that sometimes we forget just how thin the façade is. But there are always reminders. No matter if you're the child of an elder or not." Sevar balled up the letter in his fist. "You should know, Patrolman, that after your lack of discipline at Lamirna, the only reason you're not bailing swamp water out of prison at the Sonan border is that Carn says you're worth another chance. In fact, I'm going to give you your chance right now: until I say otherwise, you will serve double watch with a morning post on the east wall after your night patrol with Carn. Mark me, when you fail again you will bear the full consequence of it." Without even waiting for acknowledgment, Sevar stalked off toward the officers' tower.

All around Jhared, men went about their duties; the noises of the garrison rose and fell in a normal rhythm, but inside he was reeling.

"A second chance?" one of the Teachers drawled lazily. *"How kind. It's really more than you deserve."*

"I know," Jhared sighed as he slipped into the infirmary. The Teachers had not yet forgiven him for his lapse at Lamirna, either.

He stood in the relative dimness of the hall, breathing in the sweet-pungent odor of herbs and remedies. It was the scent of healing, and he let it flow through him. He had watched Neta at work for enough years that he could put names to many of the scents: dreamsease, bitterbalm, fefferoot, and karianta. Identifying the herbs and mentally sorting them according to their uses settled him, so that his heart slowed its pounding and he could take stock of the rest of his surroundings.

On his left, the large open chamber and high ceiling with tall windows gave the impression that the builders had tried to capture a part of the sky and pull it inside. Heavy shutters covered the windows now, casting the soot-streaked walls into shadow and making the lit hearth the brightest point in the room. A row of beds, several with occupants, lined the wall on either side of the fire. A priestess in green bent over one man, murmuring prayers. On the right side of the hall were two closed doors and a third slightly ajar.

Quietly, Jhared approached the open door and lifted his hand to knock. He paused when he heard an unfamiliar voice murmuring consolingly.

"Don't worry on it, Gabrian. Clan Amerre's petition will go nowhere. No one else on the council will agitate for the general's dismissal now. Too many in the city still remember him as a hero."

"Wrong, courier." The second voice Jhared recognized as Ino, Healer Falto's gruff, grim-faced assistant. "Amerre's elders know what they're about.

All they need do now is wait: if the general dies, they win their goal and pressure Rumar to appoint one of their own. If he lives, they call him unfit and demand he step down."

"They'll still have to put it to a vote," the courier replied.

"All right, you two," Gabrian said softly. "I'll not have such talk—"

Ino's voice barreled over Gabrian's. "A vote? Fine. So let's count it. Clan Makri and probably Rehamra will vote with Amerre. The northern five despise Clan Amerre, but they hate the Shorn more and might see the general go for his defense of Shorn soldiers. More than that, the north is furious with Rumar for the change to the travelers' tax. They'll vote contrary to anything he wants right now. Even Clan Manitar might consider it. Prefect Rumar needs the goodwill of Makri's Vintners' Guild so that her people have a place to sell their oak. That's seven heads right there, maybe eight, of the eighteen. All they need is one of the city elders and—"

"Ino, be shamed!" Gabrian's typically low, steady voice turned harsh. "You'll not talk about such things here, not with the general fighting Cael in the next room. What kind of loyalty is this?"

"Now, Gab, we didn't mean—"

"I know what you meant. I'd like to see you so brave as to speak it when the general is back on the field. You have duties, both of you, so be about them."

Chairs scraped against the floor; men muttered. Jhared scrambled away from the door. He turned quickly—and found the young priestess watching him from across the room. He froze. For several heartbeats they stared at one another. Her eyebrows arched prettily over her dark, curious gaze. He thought she would call out to him, but after a moment she shook her head and placed a finger to her lips. With a hasty bow, he thanked her, then shouldered his way out of the infirmary before the healers entered the hall. Outside, the brilliant sunshine blinded him and heated his face. The scent of illness rose from his clothes.

Clan Amerre had petitioned the council to dismiss Enrian Nadel from the guardianship of the southern towers.

The injustice of it, the utter *foolishness* of it. General Nadel was the reason Amerre hadn't lost a village to Sahiste in nearly five years. He was the reason Clan Nadaren hadn't become just another Amurian duchy. To drive him out was to put the south at risk at a time when no one could guess what violence was coming next. Why would they do it? Jhared didn't see at first what they hoped to gain.

And then he did. The pattern came clear. This was Elder Abrigado's doing.

The Minister of the Treasury had pursued Jhared to discredit Elder Trianor and thereby sting Lord Rumar. Abrigado was now going further, working his way through the leadership of Avelos to destroy those loyal to the high chieftain. Rumar had appointed Nadel to the generalship, and all the country knew that the two men were bound by friendship. What would it mean if the generalship went to one of Clan Amerre's men? Just how high was Toren Abrigado reaching?

Jhared grimaced at his own questions, and his hand sought the pouch where he kept Branlen's stone. Instead of finding the little carved talisman, his fingers encountered the note rolled at the bottom. He had avoided considering the warning since Lamirna. He fingered the smoothness of the fine paper.

They watch for your defiance.

The precariousness of his own position grew that much more salient. Lieutenant Sevar was waiting for his failure, expecting it: Lieutenant Sevar, who had mentioned Elder Trianor by name at Lamirna and accused Jhared of styling himself after an elder. Sirol had said the Legacy would trip him over the line of Shorn Law before he even realized it, and he had laughed at the scribe, confident in his own will. What if the lieutenant was a Legacy man and angry that a Shorn boy had been raised by Teachers? What if he were a part of the plan to pull Tierzen from favor? How could Jhared possibly prevail if his commanding officer meant to condemn him?

He caught his breath and reined in his catastrophic thoughts. General Nadel would accuse him of building a fortress with no stones. He had too little evidence to decide that Sevar supported the Legacy or held any grievance with Tierzen or the high chieftain. The lieutenant remained closed regarding his faction allegiance and vigorously disapproved of any partisan displays among his men.

What of the assignment to double watch? It was a just punishment. Recalling the blur of that terrible night in the valley still made Jhared's heart drum against his chest. He had lost control of a function that was as basic to a Shorn man as breathing, and as necessary. Release of the Shorn poison could only ever lead to disorder and death. In truth, he was lucky the lieutenant hadn't ordered him to be lashed.

For the rest of the day, he fought off the nagging feeling that he hadn't been lucky at all. One moment he convinced himself Sevar only meant to test his will, as any lieutenant would; the next he was certain Sevar maneuvered for his ruin; and the next he realized that none of the rest mattered; if he erred again, whoever watched him would have all they needed to condemn him—and through him, Elder Trianor. The tension set him off balance on the practice grounds, and he paid for it when Twitch slipped under his defenses and dealt him a blow to the ribs that left him gasping.

That night, while Jhared rode the boundaries of Clan Amerre with his patrol, he decided Anzo was his best hope to learn more about Lieutenant Sevar. The soldier had been in the Forest Guard for decades and knew everyone's story. Unlike Jase, Anzo seemed disinterested in gathering attention to himself, and he listened more than he spoke. Jhared trusted him more for it.

Talking to Anzo, however, meant confronting his own shame about Lamirna. It took most of the night and several false starts before Jhared convinced himself to approach the veteran. As they trotted under a deep summer sky, making the loop that would bring them back to Ravia, Jhared dared to move forward. If Anzo was going to berate him, he might as well learn it now.

He gave Brio a tap and caught up to Anzo's grey. The old soldier didn't stop the rambling tune he was whistling between his teeth.

"What I don't understand," Jhared started quietly, "is why a learned city man like Lieutenant Sevar ever joined the Guard."

Anzo stopped whistling. Their horses' hooves thudded evenly in the dark. Jhared studied the forest ahead.

"Now that's a story for them who's interested in history," Anzo observed.

"I am. If you'd be willing to share it with me."

"Maybe I would." Anzo sucked his lip thoughtfully. "It'll cost you something."

"I don't have much to offer."

"Oh, you can afford this. I need a scribe, and I hear you've a fair hand. You keep the courier busy, sure enough."

"No, I..." Jhared shifted uncomfortably. "All right. I can write a letter for you, if that's what you want."

"Well, then. A good story shortens the road on a night quiet as this one, and there's no story good as the truth, eh?" Anzo settled deeper into his saddle, looking pleased. "You want to know how our lieutenant came to Ravia, and that's a fair question. Matio Sevar was marked for the council. He should've been an elder as he's an elder's son."

Jhared looked over at Anzo. "Then why isn't he in the city?"

"His father was Elder of Guilds on the Council of Clans under Alaro Rumar, Lord Rumar's father. Elder Matien Sevar wasn't a favorite, but he was liked well enough in his circles. Not that an old clansman like me knows much about the city circles, eh? When he stepped down suddenly, the scandal reached even us in the wilds. And there went our lieutenant's plans for a place among the elders."

"Why did his father step down?"

"Ah, see. That's a tale of more smoke than substance. The loudest story was that Elder Sevar stepped aside to dodge Alaro's anger after something he did for Adan, the son who was eager to be high chieftain. Others say it was a personal thing. A grief in his family. Loss of a child, maybe. Those knowing the truth are dead or silent on it."

One of Brio's back hooves kicked a loose stone across the trail. Jhared patted the bay's neck. What had it meant for Sevar that his father stepped down from the council, throwing away Sevar's chance to be an elder? Surely the lieutenant wouldn't love the high chieftain for it. Did he nurture enough resentment to see Lord Rumar isolated in the council and weakened in the eyes of the clans?

"Did Elder Sevar send his son to the Guard to find him another road? Was the lieutenant angry about being forced from the city?"

"Hah! Fair guess, but far off. Matio ran to us over his father's protest. When he came, no one expected a gently reared city-born boy to last more'an a few months. That he showed the knack for it surprised most and annoyed some. Those with more strength than sense tried to chase him off, but Lieutenant's not the sort to retreat, is he now? To prove he'd earn his own way, he ran the temple's Tests of Rona. Passed them all, they say. Ran the whole trial in the heat of summer and on his own."

"I thought the Tests of Rona—"

"Were banned by Alaro Rumar? Mmm. Our lieutenant's not as bound to the rules as a soldier might be, eh? Seems he caught General Nadel's attention with his efforts, though. General made him commander, then lieutenant soon after, and that's when the unexpected happened. Maybe you've heard the old rumors of it?"

Jhared shook his head. Brio sensed his tension and gave a low whicker.

"Adan Rumar offered Lieutenant Sevar the Generalship of the Northern Towers."

The second most powerful position in the Forest Guard. Jhared recalled the stories that claimed Sevar rose so quickly in the Guard because of a favor the high chieftain owed his father. How would a proud man like Sevar respond to such a favor?

"Goddess, Anzo. He turned it down. That's why it's General Orn at Aglar Tower instead of General Sevar."

Anzo's eyes twinkled under starlight. "I thought you paid more attention to these things than you let on."

Jhared briefly wondered if Anzo's observation should be taken as a warning, but he needed to understand. "What did others say about why he didn't take the commission?"

"That life beyond the Sandien Mountains is fierce. That no pretty city man owns the stones or the strength to guard the northern five."

"But that's not what you think."

"Naw. Lieutenant Sevar knows what he's about when he makes a decision, and he's no coward. You've seen that by now."

Jhared nodded slowly. A man such as the lieutenant didn't want favors, and no man who could avoid it wanted a debt over him.

"He doesn't thank the high chieftain for that offer, does he, Anzo?"

Anzo cleared his throat and glanced over his shoulder. "I'm glad to see you've overcome your shyness, boy. I was beginning to think all the words in you spilled out at Lamirna."

Jhared coughed and sat straighter in the saddle.

The old patrolman leaned closer to say more quietly, "You might think on the wisdom of spilling so many words right here and now. Sevar hears you're asking those kinds of questions, and we're both likely to face something more painful than a double watch."

They crested a low hill. The horses lifted their noses into the air and moved out more eagerly, smelling home. Commander Carn kicked his mount to a canter, and the patrol followed. Jhared gave Brio a loose rein, letting the wind whip his face as they galloped toward the road to the gates.

After putting up Brio and pausing to grab a hunk of cheese and bread from the mess, he had just enough time to make his way to the eastern wall for the change of the watch. He ate as he walked through the inner yard, among buildings and figures still purple in the early light, and worked on breaking Anzo's story into pieces. "Examine each piece from all sides, like turning over rocks in a stream," General Nadel said. No matter how many ways Jhared turned it, he saw a similar picture. Sevar's refusal of the generalship might have been motivated by his unwillingness to take on a debt, his anger at his father, or his disregard for the high chieftain, but no matter which combination of emotions pushed him, by rejecting Rumar's gift, Sevar had likely burned his ties with Clan Manitar and trapped himself in his current rank forever.

Or at least for as long as Adan Rumar ruled the Council of Clans.

The gate officer, Lieutenant Imilce, was a rangy old veteran with a broken nose that jutted from under a querulous black gaze. His Clan Valador accent savagely mutilated proper Velos. The man greeted Jhared grudgingly when he reported for duty on the morning watch.

"One of Carn's 'unters, eh? Well, we've nothing for you to chase up 'ere. Keep your eyes open, your mouth shut, and 'old your post."

"Yes, sir. Understood."

Jhared lifted his gaze slowly over the ominous grey stretch of the wall. The breeze from the hills would caress the battlements, as dangerous as seduction. He wondered if he would see all the way to Laebek from the top.

"S'ere going to be a problem, Patrolman?"

Jhared looked back quickly, his stomach already doing flips. "Sir?"

"Last time I 'ad a Shorn boy stare at my wall 'at way, I 'ad a mess to clean up at the bottom before his first watch ended. If you plan to play the pigeon, you tell me now."

"Oh no, sir. I've no problem with the wall."

"Good. Because when the armies come, it's the last boundary between what you care about and the bastards 'o want to destroy it all. You treat it with respect, or I promise you, the blood 'at falls on these stones won't be Sahisten."

"I'll hold the wall as dearly as I ever would the border, sir."

"See you do better 'an that! Border watch 'as more holes in it 'an a whore's skirts." Scowling, the lieutenant pointed toward the stairs, muttering to himself as Jhared started up. "Scouts. Damn Shorn scouts."

The breeze on the wall was as soft as the dream of a woman's kiss, and when dawn broke, the entire valley stretched before him. Jhared stood motionless at the edge, eyes on the horizon, fighting off vertigo. The wind teased the hem of his tunic and played with the tail of his hair. He drew a slow breath, reaching for the stillness at his center.

No doubt Lieutenant Sevar knew exactly what this watch would do to him. The consequence fit his error too well: he had lost control of one Shorn urge and now was tested by another. *I know your kind better than you think.* Jhared stamped a foot hard to let the impact reverberate up his legs and remind him of the reality of solid stone. The man on watch at the next post turned his head at the sound. Jhared stared straight ahead: beyond the valley toward the towns of Clan Amerre and the cerulean gleam of the Jewel River.

If it was a torment to stand for hours at the edge of the wall, it grew worse as the double duty continued. His patrol gave him odd looks when he ran to join them on the practice grounds, still vibrating from the effort of holding back for so very long. His return usually provided them temporary distraction from the growing rumors about the council's petition against General Nadel. Bevan and Grion took pleasure in speculating out loud about how Jhared had earned the lieutenant's disapproval; their speculations usually included some combination of women and animals that greatly entertained the others. Jase offered suggestions about how to pass the time on a long, dull watch—which also, disturbingly, usually included some combination of women and animals. While the others roared with laughter, Anzo just shrugged and made room for Jhared in the drill line.

Amidst his other duties, Jhared struggled to find time to send his reports to Tierzen. The letters hadn't become easier. Even though he exchanged friendly words with Hendren when their paths crossed, more knowledge of his fellow Shorn only made it more difficult to determine what to say, and Jhared still avoided telling Tierzen of his own disgrace. In the face of his Teacher's continued silence, he grew increasingly uncertain.

When a letter finally did arrive, Jhared was sitting beside Anzo in the mess, using the few short moments he had for a meal to pen the note he'd promised the man. The little veteran's keen eyes followed Tierzen's letter from the courier's hand to Jhared's pocket.

"Nice thing, a note from family," Anzo observed.

Jhared made a noncommittal sound and gestured toward the half-finished letter on the table. They had been writing to the old soldier's niece.

"Was there something more you wanted to tell her?"

"Naw, naw. After Lamirna, I just wanted to let her know that her greybeard uncle still roams the south and to ask after the new colts. She raises border horses in Everen, you know." Anzo chewed thoughtfully on the end of his pipe. "All your family from the city, Denaban?"

Jhared didn't know where his family came from; none had ever acknowledged him, and his mother had never spoken of them. But he knew who mattered to him.

"Yes," he answered. "For long enough that you'd probably name them among the lost."

"Ah, well. We're all a bit lost now, aren't we?" Anzo said easily. "Some men like to brag of their pure clan blood, but that doesn't mean they know who they are. No need to be shamed by your city roots."

"I'm not." Jhared pushed the unsigned letter in front of Anzo. "Do you want to make your mark?"

Anzo nodded, watching Jhared closely as he set down his pipe and picked up the reed. He drew his family's mark and the Clan Everen ram at the bottom of the paper, then smiled as he looked up.

"Thank you for your time, boy. You've done an old man a favor bigger than the telling of rumors on a dull patrol."

Jhared averted his gaze as he put his ink and reed away, regretting his cold tone. "Tread easily, Anzo Nevia. There's no debt between us."

The old patrolman grinned at the formal phrasing and gave Jhared a jaunty nod in return. Jhared didn't need a better excuse to hurry away.

He fled to the barracks to read Tierzen's letter. It was short, nearly cryptic. Jhared recognized the elder's own hand, not Sirol's, but the cramped sentences were obviously written in haste.

Jhared,
The general's cause is harmed by increasing rumors of insubordination among
Shorn soldiers. Rumors don't match your previous correspondence. Clan
Amerre claims garrison sources of dissidence. Who?
Awaiting more news.
   —T

P.S. Remember your Anarava: A man's actions are a better measure of his
heart than his words.

The note made Jhared's chest ache. Who among the nearly two thousand soldiers and officers in Ravia was spreading rumors about Shorn men? Did Tierzen believe he could really determine such a thing in this lifetime?

The postscript confused him. Did the elder mean to remind Jhared to watch his own behavior? Did he mean the Shorn of Ravia should be judged by their actions, while their words were to be forgiven? Or was it just Tierzen's way of apologizing for such a short message? With a sigh, Jhared realized his subtle foster father likely meant all three.

He couldn't help feeling disappointed. He had hoped Tierzen would share his thoughts about the Sahisten snake ritual. He had hoped for guidance as to how to befriend the Shorn. He had hoped for some indication that he was doing the right thing when he spied on his comrades. Jhared tucked the letter away to be destroyed when he had a moment alone. The day seemed a little bleaker than it had an hour ago.

As he drew on his sword belt, Jhared's empty stomach rumbled beneath his hand. Food would have to wait. Already he would have to hurry to make it to the practice grounds for weapons practice with the Fourth.

Two weeks passed, then three, then a full turn of the moon, and Lieutenant Sevar made no move to relieve him from the extra watch. Morning light took longer to reach the wall, and when Jhared looked out over the valley, he saw Shorn women walking the fields to check the readiness of the beans for harvest. In the city and among the clans, people would soon begin to think about the Day of Dawnings and the fall gatherings.

Riding Brio toward the stable as they came off the night watch, Jhared thought about the approaching holy days. What might he do this year to shift his Path back toward good fortune and final reparation during the days when such things became possible? Autumn would mark his first Dawnings' Eve outside the city; he wondered if the little temple in Ravia would allow a Shorn man to celebrate the ritual without expecting him to play the wretch. He wondered if Riana would hear prayers for his Path from any others. Would Zia say a prayer for him?

He dismounted near the paddock with his patrol. As his feet touched the ground, vertigo rushed up from the base of his spine to break like a cold wave over his head. Jhared staggered against Brio and clutched at the saddle to keep from falling. The big gelding snorted in annoyance and turned to bump Jhared's shoulder with his nose. Jhared pulled himself straight and patted Brio's shoulder until the lightheadedness passed. Lack of sleep was making him foolish.

He groomed and watered the horse, then crossed the inner yard to the barracks. Lieutenant Imilce wouldn't expect him on the wall for nearly another hour. He might steal some needed rest. The barracks already rumbled with early morning activity: Men from the night watch pulled off their gear and exchanged words across the bunks. A couple of Shorn soldiers sat together blacking their boots. Some men sprawled on their beds and tried to sleep. Jhared unbuckled his sword belt and dropped heavily onto his bunk; he didn't bother with his boots before falling onto the straw tick.

"Do you know what you're doing wrong now?"

Jhared groaned and rolled over, pulling the blanket over his head. *"Please. Not now for a lesson. Sleeping."*

"It's time for a lesson whenever we see you need one. Tell us or we'll awaken the nightmares."

They lived within him; they knew well enough how to torment him. There was no ignoring his Teachers.

"I thought I was working hard."

"Working hard? You're counting your days on the wall and waiting for an end when you should welcome this test of endurance. Restrain the hungers of the Avelune through all adversity; that's your duty. What are you when you let those hungers loose?"

"Worse than the ancestors."

"What else?"

"Tired. Please let me sleep."

"What else are you when you give in to desire?"

"Less than a man."

"Good. The Minister of the Teaching thinks he gave you the knowledge and awareness to overcome your flaws and rule your own behavior. The Legacy believes Shorn flaws can only be masked, never overcome. Who is correct?"

Darkness beckoned him. Jhared drifted silently downward.

"WHO?"

"Tierzen, Tierzen! It must be. I possess the insight and the skills to best the weaknesses of my ancestors, and I will."

"Truly? Is that why you are dreaming through your second watch?"

"What?" Jhared shot upright, blinking his gritty eyelids, uncertain for a moment just where and when he was. As his Teachers faded from his mind, he thought he heard someone snickering. It was quiet in the hall, too quiet; most of the other soldiers were gone. Sunlight streamed through an open door.

Cursing, Jhared leaped out of bed and grabbed his sword. This was the end of him. If Sevar heard of it, he was done at Ravia. As he stood, a folded square of paper fell from somewhere beside him and floated to the floor.

He glanced quickly around the room; no one was looking in his direction. He scooped up the paper—saw his name scrawled in a familiar careless hand on the front—and pushed it into the pouch at his belt. No time to worry over it now. He hurried from the barracks, buckling his sword belt as he ran.

The morning guard was already marching up the stairs when Jhared reached the wall. He rushed to the tail end of the line, out of file. Lieutenant Imilce stood near the gate tower, scowling. He stopped Jhared as the line passed.

"My wall too dull for you to get yourself 'ere on time, scout?"

"No, sir! The wall's the last border, sir!"

"Right about 'at, boy. And just so I'm sure you know it, you'll stay on guard through the afternoon watch as well."

"Yes, sir!" Jhared saluted and rejoined the others. Imilce hadn't ordered him to be detained; that was some relief.

He found less relief as the hours crawled by. The sun glared in his face through the morning, then beat down on his back through the afternoon. By the second half of his third watch, the temptation of the open valley began to overwhelm him. He planted his feet more firmly against the stone. His gaze fixed on the hills and the road, but his thoughts wandered to another trial, the first one.

"Tell me what you learned from Iradias, Jhared."

The moon had long since set on Velantar; the elder's house was quiet; and Jhared's little room had become a live trap. For the hundredth or the thousandth time, he paced around the bed, past the clothes chest, and to the door while his body begged him to do terrible things, things that only madmen and the demon-touched would consider.

"Jhared?"

"Iradias said Clan Amerre was first among the first-clans," he panted, "and when Alende Isan gave the leadership of the council to Maravin Amerre at his death, he meant the clan to rule over all of Avelos in perpetuity."

"I know what she *said*." Tierzen's voice was quiet and gentle, with no hint of strain from the hours he'd been in that room, his back against the door, helping Jhared through the first surge of Avelune desire. "Take the cloth; it will cool you. Then take a breath and tell me what you think she *meant*."

"She meant that Clan Amerre should rule the Council of Clans!" Jhared snapped. "She's arrogant and unsophisticated. Father, please. Just a walk around Elders' Circle. I won't go to the roof. I won't go past the walls. *Please*. I can't breathe in here."

"I know it seems that way. Don't cling to that thought; let it go. It can't claim you unless you attend to it. Focus now: Luela Iradias was high priestess for nearly thirty years in a time of violent conflict among the clans. She wouldn't have survived if she had been a fool. What more subtle message might she be sending?"

Jhared's shoulders and back throbbed. More than anything he needed to stretch them. He needed to throw himself from the highest point he could find. If only Tierzen weren't in the way—

"Jhared! *Focus*."

He hissed out a breath and took another turn around his tiny perimeter. His practice sword propped in the corner caught his eye, the wooden sword he'd been given by the garrison to strengthen his arm. He hated it. He wanted it. "I don't know...maybe there are multiple messages."

"Go on. Think it through."

"She wants to *sound* as though she supports Amerre, but perhaps by writing so artlessly, she's letting the careful reader know she sees the flaws in her argument." He flung himself across the room again, ignoring the damp cloth in

Tierzen's fingers. "Perhaps by laying out such a ridiculous claim, she really lent Amerre no support at all."

"Much better. Now you're starting to understand her. Words are only the very beginning of communication. You must always look beyond the words to find the truer meaning."

Jhared closed his eyes. Dawn sang in his blood. Birds in the forest would be taking to the air as the first light opened the skies. What truer meaning could exist than the knowledge that beating wings could lift you and the wind could bear you?

"Look at me," Tierzen demanded. "Keep your mind busy and stay in control of your body. Why might Iradias deliberately flaw her argument? Come on, son. You must learn to get through this."

Jhared didn't remember exactly how it happened. He hated the sword, even when it slipped effortlessly into his grip. He needed to move, to throw all his strength into some motion, any motion. The sword was there. He swung hard. Was it only an attempt to escape the agony in his back or had there been anger in the action? He didn't know. It didn't matter. The wooden blade should merely have hissed through the air. But Tierzen had moved away from the door and taken two steps closer.

Jhared would never forget the feel of the wood striking flesh or the sound Tierzen made as he crumpled to the ground clutching his arm. Jhared's Teachers had screamed, slamming the inside of his head with their fury.

"Evil child! You've attacked your Teacher, an elder, a man willing to call you son!"

He dropped to his knees beside Tierzan. Shame and horror pounding through him. "I'm sorry! Forgive me!"

"Don't!" Tierzen gasped, his face grey. The blow had been hard enough to break bone. "Don't say it. Sorry means nothing. Changes nothing. Look at what you've done. Look closely. It is that easy for you to cause harm, boy. It is that easy for you to harm those who love you. To harm Avelos."

Desire in a Shorn man is death.

Something in the pattern of movement on the road snapped Jhared back to the fortress, his heart still galloping to outrun his memories. The lean man striding downhill was dressed in a grey tunic and breeches; he wore no weapon: he could have been a craftsman making a delivery or collecting a payment from the quartermaster. Then Jhared recognized his predatory gait and the golden warrior's tail, and he realized he had never seen Lieutenant Sevar out of uniform.

In fact, Jhared had never really considered that the lieutenant might have a life beyond the fortress at all. Suddenly, he realized how foolish that was. Perhaps Sevar was only going downhill for the brandy and music offered there, or maybe he was going to meet a woman. Then again, Ravia was the seat of Clan Amerre, who had coveted the leadership of the Council of Clans for centuries, and Matio Sevar had reasons to wish for Rumar's fall.

Jhared made the decision quickly. He owed Tierzen so much; he must find the answers his foster father needed. When his final watch ended and he hurried off the battlements to the gate, he could still see Sevar, tiny in the distance, drawing closer to the town walls. Although the guards above him would note it, he had to run. He left behind the boundaries of the fortress and welcomed the breeze against his skin as he traversed the rocky hill toward the valley. He made good time and only slowed with enough road between him and the town to make certain the Ravia clanguard didn't spot him rushing. Even so, the drowsing sentry came alert as he passed through the gates, eyeing him with a century and a half of hatred.

The seat of Clan Amerre looked like a sad jumble of children's blocks left in the rain too long. Buildings within the wooden walls leaned against and on top of one another, with balconies and stairways that stuck out at untenable angles. Plaster that might once have been painted a variety of pleasing colors now blurred into an uneven grey or had chipped off entirely, exposing the bones of the structures below. During the Exile War, the Sahistens had toppled most of the ancient construction; and later, General Maren's forces finished the job as they plowed toward the border, driving the Avelune toward death. The clan rebuilt after the war, and then rebuilt again in the aftermath of raids, but not everything could be rebuilt. Jhared knew the stories too well: women violated with Sahisten spears; men tortured over the flames; and the children… Goddess, the children. Jhared's chest constricted and he pushed the images away. Over the years, Sahiste had done its best to destroy whatever Clan Amerre created. The people of Ravia no longer strived for beauty; instead, they grasped for the strength to ensure that Sahiste made its retribution in blood.

Jhared caught sight of Sevar near the town center turning down a crooked street, and slowed to avoid overtaking him. The lieutenant didn't hurry, but strode purposefully, looking detached from the people around him. The lane wasn't busy enough for Jhared to rely on the crowd to hide him, so he moved cautiously. He knew how to avoid notice. In the garrison, a respectful man met his comrades' eyes to allow himself to be assessed; only an untrustworthy soldier lowered his gaze. In town, however, a Shorn man kept his head down, an insufficient apology for the horrors caused by his kind.

The lieutenant turned a corner and turned again. Jhared followed easily. He *did* know how to creep through Ravia, and he discovered a perverse satisfaction in observing the man who so despised him. The rhythmic clang of hammers rose from farther down the lane. Jhared tasted char. The scent grew stronger as he progressed deeper into the smithies' district, and soon he could see ropes of smoke uncoiling in the air.

Sevar approached an open shed wedged between a neat little cottage and a pen that held two horses and a goat. For several moments, the lieutenant stood at the edge of the shed, arms folded across his chest, watching the hammering going on inside. Jhared slipped into the shadow of the cottage. The clanging stopped; and a broad, bare-chested man came out, wiping the sweat off his brow with a rag that he stuck into the pocket of his leather apron. Jhared caught a glimpse of the man's smooth back as he turned to greet Sevar. The brawny smith made the lieutenant look small and oddly fragile.

"Halloo, Mat! Damn, you look beat as Cael's dog. Where on Riana's Paths have you been?"

Sevar endured the smith's enthusiastic slap on the back with a flat expression. "Nowhere on Riana's Paths, Lusian. You…alone?"

"As ever I can be," answered the smith, grinning. "The boy's delivering the prefect's horse and Grita went to help her sister with the new babe. Damn, I'm glad to see you! Too long, been far too long."

Jhared crept around the cottage and paused near the corner of the shed to better hear the lieutenant's low voice.

"You won't be so pleased when you learn why I've come," Sevar murmured.

"What is it? Not more trouble with soldiers in town, I hope. With rumors flying about the elders' petition and the general, tempers are high—"

"They're more than rumors. You needn't play as though you don't know it. You're an important man in this town now. With important connections. I've come to ask a favor."

"Aw, Mat, don't be like that. After everything you did for me and mine in the beginning, I owe you more than one favor. You know I'm glad to do it."

"This will clear your debt, then. I've a message to be sent to the city. I need your ties in Velantar."

"A message? Well, now. I've a few in the guild who'd do me a turn. But why don't you—"

"Not the guild. They would be too easily traced back to you, and then to me. It must be your clan ties."

The smith looked up with a more sober expression. "So this is Legacy business."

"Of a sort."

"Last time we spoke, you told me what you thought of that."

"The last time we spoke, I was a young fool who hoped for changes that will never come. If I were in the city right now…" Sevar opened and closed his fists. "Elder or not, I swear I would have his blood."

"Hush." The smith glanced around anxiously, and Jhared drew farther behind the building. "Your father wouldn't have approved'a that talk."

"I don't need you for my conscience, Lusian. My father lost his family, his status, and his sanity because of a Shorn child. If he'd had the courage to do what needed to be done, Abrigado wouldn't be asking for my support now."

"You forget that your father wasn't half as subtle as you and never had the strength of a sword to back him. You should consider forgiving him for that sometime."

"*Lusian.*" The danger in the one word was clear enough to make the smith flinch.

"Right. Not my place." The big man gave a shrug. "I've not the extra time it would take to be your conscience, anyway."

"I wouldn't be here if I had any other choice," Sevar growled. "But this message must be handled with discretion, so that all the right people hear it and none are certain about the source. I imagine these days you have connections who can manage those kinds of complexities."

"Aw, Mat." The smith hooked his thumbs in the front of his leather apron and sighed. "Yes. I know someone who can handle that. What message would you have sent?"

The lieutenant's stance widened as though he were preparing to take on an opponent. "Let it be heard from the mouths of the staunchest Legacy supporters that Lieutenant Matio Sevar stands by the petition to remove General Enrian Nadel from the Guardianship of the Southern Towers."

"What?" Lusian's eyes widened and he let out a low whistle. "All right, man. You'd best come into the house. I'll give you a drink to drown that fire burning in you and you can tell me all about it."

The lieutenant didn't speak, but he must have given some sign of acquiescence, for both men started toward the cottage. Jhared stared as the big, sweaty smith shepherded Sevar into the house and shut the door.

The afternoon sun beat down on the smoky lane. Jhared didn't move. He felt sick with disappointment. *A golden boy. The general's favorite. He ran the Tests of Rona on his own.* Lieutenant Sevar was a good soldier; Jhared had thought him an honorable man. How did Sevar betray the general who had nurtured him, city-born and an elder's son though he was, when so many in the Forest Guard would have seen him fail?

My father lost his family, his status, and his sanity because of a Shorn child.

Was the explanation there, locked within Sevar's bitterness? Jhared realized with a start that he might have just identified the source of the rumors against the Shorn, but all he could think about was how close Tierzen lived to such losses himself. Jhared finally understood that his Becoming had changed nothing: he would always be a risk to those he loved.

…his family, his status, and his sanity because of a Shorn child.

Abruptly, knots of dread connected together one after another, forming an intricate weaving:

You quote the histories like Tierzen himself.

I know your kind better than you think.

Elder or not, I swear, I would have his blood.

…because of a Shorn child.

Jhared stopped breathing. Around him, the clang of hammers continued. Sweat trickled between the scars down his back. "Oh, Goddess. Was it me?"

The question fell into the dust at his feet. His Teachers offered no answer. It would explain Sevar's hatred, but could it explain the lieutenant's betrayal of the general? According to Anzo's story, Sevar's father had stepped down from the council well before Jhared came to Tierzen. Perhaps the two elders had some falling out afterward. Tierzen would have been a young minister when Elder Matien Sevar was in power. Or maybe Lord Rumar's favoritism had angered the lieutenant. After all, Sevar's father surrendered his council seat for the sake of Adan Rumar, while Tierzen not only kept his seat but won his battle when the high chieftain wielded the power of sovereign right to allow him to take in a Shorn child.

If Sevar carried a grudge against Rumar, attacking the general would be a serious blow. *You must always look beyond the words to find the truer meaning.* Jhared thought of Iradias. She had argued for Clan Amerre's right to rule the council when she wasn't truly an ally of Amerre at all. What might that tell him of Sevar's declaration against the general? *You must always look beyond the words….* For all these years, had Sevar given General Nadel only the appearance of loyalty while cunningly nurturing the Legacy cause?

Jhared forced himself to start walking. He needed to talk to someone, someone whose politics he knew and whose silence he could be certain of, but no one at the fortress had given him reason for that much trust. He would write his report to Tierzen tonight. If the courier was in residence, the letter would likely go out by morning, but Jhared held little hope of receiving any reassurance from the Minster of the Teaching.

The thought of a letter reminded Jhared of the unread note he carried. He pulled it out, staring at it blankly for several moments before he registered what he held. The paper was poor quality, but the colorless seal and the scrawl matched the first warning.

When they find the right moment, they'll close like wolves. You're giving them many. It will be soon.

With a growl of dismay, he crushed the note in his fist and shoved it back into his bag. Whoever was trying to warn him with these vague threats would have done better just to wake him in the barracks this morning. At least it would have saved him another reprimand from Lieutenant Imilce.

He slipped away from the cottage and down the narrow lane leading back to the main street of the smithies' district. As he stepped out of the shadows, he nearly walked into Hendren, who was leaning against the wall of a shop, arms crossed over his chest.

Jhared blinked, caught a breath, and smiled. "Oh, hello. You're an unexpected face in town."

Hendren didn't shift his position, but watched Jhared a long, too-quiet moment. "Was there a particular face you did expect?"

Something probing existed in the other man's tone. "That's an interesting question," Jhared said mildly.

"You're in an interesting place."

When they find the right moment, they'll close like wolves.

Jhared narrowed his gaze. "Hendren, did you follow me?"

The other man lifted and dropped his shoulders. "I was in town on an errand for the commander and I saw you crossing onto smiths' street. You appeared too determined to be merely checking on shoes for Brio. I was… concerned."

Apprehension trickled through Jhared's middle. Had Hendren seen him trailing Lieutenant Sevar? "No need to be. I know my way about."

"Jhared, not so many weeks ago, a Shorn soldier was pushed off a wall by a mob. Concern is reasonable." Hendren glanced up, eyeing the street. "In fact, we'd best get moving. Come on."

Jhared realized they had started to draw attention. Across the road, a heavily muscled smith stared at them from his doorway, hammer still in his hand. Two other men joined him, their features forbidding. Jhared nodded and started walking.

"You know the quickest way to the gate from here?" Hendren asked, keeping pace.

"Think so." Jhared glanced over his shoulder. The three men left the doorway and began to follow. Others along the road noticed as well.

Hendren hissed. "For pity's sake, Patrolman, lower your gaze! Disrespect like that will get us torn for sure."

Jhared turned away. He had survived a childhood in Velantar; he knew the consequences for careless behavior. He had never seen a mob, though. That was a different thing than roving gangs of Legacy men and City Guards doling out beatings. A Shorn soldier had been killed here.

He and Hendren walked purposefully, trying to manifest the precise bearing that was neither threatening nor apprehensive. The gate seemed farther from the smithies' district than it had been when Jhared was focused on Sevar. They passed a glowering man who stepped out of his shop swinging a brace of dead pigeons hung from a rope. Limp grey wings caught the sunlight.

"You know what we must do if they come for us?" Hendren asked quietly.

"Of course." Jhared swallowed. His recklessness had gotten them into this. "You go. I'll hold them. With any kind of luck, they'll be pleased enough to snare a city man."

"What?" Hendren's features creased with horror. "No one stays! We run. Both of us. And we hope the townsfolk haven't thought far enough ahead to set an ambush or close the gate."

Jhared glanced sideways at Hendren and nodded.

The Amerre clansmen continued to follow. Someone began to chant ugly rhymes and others picked up the cry. More joined as they crossed town, including a few women, angry and fierce. *Blood-backs* they called the Shorn in the south. And *raven-spawn*. Two women grasped a board between them, brandishing it over their heads. Six small grey shapes had been nailed to the board: three pairs, roughly triangular, covered with pale down, and discolored and blackened on one side. They fluttered sadly as the women waved the board.

They fluttered.

Hendren made a horrified sound. "No, oh no. Are those…?"

Jhared couldn't stop staring at the board, at the soft grey feathers and the dried blood that discolored them. A high-pitched ringing filled his ears. "They're wings. The wings of small birds."

Hendren half-swallowed a sob. "Not birds."

Jhared's heart thudded; his severed muscles twitched. No, not birds. No birds had wings quite that shape. No fledglings were quite so big. "Don't look at them," he murmured. "Keep walking. We're almost out."

Finally, they rounded a corner onto the main road. The gate stood open, but the last steps would be the most dangerous, the time when the crowd might gather its courage and attack. Jhared strode steadily, though the open road ahead begged him to run. Three clanguard scrambled out of the gate tower. Jhared kept moving, his hands open and empty at his sides. If the guard ignited the mob, it was over. He and Hendren would end as a cautionary tale for other Shorn soldiers. The guards hurried to the front of the crowd, arms raised, slowing the first of the clansmen to reach them. One guard was grinning.

"Put the birds to flight, have you?" the man bellowed to the crowd. "Good for you! Now it's time for a drink, eh? Who's buying?"

Jhared and Hendren kept walking. The crowd roared obscenities behind them, but no one stopped them. Another clanguard growled something poisonous as Jhared passed. He didn't hear exactly what it was. They crossed out of Ravia and started up the hill toward the fortress.

When the road curved and they were finally far enough away that the crowd's taunts were no more than a rumble, Hendren stopped, panting. "Goddess, let's not do that again."

Sweat poured down Jhared's back. Shorn energy pulsed against his chest. "No. Not today."

With a faint chuckle, Hendren straightened and clapped a hand over Jhared's shoulder. "Thank you, friend."

Jhared frowned, surprised by the hand and the name. "What for?"

"Not many in my life would make that offer. To put yourself in the way of danger for me."

"Oh." Jhared began walking again. "It seemed the right thing."

"I didn't think the right thing included saving Shorn comrades." Hendren's expression sobered. "Anyway. It was a brave offer. And not a thing I'll forget."

They walked on, both quiet, the glare of late afternoon sunlight in their faces. As Jhared's heart slowed, he realized that not only had he likely found the answer Tierzen needed in the form of Lieutenant Sevar, but now a Shorn man was in his debt. He was supposed to use that debt to do as Tierzen asked of him. Could he?

As the fortress tower came into view, the troubling thought became abruptly unimportant. Something had happened. Men on the walls had their backs to the valley, away from their watch and toward the yard. A single soldier pelted along the battlements with a torch. Jhared watched him go. They were lighting the alert for the border towers. By midnight, every soldier in the south would know that Avelos was under attack. He and Hendren exchanged a sober glance.

They sprinted the rest of the way to the fortress gate, slipping through unheeded as a patrol galloped out. Inside, men ran toward the stables and commanders mustered their patrols in the yard. Jhared spotted a familiar figure running across the loggia.

"Anzo, wait! What's happened? Is it Sahiste?"

The old patrolman turned, his eyes dark and his face ashen. "Not Sahiste. Not the armies, at least. It's Orivan and Renda."

Two small villages north of Lamirna. With a knife-sharp dread, Jhared understood. "The killing winds attacked them."

"Destroyed them," Anzo replied. "Both of them. Gone."

Jhared closed his eyes: men and women, families with their children, farmers and craftsmen. Not soldiers. They worked and loved and made a life…and died. In the back of his mind, he heard them screaming. An unworthy thought flashed up to him: how many of those dead would have gladly joined the mob today? How many would have eagerly pushed him from the wall? He shook his head and opened his eyes.

Hendren's anguished gaze reflected the ache in Jhared's heart. Perhaps he heard the screaming too. Perhaps he also wondered.

Anzo nodded at them both. "You'd best get moving. We're mustering."

Hendren's voice was raw. "There's nothing we can do for them, you know. Not even for the sake of final reparation. This is beyond us, beyond all our Teaching."

Jhared discovered yet another type of betrayal in that. "We'll do the only thing we can," he said. "We'll put up our swords and go out to pick up the pieces."

13.
MESSENGERS

"Lady, wait! I must speak with you."

Nemiah continued down the crowded corridor, the faces of the acolytes and the novices that parted before her only a blur. If she moved fast enough, perhaps she could outrun the memory of the child's face.

"Not now, Clemina. The Day of Dawnings approaches and the city is filled with pilgrims whose petitions must be heard. I don't have time just now."

The footsteps behind her didn't falter. Clemina was as tenacious as a rat hound. It was for that trait, and not for intelligence or subtlety, that the Higher Circle had chosen her to be their Mistress of Messages.

"Lady, it's very important."

Nemiah turned a corner. Thanks to Kaliska's network, she already knew what the Circle thought was so important today. Not much farther to her rooms. Perhaps she shouldn't feel this way; the Day of Dawnings marked a time of transitions, after all. Death was only a transition from the Paths of the living to Riana's Hidden Paths.

"Lady!" Clemina called, hurrying to catch up.

Rom bowed as Nemiah reached her door. "The Bearer waits within," he said quietly.

Then, with the slightest flicker of his gaze, he indicated the priestess at her heels. Nemiah gave a tiny shake of her head. Riana bless him; he knew her mind without a word.

A loud throat-clearing announced that Clemina wasn't deterred. "The Mistress of Novices requests a meeting with you, Lady Nemiah. It's an urgent matter."

Urgent? Nemiah would have laughed, but the morning's petitions had revealed such a loss that it was impossible. She drew herself straight and turned.

"Sister Carian knows the way to my receiving rooms. I will be there, as ever, before the evening devotion to speak with her, or any other of Riana's servants."

"But...it's the Higher Circle that you delay."

Nemiah felt genuine pity for the girl's confusion. Clemina wasn't savvy enough to play Carian's game; she was simply trapped in the middle. Despite all of Carian's demands for a new Path, she appeared not at all pleased that Nemiah had started them moving in a new direction.

"Child, the Circle spins around the sphere that is Riana. Not the other way. You must not forget that, even if the rest have. If the Mistress of Novices wishes to contest my decision to allow our sisters to serve outside the walls for the holy days, then let her come to me. For yourself, you would serve Riana better by preparing for the Day of Dawnings."

She turned, and Rom opened the door, gifting the stunned Clemina with an unyielding frown.

Nemiah made it over the threshold: another kind of transition, there. She stepped through the antechamber and drew a shaky breath.

"A child, Leita. He was no more than four winters. A perfect, beautiful boy. Dead in his father's arms."

"Children die on Riana's Paths."

"They're not meant to die like this. Not crushed under his family's barn while trying to find protection from the knives of this storm that kills."

Merisel approached, offering tea. Nemiah waved it away, then caught the scent of boldblood and snatched it up.

"His father brought the body from Trevilan as his *gift* to Riana for the holy days. He asked what boon the Lady would give in return, now that she has his son."

"Trevilan. That's on Clan Delsio land. The storms are moving closer to the city."

"Leita! It was an innocent babe!"

"You're trying to make me lay blame, my friend, and I won't."

"This isn't about blame. It's about loss, and the grief that exists in surviving. I've rarely seen that depth of despair in a man." Nemiah moved to the chairs beside the window, where Leita sat weaving on a small handloom, and dropped into a seat beside her. Capalino was outside the walls, hunting with other temple hounds under the Mistress of Kennels; Nemiah wished she were with them.

She thought of another man who had come to her in despair long ago. Memories of Enrian Nadel had taunted her when the Trevilan farmer laid his son at her feet. She could do as little to ease the farmer's rage and sorrow now as she had done for the Forest Guard captain. Despite her words to Clemina, she was no avatar, only an empty symbol.

There had been more power once, long before her time. Before her predecessors betrayed Avelos. Before the council stripped the temple of its strength. Before she was chosen as high priestess and let the last of their influence trickle out of her hands.

"Stop that." Leita's low voice had an edge that pulled Nemiah from her self-condemnation.

"Ah, yes. I agreed to relinquish self-pity, didn't I?" She rubbed a finger against the dull ache in her head. "It's only that we began to see movement in the council last spring. I thought I awakened a few allies, and perhaps even gave Abrigado a reason for caution. Then this horror from the south. None of our little games—not mine or Rumar's or the council's—matter in the face of these attacks."

"They will," Leita said, deftly working a strand of grey yarn through her loom. It was too soon to see her pattern. "The council's idea of defense is to throw more soldiers at the borders. They have no idea how to protect Avelos from these storms. We must be the ones who find the key."

"I know." For the first time in a long while, Nemiah felt she truly did know. She had been dreaming of it since summer; she just hadn't figured out how.

Leita watched her from across the room. "If we could find a way to be near when the storm strikes, you could delve onto the Paths and seek their source. What secrets we might learn then."

Nemiah glared at the Bearer. "That's *not* what I meant. We've no need to go calling for Cael!"

Leita put down her weaving and offered a small, arch smile. "Very well. I suppose there are other ways for us to learn. Tell me about the young ones who came this morning. Are they promising? Did you sense the Paths within any of them?"

"It's too early to start counting new students," Nemiah replied. "Not all the clans have even reached the gathering yet."

"Ah." The Bearer's smile blew out like a lamp. "And how many children would there be *if* we counted?"

"Only the one," Nemiah said. The dead one. She reached out to touch Leita's hand. "They'll come. There's still time left. Surely this year they'll come."

Her encouragement was hollow, and they both knew it. In the past, the fall gathering meant families would bring their children as gifts in exchange for the chance to shift their paths toward good fortune on the Day of Dawnings. If found worthy, those children would serve as future priestesses and Arionade. At one time, some of the girls would have been sensitive enough to the Paths to learn to travel them. Nemiah had been the last of those girls.

"We must have Pathwalkers, Nemiah. We can't deny the need any longer. So much waits along the Paths. I sense their secrets, even as I must avoid them."

"Have patience. We will find them."

"Will we? None of our own women have borne a Pathwalker in years, and few people remain willing to give up a pair of hands and a young back even for Riana's blessing."

"There are many ways for us to learn. You said it yourself."

"Nothing like the Paths. You must see that. So many possibilities exist besides the simple mapping we do now. What if a Pathwalker possessed the skill to choose not only the Time and Place of the Path she traveled but also the Perspective?

Could such a walker see through another's eyes? Read their thoughts? Don't you think on what we've lost since the Exile? And what about what we still have left to lose? Goddess help us should something happen to you, when we have no other priestesses able to journey. We'd be no better than players reciting empty prayers, with no connection to Riana's power—"

"Let it be!" Nemiah said sharply. Of late, Leita grew dark when she talked about the Paths, and Nemiah couldn't face the Bearer in all her grim glory right now. She sighed and set aside her tea.

"I think the Blade is pricking you hard," she said more gently. "And no wonder with the chaos that's loosed itself on us. I'm going to the library while I have a bit of time. Perhaps there's something we've missed that will give us a key to this cursed storm—and if not, at least Clemina is unlikely to find me there. Why don't you join me?"

"You won't find what you need there," Leita said, thrumming impatient fingers against the pattern in her loom. "Not in the council library or among our own pathetic collection. The works of power are long gone."

"And what is it you suggest?"

"Go look for a Storyteller."

"Oh, Leita." Nemiah shook her head in exasperation. "That would serve us well, wouldn't it? For the Lady of Avelos to break the law by seeking some false Storyteller? If they hadn't failed so critically in their telling of the sacred journeys, Tumal wouldn't have needed to oust them from the temple. Now set your weaving aside and help me to examine what history remains."

The Bearer shrugged. "I cannot. Go without me. I've no stomach to taste the dregs Tumal's purges left for us."

"Leita, it would be good—"

The Bearer leaned over and silenced Nemiah with a kiss on the brow. "Stop worrying for me. The Blade pricks no harder than any of your own burdens. We are well-matched, you and I: we take turns walking in the light and battling the shadows. Go. Leave me to my own battle."

Nemiah brushed her friend's cheek. Leita walked the hardest road of any of them, forced to put Cael's way forward against everything she believed, all to keep her sisters on the right path. Nemiah couldn't be irritated with her.

The council library was housed in a drab stone building that squatted like an afterthought between Elders' Hall and the temple compound. The diminished collections had been shunted into what had originally served as city offices, after

Tumal's purges made redundant the large, beautiful book rooms in Elders' Hall. The newer building lacked the design to make storing and accessing the collections convenient, and Nemiah suspected that volumes and scrolls that no one had touched in years still hid in crates in some of the dusty back rooms.

The arrangement had become no more orderly under the archivist's attentions. When Rendeta wasn't giving lessons to the young ones in the high temple, the apple-cheeked woman scuttled through the halls, chittering softly to herself as she reorganized the collection in schemes only she understood. No one on the council bothered to intervene; Nemiah suspected they didn't want to look that closely into the tattered and moldering pages of Avelos's history.

When Nemiah explained she was looking for works that referenced Sahiste, Rendeta blinked at her with shiny black eyes.

"Now, my lady, you know better than that. A loyal historian would hardly waste her days recording the lore of the faithless, but if there's one or two who mention Sahiste, you should very well know who they are. You tell me."

Instantly, Nemiah was back in a hot room with ten other girls struggling to memorize the *Decisions of the Council from Tumal the Just to Matio the Giving*. It didn't matter that she had passed every novice exam at her first sitting, or that she was now the one who gave approval before new initiates took their final tests.

"No excuses," Rendeta warned, waving her skinny finger at Nemiah, "I won't have excuses."

"Iradias favored the south," Nemiah said. "Her histories of Clan Amerre might be promising. And as I recall, Sahiste served as an example for Morican's argument in *Defense of Avelos*. I thought I would begin there."

Rendeta sighed and tsked. "A partial answer won't earn you credit, Lady. Iradias and Morican, yes. But you've forgotten Anarava. I'd warrant that you haven't given due attention to Anarava. You'd do well to read them all."

"Of course, Rendeta. Thank you. If you would retrieve those works for me, I'd be grateful." Nemiah stifled her inclination to give the librarian a novice's curtsy. "I'll be in the east reading room."

The reading room was small and stuffy, with bare walls, a stone floor, and no window. A utilitarian table and a single lamp offered little by way of comfort, but Nemiah was pleased to have the room to herself. Rendeta brought two volumes—Anarava and Iradias—but expressed dismay that she couldn't find the Morican. Nemiah wasn't surprised to hear that something had been misplaced within the librarian's strange system of organization.

The binding crackled as Nemiah opened Iradias's *Victories of Clan Amerre*, and the familiar scent of aged leather and dust blossomed around her. An elegant script in ancient Velos curled across the darkened pages. Too much time had passed since Nemiah had explored the written stories of Avelos. She missed them.

She lunged into the history hungrily, but soon found herself digging through a tediously arrogant retelling of the lineage of each Amerre prefect across the centuries, through page after page of descriptions of Amerre villages and hamlets, through claims that Clan Amerre, the Rising Sun of Avelos, was the most blessed of the fifteen first-clans. Iradias revealed a slavish devotion to her subject with every entry. Nemiah wondered if the priestess had been as dull in life as she was in her writing.

Nemiah rubbed her eyes over the dense script and yawned deeply of the stale air. She pushed Iradias aside and fingered the Anarava. Char and smoke had damaged the second volume. Several pages were torn. At some point during the past century and a half, it had been saved from flames, perhaps even the flames of the purges. Ovelia Anarava was among the women appointed by Tumal to replace the executed priestesses after the Exile War, and not all thought her histories fit to be read. She'd had no formal training by the temple and no examination by the Higher Circle. She could hardly be called a priestess at all. Nemiah wouldn't have asked for her, but some instinct ingrained from childhood to obey the archivist caused her to pull the volume closer.

Compared to the cheerfully supercilious Iradias, Anarava was bloody and dark. She painted the battles of the Exile War in blunt detail. Then, every once in a while, in the midst of a passage on Avelos's losses or some narrative on the country's defenses, she wrote a line that made Nemiah think Anarava had been interested in a very different struggle from the one between Avelos and her foreign enemies.

Standing sentinel at the borders of the land and the gates of our cities, with all the treasures of Avelos behind him, the soldier struggles hardest against himself. It cannot be long before he falls prey to his own weakness and succumbs to temptations that leave our gates unguarded.

Or in another passage: *The battle being won decisively, still the people did not find peace, hungering only for retribution. Thus did they break the bonds of loyalty to one another and left themselves vulnerable to attack.*

Or another: *Weep for Avelos if any general of that terrible war experienced not a moment of horror when he considered the rivers of blood he set flowing.*

How was it possible that Anarava, who had witnessed the Sahisten invasion, visited Maren's Burn, and knew women who suffered violation and death in the war, still insisted on looking within Avelos for the source of chaos? Nemiah frowned and closed the book. Was it the woman's own guilt that moved her? After all, when she crossed the line that Tumal drew with the blood of murdered priestesses, Anarava had betrayed centuries of temple tradition.

Nemiah pushed the book away. It was no wonder the historian's work was out of favor. She'd find no help with the Sahistens here.

A great boom exploded through the library, shaking the stone at its foundation. The table shivered, sending tremors into Nemiah's hands. She stood hastily, toppling the chair behind her.

"Rendeta? What is it?"

Another quake shook the room. The lamp fell and went out. Nemiah fumbled in the dark toward the door. A wave of vertigo made her reel against the chilly stone. She tried to follow the wall to the exit, but felt only the rough stone under her hands. Cold sank into the center of her being.

"Hello, little dove. I didn't think I would see you again."

Nemiah startled and flung up her arms defensively. "Who's there?"

"Just a weary traveler pausing for a moment of rest."

"Lady? My sister on the Paths?"

"You even remember me. What an unexpected pleasure."

"Why shouldn't I remember? I was trained to hold the journeys intact when I travel."

"I'm sure you were," the voice said patiently, "yet if I crossed your Path the second time at a point before you met me the first time, then you would have no journey to remember." A ripple in the air gave the impression of a shrug. "It's no matter. The Paths are tangled beyond our comprehension."

Nemiah strained to see through the blackness, but the woman remained only sound and emotion in her head. Doors remained closed between them.

"Lady, where are we? I can't see your temple this time, and you seem… *thinned*."

"Oh, there's still as much of me as ever, not to worry." The woman laughed, but the warm richness that Nemiah remembered was missing. "Our people are dying, dove, and I've found no good way to help them."

"I know," Nemiah said in a rush. "Oh, Lady, I know. So many deaths. What can we do?"

The space between Nemiah and the priestess grew very still and quiet. "Learn," the woman said finally. "It's the only thing in my power to do. Perhaps if we understand the source of this fear, we can conquer it."

"I've tried," Nemiah insisted. "I've searched the libraries. I've found nothing of use."

"Oh, sweet, don't waste your effort on the stale slivers of memory in the archives when Riana offers access to every secret of the past, present, and future. My guide has been searching the Maps for Paths that might help me to end the fear and regain our balance. Surely, on some Path this horror was known and overcome. Somewhere."

Amazement for the woman's skill filled Nemiah once again. "You go where you choose? You've been journeying all this time?"

"All this *time*? A tired chuckle echoed in Nemiah's ear. "I can't say what time means to you, but I've spent three seasons of my own searching since last we met. As for choice? I have my Mapmaker and my guide to thank for their directions."

"What have you discovered?"

"Some things; not enough. The Paths I've found share a depressingly similar pattern: our desert neighbors keep a wisdom that we lack; our people arm themselves against the outsiders; and death spreads as quickly as hate."

"Desert neighbors? Do you mean Sahiste? Can you tell me the knowledge they keep? Will it help us?"

There was no answer. Nemiah wondered if she had fallen off the Path.

"Lady?"

"Sorry, little one." The voice returned more faintly. "I've not much in me today for traveling. Yes—Sahiste. And if I knew their secrets, I would share them with you. I suspect the harsh climates of their country have led their priests to learn to influence nature in ways that we've never imagined."

Nemiah nodded. "That's a place to begin. Don't lose hope. We work toward the same goal, you and I."

"Then may we each find our ways to it. Look to what has come before. That's the answer, I think. At one time we knew how to balance Riana's order. I must leave you now. Carry yourself safely home, little one. Carry yourself..." The woman's voice faded and went out like the glow of a doused wick.

"Wait! What do you mean *what has come before*? I don't know your past. *When* are you?"

Only silence answered.

The Path, abandoned by its maker, began to collapse. It snapped like a whip, throwing Nemiah to her knees. Another shockwave knocked her flat. She waited to be flung among all of Riana's tangled ways.

Carry yourself home, little one.

The echo caressed the dark like a gentle hand, calming the disruption and holding the Path together. The waves slowed until the road beneath Nemiah only undulated gently. She threw a thought out to the darkness.

"Lady?"

Still no answer; the other priestess was truly gone. Weariness settled over Nemiah. She closed her eyes. *Carry yourself home.* The command prodded her. With an effort, she threw herself across the blue flames, wrestled the Gate closed, and dropped back into her body.

"Carry yourself safely home."

Noise and light bombarded her as she returned to her own Path. The transition was painful. Who knew that air could hiss so loudly as it traveled around the room? Who knew that lamplight could be blinding? She groaned and burrowed her face in an arm.

"Now you're home. Easy does it. I have you now." The whispers at her ear might have been to a sick hound, not to the Chosen Lady of Avelos. Nemiah opened her mouth to say she was just fine, but then the cold rattled through her and she could only clench her jaw to keep from biting her tongue.

Arms pulled her closer, toward warmth. She smelled incense and forced her eyes open, discovering herself sprawled across Leita's lap with her back pressed against her friend's chest. They were both on the floor, Leita's cloak spread half over them. Nemiah's legs were tangled around an overturned chair. Oh, Goddess, the library. She had fallen through the Gate right here in the library. She struggled to rise.

Leita's embrace tightened and she shook her head against Nemiah's cheek. "No, dearest. You cannot, not yet. Close your eyes and take a breath. We've a Path to chart.

"Lady Riana of the Journey," Leita whispered, "the sun you gave to us, and the stars, and the flame for the darkest nights. Because of these do we seek to find balance to your order. Now, by the light of your servant, Nemiah Gabriana, illuminate for us the steps along your Paths."

Nemiah had no choice but to respond to the prayer. She tried not to think about where she was or who was holding her while she gave up the details of the journey. It didn't take long. When she had surrendered the conversation as best she could, she opened her eyes and spoke the required closing. "By Riana's ways I travel and by her ways I return."

"By Riana's ways," Leita echoed.

"Goddess," Nemiah groaned. "What have we done?"

"What we had to. Come now. Let's get you out of here before Rendeta returns. Can you rise?"

Leita shifted out from under Nemiah and crouched to take her arm.

"Of course," Nemiah said through her teeth. She had to crawl onto all fours before pushing to her feet.

"Good. Then we'll stroll out together and no one shall be the wiser."

"You should not have acted as Mapmaker."

"Would you have Bena spreading tales about the Chosen Lady falling unaware onto the Paths? Again?"

"That's what happened."

"Nemiah, you mustn't give the Higher Circle more excuses to defy you! Carian's grumbling is starting to incite the others, and we must appear united against the council."

"I will not sacrifice honesty because the truth makes others uncomfortable, Leita. Lies and fear brought us to this point."

Leita supported Nemiah with a hand on her back, but her tone held frustration. "Let us return to the temple; then we can talk."

Nemiah drew up the hood of the cloak. She needed boldblood tea and a fire and time to figure out why her control over the Gate had grown so poor, but she couldn't have those things yet. "Not to the temple. To the palace."

The Bearer's features tightened in dismay. "Nemiah?"

"I've claimed myself to be the guide of Avelos. Well, then Rumar must know of this new journey. I must go, Leita."

She could see Leita working up an argument against her, but instead, the Bearer nodded resolutely. "Very well. Carry it to him while the mystery of the infinite Paths still gleams in your gaze."

They marched across the plaza and up the wide stone steps into the high chieftain's palace. Today, the great entrance hall was quiet. A page crossed the hall, opened a door, and disappeared within. From another direction, boots clicked across the marble floor as a scion dressed in the green and silver of Clan Manitar approached Nemiah and Leita.

"Yes?" the young man asked, his voice dripping with elder-bred boredom.

"The Lady of Avelos has come to speak with High Chieftain Rumar."

The man, as tall and grey-eyed as his kinsman, gazed down on Nemiah skeptically. "The high chieftain is not seeing supplicants this afternoon."

"I am no supplicant. I carry news only the Lady of Avelos can bear. The high chieftain will want to know it."

The agent made a face as if to refuse, then seemed to think better of it. "Very well, lady. You may wait."

The clansman vanished up the stairs and along a gallery. As minutes crept by, doubt trickled into Nemiah. Had she been too impulsive? The power of the sacred journey had pushed her. She meant to reclaim some agency, to prove the words she had spoken to Rumar at their last meeting. Now that she stood in the palace hall, waiting like a hopeful suitor for some love token, she feared she had made a serious mistake. She didn't look at Leita.

Finally, the man returned. His smug expression confirmed her fear. "The high chieftain is unavailable."

Nemiah glared up at him. "You took my words directly to High Chieftain Rumar?"

"The high chieftain is unavailable," the man repeated. "Perhaps you would care to return with your petition on the day of supplicants?"

Despite the toll the sacred journey had taken on her, Nemiah drew herself up and shot her most imperious stare at the man. After a moment, he lowered his eyes, chagrin wiping some of the smugness from his features.

Without another word, Nemiah turned and marched out, Leita trailing behind her. Her face burned. Foolish, so foolish to think she had established any standing with Rumar in the past months. She said nothing to her Bearer as they reached the passage between the temple's outer gardens and the sanctuary. Sunshine turned the arched windows of the hall into half-circles of light on the floor. Nemiah didn't notice that she'd been treading on the shadowed part of the circles until the sound of hurried steps and a beseeching voice behind her made her stop.

"Lady Nemiah. Wait, please wait! This poor servant begs your blessing."

Leita's hand tightened on Nemiah's arm as they both turned to see a figure jogging awkwardly toward them.

"Grandfather, you should not be here," Leita said. "This place is for Riana's anointed. Return to the first circle and the attendants there will offer you the spiral."

"No, may it please you, no." The beggar limped closer, drawing a worn brown cloak about him. "Forgive the presumption of an old man for whom time moves ever more quickly toward, not the Day of Dawnings, but the end of days. Surely, Chosen One, you would hear the prayers of such an earnest servant."

Nemiah detached herself from Leita's grasp and pushed her hood back, trying to peer past the shadow of his.

"A servant who wishes only to change his fortunes with a Dawnings gift for the Lady," he added, lifting his hands in supplication. The sleeves of his cloak fell away to reveal long, skinny fingers. On his right hand the loyalty ring of Clan Manitar caught the light.

Nemiah drew back in surprise. "Riana does not turn away those who speak their hearts. Come to the petitions at the evening devotion and I will offer my blessing."

He shook his head once, firmly. "Hear me now, Lady, or I must walk my path without her guidance."

Leita took hold of Nemiah's elbow with a grip that urged her away, but Nemiah resisted. "Who sent you?"

Laval Astreno said nothing.

He had hurried out of the palace after them; Nemiah was nearly certain of it. She drew a breath and made a decision. "No one should walk without the Lady beside him, grandfather. Let the Bearer of Cael's Blade take you to a place where you may prepare yourself for prayer. I will see the gifts you bring."

"As you say, Lady." Rumar's steward nodded from inside the cowl. His tone changed when he looked up and said once more, "May it please you."

Nemiah pushed herself past the chill and stiffness of the sacred journey to run back to her chambers. She ordered the Arionad on watch there to find Captain Rom and send him to her receiving room. Then she exchanged Leita's dark cloak for her own warm wrap of vivid green. As she hurried back out the door, she spotted a slice of raw boldblood root that Merisel had saved for tea. After a moment's hesitation, she grabbed it and bit into the woody flesh. Even as the bitterness choked her, she felt the juices enliven her leaden body.

Astreno rose when she entered the receiving room, his hood pushed back to reveal his beaked features. Candles flickered around the chamber, casting Nemiah's shadow across the walls.

"Riana bring her order to your Path, Laval Astreno. What blessing do you ask of her?"

The steward's knees creaked as he lowered himself onto a prayer stool before her. "For the festival of the Day of Dawnings, I bring a gift for the Chosen Lady. It is a thing I offer only to you, not to the temple or your Higher Circle. Can you give your word that you will keep it so?"

Astreno seemed to have left his obsequious manner in the outer hall. Nemiah allowed herself a moment of pique. "The palace has just turned away the words of the goddess. Now I am offered a gift with conditions?"

"For the well-being of Avelos, Lady Nemiah."

No one knew the workings of the palace more intimately than the man seated before her. He had served Rumar's father for years. After Alaro Rumar died, some stories suggested he had been offered staggering amounts of silver to remain to serve the son. Nemiah wanted what he knew, but she had learned to have more caution.

"Is this gift yours to give?"

"Do not mistake, Lady. I am no traitor to Avelos, to Manitar, or to Adan Rumar. I only carry what my lord is not free to."

Nemiah sat back, absorbing the stunning implications of that. She hoped what she was about to do was brave rather than reckless: "I regret that I am not free to accept Riana's gifts in secret." She inclined her head. "For the well-being of Avelos."

Astreno looked perplexed, as though the possibility of rejection had never occurred to him. His boneless fingers pressed together under his chin, then opened, palms upward.

"Perhaps we might arrange a compromise. Choose one other with whom to share what I tell you. One whose heart you know as well as your own. You must also agree to bring this person with you when you come."

"When we come? Where will we be going?"

"Do you accept the terms?"

Nemiah bit her lip. She considered the two hearts she held most dear. Neither Rom nor Leita would approve of this bargain. "I give my word to keep it between myself and one other."

"Very well, Lady. Such is our agreement." The steward looked up from the prayer stool. A bead of perspiration trickled past his ear. "You foresaw the snakes sliding over our border, and so they have.

"And you are invited to greet them."

14.
STRANGE COMPANIONS

"Why wouldn't Astreno tell you who would come for us? I don't like it."

Nemiah tucked her arms under her cloak and pressed her back against Rigojan's warm flank to escape the predawn chill. A lamp on the courtyard wall fought through the fog to light a pale sphere around her and her Arionad.

"He said he didn't know."

Rom snorted.

"Do you think I should have rejected the invitation?"

"Reject an offer to leave the safety of the temple and the city to be led by an unknown escort to an unknown location to meet an enemy of unknown number?"

Nemiah glanced to Capalino, who nosed at a hole under an old oak tree. Neither the early hour nor the cold bothered the hound. He happily occupied himself by uncovering the mice that burrowed in the outer gardens. Nemiah gave Rom a warning look.

Her Arionad relented a little, touching a hand to the hilt of his sword. "You are safe while I draw breath, my lady."

"I never doubt it."

"Still, you should have a company of my best men around you."

"Let it be, Rom. You know why this is necessary." She offered a reassuring smile, but under her cloak, her hands clutched tightly around her waist. A Sahisten delegation had been invited onto Avelonian soil for the first time since their heinous betrayals, and she would be present to hear why they had come. Only a select few on the council were privileged with an invitation to the meeting.

The reason for secrecy, she'd been told, was for the safety of the delegation, but she knew it had as much to do with avoiding the fury and fear that would explode throughout the city if the clans knew. When Astreno offered her a gift from the high chieftain, she had expected it would be something clever and dangerous, but she had not anticipated this. What did Rumar hope to accomplish by welcoming the enemy at the very moment when the country was so vulnerable? Did he really think the clans would accept trade with Sahiste? What did he hope to learn by setting the temple beside the traitors on this first visit since the war?

Whatever his plan, he would be watching her; she had no doubt.

Rom's abrupt movement brought her focus back to the misty darkness. The Arionad stood on guard before she even registered the quick clip-clop of horses approaching.

Two cloaked men rode through the arch that led from the city's central plaza into the temple's outer gardens. One sat straight and easy on a long-legged bay of the elegant breed raised south of the Parnas; and the other, lagging slightly behind, straddled a shaggy mountain beast. The second man was tall enough to look awkward on the little mountain horse. His dun-colored travel cloak bore the red mark of the Shorn, but his twisted left shoulder announced he was no man-at-arms. Nemiah frowned at the odd pair. She had prepared herself for a detail of Rumar's guard, perhaps even a Clan Manitar elder as Rumar's perfunctory nod to her status. What had he sent her instead?

Capa trotted to her side to confront the strangers with a stiff back and raised hackles. The men stopped and dismounted when they saw the edginess of her guardians. The Shorn man took the reins of both horses and stood with eyes downcast. The other, a trim figure as clean-limbed as his mount, came forward and bent in an unhurried bow.

"Good morning, Lady Nemiah. Forgive us for making you wait in the damp."

"Wait, sir?" She couldn't make out his features yet, but his voice seemed familiar.

"Ah, yes. Of course." The man nodded solemnly, but his tone warmed, as though he welcomed her caution. He pushed back his hood, revealing neatly cropped hair of fading wheat, angled features just beginning to slacken with years, and vibrant blue-grey eyes. He drew forth a gold chain from around his neck, exposing the seal of Avelos to the torchlight.

"By the word of High Chieftain Adan Rumar, I offer you and your Arionad safe escort to our meeting with the ambassador." He gave Rom a respectful nod. "Will you give me the great honor of traveling with us?"

She should have guessed. Who else would Rumar send but the elder most steadfastly loyal to him? This ride was likely to be as much of a political challenge as the meeting with the Sahistens.

"If Riana has set our Paths together, it isn't for me to step aside, Elder Trianor. We are pleased to accept your escort."

The elder's expression clouded. "I see we are something of a shock. They wanted to send soldiers, but I thought Riana's Lady would not welcome a trip surrounded by the high chieftain's fighting men. I hope it wasn't ill-considered of me to offer my own company."

Nemiah glanced up in surprise at the man's candor. "Riana values thoughtfulness wherever it is freely offered," she said more kindly. "And so do I. Thank you, Elder."

"No debt, Lady. You are gracious. Forgive me if I hurry us on, but we've a long ride ahead." He stepped forward to hold the stirrup for her, but Rom shifted subtly to be there first. Capa gave a warning growl. With nothing more than an easy smile, the elder stepped back.

"You know, Lord Arionad, your height and your livery make you a notable figure. Let's see what we might do about that, shall we?" The elder searched through his saddlebag for a moment before drawing out a rich blue coat of a finer weave than the dark travel cloak he wore. He held it out. "The fewer people who mark the Chosen Lady's passing, the better."

Rom raised a brow. "If you have reason to expect a troubled journey, we must take more precautions than a change of coat. I will call the Arionade."

"No, no," Trianor said, waving away the idea. "Those who know of this meeting are sworn to silence. I'm just afraid in these days the sight of the Chosen Lady, her Arionad, and the Minister of the Teaching traveling together is odd enough to provoke questions."

"It does sound rather more like the start of a bad jest," Nemiah admitted. She nodded at Rom, who removed his white cloak and covered himself with the dark one. White stood for the Arionade's untainted commitment and perfect loyalty. Deep blue was the Bearer's color: Cael's color. Nemiah tried to ignore any omen in the choice. The elder was right: it was better to travel unnoted.

As Nemiah settled into the saddle, Rigojan pawed the ground, impatient to be moving. Capalino danced an eager circle around the mare. The Shorn scribe held the stirrup for his elder, then waited until the elder was settled before swinging onto his own horse. Despite the scribe's damaged shoulder, he moved gracefully. As Nemiah watched him, he was careful not to meet her gaze.

Elder Trianor led them out of the city through Travitar Gate. Although morning hadn't yet cracked through the grey shell of the sky, guild caravans already lined up at the gate, their carts loaded with grain, dyed wools, pots, plates, leather, brandy, and every other manner of craft. All waited to pay their levies before being allowed into the city's markets. The gatemen had their hands full checking guild membership and inspecting goods.

Many families who traveled to Velantar for the fall gathering avoided the city levies and the competition of the guilds by camping outside the walls. They sold their goods right where they pitched their tents, creating the largest festival market anywhere in Avelos. Clan camps dotted the hills, the banks of the river, and the newly harvested fields of the valley, identified by the mist-laden banners that drooped at the perimeters: the leaping antelope of Ontera, Hilera's rampant bear, the Mavaye of Lasla, Everen's charging ram, and Nadaren's hare. In all, Nemiah counted ten of the fifteen first-clans and twice again the number of cousin clans.

To a stranger it would look as though a disorganized siege held the city. Nemiah twitched her nose at the acrid smells of sheep and morning cook fires and nodded to herself. She saw the order in it.

The valley flickered around her disconcertingly. She set a hand on Rigojan's shoulder to steady herself, reminded that the most important part of the festival had little to do with order. All transitions were sacred to Riana—the change of the seasons, each sunrise and sunset, a maiden's first blood—and at those times, a sensitive person would feel the myriad choices crowding around her. Yet no other transition was as portentous as the Day of Dawnings, when Riana released her hold on order, and light and darkness ruled the sky equally in a perfect, precarious balance. Then was the time that the Paths converged to their closest point, making all outcomes possible. Even now the proximity of past, present, and future caused the landscape to shiver and jump. Riana's ways would continue to shift until even the least sensitive person could feel the potential for change. It was a time when small decisions could have large consequences, knocking a person from one path to another, toward good fortune or disaster. It was a time to renew oaths, to avoid debt, to embrace generosity, and to live honestly.

It was a dangerous time to deal with one's enemies, but Nemiah doubted that Rumar had considered the influence of the converging Paths when he chose to bring Sahiste into Avelos.

The thought made her head hurt, and she rubbed at the back of her neck. What had the priestess of her sacred journey said? The priests of the desert people knew ways to manage nature? Now she found herself on the way to meet the Sahistens. What did they want from Avelos? Could a country driven by hatred want anything other than blood? If Leita were here, she would have known the right questions to ask of the Sahisten envoy.

Guilt tugged at Nemiah. By now, Leita had discovered her absence. She would know it had to do with the message from the palace and would be angry and hurt Nemiah hadn't confided in her. Nemiah sighed. The Bearer had reached the point of incautiousness when she took on the Mapmaker's mantle, and yet she showed no remorse and no acknowledgment of the gravity of what she did. Even the Bearer of Cael's Blade must recognize that Riana set boundaries for a reason. Nemiah knew she had done the right thing in leaving Leita behind. Still, Riana exacted a price for every falsehood, and Nemiah already felt the loneliness that came from deceiving her friend.

"Is it so very difficult for you to leave the city, Lady Nemiah?"

She blinked. The elder had caught her glaring at nothing. "I'm afraid my thoughts are elsewhere this morning."

"I understand. It is a time to provoke reflection. For now, though, we have a few moments on this fine fall day when the road runs smoothly." He smiled, a pleasant, earnest expression.

Now that she looked around, she saw it was indeed a fine day. The fog had lifted, and the sun broke through the clouds in slender golden shafts that lit the hills. Beside the road, the Heartsblood River cut a wide trail of gleaming obsidian. Colorfully painted barges flying the leaping fish of the Watermen's Guild lumbered toward the city, loaded with Makri wine, Delsio grain, and Nadaren timber. Sailors laughed and cursed and shot insults across the decks as they worked. Along the bows of some of the vessels, bare-footed children dangled their skinny legs toward the water, grinning and pointing at the merchants' carts and family caravans heading northward.

Capalino loped beside Nemiah, periodically running down to the bank to splash in the water beneath the docks. When Nemiah whistled, he bounded back to her, tail wagging, strands of muddy riverweed hanging over one ear.

"Some model of Riana's glory you are," she murmured at him.

"He's a fine hound," the elder said, eyeing Capa's wide stance and proud carriage. "No doubt he's a joy on the trail. Did you breed and school him yourself?"

"I wouldn't have taken you for a hunter, Elder." Nemiah looked at the man riding beside her, relieved by the neutrality of the topic. "The breeding of the temple's hounds was laid out by sisters well before my time, but I raised and trained him from a pup."

"Ah, excellent." The elder sat his horse comfortably for a city man. His blue-grey gaze was calm and serious on hers.

"Then is it your belief that the traits of such a magnificent dog are impressed into the pup by the trainer, or are they characteristics that depend all on the blood of the creature's ancestry?"

She smiled and relaxed a little further. The question could have been asked by any one of the novices as they studied the breeding charts.

"The answer to your question is different depending who you ask. For myself, I believe that Madam Kanta and Lady Pahlina were correct when they said history and blood tell whether a pup has the capacity for excellence."

"Then are you saying, as some suggest, that training makes no difference? That any handler can draw out the same abilities from an animal?"

"No, that's not my meaning at all." Nemiah thought of Capalino's skill on the trail and of the hours she had spent teaching the awkward puppy. "Riana shapes the Paths that each creature travels—the environment it's given, the challenges it faces—but likewise the Paths shape the creature. What came before—a pup's ancestry—may foretell his potential, but whether you have a good hunter in the end depends on what comes after. And so, a poor trainer might ruin a promising hound, while a skilled one creates an excellent creature."

The elder nodded thoughtfully. "Just so, just so. But what of the pup born of bad blood?"

"Ah. In my experience, no amount of training can create a worthy hound from a creature descended from flawed lines," she said. "Even if the beast is successful on the trail for a time, the flaws will always out in the end—a nasty temper, distractibility, unwillingness to accept the trainer's direction. A rare few have even turned on their handlers."

"That's a thing I wonder," the elder said, guiding his mount around a rut in the road as he considered. "I know many who would agree with you, Lady. Yet, if the hound is unmanageable, how do you decide whether it is the training that has failed or the pup?"

"Once a hound has been ruined, Elder, does it matter? The creature is dangerous. Best to destroy it and prevent the same faults from continuing in the line."

A pained look crossed the man's features. "Or perhaps we must work to find a better method of training."

"Perhaps," she admitted. "You need have no fear for the temple's beasts. Their training is based on a century of wisdom and only skilled handlers work with the young animals."

"I'm sure of it, Lady. I only wish all creatures could have as much care." The elder sighed and turned his eyes to the landscape.

As the miles ran by, the elder revealed himself to be as sharp-witted as Rumar, but with none of the high chieftain's fire and impulsiveness. Nemiah wondered if his equable manner served him well in his dealings with a council that favored emotional rhetoric over careful thought. They talked about the breeding of good hounds, the favored competitors for the festival games, and the new singers who had come to offer their music for the morning of the Day of Dawnings. The elder seemed disinclined to push more contentious matters into the conversation, and for that, Nemiah was grateful. She would face contention enough when they reached the council.

When the sun touched its zenith, they found themselves approaching the bend in the river where the Clan Delsio town of Panetar lay. Elder Trianor proposed that they spell the horses and take a meal outside the town walls near the water. A little more than half a day's ride from the city and a central crossroads from the east and west, the seat of Clan Delsio was popular with travelers, who often camped for a night or two on the riverbank or beside the golden fields before making the final trek to the gathering.

"Panetar is a pretty place this time of year, if not a quiet one," Elder Trianor said, a smile lighting his face as he watched families sprawl across the sward to eat and rest near the river.

Nemiah nodded absently. Not one of those families knew the danger that entered their land. They carried all their livelihoods with them to the gathering and trusted that their homes and villages would be safe until their return. Dread clambered back onto her shoulders. The land flickered beneath her, and a woman's voice whispered in her head, *"Alende Isan's people will suffer."*

How could she forget for a moment what she rode toward?

"It will be well," the elder offered, noting her quiet. "Don't despair. This time will be marked as one of great changes."

"You speak with confidence, Elder, but these changes could throw us all into an age of darkness."

"I realize that what the high chieftain seeks is new and frightening, but it is what Avelos needs. Rumar sees clearly. He will not lead us wrong."

Nemiah pulled Rigojan to a halt and turned in the saddle. "Chaos has not loomed so close since the Exile," she declared, "and yet Rumar insists on pushing us closer. You seem an insightful man; how is it that you love him so well?"

Elder Trianor halted his bay and looked at her seriously, his pleasant features troubled. "By the manner of his upbringing, Lady, the high chieftain should be a puppet to Clan Manitar and no more. That was all he ever saw in his father and it was the purpose for which Manitar groomed him. Instead, he speaks for himself before the council and is unafraid to challenge the old ways when they no longer serve us. Regardless of who he angers. He is a better man than his rearing says he should be. He is a great man. He did not bring us to this brink of chaos, but without fear or reserve he gives all of what he is to carry us through it. For that, I love him."

Nemiah stared between the ears of her mare, nine years' worth of anger and apprehension rushing through her veins, as the noises of travel—wheels turning, mules braying, people shouting—swirled around her.

"Why do you distrust him so?" the elder asked.

"Because he has forgotten that he can only walk the Paths; he cannot form them. He has forgotten the goddess who set him on his journey."

"Perhaps he has not forgotten as much as you think."

Nemiah returned her gaze to the elder's.

Trianor smiled. "It is by his invitation you are here to represent Riana, after all."

Nemiah didn't have time to think on that before Rom cantered back to her and the elder. He pulled up sharply.

"My lady, we mustn't ride this way. It's not safe. Look beyond the hill."

"What is it?"

She trotted ahead to gaze down the other side of the hill into the small vale below them. A mass of humanity covered the landscape, stretching from the broad riverbank on her left, across the road, and halfway up the opposite edge of the vale to the walls of Panetar. Carts stopped in the middle of the road; animals jostled one another in makeshift pens; men and women, with children in tow, milled slowly through a host of vendors' tents.

Nemiah saw that it wasn't the crowd that made Rom tense beside her. In the center of the impromptu market, a speakers' square had formed. Flatbed carts at each corner of the square served as stages for anyone who fancied himself an orator. At the moment, only the stage nearest the road held a speaker, and he had attracted a large audience. She couldn't make out the words of the fair-haired man, but his voice rose and fell expressively as he paced. One fist beat the air in anger or excitement. When he paused, his audience roared enthusiastically. Beside him on the cart, two men held large, flaming torches and waved bright banners: a bloodied sword on a field of blue. During the Exile War it had been the sigil of Tumal the Just. Now it was the sign of Tumal's Legacy.

Nemiah whistled sharply, and Capa returned from his wandering to heel beside Rigojan. The elder's Shorn scribe stared toward the speaker with aversion in his eyes.

Elder Trianor only pondered the scene with detached interest. "It's naught but a festival you see, Lord Arionad. We've no reason to fear it."

"I thought the council prohibited speakers' squares," Rom muttered. "They're nothing but trouble in a crowd like this."

"In the city they're prohibited," the elder answered. "The clans still have the right to test their elders or their future elders as they see fit." He tilted his head toward Nemiah. "If you've not heard the Legacy speak recently, Lady, perhaps you should. Hear how resentment grows in those who cling too rigidly to the past."

The back of Nemiah's neck prickled at the thought of entering the smothering crowd, but she did want to know what the Legacy spewed at the people this far from the city. She had given Toren Abrigado reason to have more caution in how he treated with the temple, warning him that if he continued to use her as a tool to divert Rumar, she would willingly oblige and confess a full conspiracy between the Legacy and the temple. She had heard nothing from him since spring, but she still feared that the ambitious Minister of the Treasury would take the risk and force her move.

"Very well, Elder. Let us learn what the people have to say during this time of change."

Rom wanted to protest: every line of his body announced it, but here before the elder he only pressed his lips together and nodded.

They urged the horses into the vale. In the press of people, it was impossible to ride abreast, and soon Nemiah rode alone, with Elder Trianor in front of her and Rom and Capa close behind. Odors from penned animals, greasy food, and sweaty bodies made her queasy. A drunken man fell against Rigojan's shoulder, causing the mare to shy. He bowed an apology—to the horse—then, laughing, staggered away. A group of Arionite beggars stumbled barefoot through the crowd, mumbling blasphemous poems and moaning their grief. Some waved the dirty ropes around their wrists toward the sky, calling for Riana to free the Chosen from the mortal prisons that bound them.

Nemiah said a prayer for balance and pushed her mare onward. She could see the Legacy speaker clearly now. He was beautiful and passionate, with blue eyes that flashed like sun on ice and a voice that held the audience enthralled as he stalked across the stage. He'd had training, she thought. She wondered if Abrigado himself schooled the men who spoke for him, but she was distracted when she realized the flames on the stage didn't rise from torches; they were effigies burning on tall pikes: a Shorn man and a long-braided Sahisten, stuffed with twisted straw like the wretches that would burn on Dawnings' Eve to rid the year of bad fortune.

"My friends, through folly and faintheartedness Avelos grows weak!" the man cried. "Look at the ways Tumal's laws are mocked. Shorn women are made scribes to our elders! Shorn men are given weapons and the training to use them! These traitors, whose ancestors murdered our people, are entrusted with our secrets and entrusted to protect us. Tell me, is this sense? Is this strength?"

The crowd roared out its answer. Hundreds of feet stomped against the dirt. Flames from the effigies licked toward the sky. A little girl whimpered in her father's arms.

"My friends, there was an Exile once. Tumal cut deceit and greed out of Avelos with the blade of justice. Now that blade has grown dull. Will we let the wound continue to fester, or do we have the courage to cut it clean once more?"

The crowd roared again. Not far from Nemiah, a group of young Shorn women worked their way anxiously toward the road.

"My friends, there was a time when our prefects were chieftains in their own right, when each elder raised his own army, and the high chieftain in Velantar served the wishes of the clans. Since that time, our honor has been stripped from us, and we are led by a city man who steals the authority of ten centuries. Alende Isan made each clan chieftain the ruler and guide of his own people; how is it that Manitar has set itself above us all for so very long?"

"And in ten centuries," boomed a mocking voice behind Nemiah, "ya can be sure as Cael's balls, there's not a clan that whines louder than Amerre!"

Nemiah turned with the others to see a hulking, fur-clad man climb unsteadily onto the stage opposite the Legacy cart. The head of an axe poked over his left shoulder. The wolf's head of his cloak stared over the right. Unkempt, curly grey hair fell over his eyes but couldn't hide their overbright shine. Against the steel sky, he looked like some incarnation of Cael's Chosen.

"As spoiled as ya are soft, ya southerners, with your gentle winters and wide-open fields. And still ya mew like babes." The man spat into the dirt. "Ya complain about not owning your own armies, but I don't see ya complaining about the northern silver flowing down the Heartsblood ta pay your southern garrisons. I don't hear ya cry 'bout how my boys stand at your borders."

Nemiah drew a sharp breath. He was drunk to speak so in this crowd. The southern clansmen who filled the square did not take the words well. Makri, Amerre, and Delsio knives were loosened from men's belts.

Someone gripped Nemiah's arm. She startled and pulled back before realizing it was Rom.

"My lady, please come away. This mob is like tinder awaiting the spark."

She shook her head. The land around her flickered and spun.

"I can't leave," she breathed. "Not yet. Paths are shifting."

The young Legacy man rose to the challenge; he had the crowd with him. "Are you no longer a part of Avelos that you have no obligation to protect her? Do you think the Sahisten armies will be satisfied to sack only the south? If Velantar should fall, do you think Amuria would pause before rushing to claim the riches of the northern five? We're all in danger under Clan Manitar, you don't know—"

"Enough!" roared the northerner. "If Clan Amerre wants its own army, then ya set down your banners and take up your swords. I've enough'a my boys filling the ranks of the southern Forest Guard so ya can prance and whine like city elders!"

Several people near the northerner turned angrily, ready to prove themselves, but hoofbeats thundered along the knoll, drawing the crowd's attention upward. More than twenty men cantered down from Panetar: the Delsio clanguard. They looked a rough lot, and the expressions on their faces as they spread along the road ranged from annoyed to openly hostile. A red-haired man among them plunged his horse through the crowd, causing indignant shrieks as people scrambled out of the way. He gestured to the Legacy speaker with the tip of his sword.

"Step down and cease this agitation. You are so ordered by Henaro Delsian, Elder of Clan Delsio."

The Legacy man flashed a defiant look at the guard before bending to pick up a burlap sack beside him.

"My friends, hear me!" he shouted at the crowd. "Before I am silenced. Hear what supporters of Manitar would not have you know: Not all the enemies of Avelos are outside her borders! Right now the Sahistens crawl over our land, welcomed by the man who claims the right of Alende Isan to rule! This is the poison that Adan Rumar has loosed on us!" With a snap of his arms, he upturned the bag, sending a knot of serpents flying. A dozen sinuous bodies unwound briefly against the sky before dropping onto the crowd. He lifted another bag and more serpents joined the first. As Nemiah gasped, a third bag followed the first two.

All across the first rows closest to the stage, people cried out and leaped away from the falling vipers. The abrupt compression of the crowd traveled backwards like a wave. Men and women stumbled and fell beside the horses. Rigojan sidestepped and bumped Rom's mount, edging toward panic.

"Lady, this way." Rom jerked his head toward the river, away from the mob and the clanguard.

The men on the cart thrummed their pikes against the wood like a drumbeat. One of the flaming effigies disintegrated and fell, sending burning straw over the crowd. The flaming head of the Shorn man rolled off the cart and onto the dry, yellow grass. With a whoosh of hot air, fire leaped up and began to chew its way through the people.

The screaming started in earnest.

Nemiah hissed an urgent ward against chaos, but confusion spread as quickly as the fire. Instinctively, the people closest to the cart ran for the road, but the armed guards closed like a noose around them, and then it was too late; the flames flared into a barrier. Behind the first rows, fleeing clansmen crashed into the backs of their kin, unknowingly driving them into the fire. Orange tongues tasted girls' long skirts and fluttering ribbons. Flames crept up the wheel of a wool trader's cart and into the sacks of fleece, where the oily hair welcomed them. Penned animals charged their fences and broke free, trampling vendors' tents and family camps. A team of mules bolted off without their driver, dragging their cart until it overturned and spilled its load along the uneven hillside.

Some people cried out for buckets and water, but too quickly, the fire swallowed up the ready fuel and grabbed for more, sweeping down the knoll in a veil of smoke. People barred from the road ran for the river. A child in blue tumbled and disappeared under the feet of those behind her.

"No!" Desperately, Nemiah drove Rigojan toward the fallen child. The mare made no headway against the crowd. Fleeing people buffeted her on all sides. Nemiah choked on the smoke as Cael's power roared across the meadow.

"Make way!" Rom roared beside Nemiah. A futile effort. A woman ran past them, a child shrieking in one arm, another child dragged by the hand. One of the Arionites staggered under Rigojan's nose, beating at the flames that climbed his robe. Rigojan decided it was all too much. She half-reared and came down stiff-legged. Nemiah scrambled to keep her seat but the mare rose again, hooves battling the air. As she pounded down and rose a third time, high over the crowd, Nemiah fell. She dropped backwards out of the saddle, flames and sky blurring in an arch above her. Her body slammed against the hard ground.

Every spring, her mother had pushed the eggs of the mourning doves out of their nests in the eaves. Nemiah remembered the wet crackling sound as each shell broke open, spilling the small life within it onto the dirt.

"She's stirring."

"Goddess be thanked."

"Lady Nemiah?"

Goddess, lend an unworthy servant your strength. Nemiah opened her eyes slowly. Elder Trianor knelt on one side of her, his fine features knit into a worried frown. Beside the elder, a thin man with small eyes and wispy grey hair wrung his hands and murmured snatches of a prayer with all the wrong words. At her other shoulder knelt Rom, pale and still, with an expression she had never before seen in his eyes.

I thought there was nothing you feared, my Arionad.

She pushed against the ground to sit up, and a wave of dizziness sent her floating toward a black fog. She was a good rider; she had grown up riding across her clan's rough territory beside her father. It had been years since she'd been thrown. The experience hadn't grown more pleasant with time. She slid back down. Capa whined and snuffled his wet nose against her hand.

"Perhaps you shouldn't move yet, Lady," Elder Trianor suggested. "Elder Delsian sent for a litter and a healer."

The man beside Elder Trianor bobbed his head solicitously. "Yes, yes. Rest yourself, Chosen Lady. You had a terrible fall. I'm Henaro Delsian and I lead Panetar while our prefect and the rest of Delsio's house of elders attend the gathering. I'll see that you receive the best of care."

Nemiah grimaced as the elder bobbed and wrung his hands over her. She could see him trying to decide whether the temple would blame him for her injury or offer gifts of gratitude for tending her. If he hoped to watch her carted away helplessly, however, he would be disappointed. She glanced at Rom, and he knew what she wanted. He slipped an arm beneath her shoulders and assisted her until she could sit upright.

They had carried her up the hillside toward the town and into the protection of a small stand of juniper trees. Behind her, the elder's scribe had his hands full trying to calm the horses. Here the grass was untouched and a few vendors' tents still stood; everything below the road looked like a nightmare. Fire had scorched the knoll all the way to the river. Smoke uncoiled over smashed tents and overturned carts. A few flames still licked at patches of yellow river grass along the bank. People sat on the road, nursing injuries. Some wandered dazedly through the wreckage, picking up torn sacks of grain or spilled crates of fruit. Others tried to herd loose animals back into damaged pens. A family's earnings from the fall markets would take them through the winter. How many here had lost everything? Someone wailed, a sharp, heart-shattering sound. Nemiah found the source near a cart in the center of the field, where a woman crouched over a small figure in blue.

"I hope your healers make haste, Elder Delsian," she murmured.

"Healers, Lady? What can you mean? Clan Delsio owes nothing—"

"Look! Near the river. Is that guard *attacking* a man?" Nemiah clambered to her feet. One of the clanguard jerked an injured man upright and shoved him toward the shambles. When several other travelers stepped toward their compan-ion, a second guard cantered up to the first, sword drawn. Sword drawn!

"Elder Delsian, call off your clanguard. Quickly!"

"Lady Nemiah," the man began, "You are overwrought. It is well within the right of Clan Delsio to evict these troublemakers from our lands."

The first clanguard knocked one man to the ground with the flat of his sword. Nemiah gasped.

"Sir, by the power of Riana's sacred skies, I compel you to order your guards to stand down!"

"Very well. Very well." Henaro threw up his hands in submission, but his expression turned sour. "Riana guide my ways," he muttered, striding down the hill.

"It *is* within his right," Elder Trianor said behind her. "The old ways still give the first-clans the authority to control travel on their own lands, even if the travelers' tax now goes to the council."

"I know the law. And I'll not see these people done more injury," Nemiah declared.

"Neither would High Chieftain Rumar," he answered gravely. "Which is why he has called for the prefects to relinquish some of their power."

Nemiah remained silent, watching as Henaro waved his clanguard off the travelers. He spoke with his captain, then trudged back up the hill.

"As you demanded, Lady," said the elder when he reached them again.

"Riana witnesses what you've done to heal her order," Nemiah replied. "Now tell me what arrangements will be made to shelter and care for those who have lost the means to reach the city."

The elder went slack-jawed. "Lady! You cannot ask such a thing. We have no debts to Clans Makri or Amerre that require such an effort. Why should we aid agitators who've brought their own ruin down on them?"

"Because the Day of Dawnings is nearly upon you, Elder Delsian, and if you turn away those in need without succor, you will rue the direction of your Path in the new year."

Henaro shrank from her, resentment written across his features. "I cannot obey, even with such a curse at my feet. You must understand: we rely on Clan Manitar's goodwill in our dealings with the Watermen's Guild. We cannot succor Legacy supporters. More trouble such as this and Manitar will see to it our grain never reaches the markets upriver."

A year ago, Nemiah would have fled from this confrontation. Here she stood before it, yet still to no effect. Every bruise on her body throbbed. She closed her eyes to think.

"Manitar would have you care for the people," offered Elder Trianor. Nemiah opened her eyes to find the elder standing beside her. "You know who I am, Elder."

The man bobbed his head and looked increasingly uncomfortable. "Of course, Minister Trianor. But that matter with the Delsio Teachers was long ago and has nothing to do with this. None of the cursed Shorn babes have died since—"

"Stop," Elder Trianor ordered. "I remember Delsio's mistakes clearly enough. Now is a chance for you to demonstrate kindness toward your countrymen. You know my word is to be trusted when I say that High Chieftain Rumar will hear of it and will show his gratitude for it."

Henaro stopped wringing his hands to glance from the elder to Nemiah and back. His small eyes glittered. "High Chieftain Rumar himself? And Prefect Falina? She will know that Clan Delsio does not harbor Legacy within our walls?"

"She will," Elder Trianor assured. "If you also see to it that the Legacy speaker and the northerner are found and held unharmed."

"We'll do our best to find them, but a man who wishes to hide in this land, especially if he has collaborators..." Henaro paused and glanced at the elder's stony expression. "Of course no one in Delsio would shelter Legacy men. Be sure of it. We will find them."

"And there will be proper pyres for those who are lost here," said Nemiah.

"Consider it a Dawnings gift, Lady."

"Riana acknowledges your gifts, Elder."

Henaro bowed to Nemiah and the elder, and backed away hastily before he could be given more obligations. Nemiah watched him go. How they picked at each other, like carrion crows.

"That was well done," Elder Trianor said when the man had gone.

"Nothing here was well done," she replied, touching a hand to the knot at the back of her head. She turned to Rom.

"Captain, go to the temple. Ask for Lady Ansa and tell her we'll need whatever shelter she can provide for as many as she can provide it. Tell her to save some small space for one bruised priestess, her Arionad, and a hound."

"It's not necessary for you to stay," the elder remarked. "Henaro knows better than to break his word to me. He and his Teachers still have debts to pay."

"My hands must go to help my people. Panetar's healers won't reach everyone. If I can do nothing else, I will at least say the prayers and light the pyres. I know you must travel on, Elder. I will not delay you." She straightened and met his gaze. "I hope the changes that come from your meeting are as good for Avelos as you believe they will be."

"Lady, please understand that someone broke their oath to inform the Legacy about the Sahisten delegation. I fear what that means for the ambassador. I must get word to the high chieftain as swiftly as possible." The explanation sounded unexpectedly like an apology, and as the elder surveyed the wreckage across the hillside, his eyes filled with sorrow.

"Sir, let me go." The elder's quiet Shorn scribe stepped forward for the first time. "If the clanguard finds the Legacy speaker, you should be here. You might convince him to name the oathbreaker."

Elder Trianor's gaze lifted. "I wouldn't ask it of you, Sirol. It'll be a long night's ride, and the highwaymen are thick on the road right now for all the goods bound for the gathering."

The scribe's pale eyes shone with a will that Nemiah wouldn't have guessed in him. "Then they'll have no interest in a lone man riding south."

The elder smiled. "By now I should know better than to argue with you. Take Liset. He's faster."

"No, sir. Rimba knows me and can run all night."

"Very well. But you'll eat first, while I write a letter to the high chieftain."

With the consequences of hostility and fear all around them, the unexpected concern the elder showed for his scribe was a balm.

"Take Capalino," Nemiah offered. "Anyone who threatens you will feel his teeth. He'll guide you safely to your destination."

The scribe bowed. Elder Trianor gave her a grateful look. "Your gift means more than you can know, Lady. I'm in your debt."

The night was indeed a long one. Families who had lost their means for surviving the winter needed not just food and shelter, but a healer's care and reassurance. Lady Ansa came down to the field herself, leaning heavily on a cane for balance, but still leading Rom and her own withered Arionad. Her silver head was high as she assessed the scene. The high priestess of the Delsio temple was old enough to have seen the passing of two Chosen Ladies in Velantar; she was red-nosed and rheumy-eyed, but remained hardy as a mountain pony. She wasted no time with ceremony, embracing Nemiah tightly.

"So, Henaro wanted to play with his brother's power by ordering out the clanguard," she snorted. "He was a fool as a child and is a fool of a man; he'll be a fool the day Riana takes him."

Nemiah could have hugged the woman again. "Can you spare the room and provisions?"

"Shelter we have. Too many empty rooms in the temple these days. As for provisions, we'll share whatever's needed. I know you won't let your Delsio sisters starve come midwinter."

"You're a light on the Path, Ansa. Thank you."

With help from Rom and a handful of volunteers from among the travelers, they moved the injured to the unused novices' quarters in the Panetar temple. It was an arduous process that took all afternoon. Family members didn't want to part from their injured loved ones, but feared to leave their animals and goods. They worried that the clanguard would take its retribution if they left the camp. In the end, the Arionade's presence soothed them more than any elder's promise. Southerners believed Lord Arion to be an ancestor of their own clans, and some still held to the legends that Riana sent her lord back to the people in troubled days. By the time Nemiah headed back to the temple with Ansa, Rom was leading one young boy by the hand and a little girl clung to his shoulders as he accompanied a cart of the injured up the hill.

While her Arionad oversaw the transport, Nemiah worked beside the elderly sisters of Panetar to start fires in the dusty quarters, gather bedding, and prepare food. Henaro kept his word and sent two clanguard to the temple with a cart of supplies. The men at least had the grace to look sheepish when they asked if they could offer any assistance. Ansa thanked them and sent them away from the nervous travelers.

As afternoon light surrendered to evening's long shadows, Nemiah helped Ansa treat burns and broken bones. For some, the healer's hands were enough. Others were too far gone for any aid but Riana's to reach them. The little girl who had been trampled by the crowd lay unconscious and as still as twilight. Her mother gripped her hands and would not move from her side. They had only just arrived in Panetar, the woman told Nemiah. It had hardly been a week since she lost her husband and her home to the winds in Trevilan.

"I wish I had the Silvaye to give the child," Ansa murmured, wiping her wrinkled fingers on her apron. "The summer's been too wet and there's none to be found."

"She's so weak, Ansa. A dose of Riana's Chosen would likely send her spirit off the Path." Nemiah squeezed the old priestess's shoulder. She took the mother's desperation to give to Riana at the evening devotion. It wasn't enough, but she could do little else.

The tiny first circle wasn't half-filled by the people of Panetar when Nemiah called to Riana that evening. Among the priestesses were no acolytes or young ones at all; only wrinkled faces and clouded eyes turned devoutly to the sacred sky. No renewal had come to the temple with the Day of Dawnings petitions, not this year or for many years before it.

"I'm going to walk the camp," Ansa told Nemiah after the devotion. They were still standing under the open dome in the quiet of the first circle. "See it's safe and give a blessing."

"Of course." Nemiah's vision blurred with exhaustion. "I'll join you."

They made their way out of the city and down the dark, stony hill with their Arionade beside them. As they approached the camp, bitter murmurs began to reach Nemiah. Campfires by the river lit angry faces, and the talk sizzled with blame: for the clanguard, for Rumar, for Sahiste, and for the temple. Hostility crackled in the air like the fires that had swept down the knoll, licking at Nemiah's awareness. Ansa didn't hesitate to step into the huddled circles to listen or to offer a hopeful word, but Nemiah hung back. Distant voices growled in her ears. The faces of the travelers flickered in front of her: Young faces. Old faces. Bloody faces. Skulls. A serpent slithered past her foot. She flinched backwards.

"My lady?"

Nemiah blinked at the ground. It was empty but for the charred grass. Men and women with worried faces spoke in hushed tones around the fires. Rom's hands gripped her shoulders where she had backed into him.

"What's this?" Ansa returned from one of the campfires, her cane tap-tapping the ground. She leaned close and squinted at Nemiah. "Day of Dawnings is coming, isn't it, child?"

"With more insistence than I've ever felt," Nemiah admitted, wrapping her arms around herself as though she could anchor her awareness where it belonged.

"Time was the only journey a Pathwalker would make during the festival was a sacred journey. I don't suppose you'll tell me now what's so important that it makes our Chosen Lady risk travel while all of Riana's Paths collide with her own?"

"Have you met many Pathwalkers, Ansa?"

The old priestess thumped her cane on the ground and nodded knowingly. "All right. I figured as much. Let's get you back to the temple and I'll tell you about the Pathwalkers of my time. I've a bit of brandy that will put some color in your cheeks, and I could use a cup myself."

Nemiah hoped for boldblood tea, but made do with the liquor Ansa offered. They talked in a quiet corner of the makeshift infirmary so the healer could keep one eye on her patients. Ansa was a trove of information about Pathwalkers. She had known Dorsa, who charted more Paths than any other Chosen Lady; Pahlina, who once traveled Alende Isan's road; and the twins, Shariel and Ria, who Ansa said were so closely bonded that they could share the same Path at the same time.

"Riana no longer gifts our people as she once did," Nemiah observed as dawn approached.

"Of course not," the old priestess snorted as she reached to refill their cups another time. "She won't lend her strength where it might be used against her."

Nemiah put a hand over her own mug and shook her head. "What do you mean to say?"

"That there've always been ones among us who think that Cael not Arion should be the Lady's Consort. Those ones thrive on the kind of trouble we had today. You should be careful."

"No, Ansa. Surely your sisters are true."

"You can find darkness in any corner, child. I'm not just speaking of Panetar. There've been thefts of ancient texts from some of our chapels to the south."

"Ah, Goddess." Nemiah shook her head. "I haven't heard any such rumors since before Pahlina died. Do you really believe it's them?"

"No telling yet. Just keep your eyes sharp, child. These times breed worshipers for Cael."

The words still hung in the air when Ansa's grizzled Arionad interrupted them to announce that Elder Trianor had returned. The elder's expression was pinched after spending the night overseeing the hunt for the agitators. The Legacy speaker, he said, had cousins in Panetar who reluctantly admitted that the man had come from the city to visit, but now traveled toward his family's home on Clan Amerre's lands. Henaro Delsian dispatched the clanguard to go after him. Of the northerner, no one knew a thing.

"If there's no word by midmorning," said the elder, "I'm going on to where I can be of more use. Will you come, Lady?"

The thought of jarring her body against a saddle would bring tears to her eyes if she considered it, but Nemiah nodded. "I will mark the spirits of the dead for Riana's Pathguides and light the pyres. Then I will ride with you."

After the morning devotion, she put on the embroidered green robe she had brought to greet the Sahistens in, and went with Ansa to perform the ritual of flame for two young women, a Shorn man, and two children. All dead by the hands of their own people. Whatever their intentions, the Legacy had murdered clansmen as easily as Sahistens would, and they had destroyed the camp as thoroughly as the killing winds.

Elder Trianor brought the horses, and Nemiah said her reluctant goodbyes to Ansa.

"We must speak again soon," the old priestess murmured as they embraced. "Stay close to your Arionad, child. It's obvious the goddess wears your face for him. He'll keep you well, whatever is to come."

Nemiah kissed the woman's dry cheek and promised herself she would find a way to see Ansa again before winter took hold.

They rode off through the pyre smoke that drifted across the scorched knoll. The bright, bustling market of the day before was dreary and dead.

"It looks like the aftermath of battle," Rom muttered beside her.

"It's not," Nemiah said wearily. "It's only the beginning."

15.
OLD TIES

"You know who told the Legacy about the Sahistens, don't you, Elder Trianor?"

The second day of travel started as what was sure to be Riana's last kiss of the season. The sun glared low in the pale autumn sky. The road, deeply rutted by another moon of too much rain, caused carts to lurch and shudder and sometimes founder. Rigojan's trot jolted every bone in Nemiah's body. She was sore and angry and unable to put thoughts of Panetar behind her.

"I know who will benefit from it," the elder answered, studying a group of men on horseback as they trotted past. "That's not the same as knowing who did it."

"Toren Abrigado," she said bluntly.

"Abrigado is a leader of the Legacy, knows about the meeting, and has much to gain by inciting anger against the high chieftain."

"But?"

The elder turned to look at her. "He's more subtle than to turn to effigies and tricks with snakes. And as much as I disagree with the Minister of the Treasury, I've never known him to forswear an oath."

"He has his hounds to do his work: Gilior Rud. Lancion Makri. None have ever accused them of subtlety."

"Rumar chose carefully when he extended invitations to this meeting, Lady. Rud and Makri were not among those invited."

Nemiah remembered again that her own invitation also had its purpose, and she wasn't entirely certain what it was. She grew quiet, thinking on that. If Rumar still believed her to be acting in concert with the Legacy, then things were about to grow more dangerous for her. Someone would be made to pay for what had happened at Panetar. Manitar couldn't afford to let such dissent go unanswered.

They rode for several more miles in silence, an odd little group among all the clansmen heading to the festival markets. The farther they traveled from the city, the more stares they received. At the sign of a tiny Clan Delsio hamlet, the elder turned his horse into a grove of golden-leaved birch trees. He dismounted and bent to examine the stallion's left forefoot.

"What's wrong with him?" Rom asked, lifting his gaze from the stallion to glance back appraisingly at the passing travelers.

"Nothing. It's a good enough reason to pause if someone's watching. We're too easily followed in this crowd. I think we should leave the road. East of here, the land opens up, and we'll be crossing mostly open meadowland all the way into Everen."

"You think someone would dare to harass us?" Nemiah asked.

"No. Most likely they'll want to follow us to the Sahistens; but after yesterday, I'm not going to gamble on it. I'm sorry, Lady. You would have been better served with a patrol of Rumar's soldiers after all."

Rom said nothing, but Nemiah knew he was thinking of the Arionade they'd left behind. She nodded at the elder and they set off into the forest, under a canopy of gold and red. Rom hung back, watching for followers as the road disappeared.

It wasn't long before the trees thinned into open plains and they left the lands of Clan Delsio to enter Clan Everen's horse country. Here, where miles of countryside unrolled like a Valador-dyed tapestry, clansmen bred the elegant coursers such as Elder Trianor's Liset—and the stockier, agile border horses, which were a cross between the southern coursers and the northern mountain ponies. In the city's clan circles, it was an old joke that the border horse was the only useful thing that ever came of a union between north and south.

They crossed farms and pastureland. Small stands of trees lined creek banks with russet and burgundy. Rom circled back twice during the afternoon, but he found no evidence that anyone watched them, other than the bands of horses who looked up from grazing to stare placidly as they passed.

By early evening, they were deep into Everen territory. The day had grown steadily colder. Ahead, a bank of clouds bruised the sky green and purple. When the sun dropped to the horizon, wind gusted through the meadow grass, violating the quiet twilight with a long, evil hiss. A chill lifted the hair on the back of Nemiah's neck. As thunder rolled across the valley, she pulled to a halt and searched the horizon, uncertain exactly what she was looking for, but dreading that she would find it. The devastated village of Trevilan was less than a day's ride away—or had been.

"It's all right, Lady. The winds bring no rain when they kill. We've only the cold and wet to worry about tonight." Elder Trianor offered her an encouraging smile as he drew up the hood of his cloak. "If we hurry, we'll reach shelter before we're drenched. It's not far now. We'll meet the road over the next hillside."

They reached the road and turned south toward a village. The storm stole the remaining light, wrapping them in chill darkness. Lanterns swung furiously from their posts, casting wavering shadows along the sturdy walls of cottages and stables and one small inn. Nemiah left the hope of warmth behind reluctantly, following the elder out of the village and over another ridge of low hills.

"There's our shelter, Lady."

At the crown of a glen, surrounded by pastures and scattered trees, a walled estate stood sentinel. Lights shone at the gate and from the windows of the great house. The dark forms of horses and the smaller round shadows of sheep huddled near the trees along the banks of a stream. Nemiah caught a breath. Remnants of a tiny pyre would be long gone, but over the shoulder of the house, she could see the hill where the flames were once lit. Velanhan: *Heart's Ease*. The farm had been described to her in tender detail. What better place to hold a meeting with Sahiste than this secluded keep amidst the rolling hills of affable Clan Everen? What better place, indeed?

Something painful and long neglected turned over in her heart. She looked at Rom. He was on guard, black eyes glittering; he also knew who owned these lands.

A pair of soldiers challenged them as they reached the wall, then gave deference and quick entry in response to the elder's greeting. As they trotted toward the house, Rigojan's nervous whinny was answered by calls from the border horses in the stable and the tree-lined paddock behind it: border horses bred for the Forest Guard. Rom drew closer to Nemiah, scowling at the soldiers on watch in the yard who were bold enough to stare. Nemiah felt their eyes on her and realized how very far she was from the high temple and the touchstone of Riana's power.

Light poured across the yard as the front door flew open. Raised voices shot toward them briefly before a woman strode out. The lamp in her hand bounced golden light over her coltish figure, which was clothed in well-fitted breeches, boots, and a belted tunic. Her hair was drawn back in a tail very like that of the two warriors trying to keep up with her. From her youthful shape and energetic step, Nemiah expected a youngster, but as the woman held up the lamp to peer at the elder, yellow light illuminated the worried face of someone perhaps a decade farther along the Paths than Nemiah.

"Tierzen Trianor. Thank the Lady. Sirol reached us late last night. The men have been watching for you."

The elder swung down from his mount and was engulfed in an affectionate embrace. He returned the hug with one arm. "Madam, we're thankful to be here."

The woman's shoulders tensed, and she disengaged from the elder to glare at him. Her tall stature allowed her to face him eye to eye.

"Don't you *madam* me. Not now. I'm already furious it takes something like this to bring you here."

"Ah, Rina." The elder rubbed a hand over his eyes. "I am sorry. It's been too long. And Sarena misses you. In truth, I didn't expect to see you. I thought Enrian would have asked you to go to the city."

"Of course he did. You think I would leave him now? Leave the horses? The farm? No strangers can chase me away from where I belong. I don't care where they come from."

The two warriors behind the woman gazed on her with pride.

The elder smiled faintly. "I should have guessed. I'm glad you're here with him, after all that's happened." He laid his hand on her arm, then glanced back toward Nemiah and Rom. "Forgive me my manners. Lady Nemiah Gabriana, Lord Arionad: please meet Madam Rina Nadel of Velanhan."

Nemiah would have stumbled as she dismounted, if not for Rom to steady her. Of all the roads for the goddess to lead her down, why this one on this day? In thirteen years she had managed never to face Rina Nadel, although she knew the woman's most intimate grief and had done nothing to ease it.

At the elder's introduction, the woman sank to one knee, bowed her head, then looked up to Nemiah and the sacred sky. "Riana's Bright Star, you are the guide of us all. In your light we are sheltered. Now take shelter of your own. The warmth of our hearth and the wealth of our table are yours. Rest with us at Velanhan until you must walk the Paths once more."

How many years had passed since Nemiah heard the old formal greeting? The welcome, so genuine and so unlooked-for, touched too many vulnerable points at once. Her eyes stung as she reached out to touch the woman's brow.

"Lucky am I to walk this Path. Let Riana bless your home with the comfort of her order."

Madam Nadel came lightly to her feet. Her green eyes shone in the lamplight. Green was so rare among those not cursed that Nemiah found herself staring. Her own green eyes served as a reminder of her family's shame. Although Enrian had never turned from them, he never told her that his wife carried the same mark. But then, he had kept many things to himself, and in the end he rejected her. She and the goddess both had lost him.

"Thank you, Lady." Madam Nadel met Nemiah's gaze. Lightning flashed and raindrops began to fall. "Come inside. The storm has arrived."

A groom led the horses away, and Madam Nadel ushered Nemiah, Rom, and the elder into the house. The stone-and-timber building was laid out in the ancient style, with the high-ceilinged central hall, surrounded by public chambers—a library, receiving rooms, the kitchens—on the first floor. Sleeping quarters and the other private rooms in the house would be on the second floor.

The young soldier on watch in the hall came to attention as they entered. Rina Nadel nodded to him as she led the group through the hall and into a small, pretty chamber. Velanhan did not preen, with murals and sculptures and gilding, like the old homes in Elders' Circle; but it offered solid walls and unpretentious warmth.

"Be comfortable," their hostess encouraged them before excusing herself from the room. A girl entered soon after and served them tea flavored with anise and honey. Rom set himself beside Nemiah's chair. The elder stood by the fireplace, sipping his tea and studying an old map of Avelos above the mantle. Nemiah was glad simply to be sitting still. The fire heated the room, and the chair hugged her aching body.

"Tierzen, they want to speak with you immediately."

Nemiah lifted her head and blinked. Madam Nadel stood at the doorway.

"I imagined they would." The elder set down his cup and ran a hand through his hair. "I hope we'll have time to speak later, Rina. Lady Nemiah."

Nemiah climbed to her feet to follow. Madam Nadel moved into her way. "Lady, you've had a long hard ride. Let me show you where you might wash away the dust of the road and take some rest."

The elder turned back, frowning. "Rina, what's this?"

"They want to speak with you, Tierzen. Just you." Madam Nadel bowed her head to Nemiah, but stood as solid as oak. "I've a bath drawn that will ease your bruises, Lady."

Nemiah straightened in denial of her weariness. "Madam, Avelos needs her guide on the Paths ahead. I don't believe that a woman who remembers the old greeting sets the word of the high chieftain above the goddess."

Something akin to the storm that was beginning to lash the house flashed in Madam Nadel's expression. "This word comes from the General of the Southern Towers. And he does not share my devotion."

And so it started. Nemiah's exhaustion dragged at her. She had hoped to get through at least one night without confronting this conflict.

"Very well," she said quietly. "I accepted the hospitality of the house. I won't dispute the right of my host to close a door to me. Not tonight."

Madam Nadel's gaze remained fierce, but she bowed her head once more. The elder looked relieved; with a nod, he disappeared through a set of heavy doors on the other side of the central hall. Men's voices rose in greeting. Behind those doors were the channels to power in Avelos and the key to the dangers of Sahiste. Nemiah sighed and followed her hostess up the stairs.

The suite of rooms Madam Nadel provided were large and airy: two chairs and a short table sat under rain-spattered windows that overlooked the pasture and the front gate. On the other side of the room stood a tall bed, where her bags already waited for her. None of the rest mattered when Nemiah saw the large tub filled with steaming water that squatted beside the hearth. Another bucket warmed by the fire.

Madam Nadel moved about the room silently, drawing the shutters, smoothing the blue bedcovers. The young girl who had served them tea followed her into the room, now carrying a platter of food, which she set on the table before silently slipping away. Thunder rolled across the sky, rattling the shutters.

"He has paid dearly for turning his back on Riana, Lady."

Rina Nadel stood tall and straight as a guard. No one would know that her husband and her goddess tore her in two. Nemiah hadn't expected the wife of Enrian Nadel to remain faithful to the temple, not after all these years and all she had lost.

"I never wished him harm, madam," she answered.

"Whether you did or no, Lady, the goddess tends to her order. It could be no other way."

Nemiah nodded, wishing she could dislike the woman. For so long she had imagined someone else; her own desire painted a very different portrait of who Rina Nadel would be. "Riana has always sent him back to you; at least take comfort in that."

"I do. Even though she leaves less of him each time, I do." Madam Nadel hesitated, then looked down to meet Nemiah's gaze. "In return, I do not ask him to be other than who he is. He walks the Path he was given. Your arrival will not alter that. Do you understand?"

It was a warning. Enrian Nadel was the General of the Southern Towers and friend to the High Chieftain of Avelos. He would not hesitate to sacrifice her or the temple, if he thought it necessary for Avelos. Nemiah nodded. "I understand. And I thank you."

The woman said nothing, but her bow was formal and correct. She backed from the room and pulled the door closed.

When Nemiah could no longer hear footsteps in the hall, she collapsed into a chair by the fire. She stared silently into the flames for long enough that Rom had carried his bags into the adjoining room and unpacked her own things into a corner wardrobe by the time she pulled herself back.

"What am I doing here, Rom? I should have stayed in Panetar, where at least I might have been of use to Ansa."

The Arionad finished laying out a plate of food from the platter and set it in front of her. There were sausages and bread and warm spiced fruit with cream. "Will the general convince Rumar to keep you from the meetings?"

She pushed at a piece of bread, too tired to be hungry. "If that's all he manages, then I'm probably fortunate."

Rom's frown deepened. "If you believe he will act against you, then we must leave. Tonight."

"No. I didn't mean it that way. Enrian Nadel has the cleverness of an elder but a soldier's notion of honor. He'll not harm a guest." She leaned forward to tug off her boots; the pain that streaked down her back convinced her otherwise. She grimaced and straightened gingerly. "He will do his best to keep me from influencing Rumar. He'll have his own plans."

Rom set down the morsel of food in his hand and went to one knee at her feet. Firelight lent his gaze an unexpected warmth. He wasn't golden and handsome in the way of a Velantar aristocrat, her Arionad. His features were carved from the granite of the Parnas Mountains. His black hair and beard were curled and shot with grey. Stone and steel shaped him. As she studied him, he reached toward her.

"My Lady?"

On any night but Dawnings' Eve he asked permission to touch her. That portentous night approached swiftly, and she felt it charging the distance between them. She nodded her consent, closing her eyes and leaning her head against the chair as he drew off her boots and gently rubbed the blood back into her feet.

"The general cannot see the Paths, my lady. Tomorrow you will find a way around him. Let tonight be for rest."

She laughed humorlessly. "See the Paths? His father was a mapmaker for the Forest Guard. Did you know that? Perhaps that's why Enrian Nadel has remarkably clear vision for one so far from the goddess."

"Not clear enough that he understands the importance of what you do."

Nemiah laid a hand on her Arionad's bowed head. Here was loyalty as she would never know it again. Every Dawnings' Eve since he first swore himself to her, Rom endured the mystery of Lord Arion's Trial, facing temptation on the night when the goddess turned away from the Paths, laid aside her power, and bared her throat to her captain's blade. Every Dawnings' Eve, Nemiah accepted Rom's sacrifice—his life for hers—as he renewed his oath. She welcomed him then, even as Riana welcomed Lord Arion. Already her body trembled, remembering the moment of perfect balance between power and helplessness and the passion with which Rom chose between them.

How was it, then, that a mapmaker's son who shunned the goddess could still trouble her?

From his place at her feet, her Arionad watched her closely. He knew her too well. She glanced away.

"Let your faith in me never be misplaced," she whispered.

"You will find the strength to do what you must, and I will be beside you, fighting off Cael in whatever form he strikes." He stood and frowned down at her. "Try to sleep, my lady."

She smiled a little; he always knew when she was struggling. "Thank you, Rom. Rest gently."

As he bowed low, she brushed her fingers against his cheek and heard him catch his breath. One more quarter of the moon's turning, and Dawnings' Eve would be upon them.

Rom's eyes sparkled as he straightened. "Riana guide you, my lady."

16.
SHIFTING BALANCE

When Rom had gone to his own room, Nemiah pulled off her travel-stained robes and stepped into the bath by the fire. She melted into the water with a sigh, letting the heat soak into her abused muscles. Crushed herbs and dried flower petals gave the steam the scent of spring. Nemiah closed her eyes. Memories of Dawnings' Eve were nudged aside by images of honeyberry blossoms dripping from their boughs on the banks of the Heartsblood River outside the city walls. She was first sent to Enrian in the spring.

Enrian. The name meant *of Riana* or *from Riana.* Mothers called their boys so when they wished to draw the goddess's protection upon them. It was a powerful name, one that earned the Lady's attention and forgiveness. Had Enrian Nadel ever found a way to forgive himself?

Nemiah was newly anointed when Lady Pahlina directed her to attend the young Forest Guard captain. Too arrogant then, she preened that the Chosen Lady had picked her to attend the darling of Travitar Hill, the high chieftain's acknowledged favorite. What she saw in him those first days, however, was no charming hero of Avelos. The captain's infant daughter had died of a lung sickness in her first month, and he demanded answers for it. His anger at the goddess so shocked Nemiah that all her carefully selected teachings and clever observations went out of her head. She spoke hardly at all in their first meeting, could only listen to him roar of his wife's endless devotion to the Lady, his own acceptance of chaos as an inevitable part of a soldier's life, and his rage that such chaos could slay his babe. When he left that day, sad and spent, Nemiah knew she had failed both the man and the goddess. Yet the next day he returned, asking to talk with her again, and the next and the next, all through the spring and into the summer. They spent uncountable hours together. She saw what an agile mind he possessed, how he recognized so clearly the motives of others but twisted himself in knots to avoid acknowledging his own needs.

One bright morning beside the river, he shared the rest of the horrible truth about his daughter's death: the little girl had been born an Avelun, and he knew the curse to be his own fault. His life as a soldier caused him to walk ever in Cael's shadow, and he had passed that taint to his offspring. His babe hadn't lived to her Shearing, but it wasn't her death that broke him; it was his relief when she died. He swore he would not risk inflicting the curse upon a child ever again.

That day, Nemiah went to Lady Pahlina with a request, and Pahlina gave permission for her to offer the captain the consolation that only Riana's priestesses could give a man. Holding his hand in the courtyard one night, her own heart full of confusing emotions, Nemiah offered Riana's blessing to him, and he had refused it. Refused Riana. Refused hope. Refused her. He never returned to the temple again.

A scratching sound and a familiar woof at the outer door startled Nemiah from her memories. A heartbeat later there was a knock.

"One moment." She rose from the water and pulled on her lush robe of grey-green. The scratching came again as she belted the robe and set her feet into her slippers. No sooner had she unlatched the door than Capalino nosed his way inside. He trotted a quick patrol around the room, nipped a sausage from her plate, and leaped upon the bed.

From the doorway, Elder Trianor smiled. "He knew you were here the moment he saw me, and let me know it as plainly as if he could speak the words."

Nemiah glanced over her shoulder and the hound gave her a doggy grin, tongue lolling. "Even good training and fine bloodlines can still produce a troublemaker," she said dryly.

"Sirol wouldn't have made it through without him. I said I am in your debt, Lady, and I meant it. Can I come in?"

"You're not afraid to be seen speaking with the high priestess in her exile?"

The elder grimaced. "It wasn't the best of beginnings, I realize. There were things the high chieftain needed to know."

"Such as whether I was the one who broke faith to consort with the Legacy? Tell me, is Adan Rumar more afraid I will reenact old betrayals with the Sahistens or commit new ones with Toren Abrigado?"

The elder didn't flinch at her tone. "I told the high chieftain that the Chosen Lady of Avelos cares too much for the people to risk harm to them. This *exile*, as you name it, is not what you think, Lady. The Sahisten ambassador departed this afternoon."

Nemiah let out a breath. She cast a glance at Capa sitting on the bed before meeting the elder's gaze again.

"Forgive me. I've lost my patience for games." She gestured for the man to enter. "Please come in and tell me what happened."

The elder took a seat, stretching his long legs under the table to fit more comfortably. Nemiah wrapped a shawl over her shoulders to fend off the draft from the window before sitting across from him. Capa hopped off the bed to settle at her feet.

"They surprised us," the elder began. "The delegation arrived nearly a day earlier than we expected. They crossed the border without an escort and waited on our side of Makri Tower until the Forest Guard came to bring them to Velanhan." He flashed an appreciative smile. "It was neatly and bravely done. They wanted us to see that they'd not be helpless in our land."

"Or to show us that they can cross our borders at their whim."

"True enough," he admitted. "Nothing they do has but a single meaning. They're subtle folk."

"And was their goal to taunt us with our own weakness?" Nemiah asked. "For what else could they accomplish in so short a meeting? The council can barely finish a greeting in one morning."

"Mmm." The elder reached into a pocket and withdrew a sphere. He slid the coin agilely over his fingers as his blue-grey gaze became thoughtful. "Sahiste has no equivalent to our council. The *Camril Fi*, their great assembly of powerful families, only holds the authority to advise the king not to act. For good or ill, that means they don't spend so much time in debate. The envoy made an offer to Rumar face-to-face, so the high chieftain might judge their intentions more clearly. Then they left. They expect a prompt response."

"And the offer?"

"Open borders. Open trade."

Nemiah straightened sharply. "Why? Why now?"

Silver flashed between the man's fingers as he rolled the sphere. "The answer to that question is one of the many things the council will argue over in the coming days. My answer? They've an heir looking to his throne and trying to decide what his country needs. He's decided it isn't war. He's already brokered a cessation of violence with Laebek. The two ruling houses have sworn some bond of family—all the meanings of that aren't entirely clear; there were translation problems. Apparently one thing it means is that a younger nephew of King Javahari will wed Prince Roelof's daughter."

"Then they're looking for a daughter of Avelos for their heir?"

"Not at all. Prince Ashani is wed to one of his own people. They want access to our grain and wool and an easier road to Amurian steel and leather. An open border with us would allow them to avoid the Sonan swamps on the road to Amuria."

"You would offer Sahiste a route through the very heart of Avelos? Will you also let them inside the walls of Velantar?"

Elder Trianor lifted a hand. "Peace, Lady. There's another thing you should know. The heir himself risked the journey to come to us. Prince Ashani rode into Avelos with fewer than ten men. Javahari set the future of Sahiste into our hands."

Nemiah shivered. "If harm befalls the heir on our lands, it will be an invitation to war."

"Lady, it's something no king of Sahiste has ever done, not before or since the Exile. I think we should consider that a hopeful sign."

Nemiah owned little hope for a trusting relationship with Sahiste. "What does Rumar say?"

"He will consider all the implications of this request before giving an answer."

"You mean he'll allow the clans to speak their minds before using sovereign right to give the answer he's planned all along."

"I understand why you fear, Lady, but I beg you to consider what fear bought us at Panetar."

Nemiah sat back and stared at the man. "They fascinate you, these Sahistens, don't they? You want to know them."

The elder smiled and closed his fist over the silver sphere. "The Sahistens tame climates that would wither our stoutest crops. They carve fortresses out of mountains. And they have centuries of stories we've never heard. I don't think we can refuse the opportunity to learn from them."

"I don't think we can survive if we take it," Nemiah argued. "I've seen the end of the Path we're on. The killing winds are but one sign of it. Elder Trianor, you don't invite strangers into your home when your walls are already on fire."

"Unless they offer you a bucket of water," the elder replied. He slipped the sphere back into his pocket. "We'll not determine how to answer the question tonight, Lady. It will be the topic that consumes us in the following days."

"And will I have a place in the debates?"

The elder looked down and shook his head apologetically. "I'm afraid that's not within my power to say. Not everyone believes the temple should have a seat at the council table. Especially when the debate involves Sahiste."

She pressed her lips together. Would Riana's servants ever escape the stain of Lady Amalia's treason?

"I suppose I should be grateful to be allowed under the same roof as our elders." She rose, and the elder took her hint; with a sigh he untangled himself from his chair and followed her toward the door.

After a moment, she regretted her tone. "Tierzen Trianor," she said more quietly, "you've been straightforward and open. I am grateful for your honesty."

The elder bowed his head. "One thing more you might be interested to know, Lady. Before coming to us, Prince Ashani made a pilgrimage to seek the guidance of an order of priests, a group he called Lumati's Blessed or the Favored of Lumati. They told him it's time for the Chosen and the serpent to hunt together. That meant something important to him. If we accept his offer, I think he'll not break his word."

The ground undulated beneath Nemiah's feet. She wrapped her arms around herself.

"You're a good man, Elder. I am sorry we walk in opposite directions on this Path."

Sadness flickered in the elder's gaze, but he gave her a respectful bow. "I hope we'll have the chance to speak again, Lady. We may walk in different directions, but I believe we seek the same destination." He wished her a good night before taking his leave.

Nemiah leaned against the door, pondering the elder's words. His optimism continued to befuddle her. Was it more likely that an ambitious heir had thrown off the influence of generations of bloodshed to try some risky new gambit, or that this visit by the Sahistens was simply one more step toward their goal of destroying Avelos? Was it more likely that Sahiste's gods wished the Chosen and the serpent to hunt together—or that they intended the serpent to hunt the Chosen? What did the elder see? What did Rumar see that led him in this dangerous direction?

With a sigh, she put the thoughts aside and gathered the strength to shuffle toward the hope of sleep. She blew out the candle on the table and turned down the lamp in its sconce. Thick, soft blankets welcomed her as she nested deep into the feather bed. With a grunt, Capa jumped onto the bed, then curled up against her back. She murmured prayers for the day's closing and shut her eyes.

"Nine years she's the Chosen Lady and what good is she?" a sour voice muttered. "She's a Pathwalker who can't walk."

"A fool she was the day she was born and a fool she'll be the day Riana takes her."

"She doesn't remember the ancients," a third voice said with disgust. "We're doomed to the darkness."

Nemiah drew herself up. It was a clear, cold night in the city. The stone stairs of the high temple chilled her bare feet and icy fingers crept up her thin gown. Bena, Ansa, and Rendeta formed a half-circle several steps below her.

"I studied as hard as anyone," she told them. "Why do you mock me?"

"Studied," Bena snorted. She reached into a basket and pulled out a rock the size of a sparrow. "You never read the walls or listened to the songs."

"I read all that was given to me."

"What was fed to you, like a helpless babe. Did you ever think for yourself? Did you ever ask for more than what they gave you?" Rendeta hoisted two stones in her hands.

"Name for us the sacred place that came before Tumal," Ansa demanded, grabbing her own stone from the basket. "Before Alende Isan. Before all but the goddess herself."

"Where is held the knowledge of the ancients' power?" Bena asked. "Where might be found Riana's lost secrets?"

"I don't know this riddle," Nemiah answered, shivering. She looked from one woman to another. "I am sorry. I should never have been chosen."

The first rock struck her shoulder and knocked her backwards. She cried out in pain and surprise as the second rock hit her thigh. Her leg buckled and she sat down hard on the stair.

"But you *were* Chosen," Ansa said, "and you fled the responsibility."

The third stone smashed her cheek. Lights exploded around her. She tasted iron.

"With arrogance and ritual, you hide yourself from our people's struggles," Rendeta said.

Bena smirked and flung another rock. "There's a price to pay for cowardice."

The women scrambled for more stones. Nemiah shielded her head in her arms as the missiles smashed her body and chipped the stairs around her. One rock crushed something within her chest and suddenly it was a battle to breathe. Darkness opened its maw and she slid downward.

"Leave her be! It's not yet time for this sacrifice!"

Nemiah looked up, but couldn't see through the blood streaming into her eyes.

"Little dove," murmured a familiar voice.

"My lady of the Paths," Nemiah gasped.

"It's Altan Mar," the Pathwalker whispered. "Altan Mar is the answer to their riddle. The Palace in the sky where the ancients studied Riana's secrets. You know it. You only need let yourself remember."

The Pathwalker's tears wet her face. The woman's sadness was a whining in her ears.

"There's a price to pay for cowardice," Bena repeated.

Nemiah awoke with a start to a wet tongue bathing her cheek and a thick-clawed foot pawing urgently at her chest. She wrapped her arms around the dog's neck and buried her cheek in his ruff, waiting for the cold to take her. It didn't come. This wasn't another sacred journey. It was no more than a nightmare. Her own memory had taken the form of the mysterious priestess, reminding her to think of one name.

Altan Mar.

Mountain sanctuary of the ancients. Beloved of Alende Isan. Older than all but the goddess herself. Altan Mar, the Palace in the Sky, was abandoned when Cael's fire brought death in the form of heat and ash, and was remembered now only in song.

The residue of the dream kept pain and fear burning through her veins.

"I need to see the sky," Nemiah panted at Capa, throwing off the covers and slipping out of bed. "Come outside with me."

The hound thought it a fine idea. He paced around the door while Nemiah dressed, then dragged on her boots and cloak. Silently, she drew back the latch and slipped into the hall. She waited a moment before making her way to the stairs. Rom wouldn't understand why she needed to go out alone. Orange hearth-glow illuminated the central hall. Two soldiers were on watch there, dicing at the table. One of them lifted his head to peer at her, decided she was no threat and turned back to his game.

Outside, the wind had died and the rain had turned to a fine mist. The scent of moist dirt and moldering leaves rose in the cold. Capa bounded into the dark, toward the line of trees that marked the paddock behind the stables. His breath turned to steam as he paused to snuffle at a puddle, then looked back to see if Nemiah followed. She did. The hound was Riana's finder of trails, and she didn't know what she was looking for.

Her boots made soft smacking sounds against the wet ground as she entered the trees. Ancient oaks stretched gnarled branches old enough to have witnessed the Exile War. At the edge of the grove, a railed fence ran the length of the pad-dock. Moonlight diffused through the mist and made ghosts of the slumbering horses and sheep. Velanhan. *Heart's Ease.* How long would it stand against the killing winds? Against Sahiste?

The warrior appeared without warning in the strip of land between the trees and the paddock. Nemiah stopped short and ordered Capa to her side, hoping the shadows would conceal them. The last thing she needed was to be questioned by one of the general's men. The lean soldier patrolled the fence line silently, but with some stiffness, a tough old mountain cat determined to hold its territory. As he stalked closer, he lifted his head, as though catching a familiar scent. Moonlight limned his profile. Nemiah drew a sharp breath and pulled back against the rough bark of a tree.

The warrior went still, then without looking in her direction, he turned to-ward the fence and set both hands where she could see them on the top rail.

"Are you afraid to witness the price your goddess exacts upon those who question her?" His low voice carved the darkness like a blade. Capa responded with a warning growl deep in his throat. Nemiah shivered. She should never have come out alone.

"I'm not afraid to witness Riana's balance," she answered, stepping out of the trees.

General Enrian Nadel turned toward her slowly. The mist made it difficult to read his expression at first. Then he lifted his face, and she saw the scars. They twisted across his cheeks and into his beard. They cut down his neck and disappeared into his leather coat. They webbed his hands and wrapped his wrists.

"I will not speak of what no longer exists," he replied.

She searched for the man she had known within the ravaged features. Illness had burned his flesh and left him gaunt. There had been rumors that he would step down, that Clan Amerre had petitioned the council for it, and that one of his brightest officers had sided with the Legacy on it.

She held his gaze, as though she weren't afraid. "Then…shall we speak of why I'm here? You might just as well have convinced the high chieftain not to bring me all the way to Velanhan if you were so worried over my influence."

The detached smile he showed her at least was his. It always gave her the sense that he looked upon the world from one step outside it.

"Lady, I know Sahiste's every move before Velantar does. I'm the only one at the council table who speaks passable Sahine. And Adan Rumar holds me to his service, despite what it costs him with the clans. Do you truly believe I have reason to fear your influence?"

Honesty that, not boasting. A man with his power had no need to boast. "You believe I betrayed the Sahisten envoy to the Legacy?"

"I believe you would just as soon drown a babe as work with Tumal's Legacy."

"Then why have you convinced Rumar to shut me out of the council?" she cried, her composure shredding. "I need this opportunity to reach him. For the sake of Avelos, I must reach him!" The bruises on her back hurt when she moved, reminding her of the impact of stone.

"Nemiah." He took a swift step backwards, his neutral stance thrown off. "Nemiah, I heard what happened at Panetar. I knew what it would do to you. If you faced the clans in this state, Abrigado and his allies would tear you to pieces. I only meant to give you the night. Rina was to warn you."

I do not ask him to be other than who he is. He walks the Path he was given. She had been so sure of finding hostility; had she mistaken Madam Nadel's meaning? Or had the wife of the General of the Southern Towers intended her message to be mistaken, a small retribution after all? Nemiah wrapped her arms around her chest and closed her eyes. Capa pressed his warm body against her legs. Far away, thunder rumbled over the land. And at the very edge of her awareness, infinite Paths shifted and turned.

"I'm not your enemy, Nemiah."

As he said her name again, her perception rippled, like rings of water around a stone. Enrian Nadel was the stone, and he could crush her or gently set the pools in motion.

"You rejected Riana's gift."

"You were a child," he said gruffly, turning away to stare into the mist. "I rejected Lady Pahlina's bid to bind one of the high chieftain's men to the temple."

"Is that what you thought it was?"

He glanced sidelong at her, doubt shadowing his eyes.

For a moment, she owned the courage to step into the circle of his arms and offer him the gift he had long ago refused. But in the house a woman waited for whatever part of her love the goddess would return to her tonight. Nemiah looked at Enrian Nadel and realized Riana had taken enough. Nothing she could offer him would be a gift.

Without warning, the night turned sideways and she lost all sense of balance. Wind rushed through her hair as the world spun out from under her. Blue and red stars somersaulted at the corners of her vision.

From far away, someone called her name. Strong hands grasped her shoulders. Gently, they introduced her to the ground. She planted her hands in the damp grass, relieved for the orientation to up and down.

"What was that?" Enrian asked, removing his hands and looking her over.

"The Day of Dawnings," she said hoarsely, although the excuse had grown thin to her own ears. "The Paths twist sharply as it nears."

"When I have an officer on the lines who looks as you do, I send him off for rest before he makes a mistake that costs his men's lives."

Over Enrian's shoulder, the sky still spun. She pulled her gaze to his stable form. "Perhaps this summer has scarred us both," she said softly.

A muscle twitched in his jaw, jerking one red weal across his cheek. "You've seen the killing winds?"

"I dream of them. I walk Paths destroyed by them. I see our country blown to tatters if we do not stop them."

The soldier hissed under his breath. "I would that I could spare you the horror, but I've found no way to defeat them." Frustration steamed off him into the cold air. "For the first time in all the years I've held our borders, I am facing a foe I cannot drive out."

She looked up at him. "Sahiste has grown that strong?"

"Oh, no, this isn't Javahari's doing. If Sahiste held the key to the winds, the king would have no reason to treat with us. Whatever Javahari's planned, it will involve sword and spear and living men to wield them. The winds are darker than war."

He stilled, searching past her shoulder with a hunter's gaze for something she couldn't see. Moonlight streamed through the mist, washing his form in ghostly grey. Slowly, he drew one arm across his body like a man raising a sword.

"Enrian?"

He looked at her, his gaze raw with violence and pain. Her breath caught. Enrian Nadel might be clear-sighted and clever and sometimes charming, but she should never forget how much horror he had endured, and how much he had delivered.

She said his name again, more quietly. "I see the nightmares hunt you too."

With a visible struggle, he brought himself back, drawing a shuddering breath and lowering his arm. After a moment, he shook his head.

"A soldier could fill the temple library with his nightmares. They're nothing to dread. Only a man's attempts to make sense of the patterns of his life."

"They are shadows of the Paths, Enrian. What Path have you walked that fills your gaze with such agony?"

He gave her a ghoulish smile. "You think that two days listening to Toren Abrigado's self-serving rhetoric isn't enough?"

"Please don't," she murmured. "You shared your fears with me once."

He looked away, flexing his large, callused hands as though they pained him. When he glanced at her again, his sharp gaze had softened to something less certain.

"I don't know, Nemiah. I have burdened no one with what I've seen—for there's no response the soldiers of Avelos can make, and Rina…" He glanced toward the hill where a tiny pyre once burned. "I've already burdened Rina past the point of bearing. But your goddess cursed me with this Path. Perhaps the circle will be completed if I pass the burden to you."

The moment was hers; he was vulnerable. If she chose it, she could exploit his openness for her own purpose. Pahlina would have done it. Leita would tell her she must do it. But Nemiah had gone to him first as Riana's healer, and she could not pervert the bond that, beyond any expectation, still lingered between them.

"Tell me," she said gently.

Silence stretched between them, until she thought he would turn and stride away. Then he lifted one hand to the hilt of his sword.

"The winds caught us just after dawn. We thought it was only a fast-moving storm, and by the time we knew different, it was too late. I watched my boys sliced apart that day, and I could do nothing for them. Nightmares can't begin to capture the horror of it. It's a howling beast that beats you down and skins you alive. For hours, we knew only the noise, the pain, and the blinding, choking dust. I was addled for a time; I confess it. But, Lady, I know what I witnessed when the winds stopped their howling. It was no trick of the mind. No country holds the secret of the killing winds. They are the work of demons: Cael's messengers who care nothing for honor or love or lies and hatred, only the destruction of the bonds of men."

The words came hard to a man accustomed to overcoming challenges through his own strength and wit, but Nemiah didn't doubt them. This son of a mapmaker possessed sight that remained true, even when he closed his eyes to the goddess. Had he been a woman, he would have made a valuable guide. Nemiah suddenly understood why her Path led to Velanhan.

Altan Mar.

"You saw the demon?"

"He cursed me. Set his grey feather in my hand."

"Ah, Goddess. Your words complete a riddle, Enrian. If demons we must fight, then I know where we will find the means to defend ourselves."

"Where?" He leaned forward so abruptly that Capa let out an anxious woof. Nemiah thought he would grab her, but he clenched his hands around the rail beside her instead.

"Where?" he repeated. "What do you know?"

"It will take dedicated men to find it. Ones who can defend themselves in the wilds. And a priestess who understands Riana's ways. Can you convince Rumar to agree to such a company?"

His expression grew wary as he leaned over her. "Do not toy with me, Nemiah. You know by now that you'll not have me for a temple pawn."

"I know," she said quickly. "I know. There's no subterfuge in what I tell you. I speak of Altan Mar."

"Alende Isan's seat? That ancient place is far from Avelos and long destroyed, if it ever was more than a tale."

"No, Enrian. Somewhere it stands, though I cannot tell you how I know it. Some mysteries even you must allow."

He let out a breath and released his grip on the fence. "You don't know where."

"Alende's home lay among the rocky crags and stretched up to the sky," she sang faintly. She did remember some of the songs. She paused and sat up straighter. "What of the maps left to you?"

"My father mapped terrain for an army, not the sacred places in songs." The general frowned and cast a glance in the direction of the house. "Although his collection does hold fragments of some ancient scrolls."

"Altan Mar is out there, with knowledge we've lost. I must have your aid to find it. If I bring this to the high chieftain, he will reject the idea out of hand or drop it upon the council to let it languish."

"And it will languish," Enrian observed. "The council will debate nothing now but Sahiste's proposal for open borders."

"Enrian, you know that Rumar will heed you if you ask this of him. Choose your own men, ones who understand the urgency of this hunt. My priestess knows the history of the ancients as well as any can, and she's sensitive to Riana's ways. She'll understand how to carry whatever secrets they find."

He stared at her, his expression struck between disbelief and wonder. "You would put your lady in the hands of the Forest Guard?"

Nemiah held up her palms in a gesture of offering. "For the sake of Avelos, I must trust you in this."

She waited, hands outstretched. She hadn't expected to say such a thing, but so many things were unexpected this night. Trust was what she offered thirteen years ago, and he had seen coercion. Now she revealed her own vulnerability once more, wondering if this time he would see her more clearly.

"If these efforts fail," Nadel warned, "you will have done nothing but provide the high chieftain with a scapegoat. Rumar will see to it that the temple bears the blame. He'll have no other choice."

She looked up at him. "I know."

"Ah, Nemiah. Nemiah Gabriana." Slowly, Enrian took her offered hand and knelt beside her. His touch was a warm, sharp memory. "You truly do give all of yourself *for* Riana, and I take everything *from* her. No wonder we must ever try one another."

"We should have been a match, Enrian. You have vision that comes from her, however you might deny it."

He squeezed her fingers, shaking his head. As he let her go and drew back, she knew her Path had turned again, away from the direction of her heart.

"I will speak with Rumar. Tell your lady to prepare for travel."

17.

DAWNINGS' EVE

Velantar's streets spilled over with festival celebrations. Wandering musicians played the *Songs of Praise* and other less reverent tunes, while brightly garbed clansmen and city-born folk danced as they headed outside the walls for the day's competitions. Vendors selling skewers of roasted meat, sugared berry cakes, and mugs of wine chanted over their offerings to attract passersby. Beggars masked as foxes and bears, horses, rabbits, and all other manner of wild creatures gloried in the role of the goddess's Pathguides as they worked their ways expertly through the busy street collecting tithes, given willingly or not, from drunken travelers. As Jhared rode Brio toward the gate with the rest of the Forest Guard Fourth, he was forced to maneuver the horse out of file to avoid a half-dressed couple exchanging their Dawnings' Eve blessings in the middle of Travitar Road.

And it was only midmorning.

Jhared edged his gelding back into formation. Every house that could afford it had already lit the candles in their windows, and shopkeepers carefully lined the steps to their doors with barrels of fruit or sprigs of autumn leaves so no customers lost their way during this time when Riana turned her back to the Paths. Not that such things would protect everyone; there were deaths and disappearances every year, even among the faithful. A body would wash up on the banks of the river or would be found in the alleys behind the taverns; a wretch would go to the fire. Sometimes no trace was found at all. On Dawnings' Eve, some people who stepped off their paths lost themselves in Riana's infinite weaving.

"Goddess save me, I think I'm in love."

Other people only lost themselves in the unbridled passions of the day. Jhared smiled wryly at Jase. A group of girls waved and blew kisses at the soldiers as Commander Carn's patrol trotted from the barracks, out the city gates, toward the clan camps beyond. The boldest of the girls, tall and auburn-haired, tugged a green ribbon from her throat and tossed it to the Nadaren clansman. Jase leaned out of the saddle, caught it, and touched it to his lips. The girl smiled prettily and winked.

"Denaban, ya didn't say anything about these clanless *women*!" The tattooed clansman beamed like a child surrounded by sweets. "So daring. So confident!"

"With even more confident fathers," Twitch warned, laughing, behind them. "Better have a care whose path you stray down tonight, Jase."

"I don't intend t'try just one," the Nadaren man answered, nodding to a lady in blue on the opposite side of the street and a girl with sandy curls. "We're lucky enough t'pull a day watch on Dawnings' Eve, I'm going t'wander!"

"Just save some for the rest'a us," Esran laughed.

Anzo cleared his throat. "You boys'll want to put your eyes back in your heads," he murmured. "There's plenty in this crowd be happy to throw something other than kisses at us. This city's brittle as bad steel. Let's not be the ones to shatter it, eh?"

So Anzo sensed it too. Velantar vibrated with a tension that made lies of the smiles and singing. Dawnings' Eve was a night to cross boundaries; but the winds tearing through Avelos had already demolished many boundaries. The priestesses strolling through the crowd passing out flower petals as reminders of Riana's promises seemed small protection against the possibility of chaos. Many clansmen visiting the city had seen their lives blown to shreds; they had nothing left to lose. Everyone waited in fear for the next attack. When life grew so uncertain, did order become irrelevant?

Twitch made a jest Jhared couldn't hear, and Jase shrugged his shoulders, but they settled down a little and stopped eyeing the women so boldly. Commander Carn led them out of the city with the rest of Lieutenant Sevar's company to hold the perimeter of the clan camps. Ostensibly they were present to keep brigands from preying on the camps and to see that only effigies of the wretch went into the fires, but with the persistent rumors about Sahistens in Avelos and the growing terror of the winds, Jhared thought it likely the high chieftain wanted to make a show of Forest Guard strength to calm the clans and quiet the Legacy. He only wished that fifty soldiers didn't seem so few among the hundreds of clansmen camped across the valley.

The commander set them to patrol the borders where Velantar farmland surrendered to the forest and each clan camp set their temporary claim on part of the valley.

"Let them see that the high chieftain's rule holds steady," Carn ordered.

Jhared was glad to note that with their horses' coats gleaming, boots polished, and swords at their sides, the Forest Guard at least looked disciplined and prepared beside the ragtag collection of clanguard, who idled around the tents throwing hostile glances and occasional insults at Rumar's soldiers.

The patrol rode the camp perimeters in pairs. As they passed beneath the arches of the crumbling aqueducts, Anzo sent Jase back to ride with Lenaro and claimed the spot beside Brio. Jhared glanced at the old veteran sidelong, but Anzo said nothing. They let the horses take their time, making themselves a notable presence. The activity among the camps moved to a different rhythm from the city, one set by the families, who during the weeks of the gathering lived in the open without the shelter of the walls. Watching them, Jhared couldn't help but smile a little, warmed by the reminder of who it was he guarded. Children with mouths red from eating berry cakes chased one another around the tents and the animal pens, then, shrieking and giggling, threw little figures of twisted grass onto the fires. Mothers scolded the younger ones for playing too near the flames and sent them to sit in the circles to listen to Dawnings' Eve stories of Arion and Riana told by priestesses. Young women in brightly dyed shawls and long skirts moved in herds, pausing to listen to a musician or watch a juggler, apparently aloof and uninterested in the boys shyly stalking at the edges of their groups.

Weaving through it all like hungry crows were the wretches. The keepers of bad fortune wandered wherever they might, until some family or clan or group of strangers united to drive one off, and a chase ensued. A bold wretch haunting one camp used his unlit torch to prod a white-bearded man off a bench by the fire, then perched on the seat to scarf up the man's midday meal. The wretch grinned and flung nut shells at the old man on the ground until a dark-haired woman bustled out of her tent, all protective fury. She moved quickly in her lavender skirts, waving her arms and scolding. Still, the wretch popped another nut into his mouth and said something to the girl that made her draw Riana's spiral before she shoved him backwards off his seat.

"That one has some fire in her," Anzo said. "Young enough to be foolish, though."

The wretch scowled as he picked up his crown of twigs and bone, brushed himself off, and wandered toward the next tent.

"Don't cross Bad Fortune on Dawnings' Eve. You let him in unless you're ready for a chase." Anzo paused to scratch his whiskered chin. "You do know the lieutenant's serious about the penalty for playing the wretch?"

"Of course," Jhared said, watching as the girl helped her grandfather back to his bench. "The general forbids it."

"Forbidden or no, I've seen men lashed for it. And I've seen ones who didn't make it to the lash. It's ugly business."

Hundreds of chases would go on all morning and through the evening. The bonfires would burn across the valley all night, purging bad fortune from Avelos until the first light of Dawnings' Day. Jhared had witnessed his share of chases in Elders' Circle: howling, drunken mobs pelting after a lone man who bore the burden of the year's troubles. In the end, it wasn't always the effigy that landed on the fire.

"I'm one of the commander's hunters, Anzo. I've no interest in being some-one's prey."

"Maybe not," Anzo observed from under grey eyebrows. "Yet it's a safe bet some Shorn men will see the fire tonight."

"It does happen," Jhared admitted. "Sometimes. The crowds are drunk and men get careless."

"And this year there's more bad fortune than ever."

"True enough." Jhared turned and made a face at the little patrolman. "Anzo, would you tell me plain what you're getting at?"

"Two days in this city's two days too long for me." The veteran puffed out his jowls with a sigh. "The taverns in the clan circles are loud with stories, stories as stir trouble, and there's one seems a favorite. Maybe you heard it. Shorn soldiers are ordered into Sahiste as scouts, witness sorcery, and are bought by King Javahari to loose Cael's wrath in Avelos."

The images came back to Jhared: men bonded with the poison of vipers; a tethered raptor shrieking for freedom; forbidden boundaries tempting him. The nightmares still haunted him. It took several moments for him to climb out of the memory and absorb the full meaning of Anzo's tirade. He pulled Brio to a halt.

"The clans are blaming Shorn soldiers for the killing winds?"

"Oh, not just the Shorn. There's blame enough to spare for the high chieftain who tolerates Shorn soldiers, and the Forest Guard general who sends them into Sahiste."

"You know the men spreading those tales?"

"Naw, boy. Everyone at Ravia heard about your border crossing this summer. Those stories could'a come from one of us or could'a just been the imagination of someone who's scared. It doesn't matter where they started. They have a life of their own now."

"If it doesn't matter, why are you telling me?"

"Because last night at the Billy and Ram I heard a name attached to the story. A name I thought you might know. Trianor's Folly."

Jhared started so hard that Brio halted and pinned his ears.

"Ah. So I guessed a'right." Anzo nudged his grey past Brio toward Clan Avien's encampment. "D'you slash someone in Velantar as much as you slash Lieutenant Sevar?"

"I suppose that's one way to look at it," Jhared said ruefully. He rubbed a hand across his face and shook his head. "Were they Clan Amerre men last night?"

"In an Everen tavern during the Dawnings festival? Naw. Mostly my own people. The one who mentioned the elder was from the west. Ontaran or Nadaren. With a blessing that near masked his face, and still he cheated at dice." Anzo glanced over his shoulder. "If people here can match you with that name, boy, you'll want to keep off the streets tonight."

Jhared nodded without meeting the old patrolman's gaze. They rode along the perimeter of the Avien camp. Representation from the northern five was poor this fall; only Avien and Hilera had made the long trip.

"Anzo, how is it you reject the stories?"

The veteran chuckled. "I'm an old man. I don't have time left to waste on the gossip of drunkards."

"Most rumors start with a seed of truth. And you know more of what happened that night in Sahiste than most."

"I've known a lot of Shorn soldiers in my years, boy. With something like this you have three kinds: the ones who'd see their duty through by refusing to touch a thing powerful as the winds and doing everything they might to ease the suffering caused by them; the ones who'd turn their back, pretending they'd never seen a thing or that it has nothing to do with their duty; and the ones who'd die in Sahiste trying to slay the priests who held the winds' secret. No Shorn man or woman who's sworn the oath has brought destruction to our doors. Not you or any of our boys. I know that well enough. Sadly, what I know won't change the beliefs of people too scared to think straight."

The old soldier was right about that; it wouldn't change the thoughts of those who were scared—or of those who wanted to create more fear. Jhared shook his head. This week, fear had caused deaths in Panetar.

"You've put me in your debt on Dawnings' Eve, Anzo. What can I do for you to be clear of it?"

"Oh, I think I'll hold onto this one a while." The little veteran gave a crooked smile. "Can't hurt to have an elder's son indebted to me, eh?"

Jhared shrugged. "If I'm what you call a good debt, you'd better leave a gift at the temple tonight and pray to change your luck."

"Even a copper found on a muddy road can buy a cup of wine," Anzo said, a hint of his good cheer reappearing. "Look lively, now. That young clanguard under the Avien pennon is trying to decide whether he should start something with a pair of the high chieftain's men. Don't let him see you looking like a rain-soaked pup."

At the end of the watch, the men of Carn's patrol made quick work of cleaning up and preparing for their various Dawnings' Eve celebrations and assignations, but Jhared no longer had reason to hurry. He had hoped to track down Branlen, to spend the afternoon watching the foot races together, but he couldn't risk that now. It would be no good for anyone in the Trianor household to be seen with him. In fact, it was the best explanation he had for the lack of any message from Tierzen in response to his return to the city: the elder had to distance himself from his Folly.

Of course, the explanation would have fit better if Jhared had heard from the elder more than once in the past four months. Again and again he had sent his reports to Tierzen, but for all he knew he might as well have thrown them into the river. He closed the door on the hollow space that lodged inside him and reached for Bran's little stone. If his family was safer not seeing him, then he had to respect that boundary. Perhaps instead he would muster his courage and go to the Black Mountain to wish Zia a good Dawnings' Eve.

The thought of seeing the Shorn scribe overcame some of his low mood. Flutes and pipes played everywhere in the city, and the music made vivid his memories of her unabashed laughter and flashing green gaze. She was lovely and bold; she knew the importance of music and she knew him—not as a soldier or as an elder's fosterling, but as the son of Mahla Denaban. He grinned foolishly to himself and was supremely glad Jase wasn't around to tease him for it. Quietly humming the refrain from one of his mother's favorite songs, "Legend of Lusian," he strode around the corner of the barracks on his way to the baths. He nearly tripped over a prone soldier propped against the wall.

"Whoa there! That's not such a good place to pass out. Here, let me—" As he bent to offer a hand, he caught the scent of smoke and singed hair. "Oh, no."

The semiconscious man lifted his head from his chest and peered up blearily at Jhared, who started in recognition. Micah's face was red and blistered, his clothing burned in patches from his boots to his knees. His torn shirt revealed the old scar on his shoulder and an ugly new gash that had been caused by something blunt. A wooden staff perhaps, or maybe just a stick of firewood. Blood oozed from raw wounds around his wrists. The injuries needed careful cleaning and bandaging; burns festered easily. The pain would warrant a hearty dose of dreamsease.

"Come," Jhared said gently. "You need the healer."

"What a clever boy," Micah replied, his head lolling back against the wall. "No wonder it took an elder's home to foster him."

Jhared set his jaw and reached for the injured man's arm. "Let it be. I'll help you to the infirmary."

"Don't touch me!" Micah pulled away and scrambled to get his feet beneath him. With a groan, he used the wall to push himself up. "I'm bad fortune. They couldn't manage to be rid of me, but I cursed them. I'll curse you, too."

"From the looks of it, you're the lucky one. Lucky they didn't know how to tie a secure knot."

"Lucky." Micah laughed, a dry papery sound that ended in a choking cough. "You'll have to tell me…what that word means."

Jhared reached again for the soldier. "What are you doing, man? I've seen what service means to you. Why would you throw it away to play some angry clansmen's wretch? You of all of us, who could be the one to earn final reparation?"

"Final reparation?" Micah stared, his eyes wide and dark in his blistered face. "It seems all this time I've been wrong about you: you're not a coward; you're a child. What do you think final reparation *is*? A moment of magic when Riana appears in all her glory and our service comes suddenly to its end?"

"I know our history," Jhared bit out. "I know what reparation should look like: When Alende Isan led his companions safely out of Altan Mar. When Rona sacrificed himself to save the son of a rival chieftain. When High Priestess Elia gave up her place as Riana's Chosen and wed the Amurian duke. All those moments preserved the future of Avelos. That's the type of act final reparation will be."

"You know…you're just close enough to the truth to be pathetic." Micah was laughing and coughing again. "You want to know what it really means? Why Jech and Hendren and the rest dodge it like arrow fire?"

Final reparation. The bright star for which Jhared had reached since he heard his mother sing of it, since Enrian Nadel set a bow in his hand, and since he swore a covenant with Avelos. "Tell me."

"It is the end," Micah replied. "When we're no longer a danger. When we're gone. *All* of us. The best you or any Shorn man can do for the future of Avelos is to leave it."

Jhared opened his mouth to retort, realized he had nothing, and slowly closed it again. Was the soldier entirely unbalanced or terrifyingly lucid?

"I guess you don't have the courage for that, do you, boy? Looks like neither of us does." Micah gazed down at his raw wrists with an expression of disgust. Slowly, he straightened and drew his sword. "Maybe that's something I can still repair."

The sword rose unsteadily to level at Jhared's throat. "You can hardly hold your weapon," Jhared said, his body still, his hands open at his sides. "Even I could outdo you."

"Could you now?"

Micah grinned, and something subtle flickered in his expression. Jhared recognized the warning an instant before the injured man rushed forward, thrusting his blade at Jhared's heart. Jhared sidestepped the deadly steel as he drew his own sword. Micah thrust again, and he ducked, shifting his weight to his left and stretching low. The move exposed the length of his right leg and Micah took the opening. Jhared wrenched around to parry just in time to prevent the gliding blade from cutting his knees out from under him.

"What in Cael's unholy name?" he gasped. "You're demon-touched!"

"We all are. The others won't face it, but I've watched you. You know it." Micah swiveled and swung a fierce lateral cut toward Jhared's shoulder. Jhared met the blow solidly, his hand stinging as the force of it ran down his blade. Micah was powerful, and he wasn't holding back.

"I know only that you're disordered!" Jhared hissed.

He reeled with the irony of it as he fought for his life against a comrade, the man who was his model of Shorn soldiery. Micah pressed him hard, attacking again and again with risky maneuvers only a desperate man would try. Micah succeeded because he didn't care; he had no boundaries of fear to limit him, and Jhared wouldn't kill him.

They fought their way out from behind the stables, Jhared hunting for an opening that would allow him to disarm the man. Even hindered by his injuries, Micah moved with precision and balance. He struck and retreated as fast as a raptor.

The sword was not Jhared's weapon; it never became an extension of him as the bow did. Every combination of movements was a conscious act. Beyond his wall of concentration, he was dimly aware of shouting around him. Micah intended to die today, had tried and failed to die upon the flames. If they both perished, would that truly be two steps closer to reparation?

"We are poison," Micah panted. "The bane of Avelos. You sense it. Let this end…as it should."

He pounded at Jhared with another series of blows. Sparks flew as their blades clashed. The first ropes of exhaustion began to weight Jhared's limbs, but Micah seemed untiring. Then, as Jhared moved in to parry a diagonal cut, he saw it: the man favored his injured right shoulder. As Micah tried to compensate with the muscles in his back, the awkward movement signaled his intentions a fraction of an instant before he acted.

That observation was a gift. Micah signaled upward, and his blade followed with unexpected speed. The sword flashed in the sunlight as it carved back down toward Jhared's head. But Jhared was ready. A rush of emotions exploded within him: fears and frustrations he didn't have time to understand or acknowledge. He palmed his blade like a staff, blocked the descending blow, and shoved Micah's sword wide. Stepping inside the man's guard, Jhared twisted his pommel forward and drove it into Micah's face. There was a sickening crack. The other patrolman staggered back, blood welling from his lips and nose. Jhared released his blade and stepped in again. As he prepared to strike, he heard himself growl like something caged.

Micah gave him a bloody smile.

Cold water smacked Jhared in the side of the head, splashing over his face and filling his eyes. Instinctively, he squeezed his lids closed. In that instant, as his guard faltered, strong hands fell on him, pinning his arms and yanking him backwards.

"Enough, Patrolman! Stand down!"

Someone wrenched his wrist with bone-crushing force until he dropped his sword.

Panting and coughing, he shook his head to clear the water from his eyes. Grion and Lenaro gripped him; two more men had Micah, holding him up more than holding him back. Between them, Lieutenant Sevar stood with an empty bucket in one hand, his grey gaze blazing.

"For playing the wretch, five lashes," Sevar declared. "For engaging comrades with blades, five lashes. And for defying orders, ten lashes." The lieutenant nodded toward Micah. "Take him to the infirmary; his will wait. This one will take them now."

Micah spat blood onto the ground. "The difference between us, boy?" he snarled at Jhared. "You think only of your duty to Avelos, but I love her. You should have let me end this."

Jhared stared at the other Shorn man as the guards hauled him off, knowing with a sick certainty that Micah would never leave the infirmary except to find the pyre.

"Not even finished with one penalty, Denaban, but you must court another." The lieutenant's tone was soft and dangerous.

Jhared lowered his gaze to the ground, keeping his expression blank as Grion twisted his arm hard behind his back. Water dripped from him, painting dark patterns on the dirt.

"He wanted me to kill him. I wouldn't have."

"Wouldn't you? It looked to me that both of you were about to find an end. And then what a waste of your years of training. What a waste of the hours General Nadel spent teaching you. Is this what you learned from Tierzen Trianor about paying your debt? How to gamble it on petty rivalries?"

"No, sir." Jhared lifted his head. "Tierzen Trianor brought me to a successful Becoming. My failures now are my own."

Something shifted in Sevar's gaze that might have been surprise, but almost instantly it was drowned in cold rage. "Only the Shorn child of an elder claims failure so proudly."

The lieutenant's contempt for Tierzen was tangible. Jhared felt as if he might choke on it. He struggled to control his breathing as anger arrowed into his veins. Pride? What pride the Legacy possessed to attack the strongest defenders of Avelos for the faction's own purposes and claim it to be for the good of the country! How could Sevar possibly align himself with those who tried to drag General Nadel from the southern towers? How could any soldier justify that kind of disloyalty? Jhared couldn't speak; he couldn't look at the lieutenant for fear the man would see his lack of discipline once again.

"Let these lashes remind you that what matters in a Shorn man has nothing to do with what he reads in an elder's library," Sevar added grimly. "If you can't follow orders, you're no more useful than a rabid dog. You'll be dealt with like one. Understand me?"

"Yes, sir." Jhared straightened. Good, then. Let Sevar spend his disdain for Tierzen this way. If it kept the Legacy from hunting his foster father, let the lieutenant give him twice again fifteen lashes. The physical pain he could endure. He drew a long breath and let it out slowly as Grion and Lenaro marched him toward the bloodstone in the garrison courtyard.

"Hold!"

The guards pulled to a halt and Sevar strode up to them staring intently at Jhared. A fine weaving of scars still crisscrossed the lieutenant's cheeks and forehead, giving the appearance of a mask around his eyes. Jhared wondered what it concealed.

"Look at you," Sevar hissed, his icy tone edged with amazement. "You *want* the lash. Damn, if you're not *eager* for it. Do you think that ending Dawnings' Eve with atonement and spilled blood will transform you into Arion? Is that what it is?"

Jhared didn't flinch. "I'm not afraid to accept the punishment I deserve."

The lieutenant's gaze narrowed. "Is that so?" He gestured to the men behind Jhared. "Very well, then. Turn him loose."

As Grion and Lenaro backed off, Sevar glowered. "I won't feed your illusions of redemption, Patrolman, so here's a lash you might understand. Before the sun goes down on Dawnings' Eve, you will go to Elder Trianor, Minister of the Teaching. You will tell him that Lieutenant Matio Sevar sent you to him. And you will tell him that his Shorn experiment has failed."

18.
CROSSROADS

Jhared let himself be carried along with the crowd, his cloak pulled close against the afternoon chill. The color and music and food of the festival were no lure to him as he trod up Travitar Hill. If he was quick, Tierzen would still be at Elders' Hall. It would be a small mercy if he didn't have to face Sarena and Branlen with his news.

We are poison.

Micah's declaration was true enough, yet Tierzen Trianor had still claimed him. When even the man who had fathered Jhared fled, abandoning his mother to her grief, Tierzen had cared for him. Now their bond would be snapped like a brittle twig. Sevar was right: this penalty would cut deeper and reach farther than any lash.

The crossroads where Elder's Row intersected Travitar Road near the city's center swelled with people. A group of players had staged their performance of Arion's Trial right in the middle of the intersection, narrowing the way and netting themselves a substantial audience in doing so. Jhared eeled through the crowd, barely managing to avoid colliding with anyone. As he pulled free at the opposite corner, a tall figure jostled him. Jhared grabbed the hand sneaking toward his belt and glared up into the veiled face of one of the caelevano.

"Lost something?" he growled.

"Oh, found something!" the waylayer declared delightedly, swaying back and forth. "A gift for the guide who leads you to your destiny." Scarves of blue and green floated around the creature. His long form was robed and wrapped from head to foot; even his eyes were veiled. Only one strip of skin across his face touched the air, revealing garish green spirals painted on his clean-shaven cheeks. His wide, grinning mouth puffed the scent of cheap brandy into the cold.

On any other day, the demon-touched wouldn't risk the City Guard to harass a man in broad daylight, but today even the guard wouldn't invite bad luck by crossing a waylayer.

"You would be the guide sent for me." Jhared scowled as he disengaged the creature's hand from his belt.

"Why so sour on Dawnings' Eve, soldier?" The waylayer danced a graceful circle around Jhared, nodding up and down at him. "A young man. Strong. Fine looking enough, if you've a taste for one of the cursed.… Ahhh, tell me, have you failed in love? Shall I search the Paths and tell you which way to turn?"

"Yes, I have failed love," Jhared said, edging out of the creature's circle, one hand on his purse. "And there's nothing a demon-touched thief can do for it."

"Ow! Cut to the quick, I am!" The caelevano gripped Jhared's arm, stopping his escape. The man was tall and his grasp unexpectedly firm. "Unwise to speak to a Pathguide so on Dawnings' Eve," he muttered, offering a fey smile.

The ground beneath Jhared shivered, and he grabbed instinctively at the waylayer's shoulder to catch himself. Behind him, the audience howled as Cael's demons took the stage to fight Arion.

"Riana has cursed me already. Do you think I have cause to fear you?"

"Mmm." The waylayer made a sound of pleasure and wriggled closer, studying Jhared through the veils. "I think you fear many things. Fear makes you turn in futile circles."

You should have let me end this.

Jhared yanked out of the creature's grip, nearly striking a passerby in the face. "I'm a soldier in the high chieftain's Forest Guard and a bound Shorn man. I don't fear dying for Avelos!"

The waylayer laughed, an unexpectedly rich and resonant sound. It might have been lovely if not so bitter.

"No, you don't fear dying. You fear to live. Come, give me a gift and I'll clear the way for you to make a new start." Blue silk brushed Jhared's cheek as the creature leaned forward and whispered with brandy-scented breath. "Or do you fear taking that much action for yourself?"

Jhared scowled again at the waylayer. "All right. I know well enough what you want." He reached into his pouch for the few coins there and pulled the coppers into the afternoon light.

"I won't deny a request for aid, but I want no guidance. Not from you."

The coins promptly disappeared within the creature's voluminous robes. The waylayer heaved a sigh.

"Very well, soldier. Play the righteous, if you must. You'll come back before long, begging me to shift the road you've carved for yourself. You won't have any choice but to return, for who else will be willing to guide you?"

With another deep, mocking laugh, the waylayer spun amid a flutter of blue and green. He danced nimbly into the crowd singing the first lines of "Legend of Lusian."

As Jhared stared after the creature, a shadow fell over him. He glanced up to see the sun sliding behind the temple dome. The Council of Clans would recess soon, and Tierzen Trianor would be heading for home. On Dawnings' Eve, Sarena would be at the temple for the devotions. When she returned, Neta would serve a festival day meal, and the house would smell of meat pies, spiced fruit, and ginger tarts. Bran would run into the house late, dusty and laughing, after a day adventuring outside the walls with friends. Sarena would scold, and Tierzen would ask which clans had distinguished themselves in the competitions. Jhared would be seated next to Branlen. The elder would ask for Jhared's opinion about the course for the foot races and which runners would finish.

"A lovely scene with which to torment yourself, but will it bring you any more quickly to the elder?"

Jhared gritted his teeth and didn't answer his Teacher, but the sudden wave of homesickness was so strong that he found himself changing direction. He turned off Travitar Road, away from the city center, toward Elders' Circle and the place that had been his home.

Candles, ribbons, and pots of late-blooming flowers lined the lanes and marked the wealth of the circle. The banners of the fifteen first-clans snapped above Elders' Row. Jhared passed two City Guards, who eyed him suspiciously until he offered a respectful salute and they saw he wore no sword. Some of the families in the circle, those who kept villas outside the walls, would have their own private holy day celebrations with a selective invitation list and a priestess to say the prayers before the wretch went into the fire.

Jhared checked that no one watched him before ducking into the little alley behind Elders' Row. As he approached the Trianor home, he heard the door unlatched from inside and knew whose step it was even before the boy had both feet across the threshold.

"Sneaking out against your mother's wishes? That's bound to earn you something unpleasant."

Bran froze at the doorstep. His expression registered bemusement and caution for a heartbeat; then recognition washed over his face and he threw himself off the step.

"Jhared!" The boy reached him at velocity and flung both arms around him, rocking him backwards. "They didn't tell me you were in the city! When did you arrive? How long will you stay? Why didn't you come sooner?"

"Whoa!" Jhared laughed and hugged his brother hard, even as he continued to watch over the boy's shoulder. "Give a soldier time to recover from that attack. Damn, but you've grown, Bran."

The boy squeezed Jhared again; then, grinning, he took a step back and squared his shoulders. "Mother doesn't care for it much that I'm already taller than her. She says I eat as much as a growing Shorn boy."

Jhared's lip twisted. "Ah. Sorry for that."

"Nah. She only says it when she misses you."

Jhared didn't know what to say; he knew they should go inside, but he couldn't force himself to do it yet. When Tierzen heard why he'd been sent, the elder would have no choice but to throw him out. If there were any chance of surviving the consequences in the council, Tierzen would have to put as much distance as he could between his Teaching and Jhared's failures. These could very well be the last moments he ever shared with his brother.

"I'd like to hear what you've done since I've been gone, Bran. What are you studying? Has Tierzen found a clerkship for you at Elders' Hall?"

The boy looked askance at Jhared's sober tone, then shook his head. "First, you owe me something." He held out his hand.

"So I do." Jhared reached into his pouch for the smooth, cool stone and set it onto Branlen's palm. "Your good wishes served me well, brother. They guarded me from steel and storm. I put this symbol of our bond into your safekeeping until…I leave again."

"Let all of Riana's spheres hear the thanks of Branlen Trianor for keeping his brother safe from harm."

Branlen closed his fingers around the ancient stone face, their little ritual completed. His visage had lost much of its boyish roundness and shifted toward angles that marked him as Tierzen's son, but an innocence remained in his expression. It struck at Jhared's heart, overwhelming him with the desire to guard the boy from all the dangers that threatened to steal that last remnant of boyhood. Jhared could endure whatever punishment Lieutenant Sevar created, so long as it meant he could still stand between his brother and harm. Micah was wrong to think love and duty could be separated.

"Every time we heard that the winds hit the south, I worried," the boy said in a hushed voice. "And now with war coming…I'm just glad you're home, even if it's not for long. We'll make the most of it, right? Come with me to the competitions tomorrow."

"War? What's this? Have you been listening to the stories in the streets?"

"Not stories. It's news from the council." His brother looked up, blue-grey eyes troubled. "I thought you would know."

"I only know the rumors, Bran. I don't have access to council news anymore."

The words sounded harsh, and he hadn't meant them to. It wasn't Bran's fault that Tierzen had stopped communicating with him. He softened his tone with a hand on the boy's shoulder.

"Let's go inside," Branlen said, turning back to the door. "It's not the kind of thing Father would want me to talk about on the street."

Jhared hesitated. "I…don't want to disrupt preparations for Dawnings' Eve."

"Nothing to disrupt," the boy said with a shrug. "Father's at Elders' Hall. He's been locked in a debate with the council for days. He's hardly had time to come home to change clothes or eat. Mother's at the temple or calling on neighbors for the new year. Neta went outside the walls to Clan Everen to celebrate with kin. I was just heading to the camps myself to see if I could find Ino. Dawnings' Eve isn't the same. Nothing's the same as it was before you left." Bran looked up with a dark gaze, and Jhared saw shadows in the boy he had never seen before. "Come in. I'll tell you what I know."

The house was silent and warm. Jhared carefully wiped the dust from his boots before entering the immaculate kitchen. Branlen motioned him to a seat, then went to the sideboard, where one of Neta's lovely apple-ginger tarts sat untouched. The boy cut two large wedges and carried them to the table. Then with a mischievous smile he brought the rest of the tart to the table as well.

"Go on. Eat," he commanded, flinging himself down on the bench beside Jhared. "You look starved. And bad news is better heard on a full stomach."

The words sounded so much like Neta that Jhared stifled a smile as he bit into the tart. Then the complex combination of sharp, sweet, buttery flavors caught him by surprise, and he closed his eyes with the simple pleasure of it.

Branlen laughed out loud. "I guess that means you missed Neta's cooking."

"I forgot food could taste like that. Garrison fare is fine, if you need a strong mortar to repair the walls."

"Tell me more about what it's like at Ravia. You're the best scout in the garrison, of course."

Jhared looked down at his plate. "I'm not what you think, Bran. I..." He shifted uncomfortably. "Here. If you want a tale of a good scout, I'll tell you of a man who's been in the Forest Guard since before General Nadel ever made captain."

He told the boy stories about the men in his patrol and the routine of life on the southern border. Branlen answered questions about the histories Tierzen made him read and spoke of his father's hope to place him at Elders' Hall as assistant to the elder of Clan Everen. The boy had begged to be allowed to begin Forest Guard training instead, but Tierzen and Sarena had said *no*. Jhared suspected Sarena had said a great deal more than that. He realized that he and Bran were both leaving out parts of their stories, and regretted the distance that made them so cautious with each other. Bran went quiet, poking restlessly at cake crumbs.

"Can you tell me what's happening in the council?" Jhared asked.

Branlen huffed a breath, sending crumbs scattering. "They've not told me all of it. I don't think Mother knows all of it. I don't think even Sirol knows all of it. Shorn scribes are being kept out of the sessions. Father tells me what he can, when he can, and sometimes I hear them talking."

The boy gave up his fidgeting and folded his arms on the table to lean toward Jhared. "King Javahari wants us to open the southeastern border. He wants trade, Father says. But it looks to most elders like a prelude to war. For a week, the council's been fighting about what to do."

Jhared sat back, stunned. "*That's* why they stopped raiding. All this time they wanted us open to their message, and instead the garrison has grown more and more suspicious. But trade? I wonder what Javahari truly intends."

"To tear apart the council, maybe," Branlen said unhappily. "No one can agree on anything. Elder Varen left the debate entirely; he said this was a ploy for the south to steal more resources from the northern five and that Clan Aglar wouldn't have any part of it. Clan Nadaren says Sahiste wants our border open to spread the killing winds deeper into Avelos. And Clans Amerre and Rehamra accused the high chieftain of being unbalanced for considering permitting traitors into the country. Father is exhausted."

"Where does he stand in the debate?"

Branlen squirmed in his chair. "He thinks we should allow them in."

Jhared let out a breath and closed his eyes, trying to bring his thoughts into order.

"Of course. Let's look at it as your father might: If Avelos opens her gates to Sahiste, she might be more vulnerable for a time, but will benefit from the stimulation of new trade. Fewer smugglers. More goods flowing into the country and more people to buy Avelonian wine and timber, wool and grain. More trade means more gold, fewer taxes on the clans, and more resources to equip the Forest Guard and repair the roads. It would place us in a stronger position with Sahiste and with all the border nations."

He paused, ignoring the ache in his chest to think through Tierzen's argument. "If we *don't* open the border, with the Forest Guard stretched so thin, Javahari could likely assemble an invasion force and push into the country to take what he wants anyway. This might be the opportunity to consent to Javahari's request under our own terms." Jhared shrugged. "I imagine…Tierzen would argue something such as that."

"That sounds like Father," Branlen agreed. "It doesn't sound like you."

Open borders. Jhared rubbed at the painful place over his heart. Would Avelos truly offer forgiveness to the foreign traitors?

"Jhared?"

"No, Bran. There are good reasons why Shorn men aren't allowed to serve the council." He pushed aside his plate and turned to face his brother. "The generals will act quickly now to strengthen the border. We don't have the numbers in the south to hold off a committed force if Sahiste grows tired of waiting while the elders argue. Men will have to be pulled from the northern towers. Away from General Orn. Have you heard of it?"

"Jhared, listen." Bran put a hand on his arm. "There's more."

The torment in the boy's gaze was a warning. "What more?"

"There's been another motion…to take Shorn soldiers off duty during the negotiations."

"No." Blood beat in Jhared's ears. "General Nadel will need us. We *need* to be there. Who would possibly…?" Then he knew. "Elder Abrigado."

"That's him," Branlen answered with a grim nod. "I've never heard Father curse a man before. If the high chieftain accepts the motion…"

"I won't be going back to Ravia," Jhared finished heavily.

"Not to worry, soldier, a man of your strength and skill will always find useful service through the city labor office. Perhaps final reparation is to be found shoveling dung off the streets. Or perhaps mucking stalls for the drovers, hmm?" Sirol entered the kitchen from the great room, a scribe's satchel slung over his good shoulder, and bobbed his head to Branlen.

Jhared straightened. "A cleaner job than dealing with the dung the scribes produce. Riana shape your Path with your words, Sirol. Good Dawnings' Eve to you."

The scribe made a wry face. "I didn't realize you were back. I wouldn't have interrupted otherwise. I was only gathering some papers for the elder. Don't fear, I'll be gone in a moment."

"It's all right, Sirol." Branlen cast an apologetic look toward Jhared. "I know it's been a bitter week. Stay and have some of Neta's tart with us."

The man looked as though he would refuse, but something in his expression softened. Bruised crescents darkened his eyes, and he winced when he lifted the satchel from his shoulders. "Thank you, Master Trianor. I wouldn't mind a bit of sweetness."

With an inward sigh, Jhared nodded understanding at Bran, then reached for the tart and cut a generous slice. He slid the serving in front of the scribe.

"Well, soldier, you've managed to stay out of trouble for nearly two seasons now. It's more than I credited you. Perhaps I owe you an apology."

"No apology. There's no debt between us."

Sirol put a forkful of the tart into his mouth, chewed, and swallowed. "What news do you bring from the border?"

"Likely nothing you haven't heard from better sources already."

"I've heard little," Sirol said sourly. "They've removed Shorn scribes from duty. None of us can step foot in Elders' Hall. Elder Trianor wouldn't be so burdened if I were still at his side."

Jhared hadn't expected to hear such regret in the scribe. It caused him to feel more charitable toward the man.

"The news from the south is grim," he said. "The killing winds have spilled blood all along the border and as far north as Clan Makri. With so many people displaced by the destruction, highwaymen plague the roads and prey on the smaller villages. It's disheartening work chasing after our own people."

Sirol nodded, his expression saddened. They spoke carefully for a time. Sirol told Jhared of the events he had witnessed at Panetar: the Legacy speeches, the fear, and the deaths. Today the scribe had no taunts for Jhared about killing. As the talk continued, Branlen grew wide-eyed and solemn. Jhared looked for a way to guide the topic elsewhere.

"You'll go to your kin to celebrate tonight?" he asked Sirol.

"I have people who will share the evening with me." A faint smile pushed some of the darkness from the scribe's eyes. He took another bite of the tart. "I would have thought that you'd be out with your patrolmates, scouting for someone willing to walk a path with you. It's not a night to be alone."

Subtle as it was, Jhared still heard the mockery. He recalled Sirol's lover in Shorn Circle and couldn't help himself. "I'll not spend my night with soldiers, if that's what you mean. Not when my lady is making music for the festival."

"Oh, yes? A musician?" The scribe's fork hovered in the air as he stared at Jhared in disbelief. "How lucky for you. What's the lady's name?"

Jhared smiled. "Ziabela Marcalo."

The fork clattered onto the table. Sirol's expression steeled. Had he carried a knife, it would have been in his hand. "Here it is, then. This is the way you repay Elder Trianor for his protection. Grey feather find you for a heartless traitor, Jhared Denaban. How long has this been going on?"

Branlen gasped and turned with a stricken expression from Jhared to Sirol and back. Jhared gripped the bench to keep from striking the scribe.

"What are you *talking* about?" he hissed. "I've done nothing to earn such a curse from you!"

"Ziabela Marcalo," Sirol bit off sharply, "is Elder Abrigado's scribe. She seduced you to get to Elder Trianor."

Cold seeped into Jhared's chest. "You're wrong. It was no seduction. And we've never even spoken of Tierzen."

"I don't believe it." Sirol narrowed his gaze. "How long have you been with the woman?"

The number of times Jhared had seen Zia had nothing to do with the depth of his connection to her. He wanted to give Sirol a number that would signify all the things he couldn't say. But it was Dawnings' Eve; his fortune shifted with every step he took and every word he spoke. He wouldn't endanger Zia or himself or even Sirol with a lie.

"I've seen her twice."

"Well, no wonder," Sirol snorted. She's still grooming you. I can just imagine it: wine and quiet conversations. She runs her long fingers through your warrior's tail and whispers in your ear until you're ready to offer her a one-man Forest

Guard salute. Then, oh then, she wraps her lips around that flute of hers and makes music for you. At the end she leaves you hungry as a billy goat, and tells you to come back later."

Jhared felt ill. Heat poured through his veins. He needed to run.

"Leave it alone," he said with deadly calm. "You don't know her. She serves where she was sent. It doesn't make her a creature of the Legacy."

"Oh, I know her. I've seen how charming she can be when she's gathering information for Abrigado. Charming as Semael the serpent. Don't see her again. A creature of the Legacy is exactly what she is. Abrigado's creature." Sirol's disgust hinted at all the possible meanings behind that label.

Time shifted and split, no longer certain but suddenly open to a myriad interpretations: like reflections in the ripples of a pond. Like blood smeared across stone. The next moments offered unexpected possibilities. Jhared leaped up from the table and tackled the scribe to the floor, wrapping his hands around Sirol's throat. He leaped up from the table and slammed his fist against the wood, feeling the crack of the board and the snap of bones. He leaped up from the table and ran out the back door, heading to the Black Mountain to find Ziabela.

He was pounding toward Cirolan Hill, dread beating in his chest, when he realized that in none of those blurs of time had he said farewell to Branlen.

19.
BROKEN BONDS

Twilight folded its dark hands around the city, drawing them all toward the moment when Riana would lay aside her order and Arion would make his choice. Even in the dreary circles of Cirolan Hill, singing, laughter, and the caterwaul of lovers filled the night as people tried to drive away misfortune and fear in whatever ways they knew. At the Mountain, the doors were propped open and the shutters thrown wide, pouring rivers of light into the street and drawing in cool air for the drinkers and dancers who overflowed the place. Patrons with cups of wine straddled the stone sills and rocked to the strains of a lively tune that skipped across the shadows. A flute trilled clear above the rest, a sound as pure and painful as longing.

Jhared's insides coiled into knots, and he wiped his sweaty hands against his shirt. By the time he squeezed himself into a space against the bar, he knew he shouldn't have come. In the musician's circle, the old fiddler and the red-haired pipe player from his first visit were joined by a plump, pretty woman embracing a clanharp. Ziabela stood slightly behind them. In the lamplight, her hair gleamed as black as her Ulaye flute. Her sparkling eyes were half-lidded and her body swayed gracefully as she gave herself over to her performance.

She had known Jhared when music meant freedom and was untainted by loss. With her stories, she had returned his mother to him. If he left now and never returned, he could keep the recollection of their connection. He had given her nothing for Abrigado, after all. But he didn't want memories that were veiled by his loneliness; he didn't want those lies. He needed to see her clearly.

"Jhared Denaban, back for the holy days, are ya?" Isella peered at him from behind the bar, both hands on her hips, shaping his name with a warmth that was meant for the memory of his mother. He nodded and mustered a smile. "Back just in time by the looks'a it," she said. "You're naught but a shadow. Don't they feed ya in the 'guard?"

"Nothing as satisfying as your stew, I'm afraid, madam." Though for the first time he could remember, he didn't have an appetite.

Isella laughed and signaled to a ginger-haired barmaid, who was distributing bowls of nuts and figs and platters of cheese among the crowd. "Sosia will take care'a ya."

With a bit of an awkward maneuver on her bad leg, Isella bent under the bar and retrieved, not a jug of the house wine, but a bottle of Melandrien brandy, which she uncorked and slid across the polished wood toward Jhared.

"Festival or no, it's not a night to be out in the cold. Eat well and drink to the memory'a blessed music."

Jhared dug into his belt to see what coins remained, wondering how he could possibly afford the expensive bottle. Isella waved him away, her expression turning serious.

"Not tonight. It's a Dawnings gift." She leaned across the bar to hand him a cup with the bottle. "Walk steady on the dark Paths tonight, and never fear the maker'a your fate."

"Riana bless your ways," he answered, ducking his head to her.

She watched him speculatively, looking a little disappointed by his response to her odd blessing. Had she meant him to decline the gift? Surely not on this night. Isella shook her head almost to herself and smiled once more.

"Ay, well then. Find yourself a seat, if ya can. Zia will be glad ta see ya."

He edged his way around the dancers' circle, averting his eyes from the musicians by turning to accept the plate of cheese and figs that Sosia offered as she passed him. Couples filled the tavern tonight. And families. More than one mother rocked a babe or a small child on her knee. He smiled at a toddler bouncing to the rhythm of the music, and her mother glared at him, clutching the child close. Several other parents gave him threatening glances as he passed. Chagrined, Jhared slunk to a far corner, where he found space enough at a bench near the wall to sit alone.

The brandy was exceptional and went down easily. He drained the first two glasses before realizing how strong it was. After a moment's hesitation, he decided he liked the way it dulled emotion and muffled his Teachers' mutterings, and drained a third glass. The chaotic picture of his life grew easier to consider while floating somewhere above it. Puzzle pieces turned in his mind, and a part of the picture dropped into place: Toren Abrigado had Lieutenant Sevar to watch Trianor's Folly inside the garrison and Zia to watch him outside. It explained why Zia had come to him at his Becoming. It explained why she had been so eager for him to return.

Painful, that insight. A fist in the gut. And no amount of brandy could change it. He leaned back into the corner and closed his eyes, slipping away from his thoughts to attend to the music. The lively reels gentled, then segued into several delicate airs. One he recognized: "Rona's Glory." The beauty of it shivered through him. Most musicians celebrated Rona for his bravery when he died saving the son of his rival, Ilias Manitar, from Amurian pirates. Such interpretations of the work depended on the strength of a single voice, and every instrument took Rona's part. But Jhared had never thought of the song as a lesson in courage so much as a reminder that the heart of Avelos beat within her families. This troupe knew it, too: the complex interdependence of each part as the musicians played out Rona, Ilias, the child, and the sacrifice, celebrated loyalty and bonds, not the courage of one man.

His mother had known it. She had used the song to soothe the tempers of Clan Manitar and the northern five when the conflict between them could have torn the country in two. Mahla had been young then and skilled, and men had sought the honor of courting her, long before Jhared's birth caused her to lose her beloved and all hope of happiness.

The strains of Rona's sacrifice faded away, and the troupe picked up a faster pace once more, sending the dancers spiraling around the floor. They glided in a continuous circle around the musicians. Within that circle, each couple made their own graceful pattern of revolutions, just as each man and woman shaped their own steps within Riana's complex Paths. Timing and balance were critical to avoid collisions, and these dancers possessed some skill, turning the dance floor into a pleasantly hypnotic swirl of colors. Jhared had nearly emptied the bottle when he realized the music had paused.

"A chase! A chase comes this way!"

The tavern erupted with excited hoots and screams, and everyone rushed toward the open windows. Patrons hung from the sills to see out into the street. Others ran out the door, jugs and cups still in hand.

"Who is it? Who's the wretch? Are they gaining on him?"

"I see the torches! Here they come!"

A red-faced man at the next table leered at Jhared on his way to the windows. "Maybe we should start our own chase, eh soldier? Do ya know about bad fortune?"

Jhared was saved the necessity of a reply by a moon-faced woman who complained that they were missing the best view and dragged the man off.

It was reminder enough that this was no night for a Shorn man to be out late. When the chase passed, he would go.

Pounding footsteps and fervent cries echoed louder along the street. The wretch staggered into sight. He was a smallish man with a short stride and eyes glazed with effort. Somewhere earlier in his flight, he had lost his twig crown, and his clothes had been muddied and torn. Less than ten lengths behind him came the hunters, frenzied and screeching for blood. Their torches streamed out like an army's banners. If the wretch lasted so long, he would be run out of Cirolan Gate, where the fires and the effigy would be waiting. If he didn't last, they would fall on him in the street.

Jhared rose, more than a little unsteadily, and aimed himself toward the door.

"Jhared! Jhared Denaban, where are you going?"

His throat constricted, but not so tightly that he couldn't taste Zia's spicy scent when she grabbed his arm and stretched up to kiss his cheek. She was warm against him, her cheeks flushed, her smile touched with carmine, and her green eyes lined with kohl. His body soared to the peak of desire with a speed that left him lightheaded.

"I wasn't certain you'd be given leave tonight," she said, beaming. "I hoped for it. I'm so glad you're here." Her flute was in one hand. Her other hand stayed on his arm.

He gritted his teeth and fought to bring himself under control. "How did you know I was in the city?"

"I asked after your patrol. You don't think I would miss the chance to see you. I wanted to know..."

Something caused her to look at him more closely, and abruptly her expression changed. Without another word, she took his hand and pulled him through the crowd into the narrow back hall. It was dim in the hall, and much quieter.

"Jhared, what is it? You look terrible. What's happened?"

"Tell me what you want from me, Zia."

She blinked. Her brow furrowed; then she smiled a little and patted his arm. "On festival night, I'd ask a dance of you that we might chase off bad fortune together, but I'm not sure you're steady enough for such a chase. You've been drinking Isella's Melandrien."

He knew he should shake her hand away, but he couldn't. The heat from her fingers seeped into his skin. He took a breath.

"That's not what I meant. What is it that Elder Abrigado wants you to learn from me?"

She drew closer and her hand moved upward to stroke his shoulder. "Jhared, I'm worried for you. You're not making sense. I am scribe for Toren Abrigado, but that's only the place I was given to serve. What does it have to do with you and me?"

Against his volition, his eyes closed and he leaned into the pleasure of her touch. The room swayed around him, like the Paths that swung beneath him. Where would he land: on the road to good fortune or disaster? Spoken out loud, his words seemed very foolish. To think that a man as important as the Minister of the Treasury would shape council politics around a scribe and a Shorn patrolman? Had he succumbed to Sirol's petty manipulations again? Zia walked her fingers along his neck, kneading the muscles there. From somewhere came a small, catlike sound of contentment. He realized it was his own.

"We've found a bit of life beyond service," she whispered near his ear, "A part that is just for us. We've a connection that no one else shares."

He felt that connection like a shaft of sunlight between them. He wanted to savor it. She leaned so close that with the slightest effort he could wrap his arms around her waist and pull her to him, but the part of him that was forever questioning—was it some shadow of Cael, who loves disorder?—forced him to straighten and open his eyes.

"You knew when we met that I was the fosterling of Tierzen Trianor, didn't you?"

Her welcoming expression didn't shift. If she hadn't been touching him, he wouldn't have sensed the tension that caused her hand to pause against his shoulder. He wouldn't have felt the change when she stroked him again, more gingerly.

"Yes. Yes, I knew who your Teachers were," she said softly, "and I'm so sorry. Tonight you shouldn't have to think on such things. Sit back down and let me play for you."

"Let you use your music and wine to convince me to commit some transgression? Is that what Abrigado wants? Have I not done enough damage already? Shall I break Shorn Law for you?"

"What?" Zia darted an anxious look down the hall at the room full of noisy patrons. "Don't say such things aloud. Don't ask this of me, Jhared. Not on Dawnings' Eve."

"I must ask it on Dawnings' Eve, for it shapes my Path. Please, Zia." He stared at her, willing her to respond, but she looked away and was silent.

No one dared the dangers of a lie on this night.

"That is answer enough, isn't it?" He started to turn; the room was turning faster than he was.

"Wait! Jhared, you don't understand. I just…you don't want to know."

He looked back at her. "Elder Trianor risked his own family to take me in. I won't bring them more grief. I owe them everything."

Zia glared up at him, her green eyes flashing. "And what do you owe your own kind?"

"My own kind?" He gave a brittle laugh. "I am Trianor's Folly. There are no others like me." Immediately, he despised the self-pity he revealed with those words, but there was no recalling them. He turned and walked away, leaving her standing with her fingers clenched around the throat of her flute.

The crowd made his retreat an agonizingly slow one. Any bit of dignity he still bore tattered as he pushed through one group of revelers after another. Isella waved to him from the bar, but he pretended not to see her as he made his way toward escape. The only thing that caused him to pause was the black-bearded Shorn man, who offered him an ominous yellow-toothed grin near the door. It was the same brawny northerner from his first visit. Jhared wished the man would openly challenge him. He wished he were at the border facing an army of Sahistens. He needed somewhere to burn away the emotions that raced in his veins. It was Dawnings' Eve; there could be no running tonight.

Halfway down Cirolan Hill, wandering aimlessly among the festival performers, he realized his careless wishes might very well have altered his Path: the black-beard appeared to be following him. To test it, Jhared turned on his heel, moving rapidly back up the hill to join the audience of a flame-eater. He smirked when the burly clansman came to a bumbling halt in front of him and cast about for a reason to mask his stop. Did such a clown think he could track one of the high chieftain's Forest Guard scouts?

Fire raced through Jhared's limbs. He had already turned to confront the man when he recognized his own foolishness. Was he really going to start a brawl with a stranger while he was drunk and undisciplined on Dawnings' Eve?

There were more interesting ways to make the man pay, after all.

Jhared strode away from the performers and started north toward the city center again. The clansman hurried after him, his heavy footsteps clear to Jhared now. As they approached the next crossroads, Jhared ducked into the shadowed doorway of a temple on the corner. The priestess guiding in supplicants frowned at him as he turned to peer out. The clansman had stopped and turned to face up the hill, as though he were eyeing the group of ladies passing by. With a quick spiral for Riana, Jhared dove from his hiding spot and around the corner out of sight. Loping quickly through the people, he crossed one block east, then back-tracked south. If he was quick enough, he could circle the man and return to the street well behind him.

Tonight the goddess faced her captain's blade, the hunter became prey, and the powerless found strength. Jhared reached the street at just the perfect point. Ahead, the big man was in a frenzy, searching up and down each crossroads and muttering frustrated curses.

Jhared grinned. Watching the man curse and stomp was entertaining and made for an easy stalk. Curious now, Jhared trailed after the northerner, toward the city center, as far as Shorn Circle. Black-beard possessed persistence, if nothing else; he glared up every street and peered into every drinking house, furiously determined to find his lost prey. As Jhared crouched behind a water barrel near the walls of Shorn Circle listening to the man rant, he wondered who could possibly be so eager to hunt him down.

"Dawnings' Eve to you, Patrolman."

The scornful voice came from above and behind him. A blade touched his throat. Understanding slowly sank through his wine-sodden thoughts: they had offered him a fine distraction. He had been a fool after all.

"And to you," Jhared replied. "Nicely done. I didn't expect you."

"See, boy?" said a second man to his companion. "S'not so hard to outsmart a Forest Guard. Stick with me and you'll learn what's needed."

The second voice offered the contracted form of Velos that came from the lower circles, but the first voice was distantly familiar and precise enough to suggest a life on Travitar Hill. This wasn't a robbery. Jhared had been led to Shorn Circle for a reason. Sirol had warned him last spring what they thought of him here.

"I'm sure my small skills are nothing compared to your own service," Jhared said dryly.

"Don't give me no heart songs 'bout service," spat the second man. "I know who y'are beneath the uniform. Lift yer hands away from yer sides and stand up. Slowly."

Jhared did as he was told, keeping the barrel partially between them. His two assailants were a mismatched pair: one was in his prime, husky and powerfully built, with scarred features that suggested he was no stranger to a fight. The other man, near Jhared's years, was lanky, with red hair and a smooth brow. If not for the dagger in his right hand and the gleaming brawlers' glove that sheathed the knuckles and wrist of his left, he would fit in strolling with his family down Elders' Row. His shiny weapons and overeager expression made him look like a youngster showing off in his big brother's gear. Both assailants were dressed in bright festival garb.

Neither of them was Shorn.

That fact made a difference. A great deal of difference. Jhared began to regret the brandy.

"I've not offered myself as anyone's wretch. Why do you hunt me?"

"You were born the wretch," said the younger man in a poisonous tone. "You should have gone to the flames a long time ago."

For the second time that day, Jhared faced a blade at his heart, but this time he could do nothing to strike back. Only two paths lay open to him: endure what mischief they planned or flee.

"No wretch burns before the hunters prove themselves," he said, shifting his balance. "Shall we see if you're worthy of the chase?"

Even before he finished speaking, he was dropping backwards, out of range of the blade. His weight transferred to his right leg. With his left, he kicked the barrel hard near the top. The barrel tipped, swayed on its edge, then crashed to the ground, splashing out its contents and forcing his attackers to lurch out of the way.

"Trianor's Folly!" the redhead shouted as Jhared ran. "You *will* pay your debt tonight!"

Curses echoed after him. Then footsteps. He hadn't delayed them long. Shorn Circle curved north, and he followed it toward the high temple. An old tower wall blocked his way and forced him east, back toward Cirolan Hill. He ran at speed. People in the streets parted hastily, shouting jeers or encouragement as he passed. He laughed: they all thought it was a true chase.

Wind streamed cool and buoyant over his heated body. He reached for it and pushed himself harder, feeding his muscles on forbidden emotion. He didn't doubt his ability to outstrip his pursuers; years of trying to outrun his desires had readied him for this. As he led the men through the darkness, twisting down small alleys and crossing crowded streets, he began to understand what the chase really meant: for this one night, running was not about escape. He leaped over a cart in his path, landed in a crouch to regain his balance, and pounded on. The onlookers cried out their approval. Everyone around him believed him to be the wretch. They scorned and cheered him, both. Perhaps some even wished to join him. He laughed again, giddy with insight: *he was bad fortune.* Tonight it was within his power to let the hunters drive him away or force them to stand and face what they most feared.

He was what they feared.

He had always known it, but never before had he felt the power in it. The ground shifted beneath him. Was this what Micah felt? Was this the truth that drove the man beyond reason?

We are poison.

He couldn't think on it, tried to push past it with another burst of speed. The city twisted beneath him until he wasn't certain whether he was the one moving or if it might be the streets and circles around him. A broken flagstone caught his boot and he nearly fell, losing ground to his hunters. Their harsh breathing grew louder as they closed. They had kept up better than he expected, better than they should have. They had been prepared for him, but by whom? He renewed his efforts. His heart hammered against his chest and his legs began to burn.

Gradually, he became aware of a troubling truth: he had let them herd him into the bowels of the lower circles of Cirolan Hill, a part of the city where honest men didn't travel. The streets grew blacker and the cheering faded behind him. Dawnings' Day celebrations didn't reach this quarter. Decaying buildings and overworked balconies blocked most of the starlight above the narrow alleys. The air smelled of rot and human waste. Jhared wondered how far he might be from the Cirolan Gate. It was time to find the City Guard on watch there. He had no intention of going onto the fires.

The alley widened into a small circle, and Jhared skidded around the corner. An animal growl rose from the shadows. A warning. Jhared pivoted toward the sound too late. Movement blurred the night, and a dark figure slammed into him from the side. The blow sent him sprawling onto the stone. He just had time to pull one knee beneath him before a booted foot kicked him in the ribs from the other side, throwing him back to the ground. He rolled onto his back as the boot aimed for him again. He caught it with both hands and yanked hard. The boot's owner landed with a sharp grunt. His head made a hollow sound as it struck the stone. Jhared rolled to all fours and scrambled to his feet.

Two opponents here and two not far behind him. The one on the ground, a wide-shouldered, rotund man, groaned and sat up dazedly. The other, a compact, muscled blond, drew his sword, his eyes bright. These two weren't much older than Jhared. They didn't stink like street rats and they didn't look like fighting men, but the blond gripped his blade confidently enough.

"I told Corben you'd run," the swordsman said, frowning. "Never have seen one'a the cursed with the courage to stand and face what he's earned."

Jhared recovered his stance and struggled to catch his breath. Heat poured off his body, sending steamy ghosts of him into the cold air. He was nearly out of choices; all his Paths converged to one.

"You are ordered…in the name of High Chieftain Adan Rumar…to cease hostility against the Forest Guard," he gasped.

"Forest Guard? All I see is one ragged pigeon who's flown from Elders' Circle."

The rapid stomp of boots on the street echoed down the alley, and Jhared's hunters tore around the corner. The older, scarred man stopped beside the swordsman, but the long-limbed, redhead shoved past his companions and kept coming.

"You…earned yourself pain!" the young man panted, closing on Jhared.

He swung a fist. Jhared blocked from inside, surprised by the man's wiry strength. On another day, he would have recovered swiftly enough to throw a blow of his own or to twist the man's energy against him, but Jhared's balance was skewed with Melandrien. The impact knocked him sideways, directly into the leather-and-bronze-wrapped knuckles of the brawlers' glove. They cracked against his cheekbone. His head snapped backwards and lightning blasted in his face. The dull thud he heard was his own body slamming into the wall of a shed behind him.

"Ilvio!" the scarred man snapped from far away. "Yer to move when I say and not before!"

The boy drew back sullenly, the eagerness in his eyes changing to frustrated bloodlust. Jhared suddenly recognized that expression; he had seen it in an alley on the day of his Becoming. Ilvio had wanted to spill blood then. Here in the lower circles of Cirolan Hill, it seemed he had found an outlet for his dark appetite.

"I'm not paying you to teach me to scamper all up and down the city, Corben," the boy complained. "You said I'd have the chance to make this creature surrender what he owes."

"And I'm not teaching you to flap yer hole. Yer at the *bottom* of the hill now. My territory. You listen to orders or don't call yerself a Legacy man."

"What's he doing here?" grumbled the burly man, rubbing at the back of his head as he clambered to his feet and joined the others. "This isn't a Dawnings' Eve adventure for a wealthy man's son. This is about protecting Avelos."

The swordsman gestured toward his companion. "Encio's right, Corben. The boy shouldn't be part of this. We're not here for profit."

"Enough, Bren! Encio! All of you, attend to yer business. We got things to do, an' yer mark's thinkin'a runnin again."

Jhared did consider it, but the world seesawed violently in front of him, and with Bren fresh and the four of them to flank him, he wouldn't get far. Time now to learn what this was about. They had called him Trianor's Folly.

Bren slid a sword against his ribs. "I don't see him running anywhere."

Jhared twitched as the blade pierced his side. Ilvio laughed.

"Good," Corben said, beginning to smile in the darkness. "He's paying attention now. Y'are listening, aren't you, soldier?"

Bren pushed on the blade and Jhared hissed.

"I am a servant of Avelos. I preserve the safety of the country above all else."

"Ah, good," Corben declared. "The Law of Duty. Then you'll understand what I have to tell you. Rumar's decided that the best way to keep us safe from the killing storms is to join with the temple whores and send soldiers out to search for ancient spells. Yer patrol's 'bout to get the order."

"I know nothing of it."

"Don't matter. We do. It's a mission to find great power. If you go, you break Shorn Law." Corben threw a punch that landed hard in Jhared's middle. "S'yer duty not to go."

Jhared bent over, coughing for breath. A mission to seek the secrets of the killing winds. His patrol to be chosen? He could almost see final reparation at the end of this path, so bitterly close.

"I have no say…in where I'm sent. Why would you—"

He cursed himself for thinking too slowly. As he straightened, he tried to focus on Corben.

"You don't care if I break Shorn Law. You mean this as a message for someone. Who?"

Corben tilted his head and lifted a hand to stay Bren's blade. "Well now. Look at that. He said you'd figure it out."

Creatures rustled in the space between the buildings beside them, and Corben paused. "Encio, explain to the soldier how he'll do his part to save Avelos tonight."

The big man came around to face Jhared. His arms were fleshy and thick with muscle. Ash was smudged across his face and the scent of smoke hung in his clothes. He might have been a smith.

"Rumar's gone too far," he said. "Looks like he fancies himself king—bleeding the clans of their rule, using sovereign right to bring foreigners to our lands, putting Shorn soldiers on our borders. He's trying to set himself over us like that stone-licker Javahari in Sahiste. It's time he learns he doesn't have the power to act unless the clans say so."

"And we say y'are not going on this mission," Corben muttered. He struck at Jhared again. Jhared dodged the blow, causing Corben to stumble. Bren made Jhared pay with another jab of the sword.

Jhared bit back an outcry. Perhaps they believed they could use him to demonstrate their influence over Rumar's men, but surely they didn't think the behavior of one Shorn soldier meant anything to the high chieftain.

"That's not all of it," he gasped. "There's something more. There must be. I've no importance as a symbol."

"Oh, no?" Corben grumbled, regaining his balance. "I think there's a one who'll know how to read what we send him. He'll translate it for Rumar f'he needs to. When Tierzen Trianor sees his broken Folly, he'll know the clans are taking back their rightful rule. He'll know not to violate the Legacy of Tumal ever again.

"Ilvio, this part's what you came for." Corben nodded to the other men and stepped back. Bren twisted the sword in Jhared's side, pushing him toward an ocean of blackness. Jhared fought for consciousness as the others moved on him. By the time he recovered enough to see clearly, Encio gripped his right arm and Bren his left. Ilvio stood before him.

"It used to be my task to stone the pigeons out of the rafters in Father's stables," the boy said, smiling as he shrugged off his cloak. "You have to strike them damn hard before they give up trying to fly."

He darted his eyes over Jhared, a flush creeping over his smooth cheeks. His fingers flexed inside the glove, setting the bronze studs shining like amber tears. With his right hand, Ilvio pulled his fine blade.

"Not the knife," Corben ordered.

The boy's smile vanished. He sent a frozen look toward Corben. "You said I could make him pay!"

"He's not to die, and I don't want any accidents. F'you don't know how to do this without a blade, step aside."

Ilvio shoved the dagger back into its sheath. His eyes lingered on the ground and his shoulders rose and fell with angry breaths. Then without warning, he flung himself at Jhared.

The first blow flew so fast that Jhared hardly saw it before it landed against his unprotected throat. He staggered backwards in Bren's and Encio's steel grip. He was choking, his mouth gaping like a fish; the next blows rained in and upward into his middle, driving the air from his lungs. Bright colors swirled before his eyes. A high-pitched whine filled his head. He twisted sideways, shifting his weight against his captors, employing once more the skills he had learned on the practice grounds. He managed a solid kick that sent Encio backwards with a pained gasp, before Bren deepened the gash across his ribs and dropped him to the ground. Encio and Ilvio wrenched him upright this time. Silently, he begged

Riana that he not be used as a blade to wound Tierzen, but the moon was high on Dawnings' Eve: the goddess had turned her back on the Paths and men chose their own ways.

You should have let me end this.

Ilvio drew back to circle Jhared, studying him like a sculptor deciding where next to apply the hammer. The man didn't bother with taunts or insults, but applied himself with serene focus: a knee in the groin, a boot heel ground into the small bones at the top of the foot, bronze studs swiped across the throat.

"That's not the way a man fights," Encio murmured in disgust.

Ilvio didn't notice or didn't care what the others thought; he was attuned to Jhared's reactions. His eyes brightened at a half-stifled outcry. The shudder Jhared couldn't suppress as Ilvio stepped behind him made the boy go still. When leather and metal flayed the scars across Jhared's back, a wave of agony rolled through him that rose from beyond the moment, back to the old memory of wordless terror. The blows hammered down his back, until a low jab caused his knees to give way and shot streaks of black and purple into the night.

Corben stood back, arms folded across his chest, watching impassively. "He's not to die," he reminded the boy.

Ilvio came around to meet Jhared's eyes with his own intense gaze before backhanding him across the face with the studded glove.

How does a man count minutes of pain? Treading the borders of consciousness, Jhared saw days slip past: the sun rose, people filled the streets, life went on around him, the sun set. Temples were built, decayed, and collapsed. Riana's sphere turned and he was there, an unseen, unknown sacrifice, pushing Avelos toward darkness and disorder.

We are poison.

Blood filled his mouth with the metallic taste of guilt. And somewhere, in a deep place seldom touched, his guilt mirrored back to him as its dark opposite. Just as Riana looked into the Mirror of Night and saw Cael, Jhared released his guilt and it returned in the form of something forbidden as he began to understand.

"All right," Corben said. "Enough, Ilvio."

The boy swung again, laughing. His clothes were disheveled and Jhared's blood marred his face.

"I said, enough!"

At a sign from Corben, Bren and Encio turned Jhared loose. His legs folded beneath him, and he dropped panting to his hands and knees, his blood dripping onto the stone. He crouched there, fighting the blackness, his heart pounding. Corben had told him why they chose to attack him, but not who ordered it. Jhared had figured out what they hadn't revealed: It would be someone who knew

Tierzen and despised him. Someone with powerful connections to the Legacy. Someone who thought Jhared should be treated as a rabid dog. Someone who would know a Forest Guard assignment before it was given.

Lieutenant Sevar.

Something dark and terrible that Jhared had long wrapped in the chains of his oath shuddered and rattled, begging to be freed.

Ilvio groaned like a satisfied lover, stretched leisurely, and bent to retrieve his cloak. "Elder Abrigado keeps a pretty little scribe," he said, brushing dust off the wool. "Doesn't she blow on her flute at an inn on Cirolan Hill? I've a thought to find her and teach her to play my instrument."

"So, the little ferret has that much of a man in him," Encio murmured.

Jhared heard Ilvio shift. Ice crackled in his voice. "They say a Shorn woman's hungers are never slaked, but I'll give her something to fill her. Come along if you doubt me."

"Touch a cursed woman and you're lucky if your cock don't drop off," Bren warned.

Darkness strained against its chains. One by one they began to snap. Jhared grasped at them, wrestling emotion back under wraps.

Are you afraid to take that much action for yourself?

The little knife in his belt had been a gift from his Teacher on the day he first memorized Shorn Law. When Tierzen presented it to him, Jhared felt the bond that wrapped around them both, and he had sealed it with a word: *Father.* That bond represented all he cared for and all he owed. Now he clutched desperately to the connection to steady him.

"There's the young boy back in Elders' Circle for you, Encio," Ilvio continued. "Handsome, but soft enough still. Are you man enough to teach the way of things to the son of the Minister of the Teaching?"

"And make him beg for more," Encio said, grinning.

"Keep your cocks in your pants, all of you," Corben snapped. "We're not finished with this job yet. Our orders are—"

The ground pitched beneath Jhared and his chains shattered. Fury tore from his grasp to rise raw and unbridled. A part of him knew he was falling from the sky, but he was helpless to stop it. Before the others could reach him, he surged upright inside the guard of the man closest to him and thrust the blade toward the soft place where the ribs meet, where even a small knife could tear through muscle and find the heart.

"For the injuries done…to those before me," he gasped.

It was Bren who roared in surprise and pain as he staggered backwards. The blade deflected off bone and Jhared grappled for another angle. Then steel found flesh.

"Goddess, mercy! Stop! What are you doing?"

Jhared cried out as his Teachers' wail blasted through him and he lost his grip on Bren. Encio kicked him hard, digging into the open wound over his ribs. Red arrows flew across Jhared's vision. He tripped to his knees.

"Damn your traitor's blood!" Encio spat.

Bren lay against the shed moaning, one hand pressed to his chest. "Cael's balls," Corben hissed. "That can't go unpunished."

Corben pushed Ilvio aside and swung as Jhared lunged to his feet. Jhared just managed to block the man's wild blow and stagger inside to try one of his own, but Encio caught him from behind and struck another against his ribs.

Exhaustion and horror left Jhared empty. He backed toward the wall of the shed, trying to keep both men in front of him. He needn't have bothered; they worked too well together. While Corben stepped in to engage his defenses on the right, Encio reached him with little effort from the left. The muscles in Jhared's left side screamed each time he lifted his arm. When Corben sent a blow toward his head, he couldn't twist around fast enough to halt it. The fighting man's fist crashed against his temple and drove him into the ground. Stunned half sense-less, he lay in the street staring through a red fog. It was Ilvio who picked up Bren's sword.

"Now we'll see how long it takes a traitor to beg for death," the boy said coolly.

As Ilvio stalked toward him, Jhared saw the blurry form of the black-beard hurry out of the alley behind Corben. The first part of the trap had caught up at last.

Good. They brought a traitor to spill my traitor's blood.

Jhared recognized the order in it, but in the end, there would be no place for him with Riana; Cael would come from the shadows to feed on his flesh and devour his soul. When the blue-robed priestess glided into the street as well, he knew his Path was done. Darkness washed over him, drowning him. He had an instant to register Encio's movement as the man drew his foot back. Too many regrets to fit them all into that single instant.

Stars exploded in Jhared's head, and then the darkness drowned them as well.

20.
SACRIFICES

"I dreamed that you traveled far from me and could not return," Merisel whispered. Her hand paused with the brush still in Nemiah's unbound hair. Her wide eyes reflected silver in the polished mirror. "Then the crows came and landed on the empty altar. They tore it with their beaks until the stone bled. I wish you didn't have to go, Lady."

Nemiah reached up and slid the brush gently from the girl's fingers, surprised to find her trembling; the child wasn't prone to fear.

"Very good for remembering your dream, Merisel. Dreams are shadows of the Paths and important for that. Still, shadows are not always shaped just the same as the things they stand for, are they? I can make a shadow on the wall that looks like Capa, but does that make my fingers a hound?"

From the floor at Nemiah's feet, Capalino lifted his head to see why he'd been named. Merisel shook her head and smiled a little.

"Likewise, our dreams cannot tell us just what awaits us on the Paths. Now tell me the story of Arion's Trial while I prepare. Let me see what you understand about the things I do tonight."

Merisel settled on the floor beside Capa and looked up with a trusting gaze. Nemiah's heart stirred with affection. When the child turned suddenly to a young woman, then a blind crone, Nemiah closed her eyes and dug her nails into the insides of her palms until the pain pulled her back from the Gate.

"Lady, are you—"

"Go ahead," Nemiah encouraged faintly. "The trial will be upon us soon."

The girl looked worried, but she sat up straighter and began obediently with a formal spiral to Riana. "On that day of perfect balance, when light and darkness share the sky in equal measures, the Holy Lady saw how well General Arion led her Chosen in the war against Cael, and she called him to her. She laid down her power, turned her back to the Paths, and bared her throat before him, saying, 'If you slay me now, the spheres and the stars will turn by your order and you will live for all eternity to rule them.'

"The general saw the Holy Lady at his feet, so very beautiful, and he saw the wonder of the Paths all shifting without her to order them, and his eyes lit with desire. 'My lady, I know by the pulse of my heart that I am meant to rule the spheres, but I have given my service to you. What would you have me do?'

"'Does the sun ask the sparrow which way to rise?' she replied.

"'My lady, I have fought off Cael's armies time and again,' he said. 'Your Chosen obey me and the people love me. Why must I slay you to prove I can rule for all eternity?'

"'Can the river flow both to the mountains and to the sea?' she replied.

"At that, he drew his blade, and a host of demons rushed between them. General Arion fought his demons for many days and was injured many times, but at the end of one moon's turning, he finally drove them all away. When the last demon vanished, he fell to his knees before the Lady and threw down his sword. 'Slay me for my pride,' he begged her. 'I would end my life in your service, rather than rule the spheres alone.' But when the Holy Lady took up her power again, she did not slay him. She told him, 'This is the Day of Dawnings, because today you start a new Path as my lord. When your Path has ended, I will give you a place in my sacred skies, where you will live as long as the spheres turn. And all men will know days of hope and fear when the Paths shift without my order and they are free to choose their fortunes.'

"And so do we see Lord Arion shining in the southern sky. And so do we remember Riana's promise on Dawnings' Eve."

Merisel made a spiral and folded her hands in her lap.

"Good, child." Nemiah turned in her chair to face the girl. "Very good. And do you understand?"

"Lord Arion wanted power he couldn't have," she said. "He wanted...too much and that made him unhappy. That's why his demons came."

Nemiah smiled. "For certain, he was a man of many desires. What does that mean for us this Dawnings' Eve?"

"Dawnings' Eve must be a test. Captain Rom must prove he is as strong and loyal as Lord Arion to remain your Arionad."

"Ah, my dear, for Captain Rom, as for Arion, it is not a test but a choice: He alone must decide which Path he will walk, as all men must choose their Paths. And the important choices are ever difficult, for they are about what we lose as much as what we earn."

"What of you, Lady?" Merisel ran a hand over Capa's soft ears, her gaze growing troubled once more. "Will you choose also?"

"For me it is different. I am Chosen. Like Riana, on this night I endure the decisions of men. It is a mystery you will understand better when you take your final vows."

Merisel's lower lip trembled. "Please don't leave our altar empty," she whispered. "The crows frighten me."

Nemiah frowned and leaned forward to draw the girl to her feet. "The altar will never be left untended, child. All the sisters of the Higher Circle will guard it while Riana faces Lord Arion's choice. Come now. Cook has fresh boldblood root in the kitchen, and I could use some tea before I go. Promise me you'll keep Capa with you so he's not lonely. You can give him a run in the outer gardens if you'd like."

The girl nodded solemnly, sending butter-colored strands of hair falling around her small face. At a gesture from Nemiah, Capa rose and trotted down the stairs with the girl.

Alone in the quiet of her bedchamber, Nemiah finished her preparations. Tonight she laid down all connections to the goddess; not even a symbol would she carry. She drew the brush through her unplaited hair until sparks crackled through its length. She removed the small prism that hung about her neck on a silver chain and the exquisite silver ring that was the gift of Rom's niece. Her belted robe she replaced with a loose shift dyed by the sisters of Clan Valador, and instead of wearing her ribbon-laced slippers, she padded barefoot over the flagstone.

When she finished, she looked into the mirror and was startled by the wraith staring back at her. The gold of her hair and her deep green dress robbed the color from her face, leaving her cheeks as pale as moonlight and her lips cool and bloodless. Sleepless nights bruised the skin beneath her eyes. Only her gaze burned with life, but its source seemed borrowed rather than coming from any strength of her own, like sunlight beaming through stained glass. Tonight she could not draw upon even that borrowed strength. Soon she would make her way unguarded and alone to wait by the Ulaye in the inner garden. When Rom came to her, she would present him with the choice Riana once offered Lord Arion. If Rom did not best the two demons who challenged him or if he chose to take Riana's offer of rule, Nemiah could only abide by the outcome. That moment of uncertainty and helplessness was always the darkest moment of Dawnings' Eve for her. It was the moment when Riana's gift could be taken from her forever, leaving her empty. In the mirror, her image shuddered.

The air rippled suddenly, and the image split itself like a beam of light through a prism. Nemiah turned away to avoid catching her reflection from other Paths and murmured a prayer to seal the Gate as best she could.

Lady of Order, will you allow me to close the Gate when dawn comes again?

Since Velanhan, she hadn't been able to shut out the world's shifting from her awareness, not even in sleep, and in several frightening moments she'd become confused as to which Path was her own. Everywhere she turned, she witnessed scenes of transition that didn't belong to her own time and place. Life to death, trust to betrayal, accomplishment to decay: Nemiah knew them as warnings. She had half-hoped Enrian's agreement to collaborate in a search for Altan Mar would be enough to tug the country's Path away from destruction, but the warnings continued.

While she waited for Merisel, she wandered down the spiral stairs to her receiving room and curled into a chair by the fire. She picked up the handloom Leita had left there. The unfinished design was complex and disturbing, like the Bearer herself. Tonight it might have been a comfort to talk with Leita, but she walked among the people as a reminder of the dangers of stepping off the Path on Dawnings' Eve. Leita had been distant since Nemiah's return from Velanhan, and although the offer to send the Bearer on a hunt for Altan Mar had gone some way toward bridging the rift between them, they had lost a measure of trust. Nemiah missed her friend.

In the antechamber, the door creaked open. She was glad to hear it; she needed that tea.

"Merisel? Bring the boldblood, child."

Murmured voices and footsteps in response. Too many. Not the patter of a child and a hound.

Nemiah stood quickly, letting the loom slide to the floor. "Who enters?"

The chamber door burst open and four tall demons swept into the room. Lamplight fell upon their cruel, avian features: raven, falcon, eagle, and crow. Their midnight robes swirled like shadows as they took up places around her. Four women marched in behind them and created an inner circle that trapped her in its center.

"Lady Nemiah," Carian barked, "you have turned your back on the Paths and sundered your tie to Riana. On this Eve of the Day of Dawnings, you will bare yourself to the will of men and accept the consequences of that choice."

Nemiah gazed at the members of the Higher Circle who surrounded her: Carian, Bena, Maita, and Clemina. Leita was outside the sanctuary, as she should be, but where was Kaliska?

"You are not Chosen, Carian," she said, drawing herself straight. "You do not order the Circle."

"Tonight there is no Chosen," Carian replied. "And those with strength enough direct their own Paths. We need not be led by the feeble." She handed Clemina a length of rope. "Bind her."

The young priestess hesitated, her gaze uncertain as she looked from Carian to Nemiah.

"Don't fear, sister," Nemiah said gently. "The Mistress of Novices is correct in one thing: I have laid down Riana's power willingly."

"Or perhaps Riana's power was never in you to lay down." Carian glared at the younger woman. "Sister Clemina, do your duty to the goddess or become a part of the sacrifice."

Clemina shuffled behind Nemiah, head bowed. "Forgive me, Lady," she murmured as she reached for Nemiah's hands.

"We are all traveling together on this Path, Carian," Nemiah said. "And we will all be sacrificed if we don't change our direction."

"I know that well, Lady. I warned you of it this spring. What have you done since then? Spent your time chasing histories that no longer exist. Surrendered the Bearer of Cael's Blade to Rumar's soldiers. You are weak and afraid to fight for what is ours. It is the obligation of the Higher Circle to step toward a new Path."

Nemiah sighed. "Riana guided me to pursue Altan Mar. It is a gift we must use, and I've told you as much many times now."

"A gift? Then you found it on a sacred journey? You confirmed it with repetitions and ruled out contradictions?"

When Nemiah didn't respond, Carian snorted in disdain. "As I thought. The council would rather drive us all off a cliff than acknowledge the Higher Circle as the guide of Avelos, and you would rather jump to your death than fight."

Nemiah's heart quickened as Clemina wrapped the rope around her wrists and pulled it tight. Anxious, orderly Maita, Mistress of Ritual, watched critically, her plump fingers gripping a wine goblet.

One of the demon warriors, the falcon, shifted uneasily. On any other night they were Arionade: Rom's own men selected in secret by the Circle to play the role of Arion's demons. There should have been two, not four. They should have been waiting for her by the Ulaye tree in the inner gardens. They should have challenged Rom when he came from seclusion to confront her. Her Arionad had left that morning to prepare himself for the trial.

At least that was the message she had been given.

"What have you done to Captain Rom?"

Carian's gaze hardened. Bena shook her grey head. Nemiah thought she saw another of the demons flinch.

"We've committed no sacrilege," the Mistress of Novices snapped. "Lord Arion is ever free to decide for himself where true power lies."

"It's not the Arionad we care about," Bena said impatiently. "Give her the wine. Even Nemiah Gabriana might reach the Paths on this night, and there are things we must know."

At Carian's nod, Maita stepped forward and lifted the cup to Nemiah's lips. The familiar cloying scent of dreamsease and the bite of karianta berries caused Nemiah to draw back sharply.

"I'm no novice to be pushed through the Gate!"

"No, you're not," Bena replied. "I've known novices who traveled the Paths more readily."

"The caelevano see more of Riana's ways than you do," Maita added coldly.

Nemiah darted a look around the circle and realized they didn't know. Only Leita understood that she couldn't even walk down the hall of the temple right now without wandering dangerously close to Riana's Gate. She clung to her own place by a spider-silk thread. The drugged wine would tear apart that fragile tie and set her drifting. Perhaps forever. The Paths were endless. She twisted her head away from the cup and bumped against the chest of the demon behind her.

"You go too far, Carian. I'll not participate in this distortion of the sacred rites."

"Yours is the distortion." Carian lifted her chin defiantly. "I am the daughter of Sianale, the last true Bearer. I know stories of Lord Arion's Trial from when our Chosen Lady still owned strength and courage."

"Don't boast, girl. Half-remembered stories don't match the living of it." The ancient Mistress of Maps made a shushing gesture toward Carian before turning to Nemiah. "Come, Lady," she grumbled. "For nine years, you've avoided walking the Paths. Other than the fall you took last spring, you've given us a handful of journeys. Let Riana have her balance and give us a sacred journey to be remembered. There must be some sacrifice, at the end."

Nemiah met the Mapmaker's rheumy gaze. Knowledge hid behind those eyes. Of all the Higher Circle, Bena possessed the best understanding of the Path they traveled. She had watched Avelos spiraling toward this point for longer than any other. And she drew the maps. For Bena, this attack was about more than intimidating the high priestess back into submission.

"Who will guide me?" Nemiah asked. None of them but Leita possessed the skill to find her and pull her back if she foundered on the journey.

"Riana guides her Chosen," Carian said with a smirk.

"Ah. And if not, then perhaps she was never truly Chosen, after all, hmm, Carian?"

The Mistress of Novices stared at her stonily. Nemiah answered the woman's glare with a grim smile. Perhaps the Chosen had choices to make, after all. She turned to Bena.

"If we're to evade devastation, we must find the junctions where our Path branches toward a better outcome and determine the points of influence to get there. If I accept this journey, you will use your skill for no other purpose. Are we agreed?"

"I know my job well enough," Bena grumbled.

"I mean you must set aside your destructive rabble rousing, Bena."

"Give me the material and I will seek what is needed."

It wasn't agreement Bena offered her, but this was Dawning's Eve. "Very well," Nemiah sighed. "I have set aside my power and will not profane the ritual. I only bid you all to find Riana's order."

The Mistress of Ritual stepped forward and once again set the goblet to Nemiah's lips. "By Riana's ways we travel," she intoned.

Nemiah centered herself with a prayer; then she drank the bittersweet wine.

"By Riana's ways we will return," the others responded.

The demons marched Nemiah barefoot through the deserted living quarters of the temple. Merisel and Capa were not to be seen. Nemiah hoped Cook had kept them in the warm kitchens eating plum tarts. In the cold dark of the inner courtyard, a lone cricket, the final remnant of summer, chirped faintly. Strains of laughter and music from the city's celebrations danced over the wall. Nemiah offered no struggle as the demons bound her to the tree's trunk. The wine had begun to rush through her, tearing through every boundary that kept her intact. Behind his crow mask, one man murmured a prayer before he touched her. The others silenced him with their grim stares.

When they finished, Carian bent as though to kiss Nemiah's cheek. "The Captain of the Arionade is a wise man, Lady. He understands the ways of power. When he fights his demons, you may well find he has a different answer for you this time."

Nemiah drew back the small distance that the ropes allowed to look into the other woman's face, trying to ignore the way it warped to match the avian features of the demons. "The very bonds with which you have tied me form Riana's circle, Carian."

The Mistress of Novices looked startled at that, but if Carian had anything more to say, Nemiah didn't hear it; she drifted on an autumn breeze up through the naked branches of the dead Ulaye tree into the sacred skies. When she reached the pinnacle of the temple dome, the Gates thundered open, and she dropped through the dark flames onto the Paths.

The infinite consequences of words spoken and withheld, steps taken and not, came roaring through her. Nemiah dove deep within herself to reach the stable core where she wouldn't be swept away. She needed to direct this journey toward the Paths closest to her own, toward ways that didn't end with the country's destruction. She needed to find the forks where alternate roads were born. It was possible; her Sister of the Paths told her it was. She set her feet beneath her and took a tentative step along Riana's weaving.

A woman screams as three men drive her to the ground.

A man shares his grief: "The Bearer sacrificed herself trying to aid us."

A king touches the thoughts of his enemy and finds mercy.

A young girl binds a child's wings and knows fear.

A falcon seeks the killing winds to claim her own lands.

A goddess speaks the words of healing: "You are the body of Avelos as I am the spirit."

At first, Nemiah directed the steps she took, but the moments bombarded her too quickly, faster than her racing heart, until she lost her balance and all sense of coherence. It was like hurrying through an endless hall lined with open doors and catching fragments of the conversations within each room. Yet each of those fragments came weighted with emotion, as though she lived them. They flooded her senses until the moments that were her own, that made her Nemiah Gabriana, lost any small significance they possessed.

A fighting man confronts four opponents and wonders what choices remain to him.

With an effort that left her breathless, Nemiah strained to make that moment hers, to see Rom more clearly, but the Path wrenched away from her, leaving only echoes of rage and hatred.

"Silly bird, slow down! You'll lose yourself flitting about that way."

Something warm and strong snatched her up, and she was caught like a fish in a net. As the flood of moments drained away, Nemiah crumpled gratefully into the stillness.

"By skies and stars, it's you! My pretty dove. What a marvel you are to find me again. Your teachers taught you well. Come and speak with me."

Nemiah felt herself drawn deeper into a single moment. She knew the welcoming voice, but owned no name or face to make it real. In the dark, a warm breeze tugged her clothes. Words formed loosely in her mind, then dissipated like fog before she could speak them.

"Look at you," clucked the voice. "Dazed as a newborn kitten. Good thing I know you, Nemiah Gabriana, Chosen Lady of Avelos. Yes, that's who you are. Think on that name a bit while I steady this Path for us. It would do you no good to float off in this state."

It grew quiet, and Nemiah lay on what felt like smooth stone trying to remember herself: Nemiah Gabriana. She *was* Chosen Lady of Avelos, and she needed answers from this sacred journey.

"What is this place?"

"Welcome back, dove." Nemiah sensed a smile. "This is my escape. It's easier to recall the beauty that remains in the world when we're this much closer to the sacred skies. Yes? Besides, it's cooler up here, and the people I most want to avoid find it a difficult place to reach."

Nemiah tried to peer at her surroundings. "It's so dark."

"Really? Try looking up, sweet."

Nemiah did as she was told and drew a breath at the unending river of brilliant stars in the black-silk sky.

"So lovely," she breathed. "I could almost believe they'll take their human forms again and return to us."

"I'm glad you appreciate it. Not many take the time to study here anymore." Sadness muted the voice. "Though it could be worse. I've seen horrible, frightening Paths where the towers have fallen and every skyglass is crushed. Where no one understands the movements of the spheres or…"

The priestess seemed to register the intensity of Nemiah's silence. "Oh. I'm so sorry, dove. Let us not speak of loss, then, for this night is the first in months I've had some cause to hope."

"Have you found a way to stop the destruction?" Nemiah sat up carefully. The breeze swirled all around her. They were on a tower rooftop.

"Not *quite* so good as that," said the Pathwalker, "but I have sisters searching in the Sandien Mountains and reason to be optimistic. You gave me the thought of it, you know. In a dream you told me to look more closely at the secrets of Altan Mar, so I returned to the records of Alende Isan's Paths. The key hid among the map notes of Sister Fira. She was a thorough note-taker, that one, and it's only a small comment; I missed it the first time through. It indicates a junction of two Paths. In the first, the companions of Alende Isan survive the destruction at Altan Mar, and in the other, most perish. The note reads: 'Where High Priestess Sabela uses her skills to balance the storms, Alende's people survive to flee.'

"Fira writes that the junction was confirmed by Arria's repetition, but I haven't found Arria's notes to compare it for myself."

"Sabela." Nemiah reverently formed the name of the great lady. Legends of the migration sometimes suggested that Lady Sabela had been the one to guide Alende Isan through his peril, but her story was long ago lost. What a treasure of knowledge she had discovered in the woman beside her. "You believe that Sabela knew the secrets of the sacred skies?"

"Fira thinks Sabela had some means of controlling the storms. My hope is that the great lady recorded her skills for us, in a scroll or perhaps in stone. I've had no luck finding her Path."

"You said the Sandien Mountains? But Altan Mar is far beyond the borders of Avelos. Have you sent anyone across the sea or northeast into the true wilds?"

"We've no need to reach Altan Mar, sweet, only her secrets. Lady Sabela built a temple in the mountains where Alende Isan and the companions first landed. Somewhere in the Sandien, according to our stories."

The breeze grew chilly, and Nemiah's green wrap appeared around her shoulders. "I didn't know."

"Have you read Fira's history?" the priestess asked curiously.

"No. I mean I didn't know any of it. Nothing of Fira exists on my Path. I cannot say if she ever was...or will be." Nemiah looked down, chagrined by her ignorance. "What will you do if you don't find Sabela's temple? Or her secret is destroyed?"

The priestess made an unhappy sound and Nemiah thought she saw a hand lift in a gesture of resignation. "We have one other possibility left to us, but I won't speak of that now. Not while we still have hope that Sabela will lend us her strength."

"If it comes that neither of us have another choice…will you share it?" Nemiah asked shyly.

"If the time comes," sighed the woman. "Let us pray we have no need."

A gloomy silence descended that dimmed the stars. Nemiah regretted the change in mood and stared off the edge of the tower, wishing for clearer vision. It was a cruel thing to observe so many Paths and understand so few. She was ignorant and inconsequential, and if it weren't for the strength of this woman whom she couldn't even see, she would simply blow away like a puff of seed in the breeze. She curled her knees to her chest and wrapped her arms around them. Below, she thought she glimpsed the dark shapes of treetops, but no village lights peeked through the dark, no signs of a city. She couldn't say where in the world she sat or whether she had left the world entirely.

"Where are we tonight, Lady?"

"Near the summit on the south face of the mount my people name Remblar. Do you know it?"

"In the Parnas? Then you're from Velantar?"

She felt the other woman's surprise, then rustling, and a body moved closer to her. "Of course, sweet."

"I…I don't even know your name."

The shadow of a hand brushed the hair from Nemiah's face. She strained to see the woman, wishing for skill enough to open the final doors that separated them. As she wished, a fire crackled to life in the center of the stone, and Nemiah glimpsed a face: sun-browned skin, strands of sleek black hair, and eyes a pale grey-blue, the color of shadows on snow. Staring into that gaze, Nemiah realized she had come upon a truly ancient soul, one forged of compassion and fortified with a power she couldn't even fathom. Her heart ached with an emptiness she hadn't known existed within her. Her pulse beat with desire that only awaited the goddess's touch.

Soft lips pressed against the corner of her mouth, and she thought her heart would break.

"Lady," she murmured in awe.

"What is it, little one?"

"You're descended from the goddess herself. Forgive me. I didn't know."

Laughter filled the night, bright and sweet, like the taste of ripe apples or the sparkle of sunlight on a mountain stream. "Ah, Nemiah Gabriana. You have no idea what a gift it is to speak with you. Even if I cannot claim the honor you bestow, it is a joy just to talk with another who values knowledge and asks questions without fear."

Nemiah flushed. Beside the small fire, a sleeping Capalino appeared.

"Whoops! Careful," the priestess warned. "Or you'll bring too much of yourself to this Path."

At the sound of the lady's voice, the scent of honeyberry blossoms filled the air. "If I make myself more present in this moment, will I see you, Lady?"

Nemiah sensed a frown so quick and sharp that it hurt. "Perhaps, dove, but not without the risk of pulling yourself from the Path where you belong and injuring the body that keeps you there." The priestess paused and then asked quietly, "You know you don't belong here, don't you?"

"I'm not certain I can make myself leave," Nemiah admitted in a small voice.

"Don't talk so, dove. Many must await your return."

Another Path existed for her; she did remember that, but it was far away and not what she had ever hoped for.

"Only crows wait for me. They perch upon the altar and whisper of betrayal."

"When crows speak, something important can be learned." The Pathwalker's tone turned sober. "You will have to go back soon, or I fear you will forget the way."

Nemiah closed her eyes. For nine years she had avoided delving into the Paths for fear of the uncertain. Now that she had arrived and discovered beauty and wisdom here, would she use the sacred journey to avoid the trials that awaited her at home?

"What would you have me do, Lady?"

"Come now, little one. You know what I must answer. I cannot know the Path you walk. I cannot choose for you."

The fire crackled, throwing shadows across the stone.

"You're right," Nemiah murmured eventually. "I promised Riana I would no longer dodge the obstacles she sets before me. It's time to go back." She offered a small smile. "Besides, I carry messages now that will choke some hungry crows, and that's a thing I want to see."

"Nemiah Gabriana!"

Pain stabbed through the center of her soul and ripped apart the quiet moment. She tried to scream, but her voice shattered and dropped to the stone in pieces. The rest of her would have followed, like shards of broken pottery, but the Pathwalker flung strong arms around her, holding her intact.

"What barbarian guides you?" the priestess demanded, hugging her close. "She'll destroy you with such crude tools!"

Nemiah couldn't answer; she clawed at the burning place over her throat. Steel sliced at the pieces of herself she had carried to this place: The sleeping Capa howled and vanished. The fire died and fell to ashes.

"She's tearing you from me," the woman whispered quickly. "I must set you free. But carry this back. It will help you to remember. I am called Lia, and we will find each other again, Lady Nemiah, for our Paths have become entwined. Fare well, dove."

A gentle kiss touched her through the pain, then Nemiah plummeted back into the heart of the weaving. Men battled in the dark. Cael hovered close. Dangerous rage exploded, and bonds shattered. A man prayed.

"Nemiah Gabriana, Chosen of Avelos! Return and face the choice of Arion!"

Uttered by that deep, urgent voice, her name was a command that oriented her toward her own time and place. Mustering the remnants of her will, she dragged herself across the void and pushed through the Gate.

Her body sprawled across the ground, numb with cold and heavy as sand. A milky fog enveloped her.

"Lady Nemiah!"

She waited for the final jolt of the Gate clanging shut, but it didn't come. Through the fog, a man loomed over her, holding her down; his body radiated heat against hers, and his dark eyes flashed with emotion. His dagger pressed into her throat and a thread of warmth trickled across her icy skin. Her blood.

She pounded against his chest with her fists and writhed to escape, but he was strong and determined, and the only power she possessed remained far from reach. The mist masked everything outside her struggle, kept her outside the world. She fought more desperately, unwilling to let her Path end in this nothingness.

With a fierce grimace, the warrior batted her arms aside and drove the point of the knife deeper into her flesh. Lightning flared silver in her face. She cried out as the fog tore away, like cloth ripped from a wound. When the lightning passed, her vision returned with agonizing clarity.

She remembered who she was and what night this was.

Her gaze rose to meet her Arionad's, her body trembling beneath his. She could hardly croak the words, but she knew he would read all she did not say. Rom could always read her.

"You have made…your choice."

His eyes glistened. For nearly a decade, he had defeated his demons and bound his Path to hers, but there were other versions of the trial, versions Merisel would only learn if she were ever Chosen. In those stories, Lord Arion's decision brought his blade to Riana's throat, and the mortal man shed the goddess's blood. Not even the heretical Arionites acknowledged the story of their lord's betrayal. Or what came after.

Rom shifted his dagger, and Nemiah's blood dripped from the steel.

"I have made my choice," he replied thickly.

"Then beneath these sacred skies, let Riana know your heart."

She didn't close her eyes, but faced the blade in his hand. When he slipped the knife from her throat and put it to his own, she didn't dare to breathe. The steel slid from the point under his jaw to his chin. Warm droplets pattered against her cheek.

"I would die in your service before I see any other wield the power of Riana," he swore with a choked breath. He threw the knife from him. Then his arms came around her and he crushed her in his embrace.

"Goddess forgive me, you were lifeless," he gasped in her ear. "I thought you lost. I would not choose to wear the face of the traitor."

"Silence, Arionad!" Bena ordered beside them. "We've a journey to collect."

Rom reared up so suddenly that he nearly knocked the old priestess to the dirt. Nemiah saw him wince as he pulled back.

"You don't command me, Mapmaker," he growled. "Not on this night. Not after this sacrifice."

Bena pressed her lips together. Her gaze lifted beyond Nemiah, past the dead tree, and her wrinkled face turned grey in the starlight.

Nemiah couldn't see what caused Bena's apprehension, but she guessed what it meant.

"I carry precious secrets, Captain," she murmured, "but tonight I live by your will and you determine if we collect this journey."

She closed her eyes to grasp the images of her Pathwalk as they tried to slide away, so she didn't see the expression Rom wore when he stepped back, but she heard him rumble a warning to the Mapmaker and heard Bena's curt reply. Then the old woman forced her brittle bones to kneel, and with the prayer and the lighting of the candle, began the recording.

Reliving the myriad moments that bombarded her on the Paths pushed Nemiah toward the edges of incoherence once more. Her body ached from the ropes and the cold. By the end of the retelling, she feared she would drift through the Gate again; she dug her fingers into the bloody wound across her throat to anchor herself to the present.

"The secrets of Altan Mar," Bena echoed after they spoke the final prayer. "You have your repetition, Lady. And more besides."

The old priestess offered no apology. Nemiah supposed the richness of the journey offered the woman an excuse to justify herself.

"So it seems," she answered, wondering how Leita would feel about traveling through the Sandien this close to winter.

"As soon as possible, you must go back to find this priestess again. This Lia," Bena went on. "We can identify Place, now, but we hardly have Perspective; we have little sense of Time, and we're not close to determining the Parallel. Without it—"

"Enough!" Rom stepped in front of the Mistress of Maps and scowled down at her. "The Chosen Lady *must* do nothing for you. Tell the Mistress of Novices that Lord Arion has chosen his Path. We are done here."

Rom turned his back on the Mapmaker to lift Nemiah from the ground. He carried her, cradled against his chest, out of the courtyard, through the chilly stone halls, and back to her tower rooms. By the time he laid her on the bed and turned to build the fire, the cold had crept through her bones again, leaving her shivering helplessly.

When the flames blazed high, Rom removed his gear, his boots, and his white garments—stained now with the blood of all the night's sacrifices—and straightened slowly to reveal himself to her. Besides the wound across his throat, a bruise darkened his left brow and blood dried along a gash on his right thigh. Scars from other Dawnings' Eve battles crossed his hard body. He waited, permitting her to observe and judge him, but when he finally moved toward the bed, nothing of submission showed in his bearing or his heated gaze.

On the first Dawnings' Eve, Lord Arion reached for the goddess with desire, and she who ruled the Paths and ordered the spheres yielded to him. Nemiah trembled as Rom drew himself over her and gathered her to him. He asked no permission, but took what he needed. His touch, so certain, left no opportunity for denial. And she, still dazed and vague from the incomprehensible vastness of infinite possibilities, craved his certainty. Even as he claimed each curve of her body with his hands and lips, he marked out the boundaries of her self. His caresses reminded her where she began and ended. His kisses said this was where she belonged.

"Nemiah Rustania," he whispered fiercely. "I have known you since before the goddess marked you as her Chosen, and I will have even the parts of you that you no longer acknowledge."

He took what he desired and returned her sense of coherence, until wrapped in one another's embrace, domination shifted toward submission, and submission became a source of strength. As Rom surrendered to his need, his breaths came in short, sharp growls. His hands moved to her waist and toward the gate he longed to cross. When Nemiah closed her fingers around him, he groaned and thrust against her hand.

"Riana demands symmetry in all things," she breathed, stroking him, as the goddess's presence pulsed at her edges. "If you would have the honor of serving her, what would you give?"

"The sweat of my labor," he gasped, "the blood of my heart, the days of my life."

"So she will take from you and so you shall be given. If you make this sacrifice, your Path will be bound to her Chosen, and you shall suffer the barriers placed before me and the consequences of my missteps. Our Paths will twist together, and should Riana require it, end together. So you will be bound until the sun sets upon another Dawnings' Eve."

With a hiss, Rom moved deftly to catch the hand that stroked him and draw it above her head. In an instant, he pinned her other hand as well. As he restrained her, his body taut above her, his eyes locked upon hers with an expression so open and unguarded that if she drew upon Riana's power, the wrong words from her could slay him. They lay that way, both vulnerable and exposed.

"So I will be bound," he panted.

The bond coiled around them, and the goddess's power rushed back into Nemiah like the spring thaw into mountain streams. She opened herself to it and to Rom, welcoming him as he surged into her. They moved together, striving for balance. It was more than a bond governed by temple law that brought him to her. Nemiah cried out against his shoulder as she realized how much more. Submission and power, selfishness and sacrifice, loyalty and freedom: all of them together, when in equilibrium, formed a bond of love. Love lit Rom's features as he gave himself to her: love not for the formidable goddess, but for her. She quailed at it, and for a traitorous instant, it was Enrian Nadel who offered himself, Enrian who claimed her. She squeezed her eyes closed and begged silently for Rom's forgiveness. She was so small and fallible; she shouldn't be the reason he walked willingly into darkness.

With a sharp breath, her Arionad clasped her closer, his body stiffening. Joy and terror shuddered through her as she accepted his gift. The essence he sacrificed to her now was only a token of what might be demanded of him later.

"So let our Paths end," she gasped, clinging to him.

They descended in a long, slow spiral and lay entwined. Nemiah rested her head on Rom's chest, comforted by his deep, even breathing. Her fingers touched the dried blood that trailed from his jaw.

"How did you know to use the blade to call me back?"

He opened his eyes and shifted slightly to wrap an arm around her shoulder. "The Bearer," he answered quietly. "She said that if she wasn't near to guide you, sharp pain would likely shake you from the Paths."

"Ah. Of course."

"It's not as you think, Nemiah. She didn't come to me; I asked her. The Gate has been a shadow in your eyes since we returned from Velanhan. I wouldn't have…" His hand moved to her throat to brush the wound he had inflicted there. "I wouldn't have if I knew any other way."

She should have guessed that her observant captain would notice when she wandered. She placed a reverent kiss on his own torn throat.

"You did what was necessary. Don't rue it. After tonight, Riana will return the Gate to my control. You'll see." She laid her head back on his shoulder. A log popped on the fire. "But your men, Rom. I'm sorry."

"That was also necessary," he answered soberly. "They were not forced to it. They made their own choices. All but perhaps poor Anilo. The boy was prone to listen to his companions over his own heart."

"May the goddess find each one of them."

He leaned his cheek against her hair. His heart beat faster in her ear, and she heard his regret in its rhythm. His choice to stand beside her had cost him, but Rom would never speak of his grief; it was a part of his own sacrifice.

"You'll have to do something with Carian," he murmured.

"I know," she sighed.

He lifted his head to meet her gaze. "Nemiah, she's earned a harsh punishment."

"No," she said gently. "What she did on this night was no sacrilege. And the Higher Circle stands around her. It must be a measured punishment."

"Measured? She's faithless. And she expected the Chosen's own Arionad to be as faithless as she is." His eyes darkened. "They're whispering that Cael's Cult is growing in the city. She's the daughter of a Bearer. It might be——"

"Carian's no worshipper of Cael." Nemiah smoothed Rom's drawn brow with a finger. "She's not faithless. Her failing is that she only ever sees the Path from where she's standing. If I've failed as Chosen, and Riana has removed her hand from me, as Carian believes, then to stay by my side is to betray the goddess and all her servants. From Carian's perspective, renewing your oath to me is the betrayal. She'll be baffled by your choice."

"That doesn't make her less dangerous," Rom grumbled. "If you must temper your response, then at least be certain it's one she'll not misinterpret."

"I'll think on it. Perhaps I'll send her to Panetar. Ansa needs a set of younger hands and would keep her out of trouble for me."

"I would have her farther from you than that. Send her to the darkest corner of Avarel Forest. She can spend her time there saying prayers of protection against the Bloodless."

"Perhaps." Nemiah smiled faintly at her Arionad. Carian was bright and strong and had important ties to Clan Aglar. It would be a loss to send her away, wherever she went, but it must be done. The temple couldn't withstand the threat of a schism just now. With the Mistress of Novices put down, the rest of the Circle might return to some order, although Nemiah suspected that no matter what happened to Carian, it was likely this Circle would always be a broken thing after tonight.

She considered the evening's chaos: The strongest women of the temple had walked the line of betrayal to be rid of her. Her Arionad had renewed his oath at the cost of four of Riana's servants. The sacred journey had yielded knowledge, but she had nearly paid for it with her self.

She burrowed her head against Rom's shoulder. The warmth and closeness of him reminded her again that there was love, unlooked for and undeserved, but existent nonetheless. It was the bond that kept her tied to her Path.

"The decision need not be made tonight, my lady," Rom whispered. His strong hands slid down her back and around the curve of her waist, returning her very directly to the moment. "Dawn is still a way off, and I would travel this path with you a while longer."

She answered him with a tender kiss and shifted her body over his. As they explored the complexities of love once more, Nemiah again discovered the mystery of transforming surrender into strength. Then, sheltered in her Arionad's arms, she slipped into a dreamless sleep.

Rom's spring from the bed woke her sometime later. He lunged across the room and snatched up his sword before her sleep-sodden mind recognized the sound of footsteps on the stairs. She sat up quickly and reached for her dressing gown. Silver stripes of early light painted her Arionad's body as he leaned close to listen at the door, then grasped the latch and threw it open.

Leita hardly glanced at the naked man wielding a sword as she hurried into the room. Her dark cloak billowed behind her like wings. Strands of black hair escaped her braid and clung damply to her pale skin. Her wide eyes gleamed.

"A storm," she gasped at Nemiah. "In the south. A wall of cloud like I've never seen, and roiling like Cael in the dark."

Nemiah was already out of bed and drawing the belt tight around her gown. "Tell me."

"Near the river at the edge of the valley, and gouging through the land as it moves. It's thrumming along the Paths. Don't you sense it?" A shudder rippled through the Bearer like a memory of desire. She swallowed and shook her head. "Goddess, Nemiah, it's blowing open doors and tossing Paths from one side of the weaving to another. I never imagined such a thing. It's the killing winds."

Ah Goddess, the losses. So many losses. The hope of balance was a lie. Nemiah made a spiral in the air before daring to ask the question.

"Which way, Leita?"

The Bearer made a rapid gesture that wasn't quite a spiral and shivered again. "Due north along the river, Nemiah. They're going to strike the city."

21.
REVELATIONS

The darkness didn't frighten Jhared. Even under the stars, he knew the forest and the mountains beyond it; he knew the breeze that brushed through the leaves carrying the sweet-squash smell of autumn, the night creatures that made small sounds as they burrowed through the underbrush, and the hunters that crept unseen on silent paws. He drifted far above them all, resting on a mountain thermal. Nothing concerned him up here, although he had a vague recollection that it should.

The scents of cloves and cinnamon floated to him as though from a dream. Those scents weren't of the forest, but they had come to have meaning: bright laughter, bold stories, and unspoken promises. Somewhere close, warmth and exquisite softness waited for him. His body stirred with the anticipation of walking a road long desired but never yet explored. He stretched to draw the warmth closer.

And rediscovered the pain.

The intensity of it tore him from the place where he glided above the peaceful forest and left bits of him scattered in the world of dreams. Pain battered at the inside of his skull, blue flames that burned through his bones and bit into his flesh. He focused on the sound of his heart pounding and drew slow breaths until he could climb above the ache. When he finally opened his eyes, he found himself half-clothed and held together with bandages, on an unfamiliar bed. The room was lit by the orange glow of a brazier. Zia lay beside him, her brow tilted toward his, her gaze wide and dark.

"I knew you would return to me," she whispered.

He blinked, troubled by her words, but uncertain why. His thoughts and emotions had been snapped apart. Nothing about him was whole. Then one coherent thought came together:

Desire in a Shorn man is death.

Abruptly, despair stole the heat from his veins and turned his blood to ice. Chills wracked his body. He closed his teeth around a moan and curled up like a wounded animal.

Zia sat up, calling his name. When he didn't answer, she drew around him, offering her own warmth. It was more torment than comfort, but he didn't have the strength to move away.

"Goddess…what I've done—"

"Don't," she ordered, laying the tips of her fingers over his mouth. "Not now."

He couldn't argue; he was shaking too hard. Zia's fingers were gentle against his swollen lips, and every spot where her body touched his lit a new kind of agony. He had crossed a deadly line tonight, and now he was close to losing control in an entirely different way. He closed his eyes and pulled in on himself, breathing raggedly. She couldn't know how her touch destroyed him. Couldn't know how the thought of Ilvio's cruel hands on her had been enough to shatter his life's oath. It was a long time before he could make the necessary effort to remove her hand and slide away.

"Where…?" he said hoarsely. "How…?"

"Isella's rooms. Friends. Now hush. You've a cracked rib or two. And the wound at your side required stitches. The healer warned not to let you move about." Zia wrapped her fingers around his hand, and her eyes on his clouded with feeling. "Ah, Jhared, it's good that you're here."

So he would live, at least for a time. Until the council pushed him from the wall for murdering a man.

That realization nearly overwhelmed him again. A sound escaped his throat, a noise somewhere between a sob and a groan.

"Shhh," Zia cooed. "All will be well."

"No," he croaked, hoping she would understand everything the single word meant. He needed to know what had happened to bring him to the Mountain and how soon it would be before the City Guard pounded on the door to take him away. He needed to send a warning to Tierzen. Zia ignored his protest and kissed him gently. The darkness clawed at him again. He wondered if the healer had drugged him. Zia murmured something near his ear. He heard the word "safe" and had no strength to laugh before the darkness dragged him under.

When he awoke next, he was alone.

The transition from dream didn't tear him apart this time, although it was still the pain that woke him. He stared up at the ceiling beams in the dimly lit room and tried to catalogue the worst of it to determine what assets remained to him. After a time, he gave up and just hoped he wouldn't be required for combat anytime soon.

Instead, he made an effort to examine his surroundings. Isella's windowless little bedroom had one door, which he guessed led to the room at the back of the Mountain where he had spent a spring evening with Zia. The furnishings were simple and sparse: a rough-hewn bed, a clothes chest, and a side table topped with a lamp, a water basin, and the remnants of bandages. Woven hangings on the walls softened the otherwise austere space. They were lovely and colorful: mountain scenes, waterfalls, and one of cliffs overlooking the sea. Jhared wondered if they depicted Isella's home; he remembered a knife with Clan Lasla's stallion sigil. That prickliest clan of the northern five overlooked the Tregata Sea.

"They have the right to speak with him, Zia."

Jhared started. The commanding voice had risen suddenly from the next room.

"Shhhh. It's too soon, Elian. Tell them to wait."

Light squeezed through a crack in the doorway, and Jhared could hear movement. Glass clinked on wood.

"They're not in a mood to wait. You threw him into this. We agreed only because the goal is important enough to warrant it, but now this mess."

"This was a blessing from Riana. It brought him back to us." Zia's voice, tense and tight, might have come from a different person. Jhared pushed himself upright, hissing as his efforts tugged the stitches in his side.

"Be careful what you call a blessing," the man named Elian growled. "You cannot know how it will impact others. Already you've made a commitment for this one without his permission. He must know what that means. He might have died tonight."

"But he didn't," she said. "Bilar found him. On Dawnings' Eve, when anything could have happened, he ended here."

"Hah. Your faith in signs is strong when they show you what you want to see." Something thudded onto the table. "Soldier, tell Zia what you know."

A third voice, smooth and unruffled, joined the others. "She understands well enough where I stand on this decision, Elian."

"You've watched him, soldier. Tell her."

Nausea washed over Jhared as he stood, nearly dropping him back onto the bed. He *almost* knew that third voice, but his addled brain refused to give him the face to go with it. He clung to the wall.

"The boy seeks final reparation," the voice answered more heavily.

"Because he didn't have *us!*" Zia retorted. "He'll be grateful for what we offer."

"Goddess, woman!" Elian snapped. "You're not listening. You haven't even given him the choice. Have you forgotten the ache of turning from the oath?"

Zia inhaled sharply, the sound one makes when a knife slips and pierces flesh. "Do not ask that of me," she said. "Not ever. I pay our debts daily and you know it."

The room went silent for a long, stiff moment. Then Elian let out a sigh.

"I know," he said more gently. "Forgive me. That was unfair. But it doesn't give you the right to dice with the lives of others. He was raised by a Teacher. He's the child of an elder now."

"And that's enough to damn a person?"

"Zia, they took him in and cared for him," the almost-familiar voice said. "They didn't—"

"Throw him out?" she finished coldly.

"That's not the way I'd say it, but you might consider that if you hadn't cut those ties, we'd have no need for him. Your other connections—"

"If I hadn't acted as I did then, none of us would be here to argue about it now. Don't speak to me of any others. We have Mahla Denaban's son with us. He'll understand the importance of what we ask."

Jhared pushed the door wide and stepped into the room. The odor of cherry pipe tobacco and horse liniment filled his nostrils. "What is it that you ask?"

Three faces turned simultaneously: Standing by the fireplace with her arms wrapped defensively across her chest, Zia flinched. He saw the remnant of her anger before she offered him a weak smile. Sitting at the table, the man called Elian was the old Shorn fiddler from Zia's troupe. Although his body looked worn thin, his stare was hard enough to push past all veils. Jhared evaded the judgment he saw there by turning to the third individual, who leaned his lithe frame against the sideboard and glanced up with the mask of detached interest that he wore so well. Hendren flicked his fingers toward his chest in a lazy salute.

"You shouldn't be up so soon," Zia said, hurrying over to him. "I'm sorry we disturbed you. We would've gone elsewhere, but I didn't want to leave you alone."

"Easy there, Ziabela," Hendren chuckled. "I don't think Jhared's going to bolt off, and he looks like he could use some room to breathe." The patrolman nodded toward the scribe's hand clutching Jhared's arm.

"Hush, soldier. It'll do him no good to fall."

"I'm fine," Jhared grumbled at them both, trying to draw far enough from Zia to prove it without giving up the pressure of her hand on his body. The truth was he didn't come anywhere within sight of fine.

Still, the look of pity the fiddler gave him annoyed him. "Sir, I know nothing about you but that you're brilliant with a bow and strings. Are you the one I owe for my life?"

Zia glanced from the old man to Jhared and back. "I'll let you introduce yourselves, while I find Jhared something to wear." She smiled more brightly. "You're near to Alende's size, I think." She disappeared into the bedroom, leaving Jhared before the fiddler's appraising gaze.

"Elian Varigo," the old man said with a curt nod that suggested he wasn't softened by the flattery. "I serve as scribe to Elder Glafido of Clan Everen. I've had nothing to do with any of the events this night, although I'm glad to know that one of our own is safe from the Legacy's wolves."

Jhared frowned. "How did you know they were Legacy?"

"As you likely heard, I know some things about you. Who raised you is one. Who hunts you is another."

Hendren came to sit at the edge of the table. He had to push several wine jugs and a bowl of fruit out of the way to do it.

Jhared glanced at the men. "You all knew my mother, it seems. Was there something she owed you? Is that what this is about?"

"It had nothing to do with debts!" snapped the fiddler with sudden sharpness. "Mahla was a friend and a gifted storyteller. Do you know what it means to be a storyteller, Jhared Denaban?"

Before he could answer, Zia returned. She offered to help him don the shirt in her hands, a tunic of grey wool. For an awkward moment, he hesitated, then chose accepting her help as less humiliating than struggling to dress himself. Whoever the shirt belonged to, she had judged both their measurements well; the material slid easily over his shoulders. She'd also thought to bring his boots, for which he was grateful. This confrontation didn't seem the kind to be met in bare feet.

"The boy's had enough tests for one night, Elian." Hendren filled a cup from one of the wine jugs and offered it to Jhared. "Here. You look like you could use it."

Jhared shook his head in answer. The abrupt movement was a mistake. He closed his eyes to wait for the room to stop twirling and decided it was time to take a seat.

The loud thud of wood against wood outside the door stopped him in mid-stride. Elian and Zia exchanged a glance.

"Isella's stair!" Zia hissed.

Hendren came to his feet. Everyone froze as fierce pounding shook the door and it flew open. At the threshold loomed the black-beard.

Jhared growled in dismay. Without hesitation, he grabbed Zia and dragged her behind him, ignoring her squeak of protest, even as he reached for his blade. A futile effort, that: his sword was in the barracks and Tierzen's gift lay on a street somewhere in the Circles of the Lost. Instead, he dove for one of the wine jugs, gripped the neck, and slammed it against the table's edge. Stoneware shattered into jagged pieces. Wine splashed to the floor and dripped down the inside of his wrist as he swung around to face his opponent.

The man was big. His hulking form, clothed in the thick fabrics of the mountain clans, outweighed Jhared by a good four stone. Studded leather adorned his large wrists, which rose quickly, his fists clenched. The clansman grinned, exposing yellow teeth through his shaggy beard and moustache.

"Damn! The boy has some spirit in 'im. I wasn't sure he'd even be coming back after tonight."

"Bilar!" Zia stomped past the man to shut and latch the door. "On a night like this one you're playing games?"

"Ay. Especially on a night like this one." The clansman grinned wider and opened a meaty hand to pat Zia on the head. "Ya need reminding you're not the high priestess choosing Paths for the rest'a us."

Hendren laughed. "Hello, Bilar. Looks like the Forest Guard got the better of you again, eh? When you going to admit that being a good bodyguard doesn't make you a good scout?"

"Suck Cael's cold cock. Following this boy's like following an owl in the dark. I bet a good brandy ya'd lose 'im yourself."

The big man peered at Jhared, who swayed with confusion as he tried to wrestle down the rush of energy he'd called to meet the threat.

"This what you're wishing for?" asked the black-beard, offering Jhared Tierzen's belt knife. It was clean of Bren's blood.

Jhared lowered the broken jug, staring at the blade. "You're the one who pulled them off me. I thought you were with Corben. I thought…" He glanced at Zia and the others, and realized the depth of his error. Just how many veils warped his vision tonight? "But how did you know they would come?"

"I didn't," Bilar growled. "Ya owe Isella for that. She saw your state when ya left and sent me along ta watch out for ya. Still, it might be as ya have ta thank Cael for your life."

Zia drew a breath at the blasphemy.

The big man raised his hands. "That's the way of it! He led them on a mighty chase. By the time I found 'im, they were ready ta send 'im to the Hidden Paths." His expression sobered. "Goddess curse them for vicious brutes. It was the Dark Lady, the one as wears Cael's Blade, who kept them from it."

"How'd she manage that?" Hendren asked.

Jhared sank down onto a bench, rubbing gently at his aching head. He had thought the priestess only a part of his pain-addled dream.

"There must have been an agreement," he said slowly. "They didn't want a priestess to go to the high chieftain with word that the Legacy is interfering with the Forest Guard. It would undercut Abrigado's arguments against Rumar in the council, and could turn the people's sentiment against them. They gave me my life for her silence."

Why would a servant of Riana save a Shorn soldier who had just killed a man, when she could earn Rumar's favor by giving up the Legacy? He turned that piece over and over without fitting it anywhere, until he realized the others were staring at him: Hendren and Bilar in surprise, Elian with a spark of what might have been respect, and Zia with a flash of unease. Another puzzle, that last.

"And here I thought ya were nigh on to death during that talk," Bilar said in wonder.

"I don't know why she did it," Jhared said quietly. "I had enraged them. Even a priestess might not have stopped them if you hadn't been standing beside her, Bilar. You've given me more time on this Path, and for that I thank you."

"Ay, well. Use it wisely, eh?"

Jhared tried a smile and failed. How did he move forward now that he had broken the Law of Duty, the very heart of his oath? *I will hold each countryman dearer than my own life.* What tormented him most was the loathsome truth: he hadn't truly even struck in self-defense; he had lifted his hand with a fearsome hatred, intending that a man should suffer and be gone from the world. He had killed to sate his own desire.

"*Abomination,*" one of the Teachers muttered.

Bilar joined Hendren at the table, slapping the soldier on the back in greeting and taking up a handful of figs from the fruit bowl as he sat. Hendren gave the big clansman a genuine smile, and Jhared realized their earlier rivalry was a part of a deeper friendship. All four of the Shorn here knew one another well enough to argue and tease and laugh together. Jhared sensed how far outside their circle he hovered. Even his relationship with Zia, something unique and precious to him, was less than she knew with any of the others in this room. Loneliness pressed against his chest.

From the head of the table, Elian watched the others, like a grizzled ram standing guard over his herd.

"Where's Alende?" he asked gruffly. "The night's slipping away and we have things to discuss."

Hendren shook his head. "I've not seen hide nor hair of him."

"Probably spitting out senseless stories about destinies and Paths for some dupe as wants to be parted from 'is coins," Bilar said with disgust.

"Speak the name of a demon," Zia said, gesturing toward the window.

A blade poked between the shutters and angled smoothly to lift the latch. Jhared felt a prickle of alarm that none of the others reflected. The shutters opened inward to reveal a man veiled in blue and green silks perched on the sill like an exotic bird.

"Good Dawnings' Eve, all!" the waylayer cried, leaping into the room. Immediately, he locked the shutters behind him and began to unwrap the veils about his face and pull off his robes. In moments, a puddle of blue and green silk spread across the floor, and from it stepped a tall, golden-haired man in forest-brown breeches, tunic, and doeskin boots. He eyed the others around the table and his smile crumbled.

"Ah! Surely you've not started without me!" he cried.

"You know we could discuss nothing of import without you, Alende," Zia assured him. Bilar rolled his eyes and ate another fig.

"You're later than we expected," Elian added with concern. "Is everything well with the Kin?"

"Fine, fine. Our swamp-dwelling friends have seen us well cared for this season." The waylayer's quicksilver grin returned. "I would have come sooner, but a fool of a clansman stopped me in the street to beg a potion to bring his wife back to his bed. He offered a sphere for it, so I gave him my flask of brandy and told him that if his wife drank it off, she would be pliant as spring. But now I have no brandy, so pass me one of those bottles."

Hendren chuckled and waved a jug in the air.

The creature stalked across the room with the muscular grace of a mountain cat; Jhared stared in fascinated revulsion. In the Shorn, the golden coloring of the untainted was rare. Despite his histrionic tone and quick, fragile smiles, the waylayer carried the scent of something feral. He was dressed now as a simple woodsman, with a hunting knife at his side, but he still bore the vivid green spirals on his cheeks that claimed he could navigate Riana's Paths. It wasn't a man's place to read the Paths; only women could participate in such mysteries safely. Jhared saw the overbright gleam in Alende's eyes, and wondered about the unlikely coincidence of their afternoon meeting.

A good deal of wine disappeared from the jug before the man set it down and glided over to lean against Zia, his lips pursed for a kiss.

"Dance with me, my love," he purred. "It's Dawnings' Eve still, and we must hunt the keepers of our misfortune."

Zia turned her head away and pushed against his chest. "You're the one likely to bring misfortune, wandering the city dressed so. You're lucky no one called for the City Guard."

The waylayer crowed a protest. "What? How is it that *I'm* a danger when we have a stranger sitting at our table? A stranger who likes to play the wretch for Legacy hunters and doesn't listen to the guides at the crossroads."

"This is Jhared Denaban," Elian explained, "and he's been waiting long enough to hear what we have to tell him."

For the first time since the waylayer entered the room, he looked directly at Jhared, and his handsome face twisted with a mixture of dark emotions.

"I know who it is," the man muttered. "You've gifted us with a dead bird, Elian. He's nothing more than one of Ziabela's hopefuls. Look at him now, panting so eagerly at her side."

"Alende, please," Zia begged. "We've no time for your jealousy."

The waylayer grasped Zia's hand before she could escape and brought it to his lips to kiss her fingers. "Oh, my dear, you thrive on jealously," he said with a bitter grin. "But that's not the issue tonight. Open your eyes; I know Elian has. The boy's one of the tamed. Send him back before you disorder his small world. He's no son of Mahla's."

Jhared rose from the table, his fists clenched at his sides. "My mother befriended no one the likes of you," he ground out. "Do not say her name as though you knew her."

Surprise widened Alende's eyes, and he stared at Jhared before tossing back his golden head in laughter. Lamplight revealed a weaving of fine scars across his exposed throat.

"Now, now. Hasn't General Nadel taught you what happens to scouts who make uneducated assumptions? Carved into eunuchs by Sahiste, I think."

"Sit down, Alende," Elian commanded. "All of you. It is the eve of choices, and in memory of the one who brought us together, I will tell the story now." He cast a gentler eye on Jhared and gestured to the bench. "Please."

The fiddler's gaze was steady and straightforward. It helped Jhared to center himself. He sat beside Zia, who touched his hand distractingly beneath the table. Alende took the wine jug and threw himself down at the far end of the table, opposite Elian. The others all set aside their drinks and stopped their chattering. The mood grew solemn.

"It was in the time of Tumal that drought desolated the country," Elian began, with a voice suited to ritual. "Crops wilted, the lambs dropped stillborn, and the people died, season after season and year after year. The council had no answer for the clans who cried for aid. The prayers of the temple did not dissuade Riana from burning the land, as she did during the Great Wars. The Avelune searched for solutions, trying one after another, and all failing, until finally they offered the last option to Tumal: to bring the Sahistens into Avelos. The desert people are wise about the ways of survival when water is scarce, but Tumal's fears of the border nations caused him to spurn the ideas of our people and call them dangerous.

"In desperation, Lady Amalia and her Higher Circle of Avelune priestesses brought a Sahisten delegation into the country in secrecy, with the hope that they might teach us how to save Avelos before she withered away. When Tumal discovered them and threatened to have them executed, they struck out in self-defense. Our people failed, but Tumal did not: he executed the temple leaders and all the Sahistens; he drove the Avelune into Exile, and created the Laws of the Shorn; he brought us to war and pushed us to the edge of destruction. Since that time, our people have paid the debt for their failure and all the country suffers for it."

Elian's words held the room in thrall. Jhared stared at the table. The tale, at its core, was the same one he was told over and again throughout his Teaching, yet somehow it was unlike anything he ever heard. The veil that created it terrified and compelled him. He opened his mouth to question; Zia squeezed his hand and shook her head.

"When we failed, Avelos lost her balance," the fiddler continued. "See the damage in the decay of our city, in the conflicts among the clans, in the turmoil amid the council, and in the pain of our people. Avelos cannot stand against outside threat while she is so unbalanced within. Our existence threatens her; we do not belong here. It is time for the Shorn to leave."

The world spun away so fast that Jhared felt it ripple beneath him. He flung his hands onto the table to keep from falling, to hold tight to what he knew. "You say we owe Avelos for *failing* to kill Tumal? That an attempted assassination was meant only for the best?" He sent an incredulous gaze over the others. "You deceive yourself for the comfort of turning our betrayals into something valiant. I've read the histories. I've read some of the most ancient writings still in existence. Nothing supports such a tale. Nothing—"

"Of course not!" Elian interjected. "Tumal destroyed all images of the Exile but his own. Only the Storytellers kept alive parts of our truth through the years. And now they're gone as well."

Mahla was a gifted storyteller. Do you know what it means to be a storyteller, Jhared? With a new sense of dread, he turned to Zia; she smiled.

"Mahla gave us that story and many others," she said. "She was a true Storyteller. The last in Velantar."

"We lost a light on the Path when Mahla Denaban died," Elian added. "She gave us a different way to understand who we are." The others nodded in agreement.

Jhared didn't speak. Could it be true? Had his mother violated Shorn Law to preserve the forbidden stories of the Avelune? He reached back into memory for some small word or image of her that might have been a clue to her beliefs, some token she might have given a young child. He found only recollections of her sadness and her entreaties that he listen to his Teachers.

All these people—even the drunken, demon-touched Alende with a hero's name—seemed to share this gift of his mother, while he had little more of her than faded dreams. He leaned his head into his hands and tried to gather himself again.

"How do you intend to leave?" he asked, wanting and fearing to know. "Avelos will never let you go."

The fiddler turned his ancient eyes upon Jhared. Zia tensed and gripped him tightly. All the others focused upon him.

"Jhared Denaban, we call upon you now to fulfill your debt. Help us to obtain what we must possess in order to create a new home for the Shorn. We need you to bring us the secret of the killing winds."

Jhared lifted his head, his heart suddenly pounding. "You are disordered."

"On the contrary. It is perfectly ordered," Elian replied. "The winds' power will give us the influence we need to convince Avelos we must go."

"Influence? At least call it the threat that it is. Do you really believe you can flaunt destruction the likes of the killing winds with no consequences? Hendren, haven't you told them?"

The other soldier shifted in his seat. "I told them."

"Hendren was the first to support the idea!" Alende declared, grinning as the lithe patrolman shot him a heated look.

"Ah." Jhared tried to meld that with what he knew of Hendren. He had seen the man bleed for Avelos. The deaths of her families cut him. How did such a man plot now like the worst of their ancestors? Or was there another way to view this gambit? *"The best you or any Shorn man can do for the future of Avelos is to leave it,"* Micah had said. Could leaving Avelos actually be a route to final reparation?

Now that Jhared had proved his capacity for treachery, did it matter?

Alende drew his hunting knife, snapping Jhared's attention back to the table. The slender blade possessed a fine, brittle look, much like its owner, but Jhared suspected that, also like its owner, its edge possessed a deadly strength. The waylayer considered the knife a moment before stabbing it into the flesh of a fig.

"What was it like to sink your blade into a countryman?" the man asked, his tone deeply curious as he watched thick juice drip from the fruit. "Did it stir the fires in your blood? Did it…*hurt?*"

Jhared sucked a strangled breath. "I betrayed my oath. Of course it hurt!"

"No, no. That's not what I mean." Alende blinked at him, catlike. "I think you know it's not. Did it hurt *here?*" Without shifting his gaze, the waylayer set a hand over his left breast.

Jhared mirrored the gesture unthinkingly. Did this demon-touched creature dream of slain raptors? Did he awake terrified by the memory of arrows driving through his heart? Jhared shuddered at the thought; he wanted nothing in common with the man.

"What is it you're really asking?" he demanded.

"Alende," Hendren muttered. The waylayer ignored him.

"I am asking whether there's some life in you after all, or are you as tamed as you act? I wonder if perhaps you are afraid to set yourself against the will of Avelos because you know you will enjoy it." The creature leaned toward him and smiled slowly. "Do you long to kill your hunters, boy?"

It was too much. Jhared exploded to his feet. "Who *are* you?" he spat. "And what are you doing here? No Shorn man could mock my crimes!"

The waylayer barked a sardonic laugh.

"Jhared, wait—" Zia began.

"Hold, Zia! I warned you of this." Elian gestured angrily toward Alende. "That was unnecessary and foolish! We needn't have gone here tonight, but you provoked the boy. Now you will show him."

"It's not my fault that he fears himself," Alende said, petulance tainting his voice. "Wouldn't you rather know it now before you send him to do our work?"

"Ya're drunk, Alende," Bilar said, "and I'll have no problem helping ya ta show 'im if ya won't do it yourself."

"I'm drunk and you're daft. You see only one story. I see them all!" Alende was no longer grinning as he stood up from the table. "I'll do as you ask, Elian, and then we can all unravel together. Shall we also invite Cael and the dark Bearer who serves him to bring us faster to our end? I've told you where this story leads."

Elian rubbed at his wrist as though it pained him. The old man looked suddenly tired. "Go on, Alende."

The waylayer faced Jhared with a snarl. "What I am, boy, is so far removed from your existence I doubt it has even entered your mind. Look and expand your narrow thinking."

He grasped the hem of his tunic and yanked it over his head in one furious motion. Before he turned, Jhared saw that the web of scars across his throat marked his chest as well. They had been layered over years. Some gleamed silver across his almond skin while others still shone a vivid red. Jhared hardly had time to wonder how the man earned such wounds, when Alende exposed the ugly scars of his Shearing down his back, and then turned again. On the man's left shoulder, where the scars from his Becoming should have been, the skin was smooth and undamaged.

For a long moment, Jhared only stared, uncomprehending, then understanding struck hard.

The man was not bound.

Jhared dropped to the bench. This creature could not exist. Should not exist. He was anathema. He had failed to prove his loyalty to Avelos at his Becoming and had been sent into the wilds to die.

"How?" Jhared murmured. "How is it that he lives?"

Alende whipped around and closed the distance between them. He leaned over Jhared, his eyes glittering and his naked torso radiating heat. Under the scent of liquor, the man smelled of sweat and sun.

"Mahla Denaban," he hissed in Jhared's face. "Mahla Denaban saved my life."

The knock on the door made them all jump. Alende straightened stiffly. Three soft raps echoed against the wood, then the latch wiggled as someone fiddled with the lock.

Zia hurried over, with Bilar right behind her. When they opened the door, Isella limped inside. She glanced over the lot of them.

"Still here, my friends? With dawn on its way? The City Guard will be out soon ta clean up after the celebrations."

"We're not yet through," Zia explained. "We still have—"

Elian sighed and lifted a hand. "No, Zia. Isella's right. We must away. There's nothing more to be said. Jhared must make his decision."

Silence crept over the room as everyone turned to Jhared. Isella's eyes filled with sympathy at the sight of him. Zia seemed to be holding her breath. Still reeling from Alende's last blow, Jhared pushed himself unsteadily to his feet. They had made themselves vulnerable to him; if he told them the truth, he might not leave this place alive, but he owed them for his life. He wouldn't lie.

"I understand what you've risked tonight," he said, glancing from face to face, "and I'm honored by your trust, but despite what was promised in my name, I cannot give you an answer. I need to think. I need some time."

Zia made a small sound of dismay and turned away. Bilar and Hendren exchanged knowing glances. Alende twirled his knife and stared at Jhared with an empty expression, humming softly to himself. Jhared recognized his mother's song: "Alende's Flight."

"You've faced a difficult trial this Dawnings' Eve," Elian said. "We are not insensitive to that. We will permit you two days. Then you must come to Isella with your answer. After that, you will do what you must. As will we."

Jhared gave Elian a nod. "I understand."

"It's all we can ask for," Elian answered. The fiddler's sad gaze went to Hendren, and a look passed between them that made the hair prickle along Jhared's arms. At least he knew who would come for him when the time arrived.

"Very well, then. Our story ends for tonight," said the fiddler. "Hendren, see Jhared back to the barracks. Alende, you stay put until evening. No more antics around the city. The rest of you know where you should be."

The room returned to life. Isella limped over to talk with Bilar. Elian followed Zia to the fireplace, where he addressed her in earnest whispers. Jhared stood with his hands braced on the chair in front of him, staring at nothing.

"Come, Patrolman," Hendren said at his side. "The sun won't wait."

As Hendren nudged him toward the exit, Jhared glanced at Zia. He wanted to tell her farewell and implore her to understand why he couldn't accept all they asked. Her back was toward him, and she was shaking her head adamantly at Elian; she hadn't even noticed his departure. Feeling like the pathetic pup Alende had named him, he shoved down the urge to go to her. He was marching out of the room when he heard the faint whisper of skirts and knew that she had turned. Goddess help him, he couldn't stop himself from looking back. Their eyes met, and a wall of emotion crashed into him. Sadness, anger, and overwhelming confusion poured from her green gaze. Her confusion hurt him the most; he had believed she understood him. She had been the only one.

Afraid of what his own ruptured expression revealed, he turned and fled down the stairs into the light of the false dawn. Hendren followed close behind.

They walked in silence through the frosty city, sharing the streets with revelers crawling back to their homes and a handful of people on their ways to temple. One old woman in a green shawl paused to peer at Jhared's face and cluck her tongue disapprovingly. Jhared saw them all through a haze as he stumbled toward the barracks, trying hard not to think.

"You should be careful of Alende," Hendren said when they reached Travitar Hill and curved west toward the city walls. "The unbound are unpredictable as cats. And Alende is the worst of them. He's rather too comfortable in that waylayer's disguise, if you ask me."

"The unbound?" Jhared said dully. "There are more of them?"

The other patrolman hesitated, then shrugged and nodded. "Yes. Alende leads them, but they're to come with us. We need their numbers."

"I see." Jhared rubbed a hand across his face, wincing as he rediscovered the bruises over his brow. *Unpredictable as cats.* The odd phrase stuck in his head, metamorphosing into others:

Like a moth at the flame...
Like new-broke horses...
They'll fall on you like dogs...
They'll close like wolves...

Hendren did like his animals. Together with all that Jhared had learned tonight, one picture came clear.

"It was you. You wrote the notes in Ravia. How did you know the Legacy was watching me? Through Zia?"

"Damn," Hendren muttered, glancing up in surprise. "You're as good at this as Elian. Yes, it was me. And yes, through Zia, but...it wasn't the Legacy, Jhared."

"Then what in the Lady's name were you trying to warn me about?"

"The temple has a Shadow on you. You were being reckless and we didn't want you to prove that your Becoming had failed. That you weren't bound."

Not bound? Would the horrors of this Dawnings' Eve never end? "Hendren, I've only ever wanted to make reparation. Why would the temple think such a thing?"

"I don't know. I just know they've doubted you from the day of your cutting. It was one of the acolytes at Ravia. The small one, I think."

Jhared groaned. He could picture her: a dark-eyed girl with a clever smile who met his eyes when their paths crossed—in the inner yard, at the infirmary, walking to the mess. He had never wondered at the frequency with which she appeared.

"All this time *she* was the one watching me? And how did Zia—no, never mind. It's better you don't tell me."

How many types of betrayal could the heart endure? If he weren't so battered, he would run. He needed some way to release the agony before it unmanned him.

As they turned toward the city center, he was grateful for the effort of climbing Travitar Hill that forced him to focus on moving one foot in front of the other. By the time they reached the top, he was panting. He paused to lean against Alende Isan's monument.

"Just tell me…how you do it, soldier. How do you turn your back on all your comrades? On the high chieftain, your own kin? On Avelos?"

Hendren averted his gaze to rub a hand over Alende's boot.

"I wish you heard the stories from Mahla," he said quietly. "She learned them from a Storyteller before her, and he learned from a Storyteller before him, and on, back to the moment of the Exile, when a few people decided that the truth should be remembered. When I heard Mahla speak, I knew that's what it was: the truth. I knew that what we owe Avelos isn't the same thing our Teachers told us."

"Hendren, don't you understand? It's not just about what we *owe*, it's about who we *are*. Our place on the Paths is to serve Avelos. If not that, then what? Do you think hundreds of the Shorn will abandon their duties to follow you? Even if you could find some unclaimed territory in the wilds to settle, do you think Amuria or Laebek or even insignificant little Sona will recognize you? The history of Avelos is written in our very bones and blood. We belong to her and she to us; without her we might as well not exist at all. And maybe…maybe Avelos won't exist without us." He ran out of breath and fell silent, shivering in the chill air.

Hendren wrapped his arms over his chest, his friendly face pinched. "I can't argue like an elder, but if the Exile injured Avelos, then we're all watching her die bit by bit. If leaving the country saves her, then I've fulfilled my oath. If it doesn't, then perhaps at least some of us will remain to see the first-clans rise again."

The wind gusted, sending a precariously balanced pot of flowers off Riana's fountain to shatter on the flagstone. Jhared jumped and glanced at Hendren. The other patrolman looked just as startled. In a moment of shared understanding, they exchanged nervous grins.

Hendren wiped his palms against his thighs and shook his head. "Ah, Jhared, I'm sorry that Mahla never offered the truth to you."

"It doesn't matter," Jhared said flatly. "Tonight I broke the oath upon which I based my life. Knowing another story wouldn't change that." But the ache in his heart made it difficult to breathe. His mother had lied to him about everything she was and everything she wanted him to be, even as she committed the gravest of crimes. Did he know *anything* of Mahla Denaban?

Did he want to?

Another gust of wind shoved two more pots to the stone. Jhared's heart leaped against his chest. The prickling began at the base of his spine, reached through his weariness, and caused his stomach to flip with reflexive fear.

Without a word, he and Hendren pushed away from the statue and ran to the center of the plaza, climbing onto the top tier of the fountain for a clearer view.

North and west toward the Parnas Mountains, the predawn sky stretched empty and open for as far as Jhared could see. As he turned to the south, his insides clutched again. What he saw was so unnatural, so wrong, that he could almost deny its existence, but even from this distance he couldn't deny the scar being carved into the landscape. A wall of cloud, grey as ash and massive as the city ramparts, churned toward the Heartsblood River, uprooting whatever lay in its path—alive or dead. Nothing escaped its monstrous appetite. The killing winds flew toward Velantar faster than any natural storm.

Jhared stood still, gazing at the silent city around him. Flower petals and candle nubs from the night's celebration lay scattered across the ground. The fountain tinkled musically in its ancient basin. On the temple stairs, a man and a woman slept curled around one another for warmth and comfort after their Dawnings' Eve coupling. And above them all in the temple, Riana's eye remained closed and dark. She would not open it again until after dawn, when the goddess took up her power and the high priestess lit the candles. Unless, of course, Arion's Trial had gone very differently this year. In that case, she would not open her eye at all.

Hendren growled a curse. "The clans," he hissed. "Outside the walls and sleeping hard after the festival. They'll not have a chance."

"We have to bring them in," Jhared answered. "I'll run to Travitar Gate and rouse the garrison. Can you reach the guard at Cirolan?"

Hendren nodded, but his mask of detachment had ripped away and raw fear twisted his expression. "I never really believed the storms would reach the city, Jhared. All I love lies sleeping out there in Manitar's camp."

Jhared thought of Branlen and his family, and wondered where they had ended their Dawnings' Eve.

"They'll be all right," he promised, trying to make himself believe it. "Our men are on watch; we'll see everyone safe."

"Riana keep them," Hendren prayed, leaping off the fountain and turning to run for Cirolan Gate.

"Not likely if it's Riana who punishes you."

His Teachers struck Jhared with their anger, tearing his own anger loose again.

"Riana keep us all!" he called defiantly after Hendren.

He ran toward the barracks with everything left in him, knowing that for this chase they would all play the wretch, and no hope remained of driving off misfortune.

22.
UNCERTAIN FUTURES

Empty streets twisted under Jhared's feet as he raced toward Travitar Gate. He called warnings to the few men and women he saw, but they only turned and gawked at him. Some laughed and yelled that the hunts were over. One man whipped an empty wine jug at his head. The jug flew harmlessly past his shoulder and shattered against a wall.

It was Dawnings' Day: a day to begin new paths, a day of hope. How many people would die before the day was done?

As he approached the city wall, two sleepy City Guards stumbled out of the guardroom in the gate tower. Their eyes swept across the road before they picked him from the gloom.

"Halt, citizen!"

Jhared slid to a stop in front of their lowered pikes, his hands lifted palms outward. "Patrolman Denaban," he panted. "Under Commander Carn, in the Forest Guard Fourth. Sound the alarm! The city is under attack."

The two men looked him over, then glanced around at the peaceful streets and exchanged expressions of amusement. They were an odd pair: one man was short and solid as a boulder; the other was tall and spare as a racing hound. The tall one laughed.

"Under attack, eh? How's that, soldier? Did a pack of Sonan swamp dwellers swim upriver and scale the walls during the night?"

"Or maybe ya just mistook that pounding in your head for Sahisten battle drums," offered the round one, grinning.

Jhared ground his teeth. "There's a storm at the valley's edge. Call up to the watch on the wall. The killing winds are roaring toward the city."

The hound stopped laughing and poked Jhared's chest with his pike. "Now, that's not a thing to jest about. Could cause a panic. I should see you get a lash for that."

"Please! Listen!" Jhared begged. "We've no time. You don't know the danger."

"Damn Forest Guard," spat the boulder, "so full'a yourselves. Think you're the only ones as ever faced a threat. Well, I'll—"

A sudden gust blew a shower of dried flowers down the street. One delicate pink petal spiraled in front of Jhared and dropped at his feet. All the flowers fell and the air went impossibly still, as if the winds had sucked the breath from the city. Blood pounded in Jhared's ears. He lost the rest of the man's words. Time had run out.

Without pausing to think, he feinted two steps back from the pikeheads. Both men hastily thrust their weapons forward, but Jhared was already dropping to the ground. He rolled under the shafts and came to his feet between the guards. With his right arm bent, he drove his elbow into the shorter man's face. As the boulder stumbled sideways, Jhared spun and landed a kick that knocked the hound onto his back.

The guards shouted threats behind him as he fled to the gate tower and swung through the doorway of the guardroom. Long ropes hung in a niche that rose up the tower to the bells. He grabbed them as the sound of hooves thundered through the gate.

"Sound the alarm! Who in Cael's dark is sleeping on their watch? Ring the city bell!"

General Nadel charged into the guardroom. The gaze he turned on Jhared shone through the lurid mask of scars across his face. Blazing need burned through him. Even so, Enrian Nadel, Guardian of the Southern Towers, the man who had survived the worst of the winds' fury, still offered Jhared a gift:

"Though they come from Cael himself, they will not take our city. Not while the men of the Forest Guard Fourth fight in her defense. Ring that alarm, boy! Ring it and get to your patrol! We need your strength and courage today."

With a rush of renewed energy, Jhared yanked on the bell cords. The general disappeared; Jhared heard him roaring commands to the City Guards, then his horse's hooves clattering across the stone.

The alarm sent soldiers running out of the garrison and the circles of the city. For many of the men, speed looked to be a challenge this Dawnings' Day. They staggered toward the point of muster, calling to one another to learn what was happening. Stable boys dashed about, leading nervous mounts. Jhared collected Brio and his gear and reached his patrol in the yard outside the barracks. The others who had arrived stood in disorder, exchanging guesses about the cause of the crisis. Anzo, Twitch, and Esran hurried from the barracks looking bleary-eyed but functional. Jase arrived last, pelting down Crooked Lane still buckling his belt.

"Riana's tits!" the Nadaren man gasped. "Tell me this is some drunk City Guard's idea of a Dawnings' Day jest."

The others shook their heads or shrugged uncertainly.

"No jest," Jhared said. "The killing winds are heading for the river and moving north."

All eyes snapped around to stare at him. Esran and Twitch cursed. Jase laid a finger to his blue-marked cheek.

"Funny *you* know so much of it," Bevan said, eyes narrowed. The same sentiment registered in some of the others' expressions.

"You have connections we should know about?" Grion smirked.

"Of course," Jhared muttered. "Cael came to me in the night riding a black eagle and told me the winds were on his tail. You can see the storm from the crest of Travitar Hill! Even you would have seen it, Grion, if you hadn't been sleeping off the bad brandy."

Grion made a hostile gesture with one hand. Jase chuckled. Anzo scowled at Jhared's face.

It hurt to see the unspoken anger in Anzo's eyes, but Jhared wasn't surprised; the men all needed someone to blame, some way to make sense of this attack. The timing was heartbreakingly perfect: whoever controlled the killing winds had chosen the moment when Velantar was most vulnerable. They must have known that an attack now would tear through the heart of Avelos. Families from almost every first-clan and twice again the number of cousin clans camped outside the walls.

When Jhared considered all of the previous attacks in the context of this one, a new pattern came clear: until today, the storm targeted only small villages and the outskirts of towns. Plotted on a map of Avelos, it would show a slow creep northward, as though someone traveling toward the city had been practicing with their devastating power on minor targets, or perhaps saving their strength for something more horrible. Velantar was that horrible something.

"Riders up!" Carn bellowed, cantering to the front of the patrol. "Orders from the general, boys—we've just become shepherds! Head to the southwest and bring in our flocks!"

As the commander shouted out orders, Jhared sprang into formation with his comrades. They galloped out Travitar Gate and across the fields. Jhared glanced over his shoulder to discover that the storm had overtaken the river, three miles from the camps at most. It would strike the elegant villas at the river's edge first, then the farms just south of the city. Wind whipped the water to whitecaps and tossed the flat-bottomed barges like child's toys. In the forest beyond the riverbank, the trees bowed low, snapping branches and showering the ground with a blizzard of green and golden leaves.

Outside the storm's deadly boundary, the camps seethed with confusion and fear. People who were startled awake by the bells now rushed to pack their belongings, load carts, and herd livestock together. Some stared in shock at the wall of cloud bearing down on them. Others grabbed up their children and what possessions they could carry and ran for the forest.

Jhared grimaced at the scene. A scarce few families headed toward the city of their own will. Perhaps uncertainty caused so many to shun the walls: most of the clansmen were woodsfolk, for whom the forests meant safety. Perhaps it was the generations of tension between clan and city that made them think the winds the lesser danger. They didn't understand that the storm would slice apart every creature not sealed from its reach, like a sharp blade through a butchered lamb.

Carn raced the patrol to the edges of the camps, and they wheeled neatly around their first clan. The commander ordered the patrol to stand fast while he cantered toward the group of men who gathered around the elders' tent. The pennon that waved over the tent, a marching black bear on a field of green, belonged to Clan Hilera.

The Hileran clansmen formed around their prefect, a deep-chested greybeard who scowled and pulled his chin as Carn approached. Tierzen had once described Prefect Hilera as the essence of ambivalence. The clan made its home in the southern foothills of the Sandien Mountains, and despite the fact that most city men named Hilera among the northern five, no one could ever predict whether the clan would stand with its northern neighbors in the mountains or its southern neighbors on the plains. Today it was clear no one agreed with the order to march into the city. When Carn greeted the men from his sturdy black mare and indicated the walls, they swarmed on him, arguing in clanstongue. Carn's mount tossed her head and trod backwards until she nearly sat on her haunches. Carn stood in his stirrups, bellowing at the elders.

"What in Cael's hole's going on over there?" Twitch muttered, turning his horse in circles.

"Probably playing the northerners today," Esran said. "Which means a lot'a fussing about taking orders from the Forest Guard. What'a you expect from Hilera? They couldn't choose a boat if they were drowning."

Jhared studied the clansmen. One gestured with bravado toward the roiling cloud and others nodded in agreement. Still others pointed toward the forest. A flock of long-locked sheep bleated nervously, stomping over bedrolls and the remains of last night's celebrations while women and children hurried, with the help of several dogs, to collect them. Hilera produced some of the finest wool in Avelos. Clan Valador dyers paid handsomely for the silky fleece to make their fine bright fabrics, and other clans at the gathering would trade for ewes and lambs to enhance their own stock.

"They *have* made up their minds," Jhared said. "Can't you see? They don't want to leave the animals behind."

At that moment, Carn pulled away from the elders.

"Let's move!" he snarled at the patrol. "Women and children only. The men remain with the stock."

Esran and Twitch glanced at one another in disbelief.

"They can't!" Jhared blurted. "We can't let them."

The commander shot him a sharp look. "Not your decision, soldier. They're free clansmen. Get going."

Wives and mothers, sisters and daughters parted from their men with a hug or a quick kiss. The time for tears would be later. Jhared's heart hammered with frustration. Images of torn bodies and devastated villages filled his head.

"Patrolman! Are ya here ta help?"

He looked down to find a tall girl with white-gold hair glaring up at him while she strained to hold a clumsy, blanket-wrapped bundle. A fragile-looking old woman stood beside her. He took the bundle and balanced it across the front of his saddle. Then he leaned down and held out his hand.

"Let me help you, Grandmother. You shouldn't be made to hurry over this uneven ground."

The old woman eyed him with a gaze as bright and wary as a chipmunk's. "These feet been treading mountains since the time when the Forest Guard still gave our enemies nightmares," she grumbled. "Ya know how long ago that was, boy?"

"Uela, I just gave 'im my bride's chest," the girl said with dismay. "Ya won't let 'im ride off alone to sell it for 'imself, will ya?"

Jhared's face heated, but he waited, patting Brio reassuringly, while the grandmother pursed her lips.

"I don't have a bit'a use for horses," she said. "Can't choose your own direction if ya don't keep your feet on the ground."

"Uela, please." The girl darted a nervous glance at the storm, then at the clansmen who were starting to drive the flock toward the forest. "Father promised Churri we'd have enough for a ram and ten ewes come spring."

Jhared followed her gaze toward the clan elders. "Your father's with the sheep?"

"Of course. He'll stand by the prefect and so will my Churri. Our stock won't be trampled or stolen in the city."

The stock wouldn't be stolen, and she would not see her men alive again.

"Won't you ask them to come with you?" Jhared suggested. "The city can be dangerous for a girl alone. Surely they would come to keep you safe."

Her eyes widened. "I'm not frightened'a ya or your kind!" she cried. "Ya can't make me disgrace my family. Uela, please ride. I'll be right after."

"Fine, fine," the old woman huffed. "All of this fuss for a storm. There's nothing can beat the storms'a the north. And I've lived through enough'a *them*."

With a good deal of awkwardness, Jhared wrestled the old woman up behind him. The effort sent daggers stabbing across his injured ribs. She muttered nervously about the gelding's height and clutched at Jhared with wiry fingers.

"Come on," Jhared called to the girl, holding his hand out once more. "I didn't mean to scare you. Brio can bear three to the city."

"Nothing scares a woman'a the north!" she replied with a toss of her head. "Take care of my Uela. I have others ta see on their way before I go."

Jhared shook his head. "Riana keep you," he murmured and clapped his heels to Brio's sides.

The patrol harried the Hilera women and children toward the gate as quickly as they could manage. When a cart foundered in the soft dirt of the field, Carn forced the driver to abandon it. Twitch carried a young mother behind him. She clung to the soldier with one arm and hugged an infant to her breast with the other. All the patrolmen bore youngsters or other burdens precious to the clan.

As the winds carved their way up the hill toward the city, the tumult grew, chasing people ever faster out of the valley. The road to Travitar Gate was flooded with terrified clansfolk. People screamed and cried at the solid wall of cloud and debris working its inevitable way toward them. Panic made them mindless: they scrambled over one another and shoved just to get steps closer to the promise of protection. A woman fleeing with a child in her arms knocked a little boy out of her way and kept going. As a young man paused to help an elder, a mule cart cantered out of control and crashed into them, tossing both bodies to the side of the road in a crumpled heap.

Commander Carn took one look at the mob and ordered five patrolmen to stay with the Hilera women until they reached the barracks. No one could hear his bellowing over the winds, but it was evident when he pointed to Jhared, Jase, Twitch, and Esran that they were going back into the valley.

They had to fight through the crowd to reach a second clan. Jhared didn't know who the folk were or where they came from, but he caught up four little ones so their parents could help those who lagged behind. Brio carried the burden bravely, accepting Jhared's reassurances with a twitch of his ears and a flick of his tail as the children slipped over his withers and clutched at his mane. Carn pointed the clan toward Alende's Gate on the north side of the city, where fewer camps surely meant an emptier road. It cost them precious time, but Jhared let out a breath of relief when he helped the four children slide down at the gate and saw them scamper to rejoin their families as they entered the city.

As only a border horse could, Brio let Jhared know that going out for a third run was not an idea he favored. The gelding was already dirt-streaked and blowing hard. Still, when Jhared insisted, Brio moved out, stamping out his anxiety as they cantered toward the forests. As the storm closed on them, some villagers began to emerge from the trees—belatedly realizing their mistake. Jhared leaned close to Brio's neck, urging the gelding to greater speed. Jase's mount ran at his left, Esran's at his right; Twitch rode somewhere behind. They bounded across the newly plowed fields, the storm growling at their heels. Jhared focused on a group of men and women near the trees who were stumbling toward the distant hope of shelter.

He saw Jase glance backwards, saw his patrolmate's face turn grey, and knew what it meant. Jhared crouched closer to his horse's neck and braced himself. He knew he should pray, but no words came.

A wall of dirt and debris crashed over them like a wave. Brio stumbled nearly to his knees. A blur on Jhared's right might have been Esran's beast tumbling head over heels. Jase's roan colt bucked. Jhared saw Carn pull his mare around, saw the signal to retreat—then the commander vanished in the blackness as the storm tore open the land around him.

The winds slammed into the camps, shredding tents, tossing baggage skyward, and blasting people to the ground. Unbearable howls rent the air. Only living beasts ever howled with such emotion: predators reveling in their own vicious strength, prey dying in agony. It was the sound of arrogance and desire, oppression and despair. Jhared heard the song in it. A voice as old as the skies pounded through his blood and filled his head, compelling him to understand its source, even as its unrestrained hungers repulsed him. It sang to him. If he just stretched a little farther, a little outside the boundaries of himself, perhaps he could find—

Without warning, Brio flung his head against the bit and wheeled around. Jhared scrambled to keep his seat. He barely had time to register the immense shadow rushing toward them—part of a wall or a roof that had broken free from some stable or farmer's cottage—before Brio bugled a defiant challenge and rose to ward off the threat.

As they lifted toward the sky, Jhared knew they couldn't escape the falling wall. He kicked free of the stirrups and threw himself out of the saddle. His battered body smashed against the ground. From the edge of awareness, he saw Brio engage the wall like an enemy combatant. The gelding's hooves connected with wood, splintering beams. His feet tangled among the planks. Jhared knew his horse would lose this battle. He cried the animal's name, an impulse of hope that Riana might hear and have mercy. But mercy meant nothing in the heart of the killing winds. Storm and horse both screamed in fury. Boards snapped and tumbled around Jhared. Something heavy struck his shoulder, knocking him flat. The gelding stretched impossibly tall, and for a moment, seemed to climb into the sky. Then the chains that Jhared knew so well snapped tight, and the horse went over backwards as the wall broke upon him. The world reverberated with the impact.

And then there was only the wind.

Jhared lay under the broken planks and shards of wood, fighting back oceans of darkness as he tried to breathe around the agony in his side. Moments passed before he could rise enough to push aside the wreckage and drag himself to the place where Brio lay unmoving. Half a dozen splintered beams pierced the horse's mud-streaked hide. More boards entrapped his legs. But the mortal blow was the wooden shaft that impaled the gelding where his neck joined his shoulder, straight through to the big heart.

Jhared flung an arm over his horse's arched neck and collapsed there. Brio had been a companion since Jhared came to the Forest Guard as a trainee. The patient creature had taught him more about riding than any officer. Brio was the only one who didn't judge Jhared for the debt or look at him as a danger. He had sacrificed everything, but here in the devastated valley, his sacrifice would make no difference.

Wind whipped the long black mane into Jhared's face. He was drowning in the dust, and there was no coming up for air. He was Aberration. Trianor's Folly. He would end here with his horse, and his death would also mean nothing: the winds would continue to tear at Avelos; the clans would continue to tear at one another; and the Shorn would continue to carry their burden. The debt had not been paid.

"So it must be," one of his Teachers crooned gently. *"Close your eyes, child. You are so tired; it won't be long now."*

Jhared was surprised they had come, but he was glad not to be alone at the end. He pressed against Brio, seeking the protection of the massive body.

"Will you stay?"

"I'm right here. Don't fight. Go deeper. It will be easier soon."

Obediently, Jhared searched for the still point within him. General Nadel had taught him to find it. He wondered if the general would approve of this choice. It was almost peaceful as he floated toward his center. The howling grew distant.

"Good. Very good. Let go, boy; it's the bravest thing you can do for Avelos."

Jhared spiraled slowly through star-speckled darkness. Breathing ceased to be a struggle. Perhaps it was no longer even necessary.

"That's right. Free Avelos from the threat of the accursed."

He was so very weary of the pain.

"Stop! What are you doing? What have you done to him! We've so much more to learn!"

Jhared twitched in annoyance at the second voice. His Teachers never argued.

"Quiet! It is a necessary sacrifice. He has made the right choice for our people."

"No! This isn't right! Breathe, boy!"

"It hurts to breathe," Jhared complained weakly.

"What of your oath? What of your family? What of final reparation?"

"This is final reparation," he murmured.

"See? The boy has learned his lessons well. Leave him be."

"No! We have worked too hard to end here. GET UP!"

The voice roared in his head. Jhared startled and his body jerked involuntarily, pulling air into his lungs. He opened his eyes, coughing out the dust, but suddenly even the dust was sweeter than oblivion.

Had a Teacher just convinced him to die?

As he slowly drew himself upright, the haze began to recede. Would he give up his chance to preserve Avelos from this unholy storm just because other Shorn confused escape with reparation? Because others saw him as someone other than who he was? Zia's understanding of him was warped by her memories of his mother, a woman he never truly knew. He had imagined that the scribe saw him plainly; he desired that connection so intensely he might have given up the one thing most important to him. But he and Zia had looked at one another through the veils of their own needs, and neither had seen anything of the truth.

The sadness of it tried to undo him, but he clung to the single thing he knew to be true: he *was* different from the others; he was Trianor's Folly. If being an aberration meant he walked the path alone, perhaps it also meant he needn't walk in the same direction as others. He needn't repeat the betrayals of his ancestors, as Hendren and Zia did, or sacrifice himself in vain, as Micah did.

He needn't die here when he could stop Zia and her people from tearing Avelos apart. He mustn't die here.

"Move, fool!"

His Teacher's cry shoved him out of his head and back into the storm, where he lay against Brio's dust-caked neck. He paused, gathering his strength, then with a murmured prayer, he patted the strong withers for the last time and heaved himself to his feet.

The wind did its best to beat him back to the ground, and Jhared realized he had little chance of walking back to the city, blinded as he was by the storm. It would be all too easy to misjudge the distance and end up in the river, or to turn in circles until he couldn't go on. He closed his eyes and tried to picture the valley from where he stood: farmhouses scattered across rolling fields; patches of forest standing between hamlets; the river winding its way south from the city. The river. He grasped that image and held it. On this side of Velantar, the farmers walled their fields near the river to keep the rich dirt from running away with the rain. If he could find the wall, then he could follow it north, nearly all the way back to Travitar Gate.

The river lay a quarter mile west of the city, so with a trickle of new energy, he oriented himself as best he could, tucked his head against the storm, and started trudging westward. He counted his steps to judge the distance he covered, dragging himself on until he was certain he had gone well beyond a quarter mile. His feet didn't slope toward the riverbank and he saw no shadow of a wall. As his gait grew increasingly uneven, he gave up the counting as meaningless. Fear that he had turned too far south weighted his already leaden steps. Had he missed the wall entirely? His eyes burned and every breath was a labor. The wind pounded against him, scouring his flesh. He didn't know how long it was before he realized he had stopped moving; he had bumped right into the stone.

It hit him at the waist, a solid, reassuring formation constructed over years with rock the farmers dug from the fields. Now it was a lifeline. He set one hand on top to guide him, squeezed his eyes closed, and stumbled north. Not more than a hundred paces later, he tripped over something in his path. It yielded under his weight as he fell, and he recoiled at the contact. It was a body.

He rolled to his feet and turned to squint at the figure of a woman bowed against the stone. As he bent to check for life, her hand shot toward him and caught his wrist. Reflexively, he jerked backwards, dragging the woman halfway to her feet.

Her fingers gripped him like talons. Her bloody face contorted in desperation as she gestured toward the ground. At the base of the wall crouched a small child. She had been shielding the little one with her own body.

Goddess mercy. Jhared brought his free hand around to pry her fingers from his arm. Madness glazed her large blue eyes as she fought, clutching at him as though afraid he would abandon her. Only when he bent toward the child did she finally allow him to move.

It was a boy of five or six winters. Jhared set both hands on him, and was relieved when the child uncurled, looking up with eyes as blue and terrified as his mother's. Jhared crouched to offer his back, and the boy didn't hesitate to clamber up, wrapping his arms in a death grip around Jhared's neck. The boy's left heel dug hard into the blade wound over Jhared's ribs. Jhared staggered against the wall, clinging to the burden on his back. It took an effort of will to lever himself upright. With one hand he drew the woman close, so as not to lose her. She twined her fingers around his arm and pressed her face into his shoulder. He felt her nod against him that she was ready.

Misery defined every step toward the city. The woman limped slowly, too slowly. When she stumbled, Jhared grasped her elbow to keep her from tumbling to the ground. Each time, she gathered her feet beneath her and hauled herself onward. He squeezed her arm, urging and encouraging her. He wasn't certain he still owned the strength to pull her up if she fell. The boy stuck to his back like a burr.

I will preserve the safety of Avelos above all else.

I will devote myself to service.

I will hold each countryman dearer than my own life.

No irony echoed the words in his head. The Law of Duty became the litany that helped him to keep moving. The safety of child and mother was the only thing that still mattered. Blindly, they followed the farmers' walls across the valley.

So close. Very close now. The world narrowed to a tunnel of darkness and sound and overwhelming sensation. Jhared didn't know how he got them all through the city gate and into the barracks; one moment he was battling a force that sought to drive him beyond oblivion, and the next the resistance vanished.

In the shelter of the thick stone walls, he stood, gasping for breath. The barracks reeked of fear and churned with dazed and dust-covered clansmen. Some searched urgently for family and friends, stepping over those who huddled on the floor or sprawled across the bunks. Prefects called out to their scattered kin, while soldiers attempted to keep people from trampling one another. In a far corner, a bedraggled and bewildered elder of Clan Valador stood on a bunk waving his clan's tattered banner and desperately calling out over and over, "To me, Valador! To me!"

Ziabela wanted control of the killing winds.

The woman at Jhared's side coughed and shuddered. She needed care and a place to rest. With his arm around her waist, he shouldered through the crowd, hefting the weight of unfriendly stares as he moved through the room. Three clansmen had commandeered his bunk, and they glared as he approached, until they saw the woman and grudgingly made room enough that she could sit with her child.

As soon as she settled, the little boy dove off Jhared's back and burrowed for safety in his mother's arms. She shivered, teeth chattering, as she held her son tightly.

"Easy," Jhared soothed as he knelt beside her. He looked over the room; it would be hours before the handful of healers made their rounds to all who needed them, and in the past months he had watched too many people die from the injuries the winds had dealt them. He held out his hand tentatively. "Can I look?"

She frowned at first, then nodded. He murmured calming words as he surveyed her wounds. From what he had observed throughout the summer, three types of injuries were the most likely to cause death after exposure to the killing storms: the deep gashes inflicted by the knives of the winds that caused bleeding; the broken bones or shattered skulls caused by falls and flying debris; and the most insidious and unpredictable, the overwhelming horror and shock that drove the spirit out of the body. The myriad cuts across the woman's limbs and face were straight and neat, as though made by a fine blade. Some dragged long paths across her skin, but none were dangerously deep. She moved well enough to suggest she had no broken bones. It was the horror that made her tremble now.

"We were so…lost," she said, stroking her child's back as Jhared pulled a blanket from his clothes chest and wrapped it around her shoulders. "We were separated from my family. Ended up walking in the wrong direction. That storm, it's unholy. But I wouldn't let it take my son. I wouldn't…"

"You're both safe now," Jhared said, his voice thick with dust. "The ancients built this hall. I've not yet seen the winds touch ancient stone."

The child was already falling asleep against her shoulder, small chubby fingers wound around a lock of her hair.

"Let them howl," she murmured, defiance edging her tone. "I'll do whatever I must to keep him safe." She kissed the boy's dusty forehead. "Whatever I must."

Jhared rubbed at his wind-scoured eyes with the back of one hand. It took a moment before he could look at her. Without concern for the cost to herself, she had put her body between her child and death. He had never seen such a thing.

"Your people are Everen, yes? I'll let them know where you are."

She nodded over the child's head. "Tell them Talia and Nian are whole."

"Of course." He nodded and turned to go.

"Wait," she called. "What's your name, soldier?"

He hesitated. "Jhared Denaban."

"I owe you for my life and the life of my child, Patrolman Denaban."

"No, madam," he said, bowing his head to her. "Your lives are a part of the debt repaid."

"Denaban! Denaban, over here!" Jhared lifted his head to see Anzo waving a hand from across the hall. The old patrolman pushed his stocky form through the crowd. Dirt so crusted his face that only his bright black gaze was recognizable.

"'Bout time I found you, boy. We need your strength. Commander's put us to work making room in the stable. And we've got…Cael's balls! Look at you."

Jhared glanced down to find whatever made Anzo stare. A black-brown patch spread across his shirt, from under his left arm all the way across his side: blood mixed with the grime that coated him.

"Brio went down. I fell badly." He mumbled the half-truth.

"Ah. I'm sorry for that. Plucky little bay, that one." Anzo peered closely at the blood, then glanced up. "Why don't you sit down. Get a healer to see to it. I'll tell Commander—"

"No need. I'm well enough. Let's go."

"Jhared?"

"Do you see another Shorn soldier pampering his injuries? It's been some time since I've had a mother, Anzo. I don't need one now!" The little patrolman's expression widened, and Jhared fought against a stampede of emotions that suddenly threatened to bowl him over. "I'm sorry. I didn't mean…It's just…"

"I know, boy. Don't worry on it. Cael's brought chaos to our doorstep."

Jhared was grateful just to accept the clansman's help in finding Clan Everen's prefect. Once Jhared kept his promise to Talia, he followed Anzo to the stable, where Commander Carn had put the patrol to work. They hauled hay bales down from the loft to provide bedding for the injured and make room for more of the refugees. They carried buckets of water to the healers. They rationed out blankets and tried to prevent brawls among the frightened folk.

The mindless work left Jhared's thoughts free to race from Zia and Elian to Tierzen and his family and back. He wanted to know they were safe. He desperately needed to speak with them. He feared to face any of them. His fears chased one another fruitlessly. He knew what he had to tell Elian, but he didn't feel ready to face the events his answer would set in motion.

"Watch out, man!"

Jhared collided with something unyielding that he belatedly identified as a shoulder. He staggered backwards, the buckets in his hands swinging and sloshing. With muttered curses, Jech bent over to pick up the bundle of horse blankets scattered on the ground. The world careened, and Jhared struggled to keep his balance. Jech had always mocked and shunned him. Was he a part of Zia's plotting as well? How many of the Shorn of Ravia had chosen to betray their oaths?

"What's wrong with you?" Jech growled.

Jhared blinked. Nothing around him looked as it should. Even the halls he had walked for the last five years seemed different.

"I just…didn't see." The other soldier scowled at him. Jhared tried to steady himself. "Is Hendren back in the barracks?"

"Manitar didn't make it back," Jech replied. "Rafel saw him go down under a tree. Shame. But no more than any of us can expect, when it comes to it."

"Oh…" Jhared choked on a breath and had to clear his throat hard. "Goddess gather him."

"Right. Say a prayer for us all, long as you're at it. Aren't none of us getting out alive." With a snort, Jech grasped up the last blanket and disappeared down the hall.

A rivulet of blood tickled Jhared's side and dripped to the stone. He watched it spatter into a complex pattern. Grief drifted over him like ashes, but he couldn't have named all the things he mourned. What had Hendren been to him: the friend who helped him escape a mob or a traitor who only meant to use him? He would never know for certain. He remembered the agony in the man's eyes whenever they learned that the winds had torn apart another village. He remembered the soldier's raw fear when they saw the storm approaching Velantar: *All I love lies sleeping.…* Hendren's decision to leave Avelos hadn't been made lightly. He had claimed that he listened to Mahla Denaban and heard truth.

Dizziness twisted the world again. As Jhared tried to make the ground stop bucking out from under his feet, he realized something was missing: the grinding of the winds over the stone of the barracks. The storm had come to its end. It was time to go home.

23.
UNEXPECTED LOSSES

Slipping away from his patrol wasn't difficult. Every able soldier and clansman poured out of the barracks to see what the winds had left of Velantar. Jhared let the crowd press him toward the parade grounds and into the street, then he ducked into an alley off Crooked Lane.

Death had kissed the city and she had fallen. One after another, the homes and shops of the lower circles had folded in on themselves like wet parchment. Jhared clambered over the ruins of a gaming house that blocked the alley, then turned south to avoid the debris from the collapse of an inn. In a little plaza past Crooked Lane, a Dawnings' Day market had been caught preparing to open. The vendors had fled for cover, but their stalls were flattened and the contents crushed. Cages of rabbits had smashed to the ground along with their occupants. Sheep and goats lay butchered in the alleyways.

As people realized the storm had passed, they stumbled from their homes or crawled out of the wreckage, looking bewildered. An old man stood in the middle of the street wearing only breeches and one shoe, staring at the mound of firewood that had been his home. A ragged little girl sat on the ground, shedding silent tears over the dead kitten in her lap. The winds had caught most city folk still in their beds. People here hadn't faced the knives, but they had had no chance to seek the safety of stone. Muffled wails rose from the debris where people were trapped.

Jhared let it all fuel his anger. No retelling of the Exile could justify wielding this force. Zia and Elian might gild their tale with promises of salvation, but the killing winds had nothing to do with healing.

As he climbed out of the lower circles up Travitar Hill, Jhared found Elders' Circle to be relatively intact. Only when he entered the district did he see the wounds at its heart: shutters torn from hinges, windows blown out and shattered, roof tiles flung into the streets. On Elders' Row, the fifteen first-clan banners hung in shreds from their poles or lay in the muck on the street. Only one banner remained aloft and nearly whole, its rising sun blazing defiantly amid the wreckage. Jhared's jaw tightened at the sight of the Clan Amerre sigil.

Glancing over his shoulder to see that he went unnoticed, he jumped. His fingers brushed the edge of the pennant, setting it to swinging; then the ground pulled him back with a jolt. He took a breath and threw himself skyward once more. This time, he grasped a handful of fabric. The banner hissed in protest as he ripped it from the pole.

"That's for General Nadel," he declared, dropping the pennant to the ground.

He hurried across the street and into the alley behind Elders' Row. To his relief, Tierzen Trianor's home looked battered, but sound. Splinters of glass from the kitchen window sparkled across the alley and crunched under Jhared's boots. In Sarena's garden, the bloody body of a dog lay with its nose and front paws half-buried in the dirt.

He leaped up the back step. The door was unlatched.

"Branlen! Elder! Madam Trianor!"

His words hit the walls of the kitchen and died. No one answered. Alabaster the kitchen cat ran into the room and leaped onto the table to sniff at the half-eaten apple tart that still sat uncovered with three dirty plates. Jhared strode into the great room.

"Bran!"

A slow creak came from the upper floor. Jhared spun around and took the stairs two at a time. The hall was vacant, as was Bran's small bedchamber. He peered into the room Sarena and Tierzen shared. Empty. A shutter swayed from one squeaky hinge.

"Goddess keep them," he whispered. His vision flickered, and he leaned against the doorframe, shoving back dread as he tried to reason through his family's likely whereabouts. It seemed years since Branlen had hugged him in the alley and they exchanged their talisman. Bran had said that Sarena was visiting neighbors and making her vigil at the temple. She hadn't been home yet, or there wouldn't have been dirty plates and crumbs. That was somewhat reassuring; if she had stayed within the stone of Elders' Circle or the temple, she would be safe. Likewise, if Tierzen had spent another night in debate at Elders' Hall, then the stone would have protected him. But Branlen. Bran had planned to go to the camps with his friends. The boy was of an age to seek the excitement of Dawnings' Eve among the clans. He would have stayed to see the sun rise on Dawnings' Day.

Jhared swallowed against a surge of fear. If Bran saw the winds coming, surely he would know enough to run for the city. Surely he had grown past any boyish bravado that might tempt him to linger to watch the storm. Jhared tried not to picture all the ways his brother could have been prevented from reaching safety or returning home.

He limped back down the stairs. If Tierzen had returned during the night, he would have retreated to his study to relax with a glass of wine and perhaps to read for a bit. If later he heard the storm coming and ran out in search of Branlen and Sarena, he might have left evidence of his haste.

At the threshold to the room, Jhared paused uneasily, surprised to find the old constraints still in place in him. Tierzen had kept him out of this chamber where so many secrets of the Teaching were stored. Jhared reminded himself that, since his Becoming, no reason remained why he should not enter. Pushing past the doorway, he stepped across the thick rug and slid gratefully into the chair behind Tierzen's desk. The dimly lit study was peaceful, filled with the scent of old books and candles. He rested his head against the chair's padded leather back. The room was Tierzen's haven, and evidence of his presence saturated the place. Stillness crept into Jhared's bones and he began to sink.

He jerked his head up with a start. No time for rest now. He forced his gaze back to the desktop. Nearly every inch of space was covered, but it was all organized in Tierzen's way, with rows of ordered piles. On the left side of the desk lay a neat stack of letters in Sirol's hand awaiting the elder's review and seal. Jhared turned from them to the right side of the desk; at the top of that pile perched Morican's *Deliberations on the Council of First-Clans*, an ancient interpretation of the laws governing the council. Jhared found Morican a bitter, self-focused, and incomprehensible writer. Tierzen didn't care for her either, but he had marked several points in the volume with ribbon. Curious, Jhared pulled the work closer and flipped to the first mark.

The vellum crackled as he flattened the binding. A narrow, fading script in ancient Velos detailed the selection of council elders within the clans. Although each clan owned the right to choose its own elder through whatever method it determined best, over time important families gathered such power that competitions among candidates became largely irrelevant, and the positions became inherited by default. Morican took a sideways perspective on the issue, arguing that council seats should be a birthright, but only so long as the sitting family was virtuous and moral, as defined by Morican herself. Translating the priestess's circular logic from the ancient tongue made Jhared's head hurt. He flipped to the next mark.

Cold feathered through him as his eyes ran down the page.

When the Goddess removes Her Favor from the High Chieftain of the Council of First-Clans, he will know it is time to surrender his rule to one who is more able. However, if he is such a man who is blinded by arrogance or shielded by cunning, the elders of the first-clans may come together—for ever there is more wisdom in the hearts of many men joined than the heart of one man—and they must give their witness to the High Chieftain of his poor leadership. After an open accounting, the High Chieftain shall be cast out and each of the elders must give their vote for the new leader from among themselves. So shall Avelos be guarded from the rule of evil or ignorant men. This is the Law of Integrity.

Jhared read it twice, then pushed the book away with a groan. Of course Tierzen was studying this text. Jhared rested his head in his hands, wishing that he didn't understand why. Tumal's Legacy exalted many ideas originally set down by Morican; the Legacy's leaders would know this work. Here was the key to Abrigado's plotting: the Minister of the Treasury wasn't attacking Rumar's allies just to shift the structure of power in the council. He was upsetting the balance to create disorder among the clans. He wanted the people to be angry and afraid, so he manipulated them with rumor and rhetoric—tales of insubordinate Shorn soldiers, wild accusations about Sahistens in Avelos, stories that the Shorn controlled the killing winds—prodding them to turn on the high chieftain like a basket of snakes. And when they did, the Council of Clans would have reason to invoke the Law of Integrity.

Now Jhared understood just how terrifyingly far Toren Abrigado dared to reach: he planned to be high chieftain. What he meant to do then would tear the Shorn from the fabric of Avelos.

"Abrigado will abolish the Shearing. No more Teachers. No more Shorn Law. No more Shorn. A final Exile. Avelun babes drowned like kittens."

"Help us to obtain what we must to create a new home for the Shorn."

"Do you know what it means to be a Storyteller, Jhared?"

"When I heard Mahla speak, I knew it was the truth."

"Do you know what you're doing wrong now?"

"Quiet! Leave me be!"

Jhared sagged against the back of the chair. He was so tired of the voices. They picked at him like crows, eating out his heart and leaving nothing but gleaming bones. He didn't know what to do—for Zia, for Hendren, for his Teachers, or for his high chieftain. He longed for Tierzen to listen as he used to, sitting on the floor of Jhared's bedchamber, patient and calm and wise; but Tierzen wasn't speaking to him anymore, wasn't even writing to him. The bond between them had frayed. Perhaps it had only ever been a veil formed from his desperate wishes for connection. Jhared squeezed his eyes shut, but everything he feared waited inside him. He opened them again and spied the decanter on the sideboard against the opposite wall. Rich amethyst wine glowed in its bowl.

Abruptly, he was aware of the taste of dust in his mouth and the clamoring of his parched body. He made the long trek across the room. His hands shook as he filled a glass and took a drink. The wine swirled sourly over his tongue, burning his torn lips. He gagged and spat it out as his stomach pitched upward. Bent double with his hands braced on his thighs, he panted for breath, trying to convince his insides to stay put. Blood smeared the glass on the table.

Without warning, the floor tilted and Jhared discovered himself on the ground, staring up at the rows of spirals painted on the ceiling beams. As his vision darkened, he heard his own weak laughter. Madam Trianor was going to kill him for getting wine and blood on her rugs.

Somewhere far away, a woman sobbed as though her heart had broken in two. "Oh, Sacred Lady, is he alive?"

"Help me get him onto the table," a man replied, the familiar voice of one long loved. "Careful. Watch his head."

"Is the healer coming?"

Tierzen made a small, tortured sound. "I...couldn't find him. I left word."

No one touched Jhared. He lay alone, staring at the dark in confusion. Many people were dying in Velantar tonight.

Branlen.

He dragged himself to full awareness and wrenched his body upright. Tierzen's side table held him up for several moments before he hazarded his way toward the great room.

Night had fallen, and cold air crept in through the shattered windows. Two lamps threw wavering light over Tierzen and Sarena as they hovered over the long oak table and Branlen. Even from the shadows, Jhared saw that the boy had been torn. Dirt and blood matted his wheat-gold hair. His chest rose and fell at irregular intervals.

"Blankets," Jhared said hoarsely. "He needs to be kept warm. Quickly. Then hot water, bandages, and bitterbalm if you have it."

Madam Trianor jumped and turned, tears streaked down her face. "You? What are you doing here?"

"Jhared?" Tierzen's eyes were red with exhaustion and grief. "How did you...? No, never mind. Not now." He nodded at his wife. "Hot water. I'll get the blankets."

Opposing emotions wrestled for control over Sarena's expression. "He mustn't act the healer. It's dangerous. Against Shorn Law. He'll bring trouble to this house...."

"Madam, I watched men treated for these injuries all summer. I've nothing of a healer's knowledge, only a soldier's field skills, but I can help." Jhared's voice broke on the last words.

Sarena's lips trembled into a frown, then she glanced at Branlen, and Jhared saw her decide.

"Remember how he loves you," she demanded. "You owe him."

Jhared hobbled to the table. "Neta keeps the bitterbalm in the cupboard with her herbs. Please hurry."

As Tierzen and Sarena rushed to their tasks, Jhared examined Branlen. The boy looked so vulnerable stretched under the flickering light. Blood and bruises violated his pale skin.

"You're home and safe, Bran. We'll see you well. You'll be well." He reached for his brother's hand. Clenched in Branlen's left fist was the little grey talisman. It sparkled innocently in the pale light.

Jhared pulled in a deep breath. "Keep holding that for luck," he said, folding the boy's fingers around the ancient stone once more.

He drew his hands down Branlen's limbs, feeling for the swelling that meant a broken bone, then he did what he could to assess the gashes through the blood and grime. He worried most about the blow to the head the boy had taken and wished for Healer Falto or Gabrian to be here.

Tierzen stepped up quietly behind him.

"His bones are whole, sir. Several of these cuts are deep. I'll clean them and bind them as best I can, then we should move him to his room. It's important that he feel safe." Jhared paused awkwardly. "That is…I will if you will let me."

"I trust you, Jhared," Tierzen answered. "I know you would never do anything to harm this family."

Jhared nodded wordlessly, unable to meet Tierzen's eyes. Now wasn't the time for all he needed to say to the Minister of the Teaching.

Madam Trianor carried in the water and rags on a tray and came around to hover near Branlen's head. No bitterbalm was to be found to purge the wounds, so Jhared asked Tierzen for a bottle of brandy. The elder said nothing when he returned from his study with the bottle, but Jhared felt the intensity of the man's gaze.

Under his Teachers' close watch, Jhared set to work. The tasks of caregiving fostered a steadiness that he would never find in the flight of an arrow or the hiss of a blade. While he labored for his brother's sake, he forgot his own hurts.

Branlen stirred as Jhared washed the grit from a gash on his forearm and doused it with brandy.

"I'm sorry," Jhared whispered. "I'm almost finished." In response, there might have been the hint of a grimace; the boy's lashes fluttered.

Afterward, Jhared carried Branlen up the stairs. He staggered over the threshold to the boy's room, and only Tierzen's quick hand saved Bran more bruises. They lowered the boy onto the bed. From there, Jhared's legs were disinclined to haul him back to his feet, so he sat on the floor by the head of the bed, one hand stretched up to rest on his brother's shoulder.

"I think we could use some tea," Tierzen said above him. "Sarena, is there boldblood?"

"Sleep, husband. Do you recall the time when you used to sleep?"

Tierzen glanced at his wife with a sad tenderness that made Jhared feel even more the intruder. "One day you'll remind me of it, but not tonight, love."

With a quiet snort, Sarena shook her head at him. She leaned over to touch Branlen's cheek before going back down the stairs.

The room grew quiet. Bran's breathing had steadied, and he seemed to have risen from unconsciousness into a fitful slumber. With a sigh, Tierzen folded himself onto the floor at the foot of the bed.

"It's one thing to hear a man speak of the killing winds," the elder mused, touching the back of his hand to a cut on his face, "but altogether another to feel them flaying the flesh from your bones. I learned something about fear today."

Jhared smiled faintly. Who but Tierzen Trianor could sit in his broken city beside the sickbed of his son and talk about what he had learned?

"I'm sorry, sir."

"Sorry?"

"That it was something you had to learn. That Branlen…" His hand tightened on his brother's shoulder. "I would have done anything if I had but known how to stop it."

Tierzen stared in silence, then shook his head wonderingly. "I really did create something different when I raised you, didn't I? I didn't expect you to stop the killing winds, Jhared."

"No?" Jhared looked down. "I haven't forgotten what I owe, sir. You taught me how to put the self aside to pay the debt."

Tierzen's eyes moved from Jhared's bruised and filthy face to his torn and bloody uniform. "Yes. Yes, I did do that," he said quietly.

Jhared evaded his Teacher's gaze. "I know I haven't lived up to your Teaching."

"The weakness is in your blood, boy. You'll always struggle against temptation, even with all you've learned. It's a battle you can never win, but must always fight, for none of us can afford for you to lose."

Jhared nodded, wondering if it were already too late.

The elder sighed and rubbed a hand over his face. "I might have helped you more had I not been so consumed by council matters. I shouldn't have asked you to watch in Ravia."

"I'm a terrible informant. I'm sorry."

Tierzen gave him an odd look. "No. You're too good."

"Sir?"

"I should have known better than to loose the rein on your skills of deceit. Eavesdropping on the conversations of council couriers? Spying on your superiors?" The elder grimaced. "But you're past that now. There's no more need. We know who started the rumors about the Ravia Shorn."

Jhared drooped against the bed. Even when he followed the orders his Teacher gave him, his nature led him wrong. But how could he have done otherwise? How could he have refused the Minister of the Teaching? In all these months, why hadn't Tierzen offered some warning? Jhared shoved away his confusion and frustration.

"You know who did it? Can you tell me?"

"Toren Abrigado's Shorn scribe. A girl named Ziabela Marcalo."

"It can't be…!" Jhared coughed, barely diverting his exclamation. "Can't be one of the Shorn."

"It looks as though it is. She likely organized the Legacy speeches in Panetar as well." Tierzen shook his head. "She always was a clever thing."

"It was Abrigado," Jhared insisted. "She must have been acting on Abrigado's orders."

Tierzen lifted one hand in acknowledgment of the point. "That's an assumption I haven't discounted. The Minister of the Treasury claims he suspected his scribe of causing mischief to smear his name, so he set a watch on her. He caught her sending missives under his seal. If he ordered her to it, then he covered his tracks well, for he turned her in to the council himself."

Jhared tried to think clearly. What had Zia been playing at? How much did Abrigado know of her plans? How far could Jhared go before he told Tierzen the truth? "Who did she write?"

Tierzen made a face. "Men loyal to Abrigado and willing to carry out unpleasant tasks."

"But…how? How could she *do it?*"

There it was: the desperate note he couldn't keep from his tone. Tierzen heard it. Jhared saw the elder's expression change, and knew his time was up. He took a breath.

"Sir, it's just that…I've met her. Sirol warned me afterward that she works for Abrigado. I didn't know."

Tierzen paled. "Ah, Jhared. I don't need to tell you what Abrigado will do if he discovers it. Will people link you two? Are you *courting* her?"

"No, sir! I've been to the inn where she plays. That's all. We've never spoken of you or anything to do with this family." The lie came too easily…*your skills of deceit.* Jhared flicked his gaze upward. "What will happen to her?"

"If she survived the winds, she will be detained and questioned. Afterward, it will be for the council to decide. She usurped an elder's authority. Abrigado's accusing her of treason."

Jhared closed his eyes. Wasn't this what he wanted: for Zia to be prevented from tearing apart the country? Wasn't he about to tell Tierzen the rest of what he knew of Abrigado's Shorn scribe?

"Jhared?"

If he spoke, he would condemn them to death: Zia, Elian, Bilar, Isella. People who had saved his life. People his mother had loved. If Abrigado had his way, perhaps all the Shorn. But if he didn't speak, he would deny his Teacher's need. Deny Avelos in her time of peril. Such a lie would sever the last of whatever bond existed between him and the man he called his father.

He saw Ziabela's glittering smile. Passion and energy radiated from her until others seemed like guttering candles to her bright fire. She lit the cold, hollow places inside him. She awoke the music long dormant within him. Jhared wondered if it was her passion that had also drawn Mahla to her. His mother took her in and claimed her as a student. They had spent hours together at the Black Mountain, telling stories and recalling the old songs. Telling stories that shouldn't have been told.

Goddess help him. Zia claimed that Mahla held the forbidden knowledge of the Storytellers. But if his mother had believed the tales, why didn't she give Jhared some sign rather than stand like a shadow between him and the truth? She had begged him to listen to his Teachers. She sang to him of final reparation. Had she set him running toward a goal she didn't even believe existed? Why? How could a mother hide herself and everything she believed from her only son?

Unless everything she believed would kill him.

An unexpected image entered his head: Talia, beaten by the storm, her body curled around her child. She would have died to save the boy. Could a mother love her child that much? What if keeping him ignorant had been Mahla's way of putting herself between Jhared and danger? If she actually possessed the secret truths of the Exile—truths that Tumal the Just endeavored to conceal—could she have sought to protect Jhared from accusations of treason? From failing the Becoming?

Tierzen watched him with a concerned gaze, and Jhared glanced away with a rush of guilt.

Could he be the cause of so many deaths if his mother had known the truth?

"Jhared, are you all right?"

His hand came up to press against the place where an arrow had pierced his breast. "Of course, sir," he said hoarsely. "Your Teaching keeps me where I'm meant to be."

A sudden noise from downstairs brought Jhared's head up. The noise came a second time: someone pounding on the front door.

Tierzen stood. "The healer. You stay with Branlen."

When the elder left, Jhared pillowed his forehead on his folded arms at the edge of the bed. If Mahla spoke truly, it was for the love and protection of Avelos that the Avelune attempted to murder their high chieftain. Did that make the death and war that tore the country afterward any less terrible? Jhared had sworn to protect Avelos above all else, and had sworn not to follow the footsteps of his ancestors. Now he found that those vows ran along the same road: if he upheld one, he must break the other. He found that his kind were doomed to cause chaos, even when they acted in the name of love. If he were to evade their legacy, he must forge a new path.

Here it stood: he would neither turn over Zia's group to the council nor would he seek the winds' secrets on their behalf. The decision would cost him: it would destroy his tie to the Shorn just as he was discovering them. It would sever him from the family that sheltered him when no one else would. The thought of losing his family, losing Bran…he gasped a ragged breath.

The bedcovers stirred. Fingers patted his hair.

"You're a right mess, brother."

"We're two of a kind then." Jhared lifted his head. "How do you feel, Bran?"

The boy groaned. "Like I've been rolled over by a rockslide."

"I'm afraid you're going to feel that way for a while. Don't rush to get up."

"No worries on that score." The boy shuddered under the blankets. "It was worse than anything…anything I've ever known. People screaming. The winds tearing through us. Ino and I were in the forest, and we knew we wouldn't make it back. If we hadn't stumbled onto the Manitar estates and found the shed…if we hadn't…"

Jhared closed both his callused hands around his brother's smooth ones. "Look at me, Bran. Don't stay there. Be here. You're safe now."

A light step sounded on the stair. Jhared straightened as Madam Trianor entered the room.

"Jhared, there's a soldier at the door who claims he has orders to fetch you— Branlen? Oh, thank the Lady! Husband, come quickly. Branlen's awake!"

Tierzen's eyes shone as he entered the room and swooped down to embrace his son. Sarena murmured a prayer and held the boy's hand.

As the three of them celebrated their reunion, Jhared climbed to his feet. So many things remained to be said to Bran and to his Teachers, but he was out of time. Silently, he watched them, wondering how to say goodbye. It was Branlen who finally looked beyond both his parents.

"Jhared, does this mean you have to go?"

His Teachers turned to peer at him. Tierzen looked a little chagrined. "The man says he's a patrolmate with orders from your lieutenant. Nevia is his name."

Of course perceptive Anzo had figured out where Jhared had gone. "Then I must be on my way."

"You should eat something before you go." Sarena's blue eyes shifted with a mix of emotions. She hadn't relinquished her fear of him, but neither would she ever abandon her duty as a Teacher.

"I'm sorry," Jhared answered. "It won't go well if I'm counted as a deserter."

"Come back soon, brother," Branlen whispered.

Jhared couldn't answer. He bent and gave Branlen's hand a squeeze.

Meeting Tierzen's gaze proved the most difficult. Regret reflected from his foster father's expression, and Jhared knew he was the cause of it.

"Don't give ground, my boy. The important battles are never easily won."

This was the ending Jhared had expected after his Becoming. This time, his own choices cut him off from the people who loved him. If no shelter waited for him here, it was because he rejected it.

The pain of that truth arrowed into him. It wasn't too late to reveal everything he knew about Zia. Confiding in Tierzen would allow him to remain the boy who deserved his Teacher's trust, the Shorn man who followed the path required of him.

He bit down hard on the words and turned away. His footsteps echoed down the stairs.

Anzo stood awkwardly in the front hall, his arms wrapped across his barrel chest as though he feared he might break something. He was bruised and cut up, but the layer of wind-driven dirt had been scrubbed away and he wore a uniform that was more intact than not.

When they made it to the street and Tierzen's door shut behind them, the little patrolman took one look at Jhared and shook his head.

"Ah, boy. You shouldn't have gone back. They never know what to do with you when you go back. Come here, now. Give me your arm. We'll take it slow."

The storm had extinguished all the streetlamps on Elders' Row, but the City Guard stalked through the circle with torches, discouraging disorder. From farther away, Jhared heard hammering and the *scrape-scrape* of shovels. The cleanup had begun.

"Where are we going?"

"To the high temple."

Jhared tried to pull away. "I'm not dying, Anzo."

The little patrolman's chuckle was subdued. "'Course not. We're going to the temple because that's where Lieutenant ordered us. We've got ourselves a new assignment. I think you'll like it."

"We're to hunt the secret of the killing winds."

Anzo harrumphed. "Well, now. And I thought you'd be surprised. I should have guessed the elder would get to you with it."

"No. Someone thought they would use it to get to the elder."

"That so." Anzo went silent and looked sidelong at Jhared's face. Jhared wondered if the observant patrolman understood more than he was meant to. "Well, you'll have a chance for rest at the temple," Anzo said. "And in the wilds you won't have to worry about elders and their intrigues. You'll be back among the Guard where you belong."

Jhared leaned against the veteran, grateful Anzo could restrain his disgust to support him. All he wanted right now was to return to the life for which he'd been trained. He was a soldier, nothing more. In the wilds, he would be too far away for the Shorn to ask for his betrayals or for Elder Abrigado to use him against Tierzen.

And pursuing the killing winds would allow him to assure the safety of those he loved, even if he had already broken his oath to them. He peered through the darkness at the wreckage.

"Anzo, do you think we have a chance to do what they're sending us out for?"

"For certain I do," the man answered with uncharacteristic reverence. "Someone at the temple put us to this task, so Riana's got her eye on us. I don't see as the Good Lady's going to let Cael tear apart everything she helped Alende Isan to build. And besides," Jhared heard the Everen clansman grin, "who better to stand between Avelos and danger than Commander Carn's hunters, eh? We'll track down what we need and put an end to those cursed storms. I'd wager our blessed Nadaren on it."

Jhared wished he felt as confident as Anzo. He wished that the ache in his heart didn't tell him he had just lost the only people who cared for him to make a deal with Cael.

24.
Cursed Choices

Jhared endured the remainder of the walk to the high temple, where he and Anzo were permitted entrance to the Arionade's quarters. The world had blurred again, and everything around him became no more than elusive possibility. It was like the moments just before dark, when everything was so soft-edged and ill-defined that even a border guard couldn't trust his senses.

He recalled Anzo leading him down dimly lit stone-carved halls. And the baths he remembered, for the hot water awoke every bruise and gash on his body, forcing clarity on him long enough to note the little patrolman's displeasure.

"I fell badly," he mumbled, fairly certain that was the excuse he had offered earlier.

"Naw," the old man grumbled. "You fell exactly right. Right onto someone's blade and into someone's fist. You going to tell me about that?"

"No. Where are the others?"

Anzo snorted. "Jase, Esran, and Lenaro are offering prayers in the first circle. The rest are getting a bite of food or've passed out in the barracks."

"When do we leave?"

"Soon as we can is all I hear. High chieftain gave lieutenant the word himself."

Jhared sank deeper into the water. "Lieutenant Sevar's coming with us?"

"Sure, boy. This isn't just any night patrol to catch village raiders."

The heat of the water leeched the very end of Jhared's energy, and if not for Anzo, he would have fallen asleep in the bath. The older man pulled him out of the tub, handed him clean clothes, and guided him back through the halls.

Riana manifested just as they reached the arched entrance to the barracks. Her back, imperious and lovely, was turned to Jhared, but it was the heartrending gaze of the man offering a devotion before her that took his breath. With murmured words of awe, Jhared stumbled to a halt and started to go to his knees. Anzo kept him upright.

"She'll hear your prayers from bed, boy."

"But Anzo…"

Only upon a second look did the goddess and the man become stone. A sculpture of Lord Arion's Commitment. Stone couldn't diminish the intensity of the Holy Consort's passion for the goddess. His body yearned toward her with love and desire. His proud head bowed in veneration. But a sharper emotion carved his fingers into the fist that gripped his sword and pain brought life to his eyes. It was something Jhared never saw in other representations: grief. In the moment that Arion swore to serve Riana, he lost all connections to his mortal life, and he mourned his decision as much as he rejoiced in it. Jhared wondered if the ache ever faded, or if Arion would carry it through eternity.

"That sacrifice deserves a lament," he breathed.

Anzo only mumbled something about the problem with soldiers who thought themselves bards and dragged him away.

After that, there might have been food he didn't want and then a bed he desperately needed. As soon as his body stretched across the straw tick, he plummeted fast and far into oblivion.

When something reached through the darkness to press against his chest, he twitched to the edge of wakefulness. Cold touched his skin.

A stranger's hand.

His eyes flew open. Lamplight dazzled his vision. Blindly, he swept one arm across his body, knocking away the grip that held him. With his other arm he grabbed for his assailant's throat and sunk his fingers into flesh.

"Riana's ways," a woman choked. "Jhared Denaban…let me go!"

He squinted up at her. The lamp shadowed her features. He loosened his grip, but didn't let her free. "Who are you?"

"Madam Kaliska. Riana's healer. They told me you needed tending, but I daresay…you're doing quite well."

"Oh, Lady." Jhared released her hastily and lifted a hand to shield his eyes from the light. "Forgive me."

"Shhhh." She looked around the room, where most of his patrol and a handful of Arionade were sleeping. "You can walk?"

He nodded uncertainly.

"Good. Come with me."

"No, I…I only need sleep." What he really didn't need was to answer questions from Riana's healer about his injuries.

"Quiet. Come along." She didn't give him another opportunity to protest, but took the lamp and headed down the row of bunks. He wondered if she would return to harass him if he didn't follow; she seemed the sort who would.

Biting the side of his cheek against a groan, he pulled himself out of bed and padded after her. She took him to a small infirmary just outside the barracks. Two beds lay against one wall with a narrow table between them. A large many-drawered chest topped with an array of bottles sat against the opposite wall. The air smelled of mint and bitterbalm.

Pushing strands of long silver hair away from her face, she slipped a black satchel from her shoulder and nodded toward a bed. "Sit down."

"Madam, so many others need your care more than I."

She turned to look at him directly. She was past her prime, but straight-backed and even-featured. Her eyes were a remarkably clear grey, so clear he sensed that they revealed nothing of who she was.

"You're right about that, boy, but I can't help all of them. I can help you. Take off your shirt and let me see if you've ripped out my work entirely."

Jhared went still, a prickle of alarm running up his spine.

She glanced back at him. "Don't try to tell me you're fine. I can see you're bleeding again. The stitches have pulled free."

Madam Kaliska, a temple healer. The healer who had tended him at the Mountain. Jhared felt like a fox caught in a snare. How many others played a part in Elian's plot?

He tried to gather himself. "It seems I already owe you my thanks."

"No debt," she said, pulling jars from her satchel and uncorking bottles on the chest. "I bring ease when Riana and Cael allow, and Zia is a friend. Sit down."

The bed was soft, and more than anything Jhared wanted to close his eyes and tumble back into the nothingness, but he needed to think coherently now. Elian had said they would give him two days, but Zia had seen his face when he left the Mountain. What had she guessed? Would a healer take his life to protect their secrets?

She came at him with a vial full of foul-smelling liquid. "Drink this."

"What is it?"

"Something to return your body to its proper balance."

He glanced at the concoction doubtfully. "What's in it?"

"Sacred Lady of all the spheres! I've no time for lectures on the brewing and fermentation of restoratives. Drink it and let me look at you."

Let it be as Riana wills. He wasn't certain whether the thought was his own or a whisper from his Teachers. It didn't comfort him, but he had little other choice. He took the drink from her hand, sniffed it. Some dreamsease in there, enough to dull his senses but probably not enough to kill him. All else was masked by the odor of decomposing vegetation. Bracing himself, he poured the draught down his throat and swallowed.

"Good," she said, smiling a little. "Not as bad as you thought, mmm?"

"Delicious," he said through gritted teeth. Other than the taste—which fell somewhere between boiled cabbage and rotten spinach—it didn't appear imme-diately harmful. He relaxed a little; he couldn't imagine a woman smiling that ironically at a man she had just poisoned.

"Now." She gestured at the place on his side where blood had once again seeped through his shirt.

He drew up the fabric to expose a spectacular display of purples across his chest and ribs. The knife wound gaped in an ugly snarl.

The healer inhaled. "I'm sorry I have no Silvaye for you. I used my last in the city this evening."

"As it should be, madam."

One silver brow rose sharply. "You don't believe in the strength of Silvaye?"

"It can only cause harm to touch a Shorn man with Riana's Chosen healer. Healer Falto would tell you the same."

"Foolish." She pushed him back with a firm hand until he lay flat on the bed. "The Chosen can be dangerous for anyone when in the hands of the untrained. Used with knowledge and care, it is a gift. Old Falto means well, I suppose, but he's a soldier, with a soldier's prejudices."

"He understands how to put a man back together well enough to sit a horse," Jhared said, grimacing as she probed too close to a gash. "All I need is to be able to ride out of Velantar with my patrol."

"We'll see," she said, frowning over him. She left no part of him untouched: prodding at his injuries, both those from Ilvio and the newer ones from the winds. He turned reluctantly when she insisted upon examining his back and shuddered as her hand ran over his scars. Finally, she wiped her hands on a cloth and turned to gather items from the wooden chest behind her: a curved needle of bone, fine thread, and a clay pot that held a paste with the familiar acrid smell of bitterbalm.

"Your spirit's taken as much hurt as the rest of you," she murmured, "but I'm afraid we've not the time for that kind of healing tonight."

She cleansed his wounds, then picked up the needle, threaded it, and dipped it into the bitterbalm pot.

"So you'll help them?" she asked, pushing the needle tip through Jhared's inflamed flesh.

He exhaled forcefully. "I...don't know."

"They've long hoped for a chance such as you offer. They did not bring you into this lightly."

"Yet some of them decided my part long before I had any say in it."

The healer's lip turned upward as her needle pushed through again. "Don't fault Zia for her eagerness. She's missed you these long years."

"She needn't have." He dug his fingers into the mattress. "I was here."

Through all his years in the elder's home, the Shorn had left him alone, with no connection to any of them. Until now, when they saw a use for him. He had decided not to be used. What they wanted would cause more damage than the Avelune ever had.

As he watched the healer's fingers draw the needle back and forth through his torn body, it came to him that she was of an age to have served Riana since before he was born. Her Guardians might have attended his birth and carried him to the temple. Her hands that sewed him together now might very well have wielded the knife that cut him apart. The thought sent black snowflakes sparkling across his vision. Cold sweat trickled down his neck.

"Close your eyes if it bothers you," she said. "There's no shame in it. I've known plenty of fighting men who blanched to see themselves torn open."

"How do you do it?"

Madam Kaliska tilted her head. "It's a thing you grow accustomed—"

"No. You've seen the destruction in the city. You're a healer. How can you allow them to threaten the country in order to do…what they would do?"

"You have been Shorn," she said quietly. "How can you not?"

He blinked at her in confusion. So many reasons cried out in his head—his oath, the debt, the violence of the winds—but in the face of her calm certitude, all his thoughts lost their coherence.

"Because we are the cursed," he finally managed.

She finished knitting him together, knotted her work, and snipped the thread with a small knife.

"You've been beaten long and brutally," she said with a sigh. "Rest now. You need not think on this more tonight."

Perhaps not tonight, but now that she knew his intent, it would reach whoever yet lived to carry out their plans. Someone would come for him.

She made him sit while she bandaged his ribs. Then she stowed her tools in her satchel and pulled it onto her shoulder.

"Sleep here. You'll rest better without the noise in the barracks." She set her cool hand to his cheek and looked at him with her clear grey gaze, a gaze that told him nothing. Hendren had warned that the temple was watching him. What did she know about him?

He shivered as her hand brushed his jaw and she drew away. He thought the pain would keep him awake, but his eyes were closing even before she turned down the lamps and snuffed the candles. He didn't hear her leave the room.

The dark figure slipped into the infirmary sometime later. He opened his eyes to find her standing by his bed gazing down at him, her slender form draped in a cloak and deep cowl.

"Many roads wait to be traveled," she murmured. "Will you be the one to walk the dark Paths, Jhared Denaban?" Her voice was low and husky. He thought of crows cawing in the distance or the rustle of a forest at night. It sent a familiar chill through his core. She had come to him before.

"Are you a priestess?" he asked.

"I am the shadow of a priestess," she whispered.

"Have you come to feed on my soul?"

She laughed, the sound of cool water bubbling up into dark caverns. The sound of mysteries he could not fathom, but wanted to learn. He wished he could see her eyes.

"As you desire," she said, lifting her long-fingered hands. Slowly, she slid back her cowl.

He screamed.

"Denaban? Denaban, ya going t'sleep through the rest of the new year?"

Jhared opened his eyes. Arrows of sunlight pierced the corners of the room and drove into his skull. Jase grinned in his face.

"What time is it?" he asked, squinting against the brightness. His mouth was thick and tasted sour.

"Past midday. Commander sent me t'find out if ya was still alive."

A demon laughed in his head. Jhared grimaced and pushed himself upright. "I'm not sure yet. What orders for us?"

"Lieutenant's trying to organize provisions for the journey. That's a tricky thing with the mess out there." Jase frowned and nodded toward the city.

"I imagine he'll have help." Jhared leaned against the head of the bed. "The high chieftain will want us to be on our way. He'll want the people to know there's hope for an end to this terror."

"*I* want t'know it." The Clan Nadaren man tapped at the tattoo on his cheek. "Why anyone thinks a band of soldiers like us has anything t'do with fighting such magic, I can't guess."

"I suppose the temple will tell us. That's why we're here, isn't it?"

"Do ya think it's Sahiste? Who's brought this down on us?"

"I don't know." Jhared rubbed both hands over his face. He could have slept for another week.

"Because they're whispering that Rumar's going t'open the border for Sahiste. And if ya ask me, it sounds like the man's bewitched t'consider opening the door wide for our enemies—"

"Jase, I really don't know."

The clansman looked skeptical. "With the Teaching and all ya learned about that history? Surely, ya know things the rest of us don't."

That history. Jhared grimaced. He didn't want to think about Sahistens in Avelos. "Right now all I'd like to know is where a man might find something to eat. Do you think there's someone to feed us in the mess?"

At the idea of a meal, Jase brightened a little and dropped his speculation about the winds to join in the search. Sweat glossed Jhared's face by the time he sank onto a bench in the Arionade's mess. The bean soup and dark bread in front of him was no longer tempting, but he forced himself to eat a few bites. Jase willingly finished the rest as he answered Jhared's questions about the damage in the city.

"Hundreds dead outside the walls," the clansman said soberly. "Not enough priestesses t'make proper death masks for 'em all before they go to the pyres. I don't know how the Pathguides'll ever find 'em to lead 'em to the Hidden Paths. Those poor spirits'll wander as Bloodless in the twilight."

Inside the walls, chaos reigned. General Nadel had converted the barracks into a temporary shelter for people displaced by the winds, but some families refused to leave the ruins of their homes. Makeshift tents sprang up in streets and lanes. Rescuers continued to search for people buried in the wreckage. In some circles, arguments over the property scattered through the streets turned violent.

"Never imagined it could be so bad," Jase said, tapping a finger against his cheek. "This must be what the valley looked like during the Exile War."

Jhared's chest ached. He wanted to run into the city, where he should be helping to rebuild, but he discovered himself fit for nothing more strenuous than stumbling back to bed. Rather than return to the isolation of the infirmary, he reclaimed an empty bunk in the Arionade barracks. The voices and clatter of men preparing for duty were familiar and comforting, and he hoped they might drive off the demons from his nightmares.

Sleep pulled him into darkness, and he didn't resurface until the edge of dawn the next morning, when he ate a bit more and took a slow walk through the Arionade's quarters. The next several days became a dull routine: sleep, food, and as much exploration of the temple as his body would tolerate and the priestesses would allow.

The first thing he discovered in his exploration was that the stone-carved halls of the high temple were not only unexpectedly beautiful, but fascinating, filled with the stories of Riana and the creation of Avelos. Depicted in finely worked silver- and rose-colored granite were the legendary battles of the Great Wars, the lordly chieftains who ruled at Altan Mar, and the ancient mountain city before ever Cael's fire destroyed it. Studying the walls was like reading one of the histories, and like the histories, the walls had been sorely damaged. It saddened Jhared to see great pieces hammered away from the depictions of Riana's Chosen. The Aye marched in wounded glory over the battlefield before seeking one last refuge within the bodies of mortal creatures. The story of the migration had been almost entirely destroyed; only Alende's legs, his staff of warding, and his hound Rodleto remained.

As Jhared walked slowly down a passage, another scene caught his attention, where flakes of gilding reflected the light of the hanging lamps. Rendered in poignant, painful detail was a beleaguered warrior fighting a host of Cael's messengers. Their wings beat against the hero, driving him to one knee, and their beaks pierced his body, but he defended the city behind him with the last ounces of his strength. *That* was the image Jhared held when he so boldly promised Cael at his Becoming that he would make final reparation. But in all these months, the enemy had never stood before him so clearly. From whom was he meant to protect Avelos now? From threats within or outside the borders? From the winds? From his kind? From the Legacy? From himself? What did his silence about Zia prove about him?

You're so afraid of doing the wrong thing you do nothing.

Micah's words rang in his head. When he swore to sacrifice himself for Avelos, he imagined he would die on a Sahisten spear or a Laebeki sword in the midst of battle, like the heroes of the songs or the warrior carved on the wall, but perhaps sacrificing himself meant something other than just shedding blood. Perhaps he had been too frightened to recognize it. Arion had given up his family, his home, and his world to fight Cael for the goddess.

Leather creaked and boots slapped stone, causing Jhared to slide into a defensive stance before he spotted the company of Arionade marching around the corner toward the city. He laughed at his vigilance; it was as useless as his ruminating. Nothing better than an inglorious end would find him when Elian's people arrived to protect their terrible secrets. They wouldn't find it difficult: Kaliska could reach him easily and be done with him quickly. The hulking clansman Bilar owned the will to kill a man; Jhared was sure of it. How many others in the city—in the temple itself—were part of their plotting?

Waiting for them to come kept him vigilant and made him even more ambivalent about the white-coats who were following him. Under stern orders from their grim-featured captain, the Arionade tolerated Rumar's soldiers, but Jhared felt the weight of their contempt. As pathetic as he was, he couldn't imagine what they feared in him that made them keep him under watch. Occasionally, he resorted to slipping his guard and wandering the halls on his own. It wasn't much of a challenge: the men trained to protect the priestesses learned how to be conspicuous and imposing. They didn't understand stealth.

Days passed, and no orders came to move out. He began to receive strange looks and unfriendly glowers even from his patrolmates. He didn't blame them if they resented his idleness when they labored to prepare for the journey. He wished Lieutenant Sevar would just get them all on their way. The longer he lingered at the temple, the more likely Elian's people would find a way to reach him or Toren Abrigado would learn of his link to Zia. He needed to get out of the city.

Late in the afternoon near a moon after the winds' attack, Jhared found himself pacing the barracks in boredom. Although plenty of daylight remained, the rest of his patrol sprawled on bunks or sat around game circles. Jhared strode to the place where Anzo and Esran were throwing dice on the floor between beds.

"Why are we still in Velantar?"

"Been a bit of a delay," Anzo said, frowning at the abysmal roll he'd just thrown.

"What delay? Jase says we're ready. How can we waste another day?"

"Seems our Shorn patrolman hasn't been fit to travel."

Jhared sat down on the bed above the two men. "I'm not reason enough to make the lieutenant wait."

"Sure enough ya're not," Esran agreed, scooping up Anzo's coins. "And I wouldn't cross 'is path if I was ya. He's like t'take off your head and be done with it."

Anzo shrugged at Esran and passed the cup. "You know the lieutenant, boy. He would just as soon load you onto a horse still bleeding or simply leave you behind. Apparently, the healer said no to the one and the priestess said no to the other."

"What priestess?" Jhared asked, fearing he knew. "Why didn't I hear of it?"

"Denaban, you've spent most of the last days unconscious. The lady that's joining us, the one that bears Cael's warning, came to look us over and tell us that we're heading for the Sandien Mountains. Some ancient temple there what holds the secrets of the sacred skies. According to her, the patrol needs its Shorn boy. For balance."

"The dark priestess?" *The one who saved my life and slides like a demon into my nightmares?*

"That's her," Anzo said. "Have you seen her in the first circle? Pretty little thing. Moves quiet as a shadow. Make a good scout."

Esran shook his head as he tossed down the dice again. "Only ya could compare Cael's Bearer to a border guard, Nevia."

"I haven't seen her," Jhared murmured.

"I wouldn't fancy her eye turning in my direction," Esran said with a shiver. "But I suppose one'a your kind can't help but draw the things what's cursed."

Anzo looked up at Jhared and raised a brow. "Now that you're pawing the ground to get out of here, I'd guess they'll be moving us out quick enough. You'll be seeing her then, and for some weeks to come."

Here was the cause of his patrolmates' odd glances, then: the interest of Cael's Bearer. Jhared decided he wasn't going to wait to learn more about her.

He had not attended a devotion since before his mother's death. Madam Trianor didn't believe Shorn children belonged in the sanctuary. But with the chaos his life had become, he owed Riana his prayers. And he wanted the opportunity to watch the woman who had been watching him.

The first circle was already crowded when he arrived for the evening devotion. Jhared found a place to stand near the back under Riana's eye. People continued to file in, filling the spaces under the dome between the columns, even as the acolyte stepped forward to light the candles. A family with children in tow tumbled in behind him. A man cloaked and hooded in Forest Guard green limped up slowly beside him. Jhared gave the tall soldier a nod and made room.

"This flame to light the Paths before us."

The acolyte's well-modulated voice projected solemnly over the murmuring crowd. Silence fell. She began a graceful circle, her eyes focused only on the candles and Riana's endless ways.

"This flame to light the Paths behind us."

The soldier beside Jhared bowed his head. Jhared made a spiral. When he was a child, it was the morning devotion that delighted him, with its greetings to the sacred skies and the promises to Riana to maintain her balance. The sunrise prayers had matched his childish intentions to prove he was a creature of order, unlike his ancestors. Since his Becoming, so many veils had been ripped away that he hardly recognized his world and himself. The evening devotion meant something to him now it never had before.

"This flame to light the Paths beneath us."

The flame could be extinguished so easily.

To the left of the high priestess stood the Bearer of Cael's Blade. As she glided from the altar, a fluid figure in midnight robes, Jhared saw that Anzo was right: she moved like twilight over the valley. She met the acolyte at the edge of the circle, and with the palm of her hand, snuffed out the candle. All the candles around the circle flickered and died. An audible intake of breath came from the worshipers. Someone cried out.

The Bearer's head came up. Her large eyes swallowed the light as she stared over the crowd. Jhared lowered his gaze, overwhelmed by the feeling that she was searching for something and filled with dread that it might be him.

Next to Jhared, the tall soldier shifted closer. Without warning, the man's hand clamped around his forearm.

"A gift for the guide who leads you to your destiny?"

Jhared recoiled. "What are you doing here?"

"Praying," Alende murmured pleasantly.

"Go away. You defile sacred ground."

"Ah, he cuts me like a dull blade," mourned the waylayer. "Yet he's the one who waits for days before coming to ask Riana to return peace to her fair city."

A matron shushed at them. Jhared ground his teeth.

"Very well, Forest Guard," Alende whispered. "I'll leave. If you speak with me first."

Jhared would rather have torn open his wounds once more, but who could guess what this unbound anathema would do in the crowd of grieving folk? He had been expecting something like this; he just hadn't expected it to be Alende in the first circle.

As the high priestess began to intone the promises, Jhared slid out from among the devoted and led the waylayer from the circle and into the outer gardens. The sun had nearly set. Only a few spears of red still pierced the dusky

sky. He darted a gaze around the space. It must have been a tranquil place for contemplation before the winds ripped it apart. It was a sad mess now—flowers dragged out of the soil, fountains toppled or clogged with debris, broken branches littering the paths—but they had it to themselves.

"We haven't long. They're keeping a watch on me. What do you want?"

"I wanted to see you," Alende said sweetly, lowering his cowl to bat his lashes at Jhared. Despite his modest dress, his cheeks still flaunted the vivid green waylayer's spirals, and he studied Jhared with the same feverish, green-eyed gleam. He no longer limped. "After all these days, you must have worried for me."

"I could expose you right here," Jhared said darkly. "They'd push you off the wall before morning."

Alende offered his brittle grin. "You won't."

"Why do you think so?"

"Your mother saved my life."

Jhared clenched his fists. He didn't know what that meant for him yet, except that if it were true, his mother was a traitor in ways that went well beyond the telling of illicit stories.

"Did Zia send you?"

"No, not our lovely Ziabela," the waylayer said, one hand moving to his belt. Jhared tensed, but Alende only pulled out a flask. He took a deep draught and licked his lips. Jhared smelled brandy. "I haven't seen her since the winds blew their last over Velantar."

"Then do you know Abrigado's been observing her? They discovered she's been using his seal to stir trouble. She's going to be arrested."

"Ah, well, it was bound to happen. Our Zia likes everyone to move to her order, and stolen power makes her reckless. She craves it." Alende looked at his open palms, and his expression shifted to one fit for locked bedchambers. "Shall I tell you what else she craves?"

"I tried to kill a man who did as much."

Alende's golden brow lifted. "Oh my, she has done her work well this time, hasn't she? I can't recall any of the others actually *killing* to be with her."

Jhared's heart pounded. It would be no breach of his oath to slay this creature. He drew a breath. "She'll be executed if they find her guilty of treason. I know you care for her. Can't you find her? Warn her?"

"Elian will have heard it through his elder. He has ways to get messages to us. He'll reach her."

"Do you even know if Elian's alive?"

Alende drifted closer. His body radiated heat and smelled of the forest. Twilight painted silver across the scars on his neck.

"Oh, yes. In this story, the Mountain still stands. It was our luck to remain with Isella after you and Hendren left. We waited out the winds together.

Quite a bit of nastiness that was. Although I see you kept yourself in one piece well enough."

"Hendren wasn't as fortunate," Jhared said, the grief settling in his middle again. "He died in the valley."

"Alas! A great loss for us all!" sang the waylayer. "He was a tamed man, but one who knew how to appreciate a good brandy."

"You call us tamed," Jhared growled, "but you're a beast with a beast's shallow feelings. You've forgotten what it is to be a man."

"On the contrary, I know exactly where the boundaries lie between beast and man. I just see no reason to fear crossing them." The waylayer took another drink. "You're the one who must cross a boundary now. Cross it and take up the secrets of the killing winds."

Jhared straightened. Here it was. "I won't touch their power."

Alende met his gaze. "It's no longer a request. You must."

"No. If the Shorn want to leave Avelos, they must find a way to do it without the threat of devastation."

"Blind as any of them," the waylayer hissed. His eyes caught the last of the light, and Jhared saw the rancor in them. "I'm not here for the tamed. I don't answer to them or do their bidding. There are more important stories before us than the ones Elian believes."

"Alende, I know they sent you to see that I either agree to give over the winds' secrets or that I can't go on to spill their own. I've been waiting for you."

"Give them the winds; don't give them the winds!" the man spat furiously. "They'll find another way to bleed this country if you don't come through. But do not mistake: I have no bond to Avelos and none to the tamed. No one claims me!"

Jhared stared at the unbalanced creature. "Then why?"

The waylayer's stance was rigid. With one hand he rubbed at the place over his heart. "Because I know what true chaos is. I have seen past the edges of reason and traveled to the places where the only reality is disorder. It's a horror you, with your sheltered life, can't imagine. And this woman who will travel with you, this creature of the dark, a blasphemy before Riana's altar, worships that chaos."

"The Bearer? Goddess, man, she's meant to be a terror. What good are her warnings otherwise?"

Alende laughed his beautiful, lonely laugh. "I have lived in the fetid corners with the outcasts. I know how she spends her nights among the waylayers. I have seen too many stories of her making. She owns the secrets of blood. She wants the winds for herself."

A pain stirred over Jhared's heart. He had the urge to press a hand to his chest; he resisted.

"Tell me what you've seen."

"I've seen the waylayers who turn to her embrace, desperate for a moment of escape from madness. The escape they find is blood-filled. I've seen their lifeless bodies after. She's searching for the strength to overthrow Riana's order, and those who do not fill her need do not survive to reveal her secrets."

"That's lunacy," Jhared said. "I've no reason believe you. You're unbound and she's a servant of Riana."

"She's the avatar of Cael! Can you tell me truly that you've never felt the demon's eyes upon you?"

The long vigil of his Becoming. A demon tempting him to betray his purpose. *I am Cael. I know you. I know the things you desire.* A shadow priestess watching by his bedside. *Will you be the one to walk the dark Paths?* He shook his head to clear it. They were only dreams and visions.

"Alende, what do you hope to gain from all this?"

"Gain?" the man snarled. "Because I did not sacrifice my heart to Avelos you think I have no heart to lose? Is it beyond your ability to conceive that I do not wish to see all the lands from the wilds to the great waters flung into disorder? This goes beyond the welfare of the Shorn and all our battles with Avelos."

Silence fell between them. Twilight turned Alende into a sculpture of black marble. In the darkness, Jhared began to see.

"You're not telling me to learn the secret of the winds. You're telling me to keep the secret from her."

Alende drank up the remains from his brandy flask. "If you still wish for day to follow night and spring to follow winter."

"And how do you think a bound Shorn man might do such a thing?"

The waylayer chuckled wryly. "A Shorn man who can lie to the face of a council elder, who can spy upon Forest Guard officers unseen, and who's willing to put a blade into the heart of a countryman? Such a *bound* man would find a way."

Jhared stood immobile. "No. I'll not be a tool for you to act on your drunken visions. Leave this holy place."

Alende lifted his head to the stars and released a long breath, like a night creature awakening. Jhared sensed anticipation in the man's still form.

"As you command," Alende murmured. He shrugged his cloak to the ground. Then he was moving.

He spun and leaped, as fast and as graceful as a mountain cat. His hunting knife flashed into his hand. The knife with foreign steel the shade of twilight. The knife it was forbidden to bear in the temple.

Jhared swore as the blade came at him. He used his right arm to block it, stopping Alende neatly at the wrist. Too high. With a flick of the man's hand, the knife sliced across the back of Jhared's forearm. Jhared inhaled sharply and followed his block with a left-fisted blow. His knuckles collided with the waylayer's chin, but his strength wasn't yet what it should have been. Alende blinked and shook off the impact like a hound shaking water from its coat.

With a growl of frustration, Jhared pulled out of range, casting about in search of a weapon. As Alende sprang again, he dropped to one knee, snatched up a broken branch from the ground, and swung it toward the waylayer's shins. Alende leaped the branch and landed above him. Panting with the effort, Jhared drove upright, whipping the branch around to catch the next strike of the blade. He missed the blade, but slammed into Alende's middle. The man coughed as the air rushed from his lungs. Jhared didn't wait, but swung a third time. The branch cracked against Alende's knife arm. The waylayer yelped in pained surprise as the knife flew from his fingers and fell into the dirt several paces away.

An instant of pause. Jhared's eyes locked onto Alende's. The man was at least ten years older, but they were of a size and weight. In the dusk, only Alende's bright hair and the green spirals on his cheeks distinguished him. Both of them had loved Mahla Denaban, and both of them had become pawns for Ziabela Marcalo. Alende had failed Avelos, but what road was Jhared walking now? Alende's green eyes reflected someone unchained and alone who longed to escape the borders that held him. Someone horrifyingly familiar. Jhared gritted his teeth.

"That's *not* who I am!"

Alende smiled knowingly. And dived for the knife.

Jhared dived after him. They landed in the dirt together. Alende's fingers found the hilt, but Jhared was on top and grabbed the man's wrist. They wrestled over the ground. Jhared pulled a knee beneath him and bore down on Alende's chest. Gasping for breath, the waylayer surrendered some of his hold on the blade to try to throw Jhared off. Jhared took the advantage, wrenching the man's arm backwards. The knife dropped out of his grasp. With a cry of victory, Jhared seized it and shoved it under Alende's chin.

"Ah, there it is," the waylayer said breathlessly as the knife tip dimpled his flesh. "You've the beast in you, after all. You could slay me now; I know how vile I am to you. But then, it's far safer for you to turn your hatred on me than on the ones who chain you, isn't it? What happens to the dog that bites its master, eh? A bit of poison meat? A blade across the throat?"

Alende glanced down at the blade against his own throat and laughed.

Jhared tightened his grip on the knife. Anger roared through him. "I loathe you because you didn't possess the strength to serve Avelos loyally and you didn't own the courage to die."

"Strength? Loyalty? You hardly understand what those words mean. Mahla knew. She owned all the courage her son lacks. Kill me now if you would do what the goddess did not. But first consider why you're willing to dismiss what I say: do you sincerely believe my words are false? Or is this the way you take vengeance upon your captors, by letting them face Cael's wrath? This decision is too important to be made through a veil of hatred, Jhared Denaban."

"Of course you're false! You're a waylayer who lies to men to drive them off their proper paths!"

"If you think I lie, then go ahead. Send the blade home." Alende lifted his chin for the knife. "Be brave enough to do it yourself. Don't leave it to the council. Prove your commitment to Avelos by slaying me."

Jhared's hand remained tense and still. He had seen the demon. She had come to him. Alende wasn't demanding the winds for himself or for Ziabela. What personal gain could he possibly win by telling Jhared to keep the winds from Cael's Bearer?

"Go on, boy! I see the dark hunter you are. All you need do is ignore my warning, and you'll spill the blood of your keepers. Allow the Bearer of Cael's Blade to claim the winds' secrets for herself and you'll bring chaos to our world. What glorious power that gives you! You must—Oh, Goddess. Goddess, mercy!"

Alende's voice twisted into a tortured moan. His body convulsed and his face went deathly grey. He shuddered with an intensity that Jhared thought would tear the man in two. Terror glazed his eyes, and his fingers scrabbled at the dirt as if to keep himself from falling off a cliff.

"Not now," the waylayer pleaded in a broken voice. "Riana, mercy!

"*Not now!*"

With a gasp, Alende reached forward and grabbed the knife hilt. Instead of ripping it from Jhared's grip, he held it fast, and with a vicious twist of his head, scored a bloody line across his throat. Jhared cried out in surprise. A wave of vertigo crashed over him, spinning him out over a chasm where the ground used to be. As he scrambled for balance, Alende wrenched himself upright and drove the knife into his own flesh once more.

Blue flame flashed across Jhared's vision. He might have fallen into unconsciousness for a span of heartbeats, or perhaps it was only the strange flare that blurred his thoughts. When he opened his eyes, Alende was panting hard beneath him, his eyes wide and wild, blood dripping from his throat. The waylayer clutched the knife.

"Soldier, where are you?" The woman's voice came from somewhere along the loggia. It was throaty and deep, the sound of crows cawing in the distance. "Jhared Denaban!"

Jhared flinched. Alende laughed madly. "Already? If she knows I've warned you against her, she'll find a way to be rid of you."

Jhared struggled to get himself upright. Freed from Jhared's weight, Alende flipped to his feet.

"Call out and I'll come for you!" The voice was moving closer. "I can help you!"

"You must choose," the waylayer hissed. "You could prove right now that you are truly Mahla's son."

Jhared glared at the man through the darkness. "Don't *ever* use my mother against me. You are caelevano. Be gone from this temple!" He took a tentative step toward the loggia, wondering if the ground would drop out from under him again.

"Here! I'm here," he called to the priestess in a strangled voice.

Alende smiled sadly. "Call me demon-touched if it comforts you. It won't change the reflection you see in the mirror. This isn't ended, boy. It can't be."

"Soldier?" Light footsteps pattered over stone and then onto dirt. Alende turned and fled toward the shadowed archway that led to the city center. Jhared fought the instinct to do the same. The priestess hurried toward him, her midnight robes fluttering behind her. As she entered the garden, one hand went to her side and she drew the long curved knife. Cael's Blade.

Jhared backed up several steps in alarm, until his heel found the knot of a large tree root and he stopped in the crisscrossed shadow of an oak. He thought he heard Alende's laughter. What were his choices against a servant of Riana?

"To die quickly under her Blade or attack her and die slowly at the hands of an Arionad," murmured a Teacher.

The heady scent of incense filled his lungs as she closed on him. With long-nailed fingers she grabbed his arm. As she stared up at his face, her eyes shone the deep blue of the false dawn. Reflexively he jerked free of her and lifted his hands. The knife rose.

"All right," she murmured. "I have you now, soldier. Do you know where you are?"

The tree limited his movement, but he sidled another wary step away from her. "Forgive me, Lady. I didn't mean to trespass. I thought the outer gardens were allowed to me."

She followed him, her expression perplexed. "Look at me, soldier. Are you well?"

"As well as any man who's confronting a naked blade."

She came to a halt, the curved knife still ready in her hand.

"Answer me this," she demanded. "Have you been wandering in places you should not?"

"No, Lady. At least…not intentionally." Apprehension edged his tone. She wanted something more; a hunger he didn't understand haunted her expression.

"No, of course. Not intentionally." She sighed. "I thought I felt a shift…but I must have been mistaken." Finally, she lowered the knife and slid it back into its place at her side. As it slipped into its sheath, the woman seemed to grow smaller. She shook her head and looked up at him. "You're a restless one, aren't you? Restless enough to slip your guard again."

Jhared cursed himself for his carelessness. Why hadn't he considered who it was that set the watch on him? "I'm sorry, Lady. I was only—"

"You were bored and thought you'd divert yourself by exploiting our men's weaknesses," she said. "You needn't be ashamed. No doubt the Arionade have learned a thing or two this week. You might, however, consider the wisdom of losing a guard intended to ward you when you've not the strength to ward yourself."

He stared at her. Her expression held no anger. In fact, he saw only an unexpected combination of amusement and concern.

"A ward? For the lowest Shorn soldier in the Forest Guard Fourth? You mock me, Lady."

"Not in this, Jhared Denaban." Her features grew more serious. "The temple is not a place of peace right now, and you are needed."

She had saved his life and now she guarded him with the temple's own men. "Why?"

"Because balance is essential if the mission we set upon is to succeed."

He cast a dubious glance in her direction. "I've never known a Shorn man to be considered a symbol of order."

She laughed. The sound was as complex and beguiling as her laughter in his dream, bubbling up from somewhere cool and dark. She possessed a cleverness that reminded him of Zia, but he sensed this priestess owned a far deeper understanding of the world.

"No, for certain not," she agreed. "But I've met your Lieutenant Sevar. We'll need no more order than what he brings to us. You and I offer something very different. Something overlooked for too long."

He held his breath, not knowing how to answer and afraid of what she would say next.

"Someone must walk the dark Paths," she finished. "Someone who knows his way amidst chaos."

The gleam at the edge of the archway caught Jhared's eye first. He didn't wonder at it; he knew the particular flash of starlight on steel. With that small flash, he understood the choice that towered suddenly before him. In a breath, she would be slain, the one who wanted him to walk the dark Paths. The demon from his nightmares. He need do nothing at all and she would be gone.

The knife flew.

"Lady, get *down!*"

He leaped forward, astonished to find the priestess dropping to the ground even as he threw himself in front of her. He heard the sigh of steel slicing air an instant before the blade bit his shoulder, knocking him backwards and clattering to the ground.

With a roar of disappointment, Alende hurtled into the garden. Jhared scrambled to regain his footing, flinging himself into the path of the waylayer.

"Arionade!" cried the priestess. "Betrayal in the gardens! We are attacked! Arionade!"

Jhared slammed into Alende with all the force of his anger. It barely halted the man. The waylayer drove a fist into Jhared's middle and twisted sideways to break for the Bearer. Wheezing for breath, Jhared could do nothing but cling like a street brawler. They grappled in the dark, Alende growling and spitting as he tried to tear his way free.

"Fool! She's marked you for her own. Let me do what's needed."

"I won't twice betray my oath," Jhared panted. He hooked one leg behind the man's ankle, yanked hard, and they both went down heavily beneath the tree. A root smashed against the base of Jhared's spine.

He knew he couldn't hold out for long. Alende battered and bit at him like an enraged beast, and Jhared's half-healed injuries betrayed him. It was frighteningly clear that Alende had been holding back during their earlier struggle; he had *allowed* Jhared to gain control of the knife. That meant something important, but Jhared couldn't think on it because Alende wasn't holding back now, and death gleamed in his eyes. The priestess called out again. From far away, men shouted. Booted footsteps pounded over stone. Jhared clutched at the waylayer like a lover: determined to keep him from the Bearer, determined to see him face the chains he had evaded for so many years.

"Not today," Alende hissed. "No man will put his binding on me today."

The waylayer wrenched back his fist. He knew Jhared's most vulnerable point, and his aim was true. The blow cracked against Jhared's ribs, just over the place where Kaliska's stitches still held him together.

Lightning blazed across the night. Jhared labored for breath. His limbs refused to obey him, and Alende was already retreating.

"To the Lady!"

"Hold the traitor!"

The garden filled with the ring of swords and the sharp voices of the guards. Jhared struggled for enough clarity to lever himself off the ground. The night reeled drunkenly.

"I said hold him!"

Unexpectedly, he *was* off the ground as two sets of hands yanked him upright and shoved him hard against the tree trunk. Air rushed from his body in a painful flare of red fire. His head was still spinning when he found himself with two swords pressed against his chest and the hate-filled gazes of two white-coats burning into him.

"Tezio! Yoel! Leave him be!"

"But, Lady, he—"

"By the shadow of Cael whose Blade I bear, stand down!" Even raised in anger, her voice did not go shrill, but kept its depth and power. Her words shook the very ground beneath Jhared, and he was glad to have the tree to support him. The burly Arionade, both grizzled with their years of service, flinched and lowered their swords.

The lady spun to the third guard who stood at her side. "The boy was *attacked* by one of the caelevano. One who even now escapes into the city. A golden-haired man with the mark of the waylayers on his cheeks. Commander Evorales, I will have this man before the altar."

The commander bowed. Uneasiness made his reverence look stiff. Jhared wasn't certain whether it was the Bearer or the waylayer that made the guard uncomfortable.

"You heard the will of the Lady!" he bellowed at his men. "After him! Take apart Shorn Circle, if you must."

The Arionade saluted smartly and hastened toward the archway. Two men so accustomed to the structure of walls had small chance of catching a creature as feral as Alende.

"He's injured," Jhared called to them hoarsely. "A slash across the throat. There'll be a blood trail." The guards paused, casting black looks at Jhared, then one relented, nodding before they both moved into the night.

"There should have been guards at the arch, Evorales," the priestess said, her shadowy gaze turning full on the commander once again.

"It's true, Lady," he answered nervously. "If I had the men for it. Most of us are in the city helping with the rescue and cleanup. The barracks are near empty. What guards I have are stupid with exhaustion."

The priestess pressed her lips together. "If a man isn't safe in Riana's own temple, then her servants aren't attending her adequately. See this Forest Guardsman to Madam Kaliska, then go to Captain Rom. Report what the lack of vigilance at the outer gardens has earned us and see that Tezio and Yoel receive what aid they need. This is important, Evorales. I tell you so with all the authority of a Bearer's warning."

In the starlight, the Arionad grew increasingly pale. "Yes, Lady. I'll see it done." He glanced at her with tentative concern. "And you'll let me see you safely to the sanctuary?"

Her smile was lovely, in the way that a starless sky or a bottomless pool is lovely. "I've protection enough here," she said, laying a hand on the Blade. "And I've my own tasks to attend to. Go now. See that the boy draws no more danger to himself. Darkness calls to darkness, and we need him with us."

The Arionad gave Jhared a sidelong look of aversion. "As you will, Lady."

He was not of the darkness. Jhared might have shouted it had he the breath. He had maintained his oath to preserve the priestess, and she didn't even realize that Alende had intended to kill her. She didn't recognize Jhared's effort, only the foulness of his blood.

Someone must walk the dark Paths.

He was tired, so very tired of the fear and suspicion that dogged him. The priestess, Alende, Sevar, Sarena, and even—though it hurt him to acknowledge it—even the Teachers within him knew the danger he could inflict upon Avelos. They knew him for a cunning hunter, an undisciplined beast, a weak-willed creature, without integrity or strength to resist the whims of desire. And after all, he had done more than enough to satisfy their visions.

A Shorn man who can lie to the face of a council elder, who can spy upon Forest Guard officers unseen, and who's willing to put a blade into the heart of a clansman?

A shudder ran through him at the memory of Alende's words and the mirror of the man's green gaze. He would not be that creature. He would not!

"Lady, wait!" He felt the Arionad's glare as he whirled to face the priestess. "Please don't go without an escort. The knife was meant for you. The waylayer wanted to reach *you*."

She startled, deep blue eyes widening, and darkness gathered in her expression. "How do you know this?"

He had made his decision irrevocably at the moment when he cried out to warn her. If he were wrong, she could end him with her Blade, but she had saved his life once already. Slowly and painfully, he inhaled.

"He came to the temple tonight to warn me that you mean ill to our world."

Behind him, steel hissed against leather and a sword poked forcefully at his back as the Arionad cried out, "Lady! Let me punish him for his heresy!"

"Stand fast, Commander." She held Jhared's gaze with unwavering intensity. "What else did he tell you?"

"That you should not be allowed to know the secret of the winds," Jhared said, feeling the icy steel against his fevered skin.

"Because I intend to use the winds to overthrow Riana and bring the Great Wars to our world once again? One of the demon-touched told you this?" She laughed softly, lifting her head to the skies. A breeze fluttered strands of black hair around her pale face. "Did you believe him?"

Jhared straightened. "What reason have I to do so?"

"Ah. I see. He was convincing, then." She stopped laughing and brought her eyes, vast as the sacred skies, to settle on Jhared's once more. "I could be dead now. You didn't have to warn me."

With a gasp, Jhared sank to his knees, feeling power surge around him as he had only ever experienced at his Becoming, and knowing himself unworthy to stand before it. Mysteries worked here that he longed to understand, but shouldn't even dream.

"Yes, Lady. I did," he said breathlessly. "I have shed blood and given my oath: your life held before my own. I will not be forsworn."

She made a small sound of surprise and stretched out her hand to lay it atop his head. As her cool fingers brushed his brow, a tremor ran through him. She smiled.

"What an unexpected treasure you are, Jhared Denaban. The Forest Guard should take better care not to lose you."

His heart kicked painfully against his chest.

Behind Jhared, the Arionad cleared his throat. "Lady, this changes things more than a bit. I need to get you into the sanctuary, and the captain needs to hear it right away. He's going to want to talk to the boy."

The Bearer of Cael's Blade looked up, her expression calm as twilight. "First to the healer. Then you and I will see to Captain Rom. I want no confusion about what this soldier has done here tonight."

"As you will, Lady." The guard gestured ahead as he glanced warily around the garden. "Quickly, now."

They found Madam Kaliska in her workroom near the infirmary. It was a large, high-ceilinged chamber with a desk at one end, a smoke-blackened fireplace at the other, a long table in the center, and shelves and shelves of scrolls and remedies along the walls. Sweet-herbed candles masked some of the rotten-vegetable odor of the restoratives she made, but not all. She gazed up at the three of them from the table where she was pouring a brown, viscous fluid through a funnel into vials. Curiosity flickered briefly in her grey eyes before her expression shifted to one of concern and she came to greet them.

The Bearer handed Jhared over to her. "Guard him well, Kaliska. He's done the work of an Arionad tonight."

When the priestess and the commander left to speak with Captain Rom, the healer pushed Jhared onto a stool and began at once to examine his wounds.

"I presume that the news of a knife in the gardens has something to do with these new injuries. Tell me what you've done. For good or ill, the attention of one of the most powerful women in Riana's service has settled on you."

Whatever the source of her information, it was speedy. If the news had already spread so far, no hope remained that Jhared could deny it. He told her.

"Ah, Alende," she sighed when he finished. "There's a spirit who's wounded beyond my ability to heal. You do know that he's unbalanced."

Jhared recalled the man rending his own flesh. "I know."

"You took a blade for our Lady Bearer?"

"There are things I must set to right. That was a start."

"The Lady spoke truly, then: it was the action of a sworn Arionad. No wonder the commander had daggers in his gaze for you."

"I'm Shorn. I'm no Arionad." Jhared shrugged out of her grip and got up from the stool to pace around the room. He had survived Alende's assaults, and the Bearer was safe, but other things must still be accomplished if he was to reclaim his oath. The urgency of it beat in his veins like the power he had sensed from the priestess in the garden.

"Madam Healer, I must ask you to send a message to Elian for me."

The healer laid the bandages in her hand onto the table and watched him pace, her features still.

"I know you have ways of reaching him," Jhared said. "Alende told me. I'm leaving Velantar soon, and there are things Elian must know."

"You mean to tell him about Alende."

"Yes."

"And that you'll deny what's been asked of you."

"Yes," he said more quietly. And at least one thing more, if he could convince her to carry the letter.

Sorrow drew across her face, deepening the lines there. An old sorrow, this one; he hadn't seen it before, so well hidden it was beneath her limpid gaze.

"They will die trying to leave Avelos, you know. With no strength to back them, they'll be hunted down and slain."

Zia's image floated to Jhared unbidden: her lips warm against his skin; her spicy scent filling his head; the weight of her body curled around his. He strode to the fireplace and threw his gaze upon the flames that danced there—such a beautiful, dangerous thing, fire. Riana's most precious gifts were always dangerous, Kaliska had told him.

"The *killing winds?*" he pleaded. "There is no benign use for them. They would tear apart all we know."

"Elian would not use such a weapon unless forced to it. Unless given no other choice."

Jhared turned. "It is his *choice* to be forsworn! If they would forsake Avelos, let them first make reparation!"

"Reparation?" She sank onto the stool and gazed up at him. "Oh, Jhared, you have been cruelly bound to an impossible task. The Shorn have already paid in blood. I've seen it, for that blood is on my own hands. Your blood." She lifted her capable, roughened fingers. "How can you not embrace what they offer you?"

It was the second time she had asked the question. This time he didn't let it overwhelm him. He had answers for her in plenty: he could tell her how well he understood his own weaknesses, and what a danger he was if he abandoned the oath that made him whole. He could tell her of his forbidden desires never fully subdued, of a knife wielded in hatred, and the pull toward self-destruction. But those things did not touch the heart of the truth.

It wasn't fear that made his choice for him now; he didn't find the answers in Zia's passion or the darkness of his yearning. Instead, he found them in the earnest smiles of a man who risked himself over and over, the blue gaze of a woman who struggled with terror, and the trust of a boy who gave his heart freely, all so an orphaned Shorn child might not be left alone in the world.

"Because I have been loved," he told her. "And I love. And to that bond I must, in the end, be true."

She studied him a long while, her left hand fingering one of the vials on the table. Jhared wondered if she knew what his next steps must be and if she was considering the value of silencing him, after all. Then he saw the trails of silver down her cheeks and knew his thoughts unfair.

"I will send your note to Elian," she said. "You will write it, seal it, and put it into my hand before you leave this room."

"Thank you, madam."

She gave him ink and paper from one of the many drawers in the polished wooden desk and allowed him the silence to work. Even so, it was a chore to select the right words. Micah had known him truly: fear of taking the wrong step had too long kept him from moving at all. Now that he dared go forward, terror and regret thrilled through him, but also a deep sense of the necessity of his decision.

Afterward, the sealed letter lay between them like a chasm.

"You'll see it reaches Elian and no other?"

"As soon as I'm able." She slipped the letter into the depths of her desk, then returned to the worktable. She picked up two of the newly sealed vials and held them out to him.

"They're not Silvaye, but they'll give your body some of what it needs to heal."

He took them, murmuring his thanks, and moved stiffly toward the door.

"Don't close your heart to her," Kaliska called. "Zia may yet offer something to help you understand who you are and where you come from."

He met the healer's gaze. "I come from those who spilled the blood of innocents," he said. "Whether they were moved by love or hatred, they betrayed our country all the same."

Kaliska sighed and closed her eyes. He couldn't know what emotion might have clouded her gaze as he departed. "Farewell, Jhared Denaban. I hope you find some peace before the end."

25.
FINAL REPARATION

The quiet in the Arionade barracks was broken only by the sound of men muttering through their dreams. A white-coat sat at a table, mending his uniform by the wan light of a single lamp. He lifted his head to watch as Jhared passed.

Bone weary, but still with one more task to complete, Jhared padded to the bunk where Anzo snored under a heap of blankets. Carefully, he nudged the sleeping patrolman.

"Nevia?" he whispered.

With a grunt, the man rolled over, and opened one eye. "Sahiste's invaded?"

"No."

"Barracks on fire?"

"No. I...Anzo, I must ask a favor of you."

The little veteran grimaced. "Boy, you're not the one I'm going to be giving favors to in the night. Understand me?"

Jhared sighed. "I'm sorry for this. I know I'm already in your debt, but you're the only one I can think to ask."

"All right. All right." Anzo yawned, then sat upright, blinking and scratching at his stubbled chin. "I'm up. What's this about?"

Jhared crouched to meet the patrolman's gaze. This would be the hardest step of all. "I must speak with the Minster of the Teaching, but they've tethered me to the temple grounds. I need someone to go to Elders' Hall and ask for him."

"Ah, boy. You don't want to do that. Nothing but trouble for you there."

"Probably," Jhared admitted. "But we'll be leaving soon and we don't know when or if we'll return. I have things that need to be said."

The veteran looked skeptical.

"He was a father to me, Anzo. If you had the chance, wouldn't you leave your kin with the truth between you?"

Anzo snorted. "Believe me, boy, the truth is the most troublesome of all."

"Please. I've nothing much to offer in exchange, but whatever you ask of me, you'll have it."

"Hush that talk." The old patrolman waved a hand in the air. "You needn't go selling your spirit for it. I suppose I could wander over to Elders' Hall. Never had a reason for it before." He frowned at Jhared. "They'd let a scruffy old clansman like me in the door?"

"Act as though you know what you're about and you're unlikely to be questioned. If the guards stop you, tell them you carry an urgent message for the Minister of the Teaching from the Teachers of Ovelia and Luela."

Anzo gave him a bemused look.

"Two of Father's favorite historians." Jhared smiled a little at the old jest. "It's the wording he gave to his family should any of us need to reach him when the council is in session. You'll go tomorrow?"

"I'd better. Like as not we'll be on our way soon."

"I can't easily repay you for this."

"It's going to be a long journey," the man said, grinning. "I'm sure there'll be something you can do for me."

The knot of lies and evasions that constricted Jhared's heart loosened a little, and he drew an easier breath. The veteran waved him off and flopped back into his blankets. By the time Jhared returned to his own bunk, the man's snores rumbled through the hall.

No hope of sleep remained for Jhared, but he found an unexpected respite in moving forward with his decision, even if the outcome loomed uncertain and frightening. It wasn't for men to know all the consequences of their actions or all the ways that the road would fork.

Only Riana and her servants held the map to the Paths.

Word came the following day, just after noon: Carn's patrol would leave the city on the morrow to hunt a ward against the killing winds.

A cheer rang out in the Arionade barracks so loudly it surely echoed all the way to the sanctuary. Not only the Forest Guard cheered; the Arionade who had been toiling in the devastated city had gained a new understanding of the importance of the hunt. For a few moments, they sheathed their resentment that none of their number would protect the Holy Bearer of Cael's Blade on the journey, and Riana's guards and Rumar's soldiers shared cautious good humor and exchanged blessings for the company's success.

"I've never been to the north," Jase said, taking a drink from one of the wineskins being passed through the hall. "They say the women there know how t'keep a man warm on a cold night. Can't be so bad."

"Better hope that's the truth, 'cause it gets cold as Cael's hole in the Sandien Mountains." Twitch tugged the wine from Jase's hand. "And when you're not battling ice storms and blizzards, you're looking out that Cael's Chosen don't sink their teeth in you. The Verael hunt human flesh on moonless nights." Twitch drank from the skin and handed it to Esran.

"What do ya think, bowman?" Jase asked Jhared. "Ya going t'shoot yourself one'a Cael's dogs, like Arion's archer?"

"Not if he wants t'live t'tell the tale," Esran interjected, his blond head peering around Twitch. "Ya don't hunt the Ael if ya want t'keep body and spirit together."

"No matter," Twitch said, grinning. "From what I hear, Denaban's going to sign on as an Arionad. Dedicate himself to the Bearer of the Blade."

Quiet suddenly smothered the lively mood of the little group. Jase let out a low whistle and studied his boots. Esran cleared his throat.

Twitch glanced at them and frowned with disappointment. "Aw, you boys need to buy a sense of humor. Not even the Bearer's going to take on one'a the cursed now, is she?"

"Just as well," Esran muttered, "'cause I'm not sure which'd be worse on your heels, Cael's dogs or Cael's Bearer."

"She's a priestess of Riana and we're in the Lady's temple, so have a care," Jhared said. He wasn't clear himself which was worse. He gave them all a shrug— "I've things to do before we leave"—and walked away. It wasn't the Bearer he worried about just now. Finally, they would be on their way out of the city, but one more thing must be done before he left. The hardest thing.

And Anzo hadn't yet returned from Elders' Hall.

The messenger didn't come to him until sunset: not Madam Kaliska or the Bearer, but a somber young novice with an Arionad behind her. Jhared recognized the ruddy-cheeked girl from his Becoming. On the night of his vigil, the haughty pride of the newly anointed had glimmered in her expression. Now, nothing haughty remained in her features. Doubt and weariness eclipsed the zeal in her pale blue eyes. He wondered how her life had changed since the day they met, also at sunset, nearly two seasons ago. He wondered if, like him, she had discovered that fulfilling her oath of service was a complex and uncertain business.

"Jhared Denaban of the Forest Guard, you've a visitor," she announced as the Arionad glared silently over her shoulder. "You'll follow me."

"Is it—"

"One of the high chieftain's advisors. My lady has permitted him the hospitality of a receiving room to speak with you." She looked up and down at Jhared, her eyes flickering briefly over the place where the bandages that wrapped his shoulder made a lump under his shirt. "Perhaps you'd care to make yourself...presentable?"

A dry comment came quickly to Jhared's lips, but she didn't look in the mood for his wit, so he only bobbed his head and hurried to wash his face, draw a comb through his hair, and rebind the length of it into a warrior's tail. The preparation gave him a few more moments to consider the step he was about to take. A part of him already sang with the release the truth would bring. The weight of all he hadn't told Tierzen exhausted him, and though the telling would be painful, it would free him to recommit to his oath with a clear heart.

As he returned to the priestess, he smiled and gave her a full, proper bow. She accepted it tight-lipped and turned to lead him to Elder Trianor. They left the Arionade's quarters through the high arched doorway with the sculpture of Arion's Commitment before it. Jhared brushed his hand reverently over Arion's bowed shoulder before following the girl down the loggia. They strode silently into passages that curved around the sanctuary toward the east wing of the compound not far from the high priestess's tower. The carved walls on the east side of the temple told the stories of Avelos, just like the walls in the barracks, but so many of the major works were cut away that no story remained intact. The damage appeared oddly precise and deliberate. As Jhared looked at them, he knew that at least part of Elian's claim was true: Tumal had purged the country of the Avelune's understanding of the past. How not? He had purged the country of the Avelune.

Somewhere to the right, a man groaned in anguish. For a heartbeat, it seemed no more than a reflection of Jhared's thoughts, then his attention flew back to the moment. He followed on the priestess's heels as the passage turned. Halfway down the hall, Lieutenant Sevar leaned against a door with his eyes closed and one hand still clenched around the latch. At the sound of approaching feet, he straightened rapidly. Jhared caught the lieutenant's devastated expression an instant before a mask of fury dropped back into place.

"You were ordered to speak with him," Sevar ground out. "In my company you do not evade the consequences of insubordination. There will be a price for it."

"Sir, I—"

"Don't," the lieutenant interjected. "I've heard every excuse your kind can give. In the end, it's always the same: those who care for you pay for your weaknesses." Averting his wind-scarred face, Sevar turned and strode toward the opposite end of the hall, his boots rapping against the stone.

Dread dived for Jhared. He ran, pushing past the priestess and the Arionad, down the final stretch of hallway. The heavy door burst open under his weight and he flung himself into the room.

"Father, are you all right?"

The last of the sun's rays bled through a set of large windows and across the chamber. Jhared sensed vaguely that it was a place meant for order: chairs neatly organized around a fireplace, thick square rugs placed equidistant from the walls, nothing dusty, nothing out of place. Nothing but the broken expression in his father's eyes. Tierzen stood near a table, his back to the light. He looked up slowly.

"Oh, Jhared. You didn't tell me. Why didn't you *tell me?*" The elder never raised his voice. Not in the heat of council debate. Not in the throes of anger. Not even now. He simply stared with the shocked disbelief of a soldier who has just realized that his enemy's sword has opened his gut.

Jhared moved instinctively toward his father, wanting to bear him up and beg forgiveness. He stopped abruptly in the center of the room. His Teachers didn't touch him. Never but the once, on that rainy day when his mother's pyre burned and he was left with no one to claim him.

"I put the histories in your hands," Tierzen continued tiredly. "I gave you the knowledge you needed to understand temptation and defeat it. *Why?*"

"I was afraid to tell you all the ways I failed," Jhared whispered, "when I knew you were waiting to hear them."

"No!" Tierzen cried. "I've always shown you my confidence and trust. All these years I put the fate of our family in your hands. The fate of my..." The elder paused. His fist opened and clenched again, revealing a silver sphere that flashed in his palm. Finally, the weight of his thoughts seemed too much to bear and he sank into a chair beside the table.

"Ah, Goddess. You have indeed learned to see through veils, Jhared. Of course I doubted. The work we did together was untried, and in the end, we both know what you are. I could only hope for you to stay true. By the Lady, how I hoped."

Despite years of Tierzen's brave support, he had always expected Jhared to fail. It was a truth neither of them had ever dared voice, although in some way Jhared had always known it. Despair closed around his heart.

"Father," he croaked. "I stumbled, but I've not turned from the path you hoped for me."

"You have studied Anarava's arguments since you were twelve, Jhared. You know the ways that small deceits build the foundation for a tower of lies. Yet you concealed all this from me—the little failures and the large. How did it happen? Did I give you too much room to question what I taught? Was that my error?"

"No, sir," Jhared breathed. "It was my own cowardice. I wanted to repair my mistakes before I came to you. Somehow I thought..." He trailed off. He wanted to cry out against the unfairness of it. All his plans to confess his evasions to Tierzen would mean nothing now. The elder would see a confession as an attempt to buy himself free of his guilt. Even worse, if Jhared spoke all he had meant to, Tierzen would only see *more* evidence of Jhared's deception. How could he speak of Alende and not raise suspicion about himself? A terrible trap shut on him, and there was no escaping it intact. He had come to speak honestly with his father, and instead, he would be forced to leave with more lies between them. It was the only way to make Tierzen see he was still bound to Avelos and to his family.

Then again, perhaps he couldn't afford the comfort of convincing Tierzen he remained true; perhaps he must wield the truth and accept what came of it. A letter was already on its way to Elian. He had offered the man a bargain, and he needed to prove that his words had teeth.

Someone must walk the dark Paths.

Tierzen's thin figure bowed like a wheat stalk in the wind. Streaks of grey dulled his golden head. This summer of conflict and destruction had aged him.

"I fear for you, my boy," he said thickly. "I don't know what direction you're heading. You earned the enmity of an unforgiving man when you defied Matio Sevar."

Jhared went to the window and stared out over Velantar. As the sun dropped beneath the world, torches flickered to life along the walls, outlining the city with yellow light. If he looked closely, he could see the City Guardsmen at their posts, staring outward, as he did, toward the wilds. At one time, the walls had defined his world and meant safety from all that was foreign and dangerous; then the forbidden urges of the Avelune heated his blood and the walls came to mean constraint and torment. His control of the urges remained imperfect, and it was only because of Tierzen Trianor he had survived at all. If the elder hadn't taken him in, he might have been...Alende.

"Father, do you ever think about the Shorn who failed the Becoming?"

It was a long moment before Tierzen answered. He voice was subdued. "Of course I do."

"Do you ever wonder if you could have done something to help them survive?"

"Every single day. The schooling of each of them lay in my keeping. I knew their names and their families and the Teachers into whose hands I entrusted them."

Jhared kept his face to the window. "They were born of traitors' blood, and they proved themselves incapable of loyalty. Why do you take their failures upon yourself?"

Tierzen sighed. "Because a way *must exist* for the Teaching to counter that bad blood." The elder paused, his voice dropping lower. "I just haven't found it yet."

Jhared winced. Slowly, he turned to face his foster father. "Sir, some of those unbound Shorn still live."

The color drained from Tierzen's face. "How do you know?"

Even now, Jhared couldn't tell all. That was the bargain he offered Elian: so long as the group ceased striving for a means to destroy Avelos, Jhared would keep silent about the conspiracy shaped in Isella's inn. So long as no more manipulations of authority roused the people to anger, as at Panetar, no one would hear the names of the conspirators from Jhared's lips. The unbound, however, could not be shielded. They were anathema, and Elian and the others must see that Jhared owned the will to protect Avelos.

"A man came to the temple with a waylayer's spirals and venomous words against Cael's Bearer. When he tried to attack her, I fought him. He was Shorn. Unbound."

"You defended a priestess from a man who failed the Becoming?"

Jhared forced his hands to remain unclenched at his sides. "Yes."

"And you have reason to guess that more of these unbound ones exist?"

"Yes, sir. I believe a number of them live in the wilds, although others may lurk in Velantar itself."

Tierzen opened his fingers and flipped the sphere over his hand. As the coin caught the light, Jhared saw the elder working through the implications of what had been said and forming hypotheses about what hadn't. The coin stopped. Tierzen looked at Jhared.

"Will you tell me why you suspect this is so?"

Here was the point that Jhared most dreaded, the part that would either condemn him or absolve him. "If I do not tell you, will you trust that my purpose is to ensure the safety of Avelos?"

Silence tiptoed into the darkening room. Jhared stood very still. Tierzen rubbed a hand over his face wearily.

"Offer another choice."

Jhared forced himself to meet his foster father's gaze. "Send me to the council to be interrogated."

Tierzen choked. "I could! I could do it, Jhared! I've never made exceptions for you."

"I know, sir. And I ask for no exceptions now. All I ask is that you lend me your trust once more."

"Always you are asking. Since the day you first came to me for the Teaching. I hoped that after your Becoming you would accept more and question less, but it seems that's not to be."

The disappointment in his Teacher's eyes nearly dropped Jhared to his knees. "I do intend to keep my oath."

Quiet fell. Muffled noises came from the hall: a low voice inquiring, the guard's deeper answer, footsteps retreating from the door.

"In all these years, your intentions are the thing I have never doubted," said the elder eventually. "Anarava would call me a fool, but I always believed that your intentions would lead you right in the end. Very well, Jhared. I will take what you've given me and not press for what you will not say. I do this only because I know what you *want* to be."

In a rush, Jhared let out the breath he hadn't realized he was holding. Tierzen had given him one last gift.

"I'll see you don't bear the cost of it, sir."

"Every decision comes at a price, son, if only that choosing one thing means you never have the chance to know the outcome of another. I made this decision. I'll bear its cost. Just be certain you understand what you have chosen."

Jhared hesitated before nodding.

From across the room, the elder slid his chair away from the table, rose, and walked toward him. Jhared looked down into the eyes of his beloved foster father. Exhaustion and worry chiseled lines into the elder's gentle features.

"I'm sorry," Jhared murmured. "You have so much to face in the council now, and I've done nothing but lay more trouble at your feet."

"Don't," Tierzen chided him quietly. "You've given me something I needed to know. And the council has settled somewhat since the winds."

"How is that?"

"The high chieftain has decided not to open the border for Sahiste. He has accepted that he cannot push the clans so far right now. By refusing, he'll keep the support of his primary allies, and may even win back the west. Abrigado won't have the numbers he needs to invoke the Law of Integrity."

Tierzen's disappointment that the borders wouldn't open was evident, but Jhared felt only relief. Without the open border, the high chieftain would be in less danger of losing his rule, Tierzen would earn a reprieve from Abrigado's scheming, and Sahiste would not be forgiven her crimes.

"We'll face Sahiste's anger for this," Jhared murmured.

"Yes," Tierzen agreed. "It could very well mean war. General Orn will be ordered to withdraw the bulk of his troops from the north to fortify Ravia and Barlona."

"And while my comrades guard the border, I'll be wandering in the Sandien Mountains."

"Don't regret it, Jhared. You have important work to do." Tierzen made a face. "After what you've shared with me, it's good you'll be crossing the Sandien."

"I understand," Jhared replied. By the time the council demanded that he be questioned, he would be far from Velantar.

The elder reached out and clapped a hand to Jhared's good shoulder, the one that marked his binding. Jhared tensed, taken by surprise, before accepting his foster father's secure grip. He recalled a smoky pyre, a cold lonely rain, and the elder's fingers around his, an unspoken reassurance that he would not be abandoned.

Dawn crept into Velantar on silent grey feet, spreading a blanket of fog across the city. The stable yard smelled of horses and damp hay. Now and again, Jhared caught the stomach-turning scent of smoke from the massive pyres that still smoldered outside the walls.

The torches around the yard threw restless shadows over the stable hands moving about the pack animals. Jhared heard Lieutenant Sevar's deep voice and Commander Carn's quick responses from somewhere along the pack line as the officers made a final check of the provisions. Behind him, Jase's easy laughter rang out, Grion grumbled at Bevan, and Anzo chuckled as they tacked up their mounts and saw to their saddlebags.

Jhared tightened the girth on his saddle gently, and the mare stamped a leg in warning. He stroked her sleek flank and murmured her name. *Seravina*, the boy who gave her over said it was. *Sweet life* in ancient Velos. She switched her tail at his touch and uttered a long, irritable whicker. Someone in the temple had an odd sense of humor.

If there was no sweetness in her, she was beyond a doubt a gorgeous animal: her glossy coat gleamed the color of the mist. Where Brio had been deep-chested and stocky, she was slender and elegant. Her small head tossed on a finely arched neck. Her long, clean legs pulverized clods of dirt as she fretted. She was no mixed-blood border horse, but a southern courser, and her pure breeding showed in her conformation and carriage: she looked down upon Jhared dubiously, flicking her delicate ears.

"Sorry if you're disappointed," he muttered. "We're likely to be stuck with each other for a while, so let's make the best of it, shall we?"

She snorted and tugged impatiently in response.

Commotion at the entrance to the stable yard caused the mare to freeze, head up and ears pricked. Jhared tightened his hand on her lead to prevent her from bolting as a company of Arionade marched in, boots thudding against the ground, white coats glowing in the half-light. With no spoken order, they parted ranks to take up positions all the way around the yard. Revealed within their center were two young acolytes carrying lamps that swung from slender chains, followed by the Lady of Avelos and her Arionad.

Silence shrouded the men. As though controlled by the same string, all the grooms and stable hands offered a reverent spiral. Jhared and his patrol followed more awkwardly, with Lieutenant Sevar at the last offering only a gesture of acknowledgment.

Light from the lamps on either side of Lady Nemiah shone through the edges of her white cloak and gleamed in her golden hair, making her appear translucent. She lifted her hands to draw two spirals of blessing, and the torches flared more brightly. Somebody beside Jhared gasped.

"The journey you begin today has been mapped through the greatest of Riana's mysteries," called the lady, her imperious voice cutting cleanly through the fog. "It will lead you along difficult roads. Look for the lights she gives you to guide your way. Keep her order and you shall not be overwhelmed. You are soldiers of Avelos and the battle you fight is against Cael himself. Bring back a ward against the demon, so Riana will not be overthrown and her people will flourish.

"By the holy ways may you travel."

"And by the ways may we return!" shouted the Arionade.

Seravina shied, and Jhared allowed her to dance out her nervous energy in a tight circle. A wave of warmth beat against his chest, and his muscles hummed until he was as ready to run as the mare.

The high priestess lowered her arms and wrapped them around herself. Lieutenant Sevar approached the lady, while everyone else in the yard returned to their tasks with a will. As conversation started again, even the mists seemed a little thinner. A shadow glided closer to the high priestess, obscuring one of the swinging lamps at her side. After a moment, Jhared realized it was the Bearer, cloaked and cowled in midnight. He surveyed the stable yard, taking the measure of the Arionade at their posts. He wondered where Alende was.

"Lieutenant," Lady Nemiah began, "with the Bearer under attack from an enemy of unknown strength, she must have her own guard. I am sending a pair of Arionade with your company. She will be their only priority."

Now that the glamour of the prayer had faded, the high priestess looked small and delicate; Jhared remembered that from his Becoming. With a shiver, he also remembered the surge of pain awakened by her gaze. As she turned her eyes to Lieutenant Sevar, they shone with preternatural brilliance, but the hand she laid on the arm of her stern-featured Arionad trembled. She seemed a fragile shell lit by a power from within. Jhared feared she might shatter, like an alabaster lamp burning too high.

"No," the lieutenant answered, with an intense stillness his men knew. "It is the high chieftain's will that the priestess who bears the Blade comes with us. So be it. But the only men in this company are sworn to Adan Rumar and follow *my* order. I'll not have temple-bound bodyguards confusing things. Confusion like that is deadly."

The black-haired Arionad beside the lady tensed in a way that suggested he wanted an excuse to draw a blade. Lady Nemiah's hand tightened on his arm.

"The Bearer of Cael's Blade rides on this journey because I have seen that she will be needed," the high priestess said calmly. "She must not be risked. Not for any man's pride, Lieutenant."

The slender shadow beside Lady Nemiah offered them all one of her starless-sky smiles. "My lady, no Bearer ever needed more protection than the hand of Riana and the Blade of Cael. Let the Arionade keep their rightful places at the temple. I have no fear on my own."

"You will be traveling among Forest Guard warriors accustomed to facing any form of threat," Sevar replied. "You will hardly be on your own, Lady."

"Not good enough." The high priestess turned to the Bearer. "Threats exist no man has yet seen, Leita. Bloody Paths lie ahead."

The Lady of Avelos swayed. Instantly, her Arionad moved to support her. Jhared leaned a hand against Seravina as lightheadedness made a pinwheel of the world. His struggle with Alende had done nothing to aid his healing.

The Bearer set her own hand over the high priestess's, but her gaze flicked toward Jhared.

"Lieutenant Sevar," she said softly, "the sword of the Shorn belongs to the high chieftain, but his oath is as much to Riana as to Avelos, is it not?"

Sevar's lip curled in an expression that might have been a smile or a grimace. "True enough, Lady."

"And your Shorn boy has proved his worth to the goddess already," said the Bearer. "Make him my guard and you need not worry over Arionade or unknown threats."

The lieutenant met the Bearer's gaze, his sharp eyes appraising her. His ambivalent expression settled into a forbidding smile.

"Denaban!" he barked over his shoulder.

An abyss opened between the place where Jhared stood with his patrolmates and the circle where Sevar spoke with the priestesses. All around him, his patrol went silent; they had been listening, too.

"I'll hold the horse," Anzo murmured, slipping Seravina's reins from Jhared's hand. "Better move."

The lieutenant scowled as Jhared approached and snapped a salute. "Since you have nothing more to do than eavesdrop upon the conversations of your superiors, Denaban, you're aware of the order I'm about to give you."

The abyss grew deeper. "Yes, sir."

"Good. You will see to the needs of the Bearer of Cael's Blade on this journey. Should we face danger, your duty is to see to her protection."

"As ordered, sir."

Sevar gave a nod to the high priestess. "This Shorn soldier is bound to defend your Lady Bearer unto death. No more could you ask from any temple man."

Lady Nemiah stared at Jhared until he felt himself tumbling into the center of her preternatural strength. "Keep her safe," the priestess commanded, her voice resonating with power. The events of the next moments blurred into overlaid images, as though he watched them through a prism. A myriad high priestesses turned and agreed reluctantly with a myriad lieutenants. A myriad Bearers embraced Lady Nemiahs, their faces torn with a myriad emotions. Blue-red light swirled around Jhared, leading him away from the scene, across an expanse of nothingness, toward a bright boundary.

Pain, sharp and sudden, burned away that boundary. Jhared looked down, startled to find the Bearer's hand digging into his forearm where Alende's blade had found its mark. It was the second time she had touched him. The lieutenant was striding off toward other tasks; the high priestess and her Arionade had gone.

"I'm sorry, Lady. I…" He shook his head. "I'm sorry. May I help you to horse?"

The priestess released him. "Yes. You need to be moving."

Her mare was a blood bay, a courser like Seravina, although neither as tall nor as evil-eyed. The beast whickered familiarly at the priestess as they approached, and the Bearer crooned back sweetly.

"She's a fine hunter," Jhared said, searching for safe conversation. "But we'll be climbing through the mountains. Rough terrain compared to what she's accustomed to in the valley."

"Arania is a daring creature," the priestess replied, patting the animal's withers. "No need to worry, she'll keep up with your Forest Guard mounts."

"No doubt." Jhared let the mare snuffle at his hand. "Though you needn't burden her with so much baggage. The pack animals would take these." He gestured toward several bundles behind the mare's saddle and a cloth-covered, rectangular basket snuggled against her left shoulder. The basket made a whirring sound.

The Bearer smiled indulgently. "The Forest Guard may be accustomed to dealing with any form of threat, but I don't think you're accustomed to traveling with a woman in your midst. I'll just keep a bit of privacy for myself. Arania doesn't mind."

Jhared flushed. "Of course, Lady."

At any other time, he would have found a way to flee, but from now on, wherever she went, he went. It was a new bond he did not desire but would have to manage. Together, they led Arania to the edge of the yard, where Anzo was deep in conversation with Seravina.

"Well now!" cried the Everen clansman, turning to grin at Jhared and the priestess. "What a fine filly you've been gifted with, boy."

The ironic expression that carved the little patrolman's features made Jhared glare at the man. Anzo's grin broadened, but his bow to the Bearer as he left them was entirely proper.

If the Bearer felt any discomfort under the stares of the men around her, her infinite calm revealed nothing. With a keen blue gaze, she watched the final preparations. She watched the horses. She watched Jhared.

"Your mother in the sacred skies must be proud of you, soldier."

Jhared stiffened. What could she know? He forced himself to look at her. "Lady?"

"You made promises once," she whispered, "at the cusp of a dawn as uncertain as this one, and here you are near to fulfilling them."

"As you say, Lady." He remembered the demon at his Becoming vigil, a voice like the sound of crows in the distance. *Her* voice. His face heated at the recollection of his own bravado: *I will be the one who makes complete the Shorn promise with final reparation. I will fulfill the debt.* Promises made when he thought he knew what reparation meant.

"Does final reparation no longer compel you?" the priestess asked.

"I cannot say, Lady. I'm no longer certain what it is or even if it exists."

The heresy came out of his mouth so easily that he didn't realize the significance of what he said until it was too late.

"Riders up!" Commander Carn bellowed across the yard. All around, men leaped to the saddle. Grooms ran down the pack line, checking the security of baggage and leads one last time. Horses whinnied; a small pack of temple hounds raced across the yard.

Jhared offered his cupped hands for the lady's knee. She accepted silently. The black hilt of Cael's Blade caught the torchlight when she settled astride.

From somewhere in the yard, tangled among all the other noises, Jhared thought he caught his name. A low call muffled by the fog. He went still, listening.

"Jhared Denaban? I'm looking for Patrolman Denaban."

On the other side of the yard, a slight figure appeared outside the reach of the torchlight, someone moving uncertainly among the stable hands and soldiers.

"Bran?"

The boy whipped his gaze toward the front of the milling company. "Jhared?" He bounded across the yard, ducked under the tethers of the pack animals, and hurried up the line. His gaze darted back and forth as he tried to identify riders in the near dark.

"Branlen, here!" Jhared caught his brother by the shoulders and swung him around.

"Oh!" The boy's gaze went wide. "I didn't think I'd find you!"

"What's happened? What are you doing here?"

"It's all right," the boy panted. "I mean, father only told me last night you were leaving. We hadn't said goodbye, and I still had this." Branlen opened his fist. On his palm lay their little stone talisman. The ancient, silvery face smiled mysteriously. "I know it's silly, but I couldn't let you leave without it. I couldn't."

Jhared picked up the stone. It was warm from his brother's grasp. He had never left the city without their ritual exchange—such a small thing, yet somehow it made visible the depth of their connection.

"Let all of Riana's spheres hear my plea: keep Jhared Denaban safe from harm." Branlen looked up and caught Jhared's gaze. "You're going to stop the killing winds," he said, his voice catching.

As the torchlight flickered over them, Jhared searched his brother's face. The boy's pale features were still shadowed with bruises and his hands were covered with scabs. Beneath the unsullied faith in Branlen's eyes shone fear, the fear of a child who had seen his own death. The killing winds had left their mark.

Jhared gripped the boy more tightly. "We will find a way to stop them, Bran. I promise it."

The boy lifted his chin and offered a brave smile. "I know you will."

Behind Jhared, the priestess's mare sidled closer. Commander Carn was roaring the order to move out. Jhared hugged his brother one last time, then stepped free and swung into the saddle.

Lieutenant Sevar's dun stallion bugled into the bleak morning as they started on their way. Several of the other horses joined the chorus. The Forest Guard soldiers let out a whoop that echoed off the temple walls and into the beaten city. Hooves clip-clopped on stone.

"You see, final reparation does exist," the Bearer said quietly. "It exists for you, Jhared Denaban. A man can create his own Path, and you have chosen this one. It exists because you made it so, in spite of your doubt. You did not have to make that promise to your brother. Just as you did not have to warn me."

With a smile at the corner of her lips, she turned in the saddle to gaze toward the mist-veiled giants of the Parnas Mountains hulking beyond the city walls. The Parnas would be their first challenge; after that lay Aven Plains, and far beyond the plains stood the Sandien Mountains and an ancient temple where they might find a ward against the killing winds.

Behind Jhared, the patrol took up a traveling song, one of the standards about the hero Alende Isan and the migration. It was a song about perseverance. Jhared glanced over his shoulder, knowing Branlen remained there watching through the fog and would see him looking back. He clasped the small grey stone in his fist.

As the company trotted across the city center, singing boldly, Alende Isan's monument rose out of the fog. From where Jhared sat, the scarred hero looked larger than life but not infallible. Alende had lost their ancestral home to Cael's fire, but with the strength of his loyalty, faith, and will he led the first-clans safely to the land that became Avelos.

Loyalty. Faith. Will. The challenges carved in the stone at the hero's feet meant more to Jhared now that he understood how dearly he must pay to keep them. He understood also that he would keep them.

High upon Alende's shoulder, shrouded in the mist, a creature stirred. A raven's low cry fractured the fragile morning as dark wings spread and caught the air. A shadow arrowed through the fog, then the raven was soaring toward the open skies.

Heat shot through Jhared's veins, and his pulse pounded out the meaning of longing. Need made his shoulders ache and his body beg for release.

With unwavering control, he averted his gaze from the clouds, found his still center, and banked desire's flame.

Dear Reader

Thank you for diving into *Shorn: Book One of the Sky Seekers*. I appreciate your willingness to take a chance on a new series. It is difficult these days for new authors to reach their intended audience. I would be grateful if you would help me by leaving a review on Amazon and Goodreads to let others know what you most enjoyed about the book.

Shorn came to me at a time when I was working intensely with children who had experienced serious abuse. Many children who have been abused see themselves as deserving of punishment. By blaming themselves, children can maintain a connection to their abusive caregivers, something that is often necessary for them to survive. Jhared's character came to me in a dream, as a young man who was raised to believe himself corrupt, dangerous, and powerful, although he had very little power at all.

In *Shorn*, Jhared and Nemiah struggle to find their ways in a world that does not allow them a voice. In the following books in the series, their paths will lead them into new conflicts and toward new friends in the midst of ongoing intrigues and the peril of the dark magic of the killing winds. Find out what they face next in *Cael's Shadow: Book Two of the Sky Seekers,* to be followed by books three and four: *Wind Witch* and *Cael's Legacy.*

To stay updated about the release of the next book, read a chapter from *Cael's Shadow,* and find an author interview about the series, please go to www.StoneRavenPress.com.

Be well,

Larissa N. N. Davila

Book Club Discussion Questions for Shorn

1. What does it mean to be Shorn? How is the marginalization of Shorn people like the "othering" of certain people in our own history?

2. What are some parallels between the political structures of Avelos and our own reality?

3. Jhared struggles with feelings of guilt and shame over his ancestors' actions. How do the citizens of Avelos reinforce those feelings in order to control Jhared and other Shorn people?

4. What does it mean to "travel the paths?" What makes Lady Nemiah especially good at it?

5. How does the religion of Avelos shape its culture? In particular, how does the concept of "balance" and the tension between the Goddess of Order, Riana, and the spirit of chaos, Cael, influence the behavior of Avelonian people?

6. Avelos oppresses and exploits Shorn people, but not all Avelonian leaders agree with this policy. Why? What are some of the ways Shorn people push back against their oppression?

7. What is the nature of Jhared's relationship with his foster family? Why is it so unusual in his culture?

8. What is the nature of Nemiah's relationships with her Arionad, Rom, and her Bearer, Leita? How do they help her see into the true nature of Avelonian power?

9. How do Jhared's talents—music, tracking, archery, healing—compensate for the limitations placed on him by Avelos?

10. What do you think will be the source of the killing winds?

11. At the end of the novel, Jhared feels confident that he will be able to "complete the Shorn promise with final reparation." Why does he think so, and do you think he's right?

Photo by Gail Spiro

ABOUT THE AUTHOR

L arissa N. N. Davila is a child psychologist and director of a mental health center for children and families at Central Michigan University, where she teaches, conducts research, and provides psychotherapy. Her nonfiction publications help therapists to prevent and reduce the consequences of adverse childhood experiences such as child abuse. In her free time, she rides horses through the arroyos of northern New Mexico. Find out more at www.LarissaNNDavila.com.